THE NEW

OLD DREAMS. NEW
NIGHTMARES.

PART ONE OF A THREE-VOLUME TAVISH STEWART
ADVENTURE

K.R.M. Morgan

MADBAGUS BOOKS

ISBN: 978-1-9164472-1-9

Cover design by MadBagus

Footnotes

Based on feedback from readers, in this second Tavish Stewart adventure, I have adopted the use of footnotes to provide the equivalent of an optional "director's cut" version of the story. Those who do not desire such additional information will be able to read the simplified version of the tale and perhaps save the footnotes for any subsequent revisits to the story.

Disclaimer

The ideological views expressed by the primary antagonists are intended to be provocative and do not reflect the views of the author or publishers.

This story was written before the Russian invasion of Ukraine in March 2022. The use of the Wolfsangel symbol in my text is related to the use of the symbol by certain groups in the 20th century. The adoption of the Z letter as the symbol of Vladimir Putin's invasion is an unfortunate example of reality copying fiction.

Acknowledgements

The author wishes to acknowledge the help and support from his wife, Maddy, without whom this book would not have been possible.

Social Media

If you enjoy reading this book, please leave a review on social media so that others can discover the adventures of Tavish Stewart.

1 SANDSTORM

(The Great Huángshā (黃沙) of '44)

"It's the sands of time that contain the bones of our ancestors." - Anthony T. Hincks

Gobi Desert
Twenty-six miles West of the Gurvan Saikhan Mountains Mongolia

15:34HRS (GMT+8), 3rd October 1944

Dwarfed by the enormity of the desolate landscape around them, a small group of six men, dressed in a mix of indigenous furs and European mountaineering clothing, struggled through rapidly deteriorating weather conditions towards a massive ice-covered mountain range in the distance. The ground that, even under good conditions, was hard going due to the mix of large rocks and uneven surfaces, was becoming obscured as airborne sand began to form thick clouds around them.

Unbeknown to the small group of travellers, several hours earlier, a rare atmospheric anomaly had diverted the regional Jetstream from its course high in the stratosphere. It created a supercharged airflow that poured down from the glacial Himalayan peaks, thousands of miles to the South West, and blasted into this desolate area of the Gobi. It lost some of its ferocity[1] as it blew over Tibet and inland China, but it still sustained the wind speed of a Super

---

[1] The Subtropical Jetstream flows at heights up to 50,000 feet, achieves speeds of over 200 mph and sustained temperatures of below -70 Fahrenheit.

Typhoon[2] and created a wind chill that made an Antarctic winter blizzard[3] seem appealing. This massive global airmass had picked up millions of microscopic fragments of sharp rock on its travels, forming what the locals call *The Huángshā*[4], an airborne sandpaper that can strip layers off sheer rock surfaces in minutes.

Due to the rapid evaporation of the moisture-laden air it gathered from the glaciers and lakes on its route, this rare weather phenomenon also had the deadly combination of a frigid ambient temperature[5] and a destructive wind force that gave it a freeze-drying capability.

When at full strength, its penetrating embrace froze every living thing it encountered, causing tissue damage within seconds and a slow, agonizing death within minutes. Even under layers of fur or specialised expedition clothing, this wind is one of the deadliest environmental conditions on earth. It rapidly causes bones to ache in a growing agony that spreads throughout the body, signalling imminent hyperthermia to those experienced enough to recognize such symptoms.

As one drew closer to the hikers, struggling through these increasingly brutal conditions, it became clear that the two men leading the group were poorly equipped in comparison to the four who followed in their footsteps. The leading pair were encumbered with enormous backpacks that dwarfed their small bodies, their feet had scant protection in locally made fur boots, and their faces were blistered and

---

[2] Super Typhoons are Asia's most extreme weather systems, often stronger than Atlantic Category 5 hurricanes, with sustained winds greater than 140 mph.

[3] Where temperatures average -40F.

[4] Huángshā literally, "Yellow Sand".

[5] Acquired from the upper atmosphere.

bleeding under their improvised face protection. While in contrast, the remaining four men wore handmade Italian Scarpa[6] leather mountaineering boots, carried hiking sticks to stabilize their strides, and their eyes were protected by Neophan[7] polarized expedition glasses, with leather side panels to prevent the flying sand from entering their eyes.

Henrik von-Gustoff, leader of this expedition, possessed those features that had become associated with the European elite over the past three hundred years. He had a long nose, receding chin, cruel blue eyes, and highly defined cheekbones graced with a deep sabre duelling scar running down its left side. He was significantly taller than his three European companions at six feet four inches and could have been mistaken for a Viking had he lived some thousand years earlier. Clumps of his dark blond hair poked through small gaps between his face mask and wide-brimmed grey canvas hat. von-Gustoff raised the Erhard[8] steel whistle from where it hung around his neck and, pulling his face covering to one side, signalled for the group to halt. He rapidly replaced his mask to escape the numerous tiny sand cuts that had instantly appeared on the sensitive membranes of his exposed lips and nostrils.

The two leading men, a stooping, sixty-three-year-old called Fung Yui and his much slighter, sixteen-year-old son, Zuing Yui, stopped their shuffling progress. Both were relieved to end their exertions with the heavy packs cutting deeply into their bodies, even through the thick fur jackets. The heavy leather straps that supported the two-hundred-and twenty-pound packs severely restricted the blood flow in their arms,

---

[6] SCARPA - Calzaturieri Asolani Riuniti Pedemontana Anonima – makers of bespoke leather boots from the town of Asolo.

[7] The European wartime equivalent of Ray-Ban. Manufactured by the German company "Auer".

[8] A brand of Austrian manufactured Alpine distress whistle.

making their already cold hands turn white where their skin protruded and bleed from under their well-worn fur mittens.

Less than a week after being hired, through a series of hurried telegrams from an expedition agency in Beijing, the elderly man was seriously regretting having become involved with these particular Europeans. Simply, they were bad "Joss"[9]. Fung had only taken this out of season contract in the hope that it would be a way for his youngest son, Zuing, to establish a reputation with rich Western tourists. Such guiding work was notoriously tough on the body. A weakness of breath that Fung had recently started experiencing made him realise this would have to be his last expedition. If his son, Zuing, could get regular work, then there was a chance he could take over supporting the Yui family and let his father finally spend the quality time he had been promising his wife, Ying Yui, for the past 20 years.

But these four European men were not tourists. They had come here looking for something very specific, and although they had not informed Fung what it was that they were seeking, the four men clearly had a secret agenda. They frequently consulted a piece of ancient parchment that they kept close to them at all times, even when they slept. Based on their clandestine behaviour, one could have dismissed them as eccentric treasure hunters, except there was a deadly seriousness about everything they did. They halted at the end of each day, seeking the highest ground in their vicinity and making daily radio contact with some remote authority, who never seemed satisfied with their progress. Fung could not understand the language that was spoken, but the voice on the radio was always angry, expressing growing desperation. Whatever it was these four strange men sought, it was of great value to someone.

---

[9] An Oriental concept of Luck and Karma combined.

From the moment he and his son had met the group at the airstrip outside the town of Bayan Nur in Inner Mongolia, Fung had a growing discomfort about these men. They had refused to respect the well-established custom of obtaining a blessing from the Buddhist shrine before starting their expedition and, worse, declined an invitation to dine from Jubal-Saikan Khan, tribal head for the Gobi region they intended to explore. Instead, after arriving at a prearranged landing strip[10], a hundred- and fifty-miles South West of the Gurvan Saikhan Mountains, they dismissively threw a small envelope of money at the feet of the Khan's representatives, who were waiting to escort their "guests" to receive the hospitality of the local ruler. This insult had not gone un-noted by the local people they had passed. Besides the dark glaring stares, the prices for basic supplies were noticeably inflated, and the quality was poor, not that these strange European men seemed to care.

As the expedition progressed, the arrogance of the visitors grew worse each day. They insisted on sleeping and eating separately from their two guides and refused to share the work of carrying their supplies, expecting the elderly father and his young son to carry two packs that each weighed more than their emaciated bodies. On one occasion, when his son, Zuing, had stumbled on the endlessly uneven ground, Fung had to intervene to prevent the tall leader of the Europeans from viciously striking the young lad with a long walking pole. The episode had only ended when one of the other Europeans had made some joke to defuse the tension; otherwise, Fung did not doubt that he would have been on the receiving end of the ruthless beating.

These four white men viewed their Chinese guides as being simple beasts of burden, calling them "dogs" to their faces

---

10 Near the modern town of Gurvan tes in Ömnögovi Province, Southern Mongolia.

and would clearly enjoy working them to death, given half a chance. It was, therefore, a relief to hear the whistle. The exhausted father and son turned towards the tall leader of the Europeans, expecting to be instructed to make an emergency camp to take cover from the rapidly deteriorating conditions.

von-Gustoff ignored the clear expectation of his two bearers as he examined a large steel and bronze compass[11] that hung from his belt and consulted two maps; one was a modern aerial survey, printed on red silk, that was focused on the local region with elevation contour markings. The other was an ancient-looking parchment with a more stylised representation of the entire world[12]. Both maps were protected inside separate transparent acrylic covers that hung from a harness around von-Gustoff's neck. The older parchment had been folded, so the exposed section showed a caravan of camels heading East along a vast valley that resembled the current terrain, towards a vast mountain citadel, guarded by clawed demons, marked as "Metropolis Diablo[13]".

The needle inside the compass case rotated wildly as magnetised rock particles filled the air around them. The surface of the highly polished folding mirror immediately started showing signs of abrasion from the tiny sharp rock particles that blasted it. Sighing, von-Gustoff closed the useless device and looked at a small watch strapped to his sleeve's exterior by an extended leather strap. The radium

---

11 A Breithaupt Kassel Marching compass.

12 This world map was constructed by Albertinus de Virga around 1411 in Venice and mysteriously went "missing" before an auction in Switzerland in the mid-1930s.

13 Also known as "Agharti, Citadel of the Djinn."

dial on the field watch[14] glowed brightly in the growing gloom and showed there were still some hours to sunset, although the gathering sandstorm made it as dark as night. He gestured for his three companions to group around him.

As the four foreigners huddled around the maps, some ten feet away from the father and son team, Fung took his heavy backpack off and gestured for his son to do the same. The weather dictated that they must set up the tents and take shelter. He could not see why these "potato eyed" fools hesitated, risking everyone's lives.

But these strange foreigners had other plans. They had noticed a series of ancient traveller's refuge points marked along the high cliffs of the valley on their precious antique parchment map. Whatever these refuge points were, one was marked on the map as being a short distance away up the side of one of the steep inclines on the left side of the valley they were following. Although the swirling airborne sand had reduced visibility so that it was impossible to see if anything existed on the sides of the high cliffs, the faith these men had in the ancient map was such they did not feel the need to seek confirmation that anything marked on the map existed. Having gained the agreement of his three colleagues, the tall leader of the group strode towards their two guides and gestured for them to pick up their packs and resume their march, but not along the relatively flat valley floor. This time they were expected to head directly up the side of the steep hillside to their left.

Under these weather conditions, such an uphill hike would not just be hard going; it would take them out of the relative shelter of the valley and directly into the path of

---

14 A German manufactured "Laco-Sport" watch. This 1940s wrist watch was specially constructed from iron, to provide protection from magnetic fields, water ingress, temperature extremes and of course sand.

what was developing into a full-blown Huángshā. Thirty years of trekking experience in the Gobi told Fung that this latest plan from the four foreigners was suicide. They all would die halfway up the slope, and their bones would become added to the countless others strewn around this infamous "Valley of the Vultures".

Fung's incredulity at the insane demand was all too visible on his face. von-Gustoff took the hesitation as gross insubordination and struck the older man violently across the left cheek with the back of his gloved right hand. As the old man fell heavily to the rocky floor, his sixteen-year-old son, Zuing, became enraged and charged full out at the tall European, fists flailing wildly. von-Gustoff responded with delight; at last, he was presented with an opportunity to show his superiority and put this insolent young cur in his rightful place.

Advancing directly into the young man's path, the tall German brushed aside the uncoordinated punches and thrust his right-hand palm hard up and under the exposed chin of the inexperienced boy, causing the lad's body to come up short from his charge and his thin neck to jerk violently backward with a loud click. The youngster's body fell lifeless to the ground, crumpling softly into a tiny heap in front of von-Gustoff's thick leather SCARPA boots.

Fung looked on in stunned disbelief from his prone position nearby before crawling over the rocky ground to kneel beside his son. The old man whimpered as he tenderly shook the tiny body, desperately hoping to get some response. When he finally accepted the terrible reality that his youngest son, Zuing, was gone, he looked up at the masked faces of the four tall foreigners that had gathered around him and, even though he could not understand their language, he could understand their callous laughter. Evidently, they found the young boy's death nothing more than a minor amusement.

von-Gustoff gestured to the two huge backpacks that now lay on their sides in the blowing sands. Seeing that there would be no burial for his son, the old guide issued a snarling growl as his hand drew the old skinning knife from his belt, and he lunged with the long-curved blade toward the tall European who had just killed Zuing.

Fung's attempt at vengeance for the callous murder of his youngest son was short-lived. The last thing he saw was a bright yellow flash emitted from the barrel of a distinctive triangular shaped pistol[15], aimed by one of von-Gustoff's colleagues, who was laughing at this display of "spirit" from the "old dog". The last thought that flowed through Fung's mind was that he would never again hold his beloved wife, Ying Yui, before he felt the hammer-like impact of a copper projectile into the left side of his forehead and sixty-three years of anger, worry, and hope dissolved into black nothingness.

Moments after the old man's body had crumpled, ending up lying over his beloved son, one of the Europeans began roughly searching the two bodies. Ripping the tattered furs from the old man exposed a small leather neck wallet containing twenty US dollar coins and a creased photograph of a pretty, smiling Chinese woman. The money was the fee that had been agreed to for the guide's services. After retrieving the US dollars, the empty wallet and photograph were cast to the rocky valley floor beside the two lifeless bodies. While the money had been retrieved, two of the other Westerners had picked up the heavy packs,

---

[15] A classic, 1944, 9×19mm Luger, manufactured by Mauser. More formally known as the *Parabellum Automatic Pistol, Borchardt-Luger System* designed by the German arms manufacturer Deutsche Waffen und Munitionsfabriken (DWM).

and the three of the men started marching after von-Gustoff, who was already heading up the steep slope.

Back in the valley, gusts of wind blew the old photograph along until it rested, momentarily, on the old guide's body, exposing that the back of the picture had some Chinese text that read

"总归我家 · 你的映月"

(Always come home to me, your Ying Yui).

Seconds later, a further gust blew the small photograph away down the valley, rapidly vanishing from sight.

Some yards further up on the steep slope, the four men had started to leave the relative shelter they had enjoyed on the valley floor. The wind became so strong that the hikers were forced to rope themselves together, and their progress became painfully slow as their bodies started to exhibit the slow agony of deep bone freezing. None of them complained, but these hard men were experienced enough to realise that they would never leave this desolate valley if they did not find shelter within the next few minutes.

Every few paces took them more directly into the full force of the weather system. The ambient temperature had dropped by fifty degrees Fahrenheit since leaving the valley floor, and the razor-sharp airborne sand particles started the inevitable process of shredding through the outer layers of their protective expedition clothing.

The rearmost member of the team, who had so brutally terminated the sixty-three-year-old Fung Yui moments earlier, was the first to succumb to this battering onslaught and fall face down into the thick sand. His additional dead weight halted the group's progress and caused von-Gustoff to stagger back from the front of the roped men to examine their collapsed colleague.

During the process of assessing the man's condition, it was necessary for von-Gustoff to remove the unresponsive team member's face protection. Without the mask, the abrasive nature of the airborne sand immediately began a gruesome process of exfoliation that would, within minutes, strip the exposed skin down to the bone.

The fallen man's lack of response quickly indicated that he would not recover, so the tall leader opened the canvas pistol case strapped to his right side and, without any sign of emotion, put a single round into the skull of his comrade. Moments after completing this grisly task, von-Gustoff heard the sound of a shrill whistle from one of his colleagues, who was excitedly pointing to a small alcove buried into the side of the cliff face, some sixty feet to their right. von-Gustoff turned back, leaving the body of his former team member to its fate, and led his remaining men to the newly discovered refuge.

Some minutes later, the men had gathered in the relative shelter of the cliffside recess. Some additional exploration of this opening revealed that the alcove was, in fact, a covering for a larger space that had been carved into the hillside at some remote period in the past. Just beyond the exterior entrance was a highly distinctive carving of some form of chimaera, part bird, part reptile, and part human. The bird-like head had a savage-looking beak that contained numerous small teeth, and the hands and feet hosted long claw-like talons[16].

After unpacking four oil lamps from their backpacks, they explored the mysterious darkness within. As the men went deeper, it was clear that travellers had used this space as a

---

16 A classic representation of a Djinn. Forget the helpful Genii of the Arabian Nights, these hideous creatures filled ancient history with terrors that are reflected in our modern stories of demons and devils.

shelter for some considerable time. The walls had slots for oil lamps, and there were some hard wood tables and chairs. Towards the back of the cave, there were six beds with primitive straw mattresses.

The furniture was of good quality but obviously had not been used for some considerable time. Every item was covered with a messy combination of cobwebs and sand. The walls had all been finished to a smooth surface that was covered with graffiti in a variety of languages[17], showing names and dates going back thousands of years. Each of the dates were around one hundred and twenty years apart. To make the best of a bad situation, the men set about unpacking the sets of specialised lamps that they had brought to assist in any subterranean archaeological work. Soon the cave was brightly illuminated and looked considerably more welcoming.

von-Gustoff sat in one of the wooden chairs and, taking a wire-rimmed notepad from one of the boxes that had been unloaded from the large backpacks, wrote the following report with a steel KaWeCo[18] propelling pencil to update his superiors on their current situation.

"Wie geplant haben Führer beendet, um den Standort der Zitadelle zu erhalten. Ein massiver Sturm stoppte den Fortschritt. Habe zwei Tage vor dem Zielort in der Höhle Zuflucht gesucht. Wird beraten, wenn der Fortschritt fortgesetzt wird. Halt."

(As scheduled have terminated guides to preserve location of citadel. Massive storm halted progress. Have taken shelter in cave two days march from target location. Will advise when resume progress. Stop.)

---

17 Including Sanskrit, Latin, Chinese, Arabic, Mongolian and Cuneiform.

18 Made by the Heilderger Pen Factory in Heidelberg.

16

He tore the page from the pad and handed it to two of his men, who took a large radio backpack[19] with a sizeable expanding wire frame aerial from a hardwood box that had also been unloaded from the backpacks. The two-person radio team exited the cave, braving the steadily deteriorating weather conditions to establish contact with their headquarters. Twenty minutes later, they returned, clearly disheartened, and reported that the interference from the magnetized storm had made the radio inoperable.

To further emphasize how nature itself seemed to be conspiring against them, the cave surfaces near the entrance unexpectedly started to drop debris down on the men. The high temperature of the modern lamps that they had fitted into the old lamp alcoves had begun to warm the surface inside the cave, expanding the rocks that made up the cliffside and dislodging the fine sands that held this artificial subterranean refuge together.

As the size of the debris falling from the walls and ceiling increased, von-Gustoff ordered his men further back into the cave, just moments before a thirty-foot square roof section collapsed, burying the entrance under several hundred tons of car-sized rocks.

The three men started an organised attempt to clear a way through the cave-in. They took twenty-minute shifts, moving smaller rocks and sand to the cave's rear, near the beds. After two hours of work, it was clear that their efforts only succeeded in using up their limited air supply more quickly. Whenever a section of sand and rock was moved, the rest of the rock fall adjusted to fill the space. They were trapped. The cave, which appeared to be their salvation, had become their tomb.

---

[19] A forty-four pound portable Torn. Fu. B1, field radio transmitter/receiver made by Lorenz in Berlin.

Each man responded to the certainty of their death in different ways. Two of the men knelt and prayed, but not to any Christian God, but instead to something much older and more pagan in nature[20]. Their prayers were not for salvation but rather that they should "die well" and not show any weakness or fear.

While his men prayed, the tall, blond von-Gustoff took a broad paged book from his private travel case and began to write what would be the final entry in his log. The linen bound book had a highly distinctive decoration on its cover, of a sword with an intertwining ribbon flowing on both sides of the long blade. The sword and ribbon were surrounded by a border of runic characters that ran right around the central motif.

Examining this strange book further, one could see the opening pages were filled with loose papers that had been carefully stuck with glue to the empty leaves. Each of these sheets had a highly distinctive eagle themed logo[21] at the top of the page and was signed by multiple signatures that were, in turn, covered with distinctive formal authorisation stamps in red ink.

The numerous following pages in this unusual travel journal showed a series of expeditions to various locations around the globe, including Tibet, Africa, and most recently, China and Mongolia. The only common theme from all these trips was the acquisition of relics. Each relic was pictured and then described in considerable detail, emphasising the

---

[20] Odin or Wotan, both are deities thought to stem from the Germanic theonym "Wōđanaz".

21 The Reichsadler is a heraldic eagle, derived from the Roman eagle standard, used by the Holy Roman Emperors and other regimes in modern times.

reported mystical or occult phenomena associated with that specific item.

The most recent entries in the book were related to gathering relics from Buddhist and Taoist shrines and holy sites within South East Asia. The notes made it clear that they expected the Gobi to contain Asia's ultimate esoteric treasure, a sacred Emerald Tablet located inside a hidden underground city that would provide proof of a lost Aryan civilisation.

As von-Gustoff reviewed the final entries in the log book, he looked over to the boxes that contained the latest relics that he had successfully acquired in this final trip. Each of the small wooden crates was stamped with the same distinctive logo that adorned the cover of the log book. When he had completed his writing, he called to his compatriots, who gathered the chairs around their leader for their final meeting.

The men sat in a small circle and made light of their impending end. From one of the crates, they opened a small flask of apricot schnapps[22] and began to sing "the Devils Song[23]" to celebrate that they would all dine tonight in the "Halls of the Great"[24].

As the air inside their tomb became noticeably worse, each man nodded solemnly to their leader. von-Gustoff stood and wound up a small gramophone player and loaded a seventy-eight-rpm record before passing each man a small packet of greaseproof paper embossed with a large IG

---

22 Marillenschnaps is a fruit brandy made from apricots. It is mostly produced in the Wachau region of Austria.

23 "Teufelslied" also known as "Marschiert in Feindesland" (marching in enemy land).

24 Valhalla is an enormous hall located in Asgard, ruled over by the god Odin.

Farben logo. Each packet contained one small round glass vial inside.

The men never heard the end of the recorded music[25]. The gramophone needle finally made a long series of clicking noises, and the oil lamps extinguished, one by one, as the oxygen was completely consumed. The darkness inside the cave would have been absolute had it not been for the strange flickering lights emanating from the relic boxes stacked so carefully at the side of the cave.

---

[25] Wagner's Götterdämmerung (Fall of the Gods).

2   THE WILD HUNT

"Then the feral howls fill the air, and the host of the wild hunt appears, all dressed in shrouds, gazing hungrily from their empty eye sockets, a fetid stench issuing from their decayed breath and the sound of their hooves as they seize their victims between the bony jaws of their skeletal snouts."
- The Raging Host [Asgardreia], Chronicles of the Vendel (550-790 AD).

Gare Geneva/ formerly Gare Cornavin, (Geneva Central Railway Station)
Place de Cornavin 7,
1201 Genève, Switzerland

12:24HRS (GMT+2), 5th Sept, present day

Dr Thomas O'Neill, formerly of the Pontifical Archaeology Department, had experienced many dramatic transformations in his life, but none like the changes that had occurred after his announcement of discovering the lost city of Agartha[26], buried deep beneath the desolate sands of the Gobi Desert.

At first, his story of a fabulous ancient civilization, which he claimed predated those of the Assyrians and Arcadians by tens of thousands of years, granted him the celebrity status he had always secretly desired. Television appearances and newspaper front pages proclaimed details of his unbelievable discovery, which was only made credible because of his academic association with Rome's prestigious Pontifical Gregorian University (PUG).

---

[26] A legendary lost or hidden city frequently referenced by nineteenth century esoteric writers.

However, it was not long before allegations of deception began to emerge, circulated by jealous colleagues who, like many academics, were only too delighted to put an end to the success of a rival. The lack of evidence for O'Neill's announcement was accompanied by leaked medical assessments that had been conducted immediately after the supposed Gobi expedition. These showed O'Neill had consumed considerable amounts of powerful mind-altering hallucinogens[27] while supposedly involved with his discovery of the fabulous lost city and its amazing technological accomplishments.

The resulting fallout was that O'Neill went almost immediately from being a feted celebrity to being a laughing stock. The requests for interviews now only came from fringe news bloggers, conspiracy podcasters and publishers of the speculative and supernatural.

Predictably, his academic department was the first to disown him, and after losing his tenured University position, he was moved rapidly to less and less demanding tasks within the Church as his tarnished reputation became more and more widely known within the small Papal city community.

He also became inundated with hate mail, some demanding his name be removed from the numerous respectable academic publications he had co-written over the decades of his academic career. Other, more personal letters from fellow clergy demanded that he quit the priesthood. The frequency of these abusive messages became such that he grew to dread opening the grey metal mail box in the

---

[27] Muscimol: a potent psychotropic derived from certain species of mushroom. Enhanced in potency by shamans in the Gobi region by being fed to reindeer and then consuming the animal's urine. This laced urine induces extraordinarily powerful hypnotic and hallucinogenic psycho-activity.

entrance hall of his apartment block, watching the cascade of envelopes fall to the floor. Knowing each one was filled with the same spiteful sentiment and delight in O'Neill's professional demise.

Finally, after being rapidly reduced to less and less respectable posts within the Vatican, he hit rock bottom with a letter assigning him to part-time "ad hoc" duties within the Deliverance section. His role was to deal with cases that his superiors regarded as too "absurd" to be taken seriously by any other church member. As the more spiteful hate mail letters pointed out, such absurd cases were perfect for "a discredited former academic who no longer had anything to lose".

O'Neill's latest "absurd" case had been assigned to him in a three-line email titled "Fontaine Incident", with two pdf attachments. The first was a Vatican accommodation voucher, and the second pdf provided an electronic economy return train ticket from Rome's Metropolitan City station through Milan and then to Geneva.

After seven and a half hours, in a cramped and dirty ITALO railway compartment shared with various fellow travellers and their irritating behaviours[28], he was enormously relieved when he finally arrived at his destination.

After disembarking, he found himself breathing in the clean mountain air and enjoying a sunny afternoon in the ancient Swiss city, although he struggled to read the station signage with his rusty high school French.   Everywhere around him, the warm weather had prompted people to dress in short-sleeved tops, exposing a mass of the UNITY barcode

---

[28] Such as consuming noisy snacks with extraordinarily strong odours, listening to discordant music or making loud phone calls where they proclaimed the obvious fact that they were travelling on the train.

tattoos[29] that had been almost universally accepted throughout continental Europe. O'Neill's dark clerical dress covered his arms and hid that he was one of the very few who had not submitted to enslavement in return for a vaccine[30].

He had travelled light, bringing only a small black Adidas sports bag containing a change of clothes, a toothbrush and the small leather bag related to his deliverance work. Since losing his academic post, the dark-haired, forty-two-year-old archaeologist had given up wearing his usual casual clothing. He now exclusively wore the anonymous black suit and dog collar that matched his sober mood and new vocation.

After a short taxi ride in a yellow and white C-Class Mercedes estate, he found himself at the Geneva office of the Roman Catholic Diocese of Lausanne, Geneva and Fribourg. The building was an undistinguished 1960s glass and metal construction, next to numerous other anonymous offices. After announcing himself to the receptionist in English, she curtly replied in French, handed him a thick, sealed A4 sized envelope and called him a taxi, clearly acting under instructions to minimize O'Neill's time on the premises. Whether this was due to the nature of his visit, or his tarnished reputation, he was not sure.

Getting back inside the very same taxi that had brought him, which, either through lucky coincidence or some foresight, had waited outside the office, O'Neill opened the package he had just received. After reading the address

---

[29] See the preceding novel, "Bridge of Souls", for more details behind these insidious barcodes.

[30] O'Neill had obtained his vaccine as part of a raid on one of the UNITY vaccination centres in Istanbul.

from a tag attached to a keyring, O'Neill informed the taxi driver of their next destination.

The sealed envelope provided information related to the case, and the keys proved to be for a single room at a Church-owned lodging house run by Visitandine[31] Nuns in the Old Town of Geneva. The small room, with its single cot bed, blue plastic covered foam mattress and communal bathroom, was as basic as the assorted cold meats, cheese and bread that formed every meal at the hostel. But the documents in the envelope more than compensated for any lack of excitement in his lodgings. O'Neill spent most of the evening reading and making copious notes related to his new case. Even if his superiors thought these "crackpot cases" were a waste of time, experience had shown him they mattered to the people who had asked the Church for help.

Studying these particular case notes, O'Neill discovered they related to the "The Fontaine Mansion", a classic, twenty-five room villa set back from Rue des Granges, in the Old Town of Geneva, within a ten-minute walk from his lodgings.

The mansion had been owned by the 1960s American movie star DeeDee Fontaine. Her recent death had caused a spate of her movies to be shown on the late-night movie channels that O'Neill had recently found himself watching when he could not escape into the oblivion of sleep. So, thanks to these re-runs, he was familiar with the actress, with her famous red hair and smouldering looks, who had starred in several big-budget movies and had been one of the early "Bond girls".

After her looks had faded and the starring roles dried up, Fontaine became a recluse and was never seen in public. Instead, she closed herself away in her large estate, located in the most exclusive section of the already exclusive Swiss

---

31 Order of the Visitation of Holy Mary

city. In the privacy of her self-imposed exile, she became involved with several esoteric groups, all of whom promised her ways that she could cheat death.   In her final years, she became involved with a mysterious cult leader who practised forms of pagan rites related to old Scandinavian beliefs.

Due to these influences, the Fontaine villa and its grounds had been extensively modified over the last decade. The documents in O'Neill's files showed that the main ground floor area had been rebuilt as a replica of a Viking Great Hall that had acted as an indoor temple for the group's pagan rituals. Some grainy photographs showed that carved into the hall's wooden walls were crude representations of male and female forms, dressed in iron age period clothing, and there were further runic inscriptions carved into the structures of the building and grounds.

The great hall had two massive wooden doors, covered in more crude wooden carvings, that led directly into a reconstruction of a sacred grove of fruit trees that, in turn, led to a small lake at the rear of the property. According to the survey report, the lake was a natural body of water left over from the last ice age and was some seventy yards long and fifty yards wide. Its depth was unrecorded in any of O'Neill's paperwork but was suspected to be connected to other glacial lakes in the region by underground caves and passageways.

Since Fontaine's death, three separate buyers had purchased the residence, only to sell it again within weeks. Although the reasons for these rapid re-sales remained undisclosed, the request for a Papal deliverance representative intimated some supernatural phenomena. As was frequently the case, hauntings were seldom included in real estate documentation, as they often discouraged potential buyers.

As O'Neill looked through the final sections of his files, he noticed that the realtors had discreetly contacted their local church who, through requests from the local Protestant bishop to his Roman Catholic counterpart, Bishop Gerard, had issued a demand for some form of intervention from Rome. The priest set to work, diligently reading and re-reading every paper and making copious notes so that he would know every detail of the case. He finally fell asleep in the small hours of the morning, surrounded by files and paperwork describing the alleged supernatural phenomena. Exhausted from the travel and the detailed bookwork, O'Neill was still deep asleep on his small cot bed when the nearby church clock struck noon.

O'Neill awoke with a start and, for a blissful moment, had forgotten the loss of his academic post. Listening to the birds singing and the warm sun streaming into his small room, he assumed the strange bed and strewn paperwork around him must be associated with a fully funded conference attendance. Then the memory of his recent fall in status returned. The realisation strengthened his resolve to make the best of what had occurred, and he gave a short thanks to God that he could still make the best use of his talents before getting up and facing the disdain of his hosts for his late rising.

O'Neill's first action after an uninspiring breakfast was to go through his notes from last night one more time and then call the real estate agent who was currently trying to find a fourth buyer for the Fontaine mansion. "Monsieur Charles, SA." turned out to be a very upper-class realty agency, clearly created to cater to the highest-profile international clients. The receptionist switched effortlessly to speaking English upon hearing O'Neill's American accent. After explaining the nature of his request, O'Neill was put through to the owner of the business, Charles Defout. Based on

Defout's manner, he did not want any publicity that would damage the marketing of the property.

Defout had a falsetto voice and affected an extreme French accent, often adopted by people who have dubious French roots. However, he arrived very promptly in front of the main gates to the property in a bright red Citroen 2 CV decorated with his company's logo. He was dressed in a colourful blue blazer with a red silk cravat and closely fitted Ralph Lauren Polo, cream coloured chino trousers and leather deck shoes, without socks. Accompanying "Monsieur Charles", on the end of a red leather leash, was "Monsieur Napoleon", a light, tawny coloured, miniature French poodle who looked as though he had almost as much grooming as his owner.

Once on the premises, O'Neill walked slowly around the house and grounds, accompanied by Defout and Napoleon, the poodle. O'Neill focused on taking pictures on his new iPhone and making extensive audio notes, especially of the indoor carvings, the line of twenty trees that made up the "sacred grove", and the curious lakeside runic inscriptions carved with great care in the granite rocks beside the water. Based on what he could see, the house appeared to be in good condition and felt perfectly normal as far as O'Neill could tell.

After the estate tour, the two men sat on a long wooden bench in the gardens leading to the front door while Napoleon continued his own more detailed exploration of the scent trails associated with the trees in the sacred grove. If O'Neill was expecting an explanation of why he had been called, he was disappointed. Defout refused to provide O'Neill with anything but the vaguest descriptions of the "horrors" that had caused the three previous owners to get rid of this attractive property quickly. But, after getting a signed NDA[32] from O'Neill, he provided the phone number of the most recent owner, who, he assured O'Neill, would provide details of their experience at the Mansion.

Surprisingly, the previous owner was prepared to see O'Neill immediately. After a short taxi ride and announcing himself to yet another of the elegant French-speaking receptionists that seemed to populate Geneva, O'Neil was escorted to one of the rooftop suites at the Grand Hotel Kempinski, where the most recent mansion owner had moved immediately after her experiences at the Fontaine estate.

Mrs Allaman was a short, silver-haired, sixty-year-old senior bank executive with Credit Swiss and not someone taken to exaggeration or fabrication[33]. However, she was cautious and clearly reluctant to describe the full details of what she had experienced in her short occupancy of the mansion. All she would say initially was to confirm that, after just three nights, she had sold the property back to the realtor at a massive loss, which O'Neill reflected was not the typical behaviour of an investment banker.

Allaman finally opened up after O'Neill indicated that he had some personal experiences with the paranormal. He also reassured her that he would keep whatever she told him in confidence. And so, sitting next to this distinguished-looking, silver-haired woman on her hotel balcony overlooking Lake Geneva while enjoying a filter coffee, O'Neill heard his first description of the phenomena at the Fontaine Mansion.

Allaman's account of her experiences started normally enough, for a haunting, with doors slamming, furniture moving, and lights and electrical appliances turning on by themselves when the house was empty. O'Neill's

---

[32] Non-Disclosure Agreement

[33] We will not digress to discuss the 2008 banking crisis.

acknowledgement that such phenomena were common in hauntings calmed Ms Allaman. It gave her confidence to continue with her account that became more unusual with her description of what she encountered when she entered the great hall after sunset on her third night after moving into the estate.

From the first evening, she said that she had noticed some distinctive and unpleasant odours in the great hall, like rotting kelp or sea weed, and had assumed that some drainage had failed under the old house. Since such plumbing investigations take time, she decided they could wait until she discovered all the other repairs and alterations that she would undoubtedly require in her new home.

But then, on the third night, while standing in the great hall, she had heard unfamiliar noises that she, at first, could not place. It sounded like heavy objects being dragged. The source of the commotion seemed to emanate from the grove of fruit trees directly outside the great hall.

Allaman paused and required further encouragement and confirmation from O'Neill that he was familiar and comfortable with such phenomena. Having received it, she began to describe how, after hearing these undetermined noises on her property, she had opened the two large oak doors that exited from the great hall. She expected to find some workmen completing some finishing touches to the estate on behalf of the realtor.

Instead, she was confronted with what she described as swathes of thick mist that had manifested what could only be described as tall forms rising from the lake. Forms that were not exactly human in shape but something between human and, she paused, struggling for words, and then, after O'Neill encouraged her, continued. She described something much longer, thinner and taller than a human, walking on two legs, like an acrobat on stilts, with long flowing light-coloured robes that, on reflection, might have been kelp or seaweed draping from their long limbs.

Allaman hesitated again and looked at O'Neill. There was something more. Something that O'Neill could sense she found so disturbing that even now, she wondered if she could share it without being thought insane.

O'Neill nodded and gently reassured his interviewee to continue. Finally, after some considerable reluctance, she pulled up her sleeve and trouser leg to reveal a series of savage bites.   After O'Neill exhibited sympathy, rather than ridicule, at her wounds, she partially pulled up her top to show that the same deep bite marks covered her stomach and, she informed O'Neill, the rest of her body.

At this stage, Allaman broke down into tears and, through her sobs, revealed to O'Neill that she did not remember exactly what had happened, only that the shapes by the lake had suddenly been much closer to her and that she had passed out in sheer terror. She had a vague memory of a figure intervening but nothing definite. She regained consciousness at dawn, lying in a bloody mess halfway along the tree-lined grove. The two massive wooden doors from the great hall were still open, and light streamed out into the garden.

She had staggered into the house and called 144. The paramedics reported that she was covered in blood, with deep animal bites all over her body. Her clothing was torn by teeth in numerous places, and she had been the victim of a savage attack from a pack of between ten and fifteen animals, probably large dogs and possibly wolves. However, Allaman insisted that there were no animals on the estate at the time.

After showing O'Neill her wounds, she permitted him to take some photos on his iPhone and then signed a short statement that was a pre-requisite for the Church to consider the sacrament of a formal exorcism. Although O'Neill now suspected that this particular case would involve an exorcism on the property and not any individual.

After thanking Ms Allaman for her time and trust, O'Neill went to the Hotel's internet café and hunted for any unusual events associated with the estate. After some searches, he found a news report of a German independent paranormal group, "Geisterjäger", who had investigated the property three years ago, immediately after the death of DeeDee Fontaine. Not much information was reported about what the group found, beyond mention that three of the four members of the team were hospitalised with severe psychotic symptoms that were suspected to be linked to intensive recreational drug use. The fourth team member was still missing, and the subject of an Interpol missing persons watch.

Continuing his internet research, O'Neill found a local journalist, Hans Burckhalter, who had written many of the news articles associated with the late movie star. A phone call and a short taxi ride later, and O'Neill was at the offices of the French-language newspaper, Le Matin, and face to face with Burckhalter. His status with the paper was obviously in decline, as his office was hidden behind numerous dead plants, discarded printers, and assorted computer components. The disarray continued inside the tiny cubicle, with files, papers, and photographs randomly scattered beside a single desk.

Hans Burckhalter was a large, balding man with thick spectacles, a walrus moustache, a wicked sense of humour and a sharp eye for detail, but, as demonstrated by the notes strewn randomly around the cubicle, poor organisational skills.

After O'Neill introduced himself and described his professional interest in the Fontaine estate, Burckhalter chuckled and informed O'Neill that he was not surprised if the house had some "bad vibrations". Although it was some years ago, he distinctly remembered the consistent rumours that dogged Fontaine in the later years of her life. There was talk of missing persons; Eastern European orphan children brought to the mansion and never seen again. There were also complaints from neighbours of lights and disturbing noises emanating from the estate's rear late at night. But no conclusive evidence could ever be provided, and the influence of a Hollywood star, like Fontaine, meant the investigations were never as complete as they could have been. Besides, the allegations ended when the movie star died.

O'Neill asked if the elderly journalist knew anything more about the people who met for the strange late-night ceremonies at the mansion and the person who led them. According to Burckhalter, the group's membership was very select, taken from the wealthy and well connected within Europe, including political leaders, internet billionaires and celebrities. The group leader was an enigmatic, powerfully built young man who claimed to channel dark forces that could grant great power on this earth. There was no clear description of the male organiser but based on the accounts of the servants who worked at the estate, the leader could radically change his appearance from meeting to meeting, presumably using a series of expertly applied disguises.

When the movie star died, the late-night meetings abruptly ceased. The journalist searched through his notes and gave O'Neill an address of an abandoned Ottoman fortress on a lake in Montenegro. The enigmatic leader had purchased this property to continue his ceremonies, using a large bequest from the late movie star.

By now, it was late in the afternoon, so, after leaving the offices of Le Matin, O'Neill made one final phone call and arranged a meeting for the following morning at the University before taking another taxi back to his lodging house in the Old Town. After another unappetising meal of the same cold meats, cheese slices, wholemeal bread and skimmed milk at the Church hostel, O'Neill spent the evening preparing his presentation and questions for a ten-thirty am meeting the following day.

After breakfast, comprising the same food from the previous evening, he made the long taxi ride to the city's Eastern section to visit Professor Novik Sackoff at the Faculty of Protestant Theology on the Uni Bastions campus of the University of Geneva. Sackoff's office was located in a narrow corridor, set off from a stone spiral staircase, in the nineteenth-century building near some well-tended parkland.   The professor was a tall, thin man in his seventies with delicate, wire-rimmed glasses and a mass of fuzzy white hair that made him look like he had just received an electric shock.

After formal introductions, O'Neill showed the pictures of the carvings and runic inscriptions he had taken at the Fontaine estate the previous day. Sackoff immediately pulled some old books and lever arch files from the numerous bookshelves that dominated the small office. On opening these references on Old Norse and Germanic pre-Christian religions, it was clear that there was an extraordinarily close correspondence between the images taken by O'Neill from the mansion and images from sacred sites in Sweden, Germany and Holland.

Sackoff informed O'Neill, in a practised lecture-like tone, that this ancient religion was polytheistic with various gods and goddesses. These gods were divided into two groups, the Æsir and Vanir, who were constantly engaged in battle. These battles were similar to the conflicts between good and evil in the Abrahamic religions, except there was not such a clear understanding as to who was "good".   The followers of this ancient religion believed that the world was populated by various other races and that these strange supernatural beings inhabited the entire natural world and its elements alongside humans.

The details of exactly how people worshipped these deities and interacted with these supernatural beings were not well documented since their traditions were oral. Still, from contemporary accounts, they could be extraordinarily brutal. From what was known, their gods and supernatural beings required blood sacrifices, made in ceremonies directed by practitioners of a form of ritual magic called, Seiðr, which many scholars described as shamanistic. In such practice, the shaman would become possessed by the entities in the supernatural world to effect change according to the desire of a group or influential individual.

With his research and preparation completed, O'Neill thanked Sackoff and returned to his lodging. In preparation for the coming evening, he slept during the afternoon and deliberately abstained from consuming anything beyond some fresh fruit and water. After a shower and a short taxi ride, he took the Eucharist in the ruins[34] of the Gothic Basilica Notre-Dame of Geneva, under the statue of Our Lady of Geneva, where he prayed for her blessing and protection for the coming night's vigil.

He had been left the Fontaine mansion keys and entered, just before dusk, without any problems, except for the unexpected presence of Napoleon, the tiny yapping poodle. The realtor had left the dog tied to the bottom of the staircase with a note attached to his collar, wishing O'Neill "Bon chance" and hoping that Napoleon would prove good company during what promised to be a long, solitary evening.

---

[34] All significant sites of religious faith had suffered great damage and destruction as part of one of the most powerful left-hand path magical evocations, intended to begin the end of days.

As the sun descended behind the mountainous horizon, night enveloped the house. O'Neill turned off the room lights, as darkness was more conducive to paranormal manifestations. He had his trusty Petzl Tikkina head-mounted torch from his time as an archaeologist, working in underground passages and ancient tombs. He was not afraid of the dark, but he quickly became glad that the realtor had been kind enough to leave his dog since the big mansion was a lonely place.

O'Neill first walked from room to room, covering the entire interior before beginning an hour-long vigil in each room, timed by the steady ticking hands of his trusty Nite watch. Its tritium illumination proved itself invaluable again, as it had on numerous expeditions over the past years, including the extraordinary adventure he had recently survived.

By midnight nothing had happened, and O'Neill wondered if he should return home to the hostel and try again the following night. Then he heard a door slam from one of the bedrooms he had just left. The sudden noise caused Napoleon to bark in alarm, but after looking at O'Neill to judge if he should be afraid, the small dog became calmer.

On opening the bedroom door, O'Neill found the lights on and the taps in the en-suite bathroom running full and already overflowing, flooding the white tiled floor. After turning off the water, he could hear other doors slamming throughout the vast, old building. He exited that bedroom to find the lights from the great hall were on, and they illuminated the entire edifice. Outside, in the grove, the torches that ran along the rows of fruit trees had been lit. They cast flickering shadows into the windows of the main mansion. Between the flickering torches, one could vaguely see tall, thin forms, causing inhuman shaped shadows on the windows that faced the grove as they strode up the rows of trees towards the big wooden double doors at the end of the great hall.

As O'Neill walked calmly towards the lights, with Napoleon still in close attendance, he began to smell a musty scent that he recognised from numerous digs on ancient sites when sealed vaults are opened. As he got closer, he heard a noise, like torrential rain and something wet and heavy, dragging slowly across a wooden surface. The musty smell transformed into a distinct aroma of stagnant water, and O'Neill was reminded of Ms Allaman's description of her experiences in the house. Not hesitating for a moment, O'Neill fearlessly pulled open the interior doors to the great hall and, unexpectedly, found the hall in silent darkness. The strange lights and fantastic figures that he had seen on his approach had gone, leaving only the musty smell and some definite marks. There was a water trail on the timber floor that led to the two massive carved wooden doors to the grove. Both doors were open, showing that the rows of flaming torches illuminated the tree-lined walkway.

On closer inspection, the same strange, vaporous forms visible from the mansion now danced through the grove. The figures were extraordinarily tall, maybe ten to twelve feet in height, wearing long flowing white robes that concealed the entire length of their bodies. But that was not their most disturbing feature- their faces were white, bleached, elongated skeletal animal snouts. Some of the skeletal faces resembled horses, others cows. Other creatures were unrecognisable, but all were deeply disturbing to behold.

Napoleon, the dog, took in the tall dancing shapes and began barking while looking at O'Neill to gauge what they would do next. Besides the loud barking, there was another noise, like a long, wet rope being pulled slowly through the undergrowth and again that strong smell of dank mould and fetid, still water.

For the first time that evening, O'Neill felt a visceral chill of terror run through his body, and as if he sensed this,

Napoleon stopped his barking dance and fell silent. O'Neill recalled his recent experiences in the Gobi that had reaffirmed his absolute belief, not just in the paranormal but also in the divine power of the Holy Roman Church that, he reminded himself, he represented. O'Neill steeled himself, remembering his purpose here. He gave the sign of the cross and walked out into the grove while reciting the Roman Ritual, accompanied by the loudly yapping poodle that danced fearlessly by his side.

"EXORCIZO te, immundíssime spíritus, omnis incúrsio adversárii, omne phantasma, omnis légio, in nómine Dómini nostri Jesu+Christi eradicáre, et effugáre ab hoc plásmate Dei +. Ipse tibi ímperat, qui te de supérnis cæaelórum in inferióra terræ demérgi præcépit. Ipse tibi ímperat, qui mari, ventis et tempestátibus imperávit. Audi ergo, et time, sátana, inimice fidei, hostis géneris humáni, mortis addúctor, vitæ raptor, justítiæ declinátor, malórum radix, fomes vitiórum, sedúctor hóminum, próditur géntium, incitátor invídiæ, origo avaritiæ, causa discórdiæ, excitátor dolórum: quid stas, et resistis, cum scias, Christum Dóminum vias tuas pérdere? Illum métue, qui in Isaac immolátus est, in Joseph venúndatus, in agno occísus, in hómine crucifixus, deinde inférni triumphátor fuit. Sequentes crucis fiat in fronte obsessi. Recéde ergo in nómine Patris +, et Fílii +, et Spíritus + Sancti: da locum Spirítui Sancto, per hoc signum sanctæ + Crucis Jesu Christi Dómini

*nostri: Qui cum Patre et eódem Spíritu
Sancto vivit et regnat Deus, per ómnia
sæcula sæculórum.[35] "*

At first, nothing happened, but then, slowly, the strange
gliding shapes noticed him and gradually, almost
imperceivably, they approached closer. It took O'Neill a
moment to recognise what was happening. Every time he
blinked, the tall spectral figures had moved, changing their
posture and position. They were always closer with their
hideous skeletal faces angled towards the exorcist, even
though it was clear that their eyes were sightless, empty
orbs.

O'Neill opened a small bottle of holy water and scattered
the liquid directly at the shapes that now surrounded him in
the flame lit grove. At close range, the fetid smell of rotting
flesh emanated from the breath of these creatures as they
snorted in evident excitement at encountering O'Neill. The
holy water and demands to depart in the names of the
Christian God seemed to have no effect on these
monstrous, dancing things. Then, the shapes were upon him
with the rapidity of an animal attacking. He could see their
elongated skeletal heads filled with rows of sharp teeth. The
rest of their bodies took the form of a thin torso, supported
by four extraordinarily long, slender skeletal limbs, hidden
by the long draping white cloth that covered each creature.
They dropped low to the ground and assumed a much more
feral form, some bounding over the grass like a pack of
wolves.

Up close, some of the monsters, those with the longest
snout, filled with malformed teeth, looked similar to the

---

[35] O'Neill is a Jesuit, so naturally he prefers his Rituale Romanum
"old school" in Latin.

traditional Celtic "White Mare"[36] associated with the year's end celebrations. Hideous harbingers of death who knocked on the doors of the living, demanding entrance on the night where the dead roamed and could cross between the veil between life and death. O'Neill screamed as he was forcibly seized by numerous skeletal forms and pulled to the ground, his bible and bottle of holy water scattered to the floor. In the violence, Napoleon whimpered and took flight somewhere, far away from the grove.

Long teeth, set in powerful jaws, now buried themselves into O'Neill's body, arms and legs and began to drag him down the grove slowly. Terrifying feral noises emanated from the creatures that pulled his body, and, in blind terror and pain, O'Neill's mind froze as he was hauled closer and closer to the icy cold lake. As he realised his body would be lost forever in the icy depths, he gathered his wits for one final time and repeated the rite of exorcism but still with no effect. In desperation, he recited Psalm 23[37], but the monstrous creatures remained immune to his attempts to banish them. As he was dragged closer to the lake's edge, his body smashed over the harsh rocky surface, ripping his vestments and removing the skin on his hands and elbows. In despair, he began reciting the ninth-century version of the Catholic Kyrie invocation[38], but still with no effect.

---

36 Called variously "Mari Lwyd" "Láir Bhán" or "Laare Vane" in different Celtic regions and countries.

37 "Yea, though I walk through the valley of the shadow of death, I will fear no evil: for thou art with me; thy rod and thy staff they comfort me."

38 "Kyrie, rex genitor ingenite, vera essentia, eleyson. Kyrie, luminis fons rerumque conditor, eleyson."
(Lord, King and Father unbegotten, True Essence of the Godhead, have mercy on us. Lord, Fount of light and Creator of all things, have mercy on us).

Seconds later, his body gave a massive involuntary exhalation as he was pulled into the lake's icy waters. The dramatic thermal shock made O'Neill's body enter a state of disassociation, where time seemed to stand still under the icy water.

O'Neill could feel an agonising pain in each of his limbs, caused by the combined force of the numerous powerful jaws and sharp incisors that had seized him in the grove. Under the water, these skeletal creatures continued to work in a coordinated manner, slowly dragging him deeper and deeper into the dark, icy nadir of the small glacial lake. As he was forcibly dragged down to a watery grave, the icy cold made O'Neill feel strangely detached as if he had separated from his body, and he could watch it being guided to the murky bottom.

O'Neill felt strangely at peace as his body began to give up the last vestiges of life and surrender to its watery grave. Then he saw them, the bodies of others who had shared this watery end, and he felt pity that their souls had been violated. He began a sincere prayer to his God that these others should not be forsaken. He was no longer concerned with his own salvation. However, like all the others he had made that night, his prayer seemed to be going unanswered as his body made one final convulsion and his lungs involuntarily took a deep breath of the ice-cold lake water.

3   THE SUMMONING

"Believed to be one of the most ancient myths of the Alemannic, [Germanic Tribe of Switzerland], the Wuodan in Wuotis Heer ("Wuodan's Army") was a terrifying procession of preternatural beings that chased the living, sought to rend them to pieces or drag them to their doom. In Viking culture, this chase was better known as Asgårdsreien: The Wild Hunt of Odin." - Occult Lore of Switzerland (1879) Uppsala University Publishing House.

The Fontaine Mansion,
Rue des Granges,
Old Town, 1204 Geneva,
Switzerland

03:33HRS (GMT+2), 7th Sept, present day

Just as the inert body of Fr Thomas O'Neill began its final journey to join the numerous other human and animal remains that littered the bottom of the icy lake, an impact disturbed the still surface of the water high above him. From his viewpoint, twenty feet down, near the rocky bottom of the lake, surrounded by terrifying skeletal creatures, who continued dragging his inert body downwards, O'Neill could only just make out the small shape that had leapt into the lake surface above him. But whatever it was, it broke some dark enchantment. It freed O'Neill from the trance like lethargy that, like a bird hypnotised by a snake, had seemed to make his death in this watery grave an inevitable, irresistible destiny.

O'Neill's disassociated consciousness was suddenly back in his body. He kicked violently with his legs and pulled desperately with his arms, slowly struggling free from the deadly grip of the skeletal creatures that held him. Once freed from the toxic grip of those jagged teeth and powerful jaws, O'Neill's body began to rise slowly towards the surface. During his ascent, he passed the mysterious object that had freed him from his stupor as it sank down, taking the priest's place in the watery grave. It was a small dog. O'Neill's sluggish mind slowly remembered the realtor's poodle, Napoleon. Floating on the surface, some small distance from where Napoleon had entered the water, was a small wooden stick, clearly having been thrown into the lake to induce Napoleon to leap after it and, by doing so, save O'Neill.

After what felt like an eternity, O'Neill's body broke the surface. A pair of strong hands immediately grabbed the back of his soaked vestments and dragged him from the water, placing him on the rocky edge by the lake in what he recognised was the classic recovery position. His body instantly began a series of violent coughing spasms that brought a recurrence of the awful choking sensation that he had already been through once that evening when he first fell into the water.

Agonising minutes passed before he finally cleared his lungs and gasped long, delicious breaths of the warm evening air. As his senses returned, he noticed a dry beach towel and an emergency space blanket placed around his soaked frame. It was only then that he began to feel how completely the icy cold of the waters had penetrated throughout his body.

His rescuer also realised the importance of getting O'Neill somewhere warmer because the same strong pair of hands that had pulled him from the icy lake now guided him to his feet, across the sacred grove, and out of the grounds, through a hole that had been cleanly cut in the wire perimeter fence.

O'Neill was helped down the steep grass verge that led from the estate boundary to a small, two-lane service road, where he was bundled through a wide sliding door and into the heavenly warmth inside a 1967, split windscreen,

Volkswagen camper van with pre-2009 Paris number plates. Under the sodium street lighting, the lower sections of the van's metallic green bodywork matched perfectly with the classic, white paintwork on the upper sections. The rear exterior of the classic vehicle was taken up by the carrying rack for a large, black, Triumph motorcycle[39].

Everything had the original period fittings for heating, cooking, and refrigeration inside the classic mini-van. The folding beds and storage bins also still respected the late 60's style of the original mini-van design and colours. On the right side of the split front windscreen, the glass was fitted with a suction cup, holding a small Garmin navigation unit that, O'Neill reflected, although not expensive, would allow the van to complete long journeys without significant challenges.

A well-used fifteen-inch Hewlett Packard laptop and an unbranded android phone were strapped in one of the many storage bins beside the driving seat. A classic black Kangol Colt, open-faced motorcycle helmet, and a pair of matching goggles were on the passenger seat. An open cupboard situated behind the driver's seat revealed some well-used books. From his standing position in the main cabin, O'Neill could identify copies of Regardie's Complete Golden Dawn, The Book of Abramelin[40], the Lesser Key of Solomon[41] and several handwritten tomes, embossed with Arabic, Hermetic, Pagan and Runic scripts on their heavily worn bindings.

Once seated on one of the two-seater benches in the rear of the van, O'Neill had his first clear look at the person who

---

[39] A Triumph Bonneville Black.

[40] A hand written 14th century Hebrew version, by Rabbi Yaakov Moelin.

[41] Also known as Clavicula Salomonis Regis or Lemegeton.

had just saved his life. The interior lights of the camper revealed a small figure whose face was obscured by the fabric from a long, dark, hooded sweatshirt with "Sorbonne Universite" written discretely, in a red text, on the front. The university hoodie was worn under an open, close-fitted, black leather Richa biker's jacket. O'Neill noted that the colour theme continued to the RST "Kate" leather trousers and a pair of calf-length, black Bering "Morgane" motorcycle boots.

Noticing O'Neill's interest, the figure pulled back their hood to reveal the face of an attractive woman in her early forties, with long, auburn hair tied into a pony tail that trailed down the back of her jacket. The hair was swept back from her temples, highlighting a refined and intelligent face that sported classic, round, steel-rimmed glasses. High cheek bones gave her a striking natural beauty that she underplayed, with a conspicuous lack of any makeup. Apart from the smell of fine leather that emanated from her clothing, now that they were in the enclosed space of the mini-van, there was also a subtle mixture of scents, orange, vanilla and white musk, that could only come from classic French perfumery[42].

O'Neill estimated this striking woman was around five foot nine inches tall and weighed maybe 120 lbs. Although, based on the way she had lifted the deadweight of his soaked body from the water, she was deceptively strong and also very physically fit.

She removed a black CORDURA latex glove from her right hand and extended it towards O'Neill. He reached forward to take the small but strong hand and went to shake it. Effortlessly avoiding O'Neill's attempted grip, the stranger instead proceeded to take his pulse while consulting the

---

[42] Guerlain's "L'Heure de Nuit"

sweeping second hand on her Mondaine[43]. Apart from the classic timepiece, her only other jewellery was a highly distinctive golden ring, decorated with some engravings, that she wore on her right forefinger. The only symbols that O'Neill could clearly make out on the unusual jewellery during the brief period that his pulse was being taken were the numbers "7° = 4° [44]".

As an implicit question passed between them, she spoke for the first time.

"Ne t'inquiète pas, tu vivras." (Don't worry, you'll live.)

Simultaneously with her response, she retrieved a glass bottle, of five-star Martell brandy, from a small drawer in the kitchen unit along with a tall, steel Thermos flask from the draining board beside the fitted sink and poured two cups of steaming black coffee from the Thermos. She added a generous measure of brandy to the cup that she offered to O'Neill. After an appreciative sip, O'Neill looked at the stranger.

"I thought I had seen everything in my deliverance work, but nothing had prepared me for that,"

O'Neill gestured towards the grove inside the mansion grounds,

"What the hell happened there?"

The stranger sat back in her chair and regarded O'Neill carefully, taking in his clerical dog collar, before replying in a

---

[43] A white faced, MONDAINE OFFICIAL SWISS RAILWAYS watch on a tan leather strap.

[44] Denotes the Sefirot, "Chesed", (Mercy) on the Kabbalistic Tree of Life and the initiatory grade "Adeptus Exemptus" in the Western Esoteric Tradition (WET).

refined accent that retained only the lightest trace of French inflexion.

"Before I explain, maybe I should learn your name?" She paused, clearly waiting for the response from the soaked figure in front of her.

"O'Neill. Father Thomas O'Neill of the Vatican Deliverance unit."

She extended her arm once again, this time firmly shaking his hand, as she introduced herself,

"Madeleine Mathers." She then continued,

"Father O'Neill, you have clearly studied your Christian principles in great depth to work in the field that you do, but you must understand that each theology has its own sets of beliefs that, over time, can, with the correct intent, create their independent realities. You just encountered one of those realities."

O'Neill found himself shivering involuntarily as he recalled the skeletal creatures that had attacked him in the glade.

"But none of the Ritus Romanus had any effect on those... those *things.*"

Mathers nodded sympathetically,

"Those so-called *things* come from a time long before your Christian faith. Put simply. They do not know of or believe in your Christ, Saints or Angels. Therefore, your rites have no meaning for them."

O'Neill became incredulous, exclaiming.

"Nonsense!"

Mathers ignored her guest's outburst and looked in the direction of the glade. O'Neill followed her glance with a nervous expression as if he half expected to see the terrifying things re-emerge.

"Father O'Neill, I am a student of more ancient theologies than yours. Those skeletal headed entities you encountered tonight in the grove were summoned into our reality by acts of ritual intent."

In the act of self-preservation, O'Neill's mind had blanked out the full implications of his having been seized and physically dragged through the grove in the bony jaws of shroud covered phantasms, that were, evidently, utterly immune to every aspect of the Roman Ritual.

The idea that someone might have deliberately summoned such *monsters* into physical existence, using rituals more powerful than those of his beloved Church, was too much for his rational mind to accept.

But Mathers' calm explanation had begun to unleash the repressed implication into O'Neill's consciousness that some dark forces and rituals were beyond any hope of Christian deliverance. As a result, O'Neill began to show the classic symptoms of post-traumatic stress. It was clear that the priest's mind was still struggling to accept what he was being told and he would soon become overwhelmed by the symptoms of extreme psychosomatic trauma.

Mathers sensed that she needed to act quickly and provide evidence of her statements. She calmly reached down the length of her right leg and retrieved a steel folding boot knife[45] with a spring-assisted opening switch that instantly brought a razor-sharp, four-inch blade into sight. The French adept reached over and clinically cut away sections of the priest's shirt, sleeves and trouser legs. The action was so rapid that O'Neill remained unaware of what had happened until after Mathers' knife had returned to her right boot.

---

[45] A Fontenille Pataud Corsican Vendetta.

Mathers' knife strokes revealed thick bands of necrotised flesh that slowly spread over the skin around his midsection, arms, and legs. These wounds corresponded exactly with where O'Neill had felt the skeletal jaws seize him.

While O'Neill looked with dumbfounded shock at the dark bands of putrefying flesh slowly spreading over his body, Mathers gestured towards the lesions.

"Tu vois ? (You see?) They were draining the Vital Life Force[46] from you."

She then saturated sections of the cloth she had just cut from the priest's vestments with the fine French brandy. She systematically applied them to the wounds, soaking the infected epidermis and causing O'Neill to wince with pain, but immediately halting the slow spread of the decay, before she continued with her elucidation.

"Yes, these ancient things have probably resided on this site since the end of the last ice age. Doubtless lying there, dormant, for millennia, until they were reawakened by the recent blood rituals conducted here."

O'Neill numbly nodded, his mind struggling to accept the terrible alternative reality that had been revealed to him, then the full implications of what Mathers had just said struck him.

"Ms Mathers, I refuse to believe that anything exists beyond Christ, my redeemer. Let alone accept that *things* like those can be summoned by a *simple pagan* ritual."

O'Neill gestured to the estate grounds and then to the gruesome wounds still in evidence on his body.

---

[46] VLF – Vital Life Force: The vibratory energy drawn from the process of breathing which, according to esoteric belief, animates the ethereal and corporal bodies.

Mathers nodded her understanding of how hard it must be for a Roman Catholic Priest to accept the alternatives of a much broader reality.

"Je connais. (I know) It is a lot to take in all at once. Perhaps it would be better to show the alternative reality here rather than to try and explain because, I promise, there is very little that is *simple* about these particular *pagan* rituals."

O'Neill shook his head and reached for the old and heavily scuffed android phone beside the driver's seat.

"There is nothing more to explain, Ms Mathers; we must call the Police. They will know what to do. They will bring guns or explosives or whatever is needed to exterminate those creatures and then retrieve the bodies of those poor victims at the bottom of the lake so that they can receive a proper Christian burial."

Mathers smiled at the naivety of the priest sitting in front of her.

"Your police will find nothing and will simply think you are insane."

As Mathers gently but firmly took the phone from O'Neill's hand, O'Neill sensed a disturbing truth about Madeleine Mathers. When he looked into her eyes, he recognised the potential for terrifying darkness and supernatural power within the person before him.

While O'Neill was silently contemplating that this inexplicable woman might be extraordinarily dangerous, Mathers returned the phone next to her laptop and resumed her explanation.

"You think *only* in terms of *Good* and *Evil*, Father O'Neill. Of *monsters* that must always be destroyed because you do not understand them. The truth is always more complex because everything is dual in nature. Whatever destroys must also create. Acts intended to exclusively create good or evil always fail because the dualistic nature of this material plane means they also manifest their cardinal opposite, often in what appears, to the uninitiated, to be the most unpredictable coincidences."

She opened one of the cupboards beside her and pulled out a large, black plastic bin liner, a jar of honey, a large salt cellar, a small loaf of French bread, and a natural coloured Le Bon Marché branded merino wool blanket. She passed the blanket to O'Neill while placing the other items in a small Longchamp branded fabric satchel.

"Put this over yourself and come with me,"

She then checked the time on her watch,

"There is less than an hour before dawn and the end of the current nocturnal alignment between the full moon and Venus. Just enough time for you to see your phantoms released from their age-old bondage to this place."

She then pulled open the van's sliding door and gestured for O'Neill to follow her as she walked up the grass slope, through the opening cut into the wire fence, and back towards the grove.

The flaming torches had dimmed considerably since the encounter, but the patterns in the grass, formed from when O'Neill was dragged through the grove, remained visible. Mathers reached down and picked up the scattered trail of O'Neill's belongings, phone, bible and an empty silver holy water bottle that she passed to him, with the instruction,

"No phone calls yet, not until you better understand what happened here. Now, there will be a blood sacrifice around... ah, yes, over here."

She walked calmly towards a tall, dark figure that was gradually revealed, standing in the shadows, to one side and behind the right-hand door to the great hall. O'Neill could make out the head of the figure through the gloom, its head slumped to one side and, to O'Neill's horror, on the top of the tall figure's head were a pair of large, bony horns. Stifling a scream, O'Neill noted that his petite companion was showing no sign of alarm, so he steeled himself and followed her as calmly as he could, all the time making ready to run at the slightest sign of danger.

As O'Neill approached closer, he could see that the horned figure was, in reality, the body of a large male goat that had been tied in an upright position before having a vicious incision made from its neck down to its groin. Its horned head lay to one side of its body, almost like some cruel parody of the Crucifixion. The poor animal had clearly died in agony, as its entrails and blood had flowed copiously over the ground beneath its dying body.

Mathers produced her boot knife again and cut the rough hemp cords tied around the fore and hind legs to let the body down from its sacrificial position slowly.

"Why had they tied the poor animal like that?" Asked the horrified O'Neill.

"It is tied in an upright stance to represent a human sacrifice,"

She commented quietly, to herself, "La chèvre sans cornes[47]",

before continuing in English,

"They could not find a suitable human in time, so they made do."

Mathers dragged the fore and hind legs of the animal across the grass, its entrails trailing behind, as they cascaded out of the open wound that ran along the entire length of

---

[47] "The goat without horns" is a Left-Hand Path (LHP) ritual Magic term implying a human sacrifice. Most frequently used in modern times within the practice of Voodoo.

the animal, along with huge clots of drying blood. The air became filled with the strong scent of iron, and dead meat as Mathers gently lowered the goat's body inside the black plastic bin bag, applied the bag's tie cords to seal the body out of sight, and left it in the centre of the grove pathway.

O'Neill was not sure if it was a trick of the flickering torch lights, but he was convinced that dark animated shadows gathered around the trail of blood and offal that traced where Mathers had dragged the goat's body. The forms looked vaguely human, but on closer inspection, that was not quite correct. The shapes were only partly human. Their limbs and heads showed a variety of forms from the animal kingdom and the darkest imaginings of renaissance artists[48].

Fear, combined with the sickening smell and terrifying shadows, began to overwhelm O'Neill. He involuntarily doubled over and fell to his knees, violently throwing up, prompting Mathers to sigh and complain under her breath, in French, about wasting her five-star Martell. Ignoring the incapacitated priest, she then walked purposely down the grove, gathering flowers while at the same time extinguishing the remaining flaming torches.

She stopped at the end of the grove and scattered the flowers and blooms she had picked into a roughly circular shape, around twelve feet in diameter. Once the circle's outline was defined to her satisfaction, she repeated the tracing around the circumference, this time pouring the salt that she had brought from the VW camper around the entire perimeter. After carefully examining her work, she made a grunt of satisfaction before pulling one of the extinguished torch stakes from its place at the edge of the

---

[48] These blood animated shadows were frequently mentioned in ancient accounts of blood sacrifice as "larvae" or "shades". Magical lore explains them as the reanimated ethereal bodies of the recently deceased (of all species).

grove pathway and sinking it into the ground within the perimeter of the circle. By this time, O'Neill had recovered enough to join Mathers at the end of the grove, close to the lakeside stone edge. She gestured for him to sit close to her, well inside the circle, and told him to remain still and silent, no matter what he might see or experience in the coming moments.

Mathers again checked her watch and, evidently being satisfied that there was sufficient time for whatever she had planned, she began. She sat cross-legged, facing towards the part of the circle nearest to the lake and slowly and methodically unpacked the bread and honey from the fabric bag she had brought from the caravanette. As she unpacked the items, she began to sing, allowing her body to sway slowly and rhythmically, in a perfect cadence to the exotic melody she was singing, in a language that O'Neill could not understand but sounded full of the joys of creation and life. In a powerful synchronicity, the start of Mathers' singing coincided with a mist forming over the lake's cold waters. The vapour grew thicker and gradually extended beyond the water's edge, spreading over the entire grove, rapidly reducing visibility until only the flowers and salt that formed the edge of Mather's circle were visible, along with the flattened grass inside the confines of the circle.

The slow cadence and lilting melody made O'Neill's exhausted body sway gently back and forth, and his tired eyes closed involuntarily. He reflected that he had never heard such a calming yet compelling song. He was about to ask Mathers if she wanted him to light the beacon beside them, but as he opened his eyes, he was surprised to find that the torch was already alight, its flames illuminating the flower circle and casting strange shadows around them in the wall of lake mist that had thickened and now surrounded them. He rationalised that the strange singing figure in front of him must have stood and lit the torch without breaking the rhythm or cadence of her haunting melody.

While O'Neill's eyes explored the thick wall of fog that mysteriously did not penetrate significantly inside the edges of the small circle where they sat, the sound of Mathers' song was disturbed by the noise of water slapping loudly against the lakeside edge. Something was disturbing the still, deep waters. The lapping sound was quickly overwhelmed by a louder disturbance. Something or, more accurately, some things, were emerging, slowly, clumsily, from the icy waters and making their way onto land. The unmistakable sounds of numerous, unsteady footsteps resonated from the cobblestone surface that marked the start of the sacred grove.

The sounds indicated a procession of some kind had made its way between the rows of fruit trees that demarked the edges of the grove and headed down the clearing on either side of the small circle. The ground trembled gently inside the circle, like a large crowd of people passed close by on their way to some important assembly. But, O'Neill's earlier experience with these entities had already taught him that these things were far from harmless wanderers; their search was for what Mathers had described in the minivan as the Vital Life Force[49] of the body or what the Roman Church terms the Spirit[50], of their victims.

Thankfully, something in Mathers' simple ritual was protecting them, as these terrifying creatures did not seem to notice the two figures seated in their midst. Some of them did, however, come close enough to the edge of the

---

[49] Nefesh in the Kabbalistic tradition

[50] Not to be confused with the immortal principle, called Ātman (आत्मन्) in the Eastern Esoteric Traditions (EET), "Soul" by the Roman Church and "Yechida" by the Kabbalists of the Western Esoteric Tradition (WET).

protective circle to partially reveal themselves through the opaque wall of fog. There was no doubt that they were the same, unusually lofty entities that O'Neill had seen earlier; the tops of their hoods were at least 12 feet above where O'Neill sat. The flickering light from the flaming torch inside the circle cast long shadows that made their perambulation past the seated pair look like stilt performers from an old-fashioned circus.

Whatever they were, their physical forms were obscured by a long, white, shroud-like covering over their entire body that draped like a parody of a long bridal train behind them. The soaking shroud dripped copious amounts of water onto the grass. It made their fabric wrappings drag along the ground as they moved, producing the hideous slithering sound that O'Neill recalled so vividly from when he had observed the tall figures in the grove earlier that evening.

One of the shrouded entities on Mathers' side had stumbled upon the edge of their protective circle. It was pushing one of its long legs towards the flower-strewn boundary, pulling back its shroud-like covering and revealing its leg's bleached white bones and, more terrifyingly for O'Neill, a long skeletal, cloven hoof.

The associations of the cloven hoof with the Christian Devil, combined with the memory of how a similar creature had dragged O'Neill to a potentially watery grave, made his blood run cold. He emitted an involuntary cry of terror, only to find Mathers' hand grasping his arm with firm, reassuring pressure that somehow made him regain some self-control and prevented him from running blindly from the circle, down the grove, and back into the mansion.

"Satan!" he exclaimed in a whisper while crossing himself involuntarily and imploring Mathers,

"You... You MUST use whatever power you possess to destroy this most ancient evil!"

"Stop such melodramatic nonsense," Mathers replied in a soothing tone that one would use with a petulant child.

"These are simple, soulless beings, animated by numerous repeated rituals, combined with blood sacrifices and informed intent. Conjured by another human being, who wished to simulate the ancient Nordic legend of Asgårdsreien."

"Azazael's run?" O'Neill's poor pronunciation and the deliberate use of a secret angelic name, purported by some in the Roman Church to be Satan himself, prompted Mathers to explain further and correct.

"You would know it better by its anglicised name "The Wild Hunt".

O'Neill nodded as if he was a leading authority on the topic.

"Yes, I have heard of this unholy rite. On dark nights, the Devil rides abroad, leading a pack of his demonic hell hounds, hunting Christian Souls to drag to Hell!"

Mathers sighed before continuing her explanation.

"In its original, pagan form, the head of the Nordic Gods, Wotan, leads the wild chase as they seek those unworthy of a noble warrior's death."

Mathers gestured to the skeletal hoof that was continuing to scratch away what remained of the salt circle.

"But I believe these phantoms are not enacting the original form of this pagan belief. Instead, they are an abuse of ritual magic that has been used to create a horrifyingly convincing display for someone or some group who needed to be persuaded about the reality of some ancient belief system. Probably to encourage rich patrons to make large financial contributions to a related cause."

O'Neill flinched as the cloven hoof moved closer, continuing its grim work removing the thin layer of salt that remained in the circle's perimeter.

"You must destroy them before they break into the circle and drag us to the lake!"

"Nonsense, the circle is all the protection we need. As you saw, I took the precaution of removing and sealing away the blood sacrifice, and since my invocation was with the positive elements of bread, salt and honey, these phantasms were not summoned by any aspect of a dark intent or bloody ritual. They have no access to blood or recently dead bodies, so they will remain relatively passive before I formally release them from their association with this location.

I would not recommend that a non-initiate like yourself leave the safety of the circle. Still, even if you were to venture outside, these creatures would probably only exhibit curiosity about you.

You must understand that such artificial entities only become dangerous when there is a body from a blood sacrifice nearby. Still, even then, their attack on you would be limited in its ferocity since the goat's body had been tethered. If the remains and blood had been spread freely and these entities had been able to have free access to those remains, well...."

She hesitated and smiled.

"Let us just be glad that will not happen."

O'Neill was not convinced. "You forget, I have first-hand experience of these so-called phantasms. I can assure you they are not passive. You have a responsibility to destroy them. Or is your ritual as impotent as mine against them?"

The French Magician smiled enigmatically.

"Father O'Neill, yes, in truth, the situation is more complex than perhaps I initially indicated.

Adepts, like myself, are prohibited from the use of offensive high magic by the Paris Council of 1682. If you know your history from that period, you will recall that there had been widespread social unrest with numerous witchcraft trials in Europe and America. After much bloodshed, it was decided that society would become more stable if the public were encouraged to disbelieve in the existence of hidden forces. So, the high council of esoteric orders[51] decreed that only passive, protective magic would be permitted, and it was agreed that there would be a moratorium on Offensive Magic. This prohibition has held for over 300 years."

O'Neill looked incredulously at his companion in the circle.

"What exactly does the prohibition ban?"

"It is forbidden to use anything other than passive, protective mechanisms, such as this circle."

O'Neill assumed a scholarly tone that he probably adopted with his students,

"With respect, Ms Mathers, that sounds like a convenient excuse to avoid humiliating demonstrations that prove ritual magic does not work. Besides, if such a moratorium existed, after three centuries, I doubt modern adepts, such as you claim to be, would even remember how to use so-called offensive techniques anymore!"

Before Mathers could respond, there was the sound of another creature emerging violently from the still waters by the lakeside edge. This unknown entity sounded much smaller and very different from the arrival of the tall, shrouded figures that were still perambulating through the

---

[51] SPLEE. Société pour la préservation des lignées ésotériques européennes.

thick mist beside the edges of the protective circle. One could hear this newcomer shaking itself dry before tiny, rapid legs scampered over the stones and onto the grass-covered grove. As this new arrival rushed past the edge of the circle, it could be seen to be a very wet, miniature French poodle; its tawny coat was no longer in its elegant trimmed form. Instead, it looked more like the hunting dog deep within its gene pool.

"It's Napoleon!" exclaimed O'Neill, only to be abruptly silenced by Mathers,

"Shhh! The last thing we want is for the dog to cross into the circle and break the protection. Don't attract its attention and avoid saying its name until this is all over," she consulted her watch, "just twelve minutes before sunrise, and we will be safe."

The small dog continued its dash along the sacred grove, barking at the shrouded entities and causing the tall skeletal forms to emit a hissing sound that sounded half snake and half-human.

Then the barking stopped abruptly and was replaced by a deep growl, interspersed with the sound of plastic being ripped and rendered apart by strong canine teeth.

"Merde! Le sang!" exclaimed Mathers as the colour bleached from her face. She turned to O'Neill and pulled him towards her.

"Get closer to the centre and keep your arms and legs well away from the edge of the circle. Things are going to get... unpleasant."

"Unpleasant? Do you mean it can get worse than having these skeletal devils clawing at the circle's edge?"

O'Neill's query was answered as the air became filled with numerous savage growls, and blood covered forms raced past the circle's edge, snarling and roaring towards each other and the whole of creation.

As if answering the feral roars of the blood-crazed monsters, there sounded a hunting horn that repeated its eery piercing blast as it approached. Within moments, the circle's edge became surrounded by shrouded beasts, covered in blood and offal. Goat entrails hung from the misshapen teeth in their skeletal snouts. Although not alive, the monsters took deep breaths as though they could smell the two people within the circle.

"That's bad, isn't it.." O'Neill clung to Mathers' arm.

"Vous avez un don pour l'euphémisme." (You have a gift for understatement)

"Mathers, you must act to destroy them..."

"I have told you; it is forbidden. Stay well inside the circle, provided nothing breaks it...."

Mathers never finished her sentence as she was interrupted by a small, rapidly moving blur of blood-stained fur that yapped and barked excitedly, as it leapt at O'Neill and licked his face, covering both of them with a mix of dog slobber and goat's blood.

The passage of the small dog across the salt and flower boundary of the protective circle brought a group of four searching skeletal snouts immediately into the confines of the small space. Multiple blood-soaked mouths, filled with twisted, bloody teeth, grabbed the terrified O'Neill by his arms, legs and torso. They pulled his screaming form out of the circle and down the length of the tree-lined grove that had become visible the instant the small dog had breached the circle's perimeter.

A second later, the air was filled with pitiful yelps as the blood-soaked miniature poodle was grabbed up into the mouth of another of the skeletal creatures, which then lumbered down the glade in the same direction as the other creatures were dragging the screaming priest.

"Fuck it." Exclaimed Mathers, as she watched O'Neill and the small poodle looking helplessly towards her with imploring eyes as they were carried away by the creatures she had only recently described as harmless.

The piercing blast of a spectral hunting horn became ever closer as the remaining gore-crazed creatures roared and stamped their hooved feet in an ever-wilder frenzy along the length of the sacred grove. Four of them broke away from the mass and surrounded the seated figure of Mathers, moving closer with every second, as they prepared to seize the French Adept from the now violated protective circle and carry her down the grove.

As if she was calmly accepting her fate, she stood, facing the gathering of four blood-crazed skeletal monsters in front of her. She slowly and deliberately stepped outside of the protective circle, outstretched her arms, so her body formed the shape of a cross[52], and then crossed her arms diagonally over her chest and bowed her head[53].

The four skeletal creatures took a single, unified pace back from this strange figure, around whom the atmosphere now hummed with an unseen power that could be felt, like the vibration of a massive locomotive that was powering up.

---

52 Known as "The sign of Osiris Slain". Denoting an adept of the second order within the traditional Golden Dawn based system of ritual magic. There are three orders within these systems, the third and highest order is believed (by traditionalists) to only be achieved by non-physical beings, who are regarded as "Masters" or sometimes "Secret Chiefs".

53 The sign of Osiris Risen. Also denoting an adept of the second order.

Mathers extended her right hand towards the heavens while her left pointed towards the ground[54]. She then brought her heels together, slightly angled to form a letter V, placing each hand on either side of her head beside her temples. She then extended her thumbs from her fists. Above her head, a sphere of opaque mist began to form and soon glowed an incandescent white, with a brightness that illuminated the entire scene like an array of spotlights. Her golden adepts ring blazed like it was red hot on her hand[55].

Mathers exhaled and uttered a single word[56] with a thunderous voice that felt like its vibrations carried to the very edge of the universe.

"Suffisant !" (Enough!)

The scene around her instantly transformed. The crazed skeletal creatures abruptly ceased their wild motions. Instead, they all backed away from her in evident terror. O'Neill and Napoleon were dropped to the ground, and their attackers fell over each other in their eagerness to depart as quickly as they could back to the lake.

---

54 The sign of Earth. Cornerstone of the Western Esoteric and ancient Hermetic Traditions. The Adept's proclamation, attributed to Hermes Trismegistus. "Quod est inferius est sicut quod est superius. Et quod est superius est sicut quod est inferius, ad perpetranda miracula rei unius." (As above, so below, as within, so without, as the universe, so the soul...)

55 The sign of Pan. Indicates a 7th degree-initiated adept of the Western Esoteric Tradition (WET), the highest grade awarded to living mortals in the more ancient (traditional) schools of the Western Esoteric Tradition.

56 It should be understood that it is the action of the will that is the key element of magic and not, as many suppose, the word or phrase that is uttered.

O'Neill was left looking confused but relieved, lying on the ground some twenty feet away.

Mathers walked slowly down the now empty grove to where O'Neill was lying. The stunned priest looked at her in awe, the bright light above her head still visible, like the halo from a medieval painting, but gradually fading until it vanished.

Mathers winked conspiratorially, saying,

"Just because something is forbidden does not mean it has been forgotten. Come on, let's have something to eat. I do not know about you, but conjuration always makes me starving."

4 AWAKENING

*"What does not kill me makes me stronger" - Friedrich
Nietzsche, Twilight of the Idols, 1888.*

*A Small Oasis, Twenty Miles West of The Gurvan Saikhen
Mountains
Gobi Desert
Southern Mongolia*

15:00HRS. (GMT+8) 8th Sept, Present day.

The exceptionally fit-looking man lay on his back. Over the
last forty-eight hours, the movements of his semi-conscious
body had caused shallow indentations in the wet, coarse
mixture of yellow sand and lighter coloured small pebbles
that surrounded his athletic frame. The man's thick dark
hair was swept back from his face and was permeated with a
mixture of perspiration, salt and sand that glistened in the
oppressive desert sun.

His head rested near some small, smooth rocks that marked
the edge of a shallow, twenty-foot square pool of water that
emerged from an aquafer buried somewhere deep beneath
the desolate Gobi Desert sands. The surface of this murky
liquid was partially obscured by accumulations of thick,
fifteen-foot-tall Burma reeds. Such reed formations are
found in the watering holes all along the ancient silk routes
of the Gobi; the reed seeds having been unwittingly
transported from oasis to oasis in the thick fur of the
Bactrian camels that have passed these same desolate and
inhospitable routes for untold millennia.

The numerous scars and injuries on the man's lean body
glistened with the dense perspiration so often associated
with recovery from a serious illness. The highly distinctive

hawk-like features of the man's face was soaked in the sweat of heavy fever, and his body jerked in a series of movements that represented some unknown activity in his dreams.

A close inspection of his fingernails showed several of them had been ripped clean from his fingers, and three of the digits on his left hand showed signs of having had the flesh gnawed away by some sharp interlocking scissor-shaped abrasion.

His "tearproof" desert camouflage[57] had been shredded in numerous areas, exposing the flesh on his arms and legs. While in other areas, the fabric tears revealed deep gouges in the hardened[58] surface of the shining hexagonal scales[59] of his body armour that covered the vulnerable areas of his chest, neck, groin and thighs. Some of the most vicious flesh wounds on his arms were fresh and marked with long serrated patterns and the pungent smell of putrefying shellfish.

The broken remains of a highly distinctive Japanese combat dagger[60] were attached to the unconscious man's webbing belt. This Tanto[61] styled weapon had a thick, white organic

---

[57] DuPont Kevlar reinforced Scorpion W2 Desert Sand pattern camouflage uniform.

[58] Wurtzite Boron Nitride (BN) surface treatment, 20 per cent tougher than diamond.

[59] Silicon carbide ceramic Dragon Skin Extreme. Alleged to resist the US DOD "X Threats" including the classified M993 7.62mm NATO armour-piercing round and some classes of grenade.

[60] The Rockstead UN-ZDP boasts a ZDP-189/VG10 powdered, hand ground, steel blade. It is widely regarded as the finest knife blade ever created.

[61] The Tanto was one of the classic Japanese Samurai weapons. Traditionally a very short sword for close combat. It has become

material plastered between the stylised Tsukamaki silk grip wrappings, completely obscuring the exquisite stingray skin covering of the handle. This disgusting white substance was also in evidence in the serrations on the top rear thumb grip and deep in the "blood groove" on what remained of the nine-inch razor-edged knife. These deposits of rotting organic matter emitted the same distinctive aroma of marine decay that was evident in many of the man's vicious wounds. The final two inches of this extraordinarily strong carbon steel alloy blade had been broken clean away while penetrating into some unimaginably tough material.

The man's Suunto ceramic ABC[62] watch had shattered into fragments, its buttons covered in the same thick white flesh and mucus so in evidence on the knife. The watch's carbon fibre band had been torn apart in several places. What remained of the sophisticated timepiece was only kept in place by the cuff of the man's uniform.

Finally, as one's gaze reached the man's extremities, one could see that his heavy boots[63] were cut to ribbons. The thick Milspec materials exhibited the same scissor-like serrations seen on the flesh of his arms and legs. His boots barely remained on his feet but had saved him from massive trauma in a series of sustained ferocious attacks from some terrifying apex predator[64].

---

popular since the 1980s as a stabbing weapon, capable of extraordinary penetration through body armour.

[62] Altimeter Barometer Compass.

[63] Warrior Aqua Sand Boots.

[64] No genetic analysis has been performed on the crustaceans (crab like creatures) that have evolved within the darkness of the vast hidden sea beneath the Gobi. Based on their extreme size and aggressive nature it is likely they are hybrids of the Malacostraca

The fever fuelled dreams of the wounded man were a confusing mix of memories from his childhood in Cairo, Egypt and more recent events in his life. His was a childhood filled with the stories of the brutality of invading nations, from the Greeks and Romans, through to the more modern epochs of the French and British. Each invading nation sacked the riches from the ancient land of the Pharaohs.

The dream images included his mother, recalling worries over the conflicts between the Israeli and Egyptian armies, the overt interventions by America and the then Soviet bloc, and the ever-present threat of an escalation into a global nuclear war. A short-lived but long remembered jubilation, with dancing in the streets of Cairo when the Egyptian army invaded Israel and the corresponding national despair when, after retreating to home territory, the Egyptian Third Army became surrounded by the Israelis. The shame of a proud Arab nation having to accept American aid in return for becoming an American puppet in the Middle East conflicts. While knowing all the time that Russia was their real ally, the one nation which had saved the Egyptian third army from even greater humiliation.

These childhood traumas faded into a mix of more recent memories; an emaciated fifteen-year-old boy running away from home, lying about his age to join the Egyptian army; followed by long boring years of learning basic drill skills and growing into a man who was tough and ruthless enough to be selected into a specialised unit[65] of the Egyptian Sa'ka[66] taskforce. There followed numerous

---

class of decapods (coconut crab) but, due to a lack of vegetation, they have evolved to become exclusively carnivorous.

[65] Unit 777 (Arabic: الوحدة 777 قتال), also known as Task Force 777. Egypt's equivalent of the US Navy Seals or British SAS.

[66] Code name: Thunderbolt

deniable operations in remote regions around the globe, alongside American, Arab and Russian elite forces. Some of these missions forced the young soldier to work alongside Soviet GRU[67] Spetsnaz[68] operatives, which led to the brutal selection process to enter the most secretive elite division of the world's intelligence services[69].

There followed memories of learning distinctive Cyrillic languages, ruthless Russian instructors, dirty cities and concrete utilitarian buildings in Eastern European capitals. Countless hours were spent training in the tradecraft of death, learning about rare and deadly substances unknown to forensic medicine. He completed years of advanced training in every form of effective combat, weapons and methods of bringing a rapid and untraceable end to an individual.

Then the dreams flowed into another, more recent series of images. A highly distinctive whirlpool logo was associated with the emotions of both pride and shame simultaneously. Another set of memories was of a dark-haired woman who was both extraordinarily beautiful and evil. This enigmatic

---

[67] GRU: Main Intelligence Directorate: the foreign military intelligence agency of the Soviet Army's General Staff of the Soviet Union.

[68] Spetsnaz is an abbreviation for "Войска специа́льного назначе́ния" "Special Purpose Military Units" for the GRU. Created during the cold war period for special reconnaissance and direct action (sabotage) attacks on foreign soil.

[69] Unit 7 of the Committee for State Security. The cold war era deniable operations section of Soviet Union's Intelligence Service. Dedicated to assassination, extortion, blackmail, kidnapping, false flag operations and disinformation. They were the equivalent of the "Increment" attached to the British Secret Intelligence Service (MI6), now renamed "E-Squadron" and no longer with the mandate for such disreputable operations, which are now entirely outsourced to private sector contractors.

female appeared in the dreams with different faces and bodies but was mysteriously the same person. These images were interspersed between an immaculately dressed Chinese Priest, who emanated such a powerful persona that it felt like the whole of creation danced in accordance with his will. And then a powerfully built Scotsman, dressed in the chainmail of a hated Crusader Knight, who carried a highly polished stone knife, covered in a series of mysterious symbols that glinted and was in some way connected with the endless searing pain in his left side.

The dreams culminated with nightmare images of endless dark watery caves filled with enormous, ghostly white, flesh-eating monsters. These monsters pursued the dreaming man in an endless battle through a subterranean world of darkness, in a battle that had tested the very limits of one of the most dangerous men in the world.

Four thousand three hundred miles to the North West of the quiet oasis in the desolate wastes of the Gobi Desert was an enormous purpose-built command centre. Its numerous facilities resulted from decades of unimaginable levels[70] of investment in research and development that had been systematically extorted from world governments. Massive diversions of tax payments and national debts, along with manipulated banking crises, stock market crashes and central bank interventions, had resulted in the creation of a self-contained complex of structures that were one of the planet's best-kept secrets. This secret location was where governments were governed, markets manipulated, and currencies controlled. In short, it was the seat of the hidden power that rules our modern world.

---

[70] Quadrillions: Thousands of billions: 10^{15} US Dollars.

It was expertly hidden, in what appeared to any external observer, to be a pristine Alpine wilderness of rugged peaks and sheer rock outcrops in the Bernese Alps, around fourteen miles outside the sleepy Swiss town of Grindelwald.

The perimeter signs surrounding the location proclaimed the whole area to be a Swiss Federally protected site for endangered indigenous flora and fauna; specifically, a rare Alpine Broomrape[71] and the Greater Spotted Eagle[72].

Tree covered walkways that were undetectable from above led from a one hundred and twenty foot long, retractable helipad[73] that could rapidly emerge from the sheer rock face and just as quickly disappear. When concealed, these landing zones looked like rugged rocky outcrops and made the entire site look completely uninhabited. There were no tracks or roads into the site, and all the approaches had been converted into impassable rock overhangs, making access by car or foot impossible.

The concealed pathways from the helipad led into a series of six interlocking, blast protected entrances monitored by a detachment of private contractors, who were highly skilled in using the state-of-the-art surveillance and weapon systems that guarded this most secret of all global locations.

The hidden passageways, carved deep into the rock, were thirty feet wide and fifteen feet high. The walls, floors and ceilings had an array of different sized openings to release

---

[71] The One-Flowered Broomrape: Orobanche purpurea.

[72] The spotted Eagle: Clanga clanga. It is classified as vulnerable to extinction by the International Union for the Conservation of Nature (IUCN).

[73] Capable of handling large transport helicopters such as the Sikorsky CH-53K King Stallion, Boeing CH-47 Chinook and the Bell Boeing V-22 Osprey.

noxious substances and projectiles. Once inside, the visitor was confronted by a series of four massive sliding doors that were recessed into the rock at twenty-foot intervals inside a one-hundred-foot-long stone corridor.

These doors were of a bespoke design by the world's leading specialist in blast protection[74], some ten feet thick, constructed from a composite of concrete, titanium and depleted uranium. They were rated to withstand the typical tactical thermonuclear blasts[75] anticipated in the most likely conflict scenarios projected to occur within a European theatre of war. Each of the four enclosed compartments formed by the doors was a "killing zone" complete with a diverse range of weapons and booby traps designed to neutralize any attacking force rash enough to attempt a forced entry into this modern fortress.

A mile under these concealed and protected entrances was a series of clinically clean sixty-foot square spaces, filled with numerous wide screen control stations connected to a dedicated super computer[76] that made the machines used by the US DOD, NSA and DARPA look like children's toys. The massive power requirements for cooling and powering this mass of silicon, gallium arsenide, glass and liquid nitrogen came from an energy generation system that was even more exotic and secret than the computer system it powered.

---

[74] Korean blast door specialist Dongbang Novoferm. Suppliers of choice to world governments and the super-rich.

[75] Anticipated explosive yields of less than one hundred kilotons from "tactical nuclear" weapons such the French Pluton, Russian OTR-21 Tochka, or the American MGM-52 Lance.

[76] A multi Zettaflop (ZFLOP : 10^{21} flops: Floating Point Instructions per Second) computer built from an array of over a billion cores with a propriety design superior to the existing IBM, Nividia, Intel and Matrix designs.

At the deepest level of this perfectly concealed global control centre lay three Magog[77] generators. These were macro geothermal electrical energy generation systems that used a technology that had been all but eradicated from existence due to its association with the infamous Dr Nissa Ad-Dajjal and her UNITY movement[78].

The complex electronic systems housed in this remote fortress were the apex of a worldwide system that monitored and recorded the activity of over four billion computers and six billion mobile devices that were active globally every day. It used data feeds from internet service providers, global software corporations, telecommunications, law enforcement agencies, and every nation's intelligence services that were ostensibly to monitor and prevent terrorist activities. However, this system was, in reality, devoted to keeping a detailed record of the activities of every person on the planet. Just like every other intelligence database created throughout history, these records had only one particular purpose. Because regardless of whatever noble excuses are used to justify the creation of such systems, they always have the same rationale. This single purpose has inspired every oppressor throughout history to create detailed records of every person they wished to control, from the secret records of the Gestapo in Nazi Germany to those of FBI head J. Edgar

---

[77] Macro GeOthermal Generation, or MaGoG uses the minor temperature differences that occur naturally around us to expand and contract a thermo-sensitive compound, which powers the motion of a simple turbine. Developed by the UNITY corporation as a free energy alternative to fossil fuels, it was the cause of a world-wide conflict between the rich and poor nations.

[78] To fully understand the evil that was associated with the late billionaire Dr Ad-Dajjal and her UNITY movement you should read the prequel to this story, Bridge of Souls: Ancient Prophecy. Ultimate Evil.

Hoover and the files of the dreaded Stasi in Cold War, East Germany.

When you know a person's peculiar vices, you have the most potent of all weapons. The fear of shame, humiliation and public ostracization will make anyone comply with even the most distasteful demands. As history has repeatedly shown, children have betrayed parents under such threats of exposure; Kings have abdicated crowns, and Premiers have betrayed their people in the most despicable ways.

The yottabytes[79] of personal data stored in this global control centre allowed the owners of this system to quite literally control any and every living person on the globe. It held carefully structured information that could be applied to exert pressure on anyone who needed to be coerced into performing some service that furthered the goals of the secretive cabal, who had taken over the supervision of what remained of the disgraced Maelstrom's intelligence and surveillance operations. After the global outrage over the revelation that Maelstrom had held the Western nations and their leaders hostage, anything and everything associated with the name Maelstrom and its signature whirlpool logo had fallen into disrepute. Like so many disgraced organisations before them, a rapid rebranding exercise was completed before business resumed precisely as before. The new leadership replaced the distinctive whirlpool logo with a German heraldic symbol, called Wolfsangel, that was believed to denote liberty, independence and fearlessness. The adoption of this unique logo, which looked like a sideways Z with a bar through it, was accompanied by a global change to the name of the organisation from Maelstrom to Wolfsangel SA[80]. Except that is within Germany, where a historical association between the

---

[79] Yottabyte: 1,204 Zettabytes, or 10^{24} bytes of storage.

[80] Registered in the Swiss Federal Commercial Registry.

Wolfsangel and elite members of the Nazi Party during World War II meant that within Germany, the organisation called itself "Sichern"[81] (meaning Secure).

The mysterious puppet masters who directed this rebranding were led by a charismatic man called "Alpha". Based on the few clues that emerged during this man's rare interventions, he resided somewhere in the Eastern Standard Time zone, but that could mean anywhere along the Eastern coast of North America or numerous South American nations. For most of the time, Alpha was content to let the surviving leaders of Ad-Dajjal's former organisation take responsibility for the day-to-day operations. On the few rare occasions when Alpha communicated, it was only to the new acting leader of Wolfsangel. Such communication was exclusively to use the unimaginable resources already built up by Maelstrom to undermine some nation or a multinational corporation.

By this rebranding as Wolfsangel, the former middle ranks of Maelstrom had come to inherit the day-to-day running of surveillance and intelligence gathering systems designed and created by one of the greatest manipulative geniuses of all time.

This global pyramid of control was coordinated from a sleek, modern board room, some forty feet long and twenty feet wide, with a large, mahogany double door at its Southern entrance. The Northern wall that dominated the view of everyone who entered the room was decorated by an exquisitely detailed and lifelike, full-length fresco that was both compelling and disturbing to everyone who looked upon it. The picture was of an extraordinarily beautiful woman whose sensuous body, flawless skin and long dark hair only accentuated her piercingly hypnotic, emerald green eyes. These drew the viewer into them,

---

[81] Sichern GmbH, based out of Hamburg, Germany.

rapidly and invariably inducing a hypnogogic state characterised by disturbing images and dark compulsions.

For this reason, and because of negative associations[82] with this former owner of the complex, there had been a series of unsuccessful attempts to eradicate the picture. First, by applying chemical paint strippers, then stain blockers and finally thick coats of paint. Each effort resulted in the same outcome; the disturbing image gradually re-emerged, looking as vibrant and detailed as before. The entire painting had been covered by a succession of tapestries, sheets and barriers. Unfortunately, none of these precautions had proven effective either. It seemed nothing could prevent the fresco from exerting a mysterious influence over the room's occupants, making them suffer from an overwhelming compulsion to remove whatever coverings had been used, exposing the fresco once more. So, it was that the painting remained, casting a dark glamour over anyone foolish enough to gaze upon its malevolent beauty for too long.

Apart from the distinctive artwork, the board room was dominated by a long steel and glass table, surrounded by twelve high backed, red leather chairs fitted with adjustable steel and leather armrests. All of the furniture in this windowless room, from the long sideboards to the board table and chairs, displayed the distinctive Pininfarina's Aresline Xten design logo on their surfaces.

The twelve-foot-high walls were painted in an electromagnetic shielded white paint that, when combined with the decorative metal sheets covering the bottom two feet of the wall surface, shielded against all electronic eavesdropping technologies.

---

[82] For example, starting a global conflict and deliberately killing 25% of the world's population.

On the long western side of the room, at eye level, were a series of Mondaine Swiss Railway clocks, showing some of the world's primary time zones.[83] Just below the highest points on the walls were the grills for the ventilation system. These kept the room at precisely seventy-two degrees Fahrenheit with twenty-two per cent humidity and barometric sea level pressure, even though the board room was nearly five thousand feet up in the Swiss Alps.

The floor covering was a handmade Ushak[84]rug with a distinctive star and medallion pattern that perfectly fitted the dimensions of this particular room. Lighting came from over one hundred Plumen LED[85]s embedded into the high ceiling. The multiple facets on these bespoke light bulbs were specially dimpled to reflect light at different angles to give the appearance of localised shadows.

Despite all the state-of-the-art technology that surrounded them, or maybe because the users of this particular facility fully understood how technology eavesdropped on every action, there were no laptops, phones or tablets in evidence at the table. The glass desktop in front of each seat was filled with a simple Liberty leather Ianthe notebook and a white, wooden Faber HB pencil. The rich red leather on the front covers of each of the twelve notebooks were embossed with the same symbol on the pencils, a highly distinctive sideways Z with a bar through the centre.

At this moment, the twelve people occupying the seats around this most illustrious table were all looking towards

---

[83] Washington D.C., UTC, Moscow, Delhi, Seoul and Tokyo.

[84] Named after the Turkish town of Usak, where the finest handmade carpets are created.

[85] The Plumen "003" has a warm-white (2400K) colour temperature, uses 6.5 Watts (equivalent to a 50W incandescent bulb) and is rated for 10,000 hours.

the Eastern side of the room, where an array of 16k high definition 120-inch LG displays showed the status of the current priorities for the most powerful surveillance systems ever created by humanity.

The first set of screens focused on the group's active income streams: insider stock market deals were targeting state pension funds, currency rates were being manipulated to negatively influence the sales of crop harvests from developing nations (ensuring they would remain heavily in debt), and finally, their most lucrative source of income in the past decade, central bank quantitative easing. QE was where trillions of Euros, Dollars or Pounds were acquired in hours, without any significant effort beyond repeating some existing threats to cowardly bankers and corrupt bureaucrats. The public had become so apathetic that they never inquired where these unimaginable sums of money went after being conjured from nothing by the press of a button in Washington, Brussels, London or Tokyo.

All middle-aged leaders gathered here were male, of a similar age, social class and elite education, and had similar corpulent bodies in the steep decline that often accompanies a life of gross excess and complete self-indulgence.

Seated at the head of the table, deliberately facing away from the disturbing fresco behind him, was a short fat man with chronic halitosis, thick gold-rimmed glasses and a badly miscoloured wig - which highlighted his hair loss and his extraordinary vanity. He was dressed in a British Army, Brigadier's mess dress uniform, with enough medals to condemn him to rapid death should he ever fall into any depth of water. Just below these rows of decorative brass, silver and gold was a black, plastic name badge that declared the wearer to be "Brigg. H. Smegett".

Smegett luxuriated back into his two-thousand-dollar chair, admiring the rapidly accumulating fifteen-digit daily income on the LG displays. He raised a Lismore cut crystal brandy glass and appreciated the one-hundred-year-old Rémy Martin Louis XIII cognac. Swallowing slowly, he focused on how the amber nectar burnt going down his throat and then, seconds later, made his body feel utterly tranquil. Such moments allowed him to savour the joys of existence more fully. Even the sensation of his thick pot belly, resting on the top of his fat thighs through the half-lined Hainsworth cloth of his dress trousers, felt unusually comfortable. He reflected on how much his fortunes had radically transformed in the past weeks.

It was only a matter of days ago that Smegget had been detained by Navy SEALs[86] at the Cheyenne Mountain Complex[87]. He had feared that his fate was sealed when he was chained and manhandled onto a C-130J Hercules transport plane at Peterson Airforce Base. This aircraft was headed to Guantanamo Bay Naval Base, where Smeggert was scheduled for hostile interrogation to determine his role in a global coup to seize power from Western governments.

But nature abhors a vacuum, and it was only a matter of hours before the mysterious "Alpha" had reached out from his hidden location and replaced Ad-Dajjal in exerting a sinister influence of blackmail and extortion over the world under the new name of Wolfsangel.

So, although publicly Maelstrom featured in a series of media witch-hunts, privately, world leaders were quickly reminded of their place in the modern world; where their corruption, misuse of taxpayer money and abuses of privilege could be made public knowledge with the press of a button. Knowing that their power, status and historical

---

[86] United States Navy Sea, Air, and Land Teams: SEALs

[87] Again, see Bridge of Souls for more details.

reputation would be lost, under a cloud of shame and public humiliation, world governments quietly released the former senior members of Maelstrom. They issued disproportionately vindictive punishments onto the lower, ordinary Maelstrom operatives, who had little or nothing to do with the attempted world coup.

Under these circumstances, the group of twelve men, currently gathered around this board table, had taken over the operational control of the newly named Wolfsangel. In fairness to them, they had tried to resume the organisation's activities from where Ad-Dajjal had left them, but all twelve of the men had been, without exception, only third-level operatives; judged by Ad-Dajjal to be unworthy for higher positions. They shared the flaws of so many who crave power, inflated egos, a chronic overestimation of their abilities and being utterly dismissive of the capabilities of others while having no scruples about stealing their work. Since they had been excluded from the decision-making processes, they lacked the background information to explain why their late leader had initiated certain ongoing surveillance operations.

For example, an array of multibillion-dollar satellites, eavesdropping technologies and cyber monitoring resources were allocated for observing a desolate area in the Gobi Desert near the Gurvan Saikhen Mountains. No one was sure what they were supposed to be looking for, so they looked for anything out of the ordinary.

Records also showed that, in her final hours, Ad-Dajjal had shown extreme interest in four individuals. Two were Vatican priests. Dr Thomas O'Neill was a discredited archaeologist who had made a series of outlandish claims about discovering a lost civilization that predated recorded history. O'Neill had lost his academic position and was currently assigned to fringe deliverance missions within the Vatican. The other priest was Fr Chin Kwon, now a junior secretary in the papal offices. He had been involved in some comparative religion projects in Tibet and Northern India. He underwent some severe psychotic breakdown and had been confined to a sanatorium for extreme personality disorders. He had apparently made sufficient recovery to resume non-taxing, minor clerical duties.

The other two were British nationals. First was Ms Helen Curren, QC[88], a highly respected barrister working from her chambers near the Temple district in London. Her medical records showed that she had also recently undergone an unspecified but severe mental crisis. She was making a steady recovery and had recently returned to halftime work at her chambers, where she coordinated one of the largest class-action suits in legal history on behalf of the former UNITY supporters.

Finally, there was Sir Tavish Stewart, a Scottish antiquarian and decorated military veteran[89]. According to their records, Maelstrom intelligence operatives had suspected Stewart of being involved in some unspecified threat and had initiated a series of covert operations to detain him. Stewart had inexplicably evaded capture from three separate teams of elite former special forces operatives and had later been publicly exonerated of all suspicion. However, Maelstrom's records confirmed that he had recently visited the region of the Gobi Desert currently being monitored by their full surveillance capabilities. So, he remained under constant scrutiny in his home in the Scottish Highlands, where he was personally overseeing

---

[88] A Queen's Counsel: QC: an eminent lawyer appointed to be a legal advisor to the government.

[89] Victoria Cross: VC : the highest award of the British honours system, for extraordinary acts of gallantry in the presence of the enemy. Often, due to the nature of the bravery necessary for this distinction, it is awarded posthumously.

repairs to the extensive damage inflicted on his ancestral home.

Four thousand three hundred miles South East from the luxurious Alpine board room, the first stirrings of consciousness returned to the mysterious man who had lain in a delirious fever for over forty-eight hours beside the tranquil reed-filled oasis.

His first sensation was of a constant, low buzzing vibration. At first, he wondered if it was tinnitus caused by some inner ear infection, but then, as his mind focused, he recognised it as the sound of flies, thousands of them. They were gathered in some mass feeding. It was then that the smell hit him—the sweet, rancid stench of rotting meat[90] combined with the unmistakable metallic scent of blood.

As he slowly opened his eyes, his vision lacked focus, and, unexpectedly, the first thing he saw was a very large, black, spiral shape slowly rotating in the sky above him. His recent trauma had triggered an automatic psychological defence mechanism, blocking any recollections that might jeopardise his fragile recovery. The slowly rotating, black whirlpool shape seemed familiar and strangely reassuring to him, but he could not understand why. The only coherent recollection he retained was of twelve Mongolian traders pulling his semi-drowned body from a group of tall Burma reeds.

His mind and senses gradually grew more focused with every breath until the dark whirlpool dramatically transformed, and his brain recognised that the shape was composed of many individual forms. These were shapes with large dark wings, highly distinctive bald heads and

---

[90] Cadaverine and Putrescine. Foul-smelling diamine compounds associated with decomposition of dead matter.

hooked beaks associated with large carrion consuming birds.

Pulling himself up slowly, the hawk-faced man could see the full extent of the terrible carnage that surrounded him. Everywhere was covered in a horrific tableau of badly decaying human bodies and thick, red, dried arterial blood. What remained of the bodies were being pulled apart by a collection of twenty giant, black vultures[91].

Staggering to his feet, he gradually overcame his body's unexpected weakness. He forced himself to search through the mass of twelve corpses, forcibly displacing the birds from their feast, hoping to find at least one survivor from this outbreak of violent haemorrhagic disease. But everyone was the same. Dead and covered in their thick blood that had violently erupted from every orifice.

---

[91] Eurasian Black Vulture: Aegypius monachus.

5 SECRET ORDERS

"There are hidden powers in man, which are capable of making a God of him on earth." - Helena Petrovna Blavatsky

Rue du Mont-Blanc
1211 Genève, Switzerland.

04.01HRS (GMT+2), 8th Sept, Present Day

After leaving Father Thomas O'Neill at the Fontaine Mansion, Mathers had driven into the commercial district of Geneva. Usually bustling with tourists and shoppers who fill the busy pavements, it was blissfully quiet and empty in the early hours of a summer morning. Searching along the deserted cobbled streets, she found one of the rarest treasures in Switzerland, a vacant parking space large enough to accommodate her VW van. The precious spot was on Rue du Mont-Blanc, near the tourist information office. After squeezing her mobile home into the space, Mathers fed the meter for a couple of hours to cover her from eight AM, when the free overnight parking ended. She then pulled the curtains around the mini van's windows, undressed, set up a grey coloured, linen cloth hammock along the entire length of the van's interior and, once lying in her cocoon, guided her consciousness into five hours of deep, dreamless sleep.

Mathers woke at nine AM precisely, just in time to hurriedly pull-on clean Chantal Thomass underwear, a white cotton T-shirt, faded Levi's 501 Jeans and a pair of white Dunlop canvas sneakers before emerging from the VW. She quickly fed the parking meter, just in time to escape the scrutiny of a team of traffic wardens, who had just started their shift, having emerged from the Cantonale des Pâquis police station on the junction with Rue de Berne. In their dark blue jackets, matching caps and grey trousers, these parking enforcement officers massed at the end of the long elegant, stone-fronted building before heading off in every direction through the city centre. One of these was a stony-faced young woman in her twenties, with severe black lipstick and short, dyed black hair that was partially hidden under her blue uniform cap. She headed towards where the VW camper was parked, moving like a guided missile and spent a good fifteen minutes minutely examining the minivan while aggressively trying to bully Mathers into admitting to having camped illegally overnight and face a two hundred euro fine.

While Mathers talked with the attendant, from the edges of her peripheral vision, she could see dirty brown and red colours dancing around the edges of the energy field that surrounded the traffic warden's body- what new age followers would term the "aura". This woman had dark passions that could easily overwhelm her rational mind and lead her into performing unusually vindictive and cruel acts[92]. Although, now that Mathers focused on the exact nature of these energies, she noted that there was something else, some external influence that played upon this woman and maybe fed these dark forces.

At one time, the occult literature was full of ominous forebodings to students about these so-called "dwellers on the threshold". A parasitic, non-physical entity that was supposed to feed off destructive emotions and, some speculated, prompted behaviours in afflicted individuals that would likely create pain, suffering and sadness. Many who followed the dark arts, the so-called Left-Hand Path (LHP), willingly accepted such parasitic attachments to their energy bodies as a part of their probationary initiation. The justification is that the new initiate is more inclined to sow

---

[92] Beyond even those normally associated with traffic enforcement officers.

discord and misery in the world around them. Such individuals were best avoided, as their sole motivation was to bring suffering and complexity into their own lives and those with whom they interacted.

Mathers provided the antagonistic young woman with the electronic parking receipts from her smartphone and allowed the attendant to note the details from her French driving licence and insurance documents. After which, the auburn-haired adept crossed the road for a leisurely breakfast in the Pouly Mont-Blanc café. Having ordered a Doppio espresso with two fresh croissants, Mathers made a point of sitting at one of the roadside tables outside to check that the traffic warden did not sneakily issue her with a ticket while she thought she was unobserved.

Having finished her small but delicious breakfast, Mathers then briefly entered the café, where she used the washroom to clean her teeth and have a quick sink wash. She then sprayed herself generously with Guerlain Vetiver, leaving her body imbued with the unmistakable aroma of orange, bergamot and lemon. After paying the café owner, she returned to her beloved minivan and drove away across the Rue du Mont-Blanc bridge, where she vanished from sight as she turned left at the end of the bridge onto Promenade du Lac.

Back on the busy Rue du Mont-Blanc Road, in front of the elegant stone-fronted building where Mathers had been parked, a tall clean-shaven, dark-haired male figure with a deep golden tan (the kind that can only be acquired in a tropical climate) walked down the steps from the Tourist Information Centre and consulted the time on his watch[93]. The air around this stylish individual was filled with the aroma of leather, fine tobacco and the distinctive fragrances

---

[93] An 18kt gold IWC (International Watch Company, Schaffhausen) Da Vinci Perpetual Calendar Chronograph.

of citrus, middle floral notes, and base notes of cedar and musk indicative of Clive Christian No 1 cologne.

He wore an exquisitely-tailored[94], two-piece, dark grey suit, with a white, thousand thread Egyptian cotton, open-necked Oxford shirt and tan coloured leather brogues[95]. This sophisticated looking gentleman was known to the exoteric world as Señor Edwardo Salvador. He was descended from Spanish nobility and one of South America's wealthiest businessmen. His family's business interests included cattle, agriculture, real estate, oil, precious metals and gemstones.

In addition to his formidable business reputation, Salvador ranked among the world's top polo players. He frequently mixed with the elite at Cowdray, Guards, Chantilly, and his home ground, Campo Argentino. Salvador was also renowned as an excellent marksman, invited to the best grouse estates in Europe and was, consequently, on first name terms with most monarchs in Europe, Asia and the Middle East. However, today he was hunting more exotic prey, related to his most profound passion, esoteric power and knowledge. For, unknown to all but a select few, Edwardo Salvador was also an active member of secret societies devoted to the study of obscure rites and rituals that promised transcendental powers through various secret sexual practices and techniques.

Although such para-sexual rituals were supposed to awaken the preternatural powers that were latent in all human beings, in reality, the real power that was most frequently associated with sex Magick[96] was the ability to recruit and

---

[94] By Casimires Rocha.

[95] By Loake Foley.

[96] Magick is a deliberate spelling, used by many practitioners to differentiate the practice of serious ceremonial ritual magic from

ensnare the rich and the powerful, who had become bored with those amusements that are permitted by law and regular society.

Typically, these respectable men and, rarely women, were approached, through what appeared to be a chance meeting with a visiting guest at one of their dull fraternal societies, and told tantalizing intimations about another group that was more exclusive and promised the *genuine* secrets that were missing from the more mainstream societies. Tempted by prestige, mystery and the alluring promise of beautiful, promiscuous young sexual partners in exotic settings, these older patrons often then attended some staged erotic rituals that were, in reality, intended to place normally respectable people into highly disrespectable settings, where they could be documented in extraordinarily detailed ways. Once trapped by such methods, there inevitably followed a rapid escalation in the depravity of the acts demanded of the once respectable person. Eventually, they became so immersed in scenarios including illegal drug use, underage sexual acts and animal blood sacrifices that they were easily blackmailed and manipulated into using their influence in politics, business, the law or the military in accord with whatever was demanded of them.

For ninety-five per cent of those involved with a Left-Hand[97] Path (LHP) Lodge, this extortion and fear of exposure is the entire extent of their association with Black Magick. However, for a select five per cent of high-ranking initiates involved with the LHP, there is a very real and potent connection with discarnate evil. For the gifted amongst

---

the types of magic that are stage conjuration for entertainment purposes.

[97] The term Left Hand Path (LHP) refers to darker methods of esoteric practice, often associated with Satanism.

these select few, there is the possibility of initiation into a much older and genuine Satanic society. Señor Edwardo Salvador was among the elite from this very privileged group.

In recognition of his exalted status, on his left lapel was a small but distinctive golden pin badge in the shape of a winged cobra, its hood extended and with its mouth wide open, fangs exposed, its thick body coiled and ready to strike. His only other jewellery was a golden ring, with a similar pentagram design to that O'Neill had noticed being worn by Mathers, except that Salvador wore his ring with the pentagram inverted, a sign that he was an advanced adept of the LHP.

He approached the traffic warden and greeted her as "parva soror" (little sister). She gasped, vividly remembering their last ceremonial encounter at the Zurich Lodge three days earlier[98]. Involuntarily, her face flushed, her pupils dilated, and her pulse increased, perspiration forming on her upper lip and other, less public areas of her body. Salvador smiled in recognition of her physiological reaction to his physical presence. It was another of the many blessings conferred on those who had achieved his status in the secret science.

She gently lowered her head in deference, but not enough to draw attention to the two of them, and quietly called him "grand maître" before handing him the notebook containing the license, insurance and registration information Mathers had provided to her earlier. She wiped the palms of her hands, which were damp from sweat, and nervously stammered something about a,

"dispositif de postage." (tracking device)

---

[98] If you are hoping for graphic details about this particular ritual encounter and its parasexual techniques, then sadly you picked the wrong book.

Salvador casually nodded, placed the notebook in his jacket pocket and walked to a long, black Mercedes S650 Maybach limousine that had just pulled in at the curb. The sleek, luxurious vehicle silently moved off once the elegant man had entered through the rear passenger door, leaving the flustered traffic attendant to resume her patrol as though nothing had happened.

Meanwhile, less than a mile away from this encounter, along the promenade du Lac, Mathers finally arrived at her destination, a large Volkswagen service centre with a sign announcing, "Garage VW Geneve, SA". The establishment was opening, and Mathers was warmly greeted by a balding, middle-aged mechanic called Albert, who was dressed in dirty blue cotton overalls.

Having left the minivan in Albert's expert care, in preparation for returning to Paris overnight, Mathers walked the short distance from the garage to the edge of Lake Geneva. Here she enjoyed the early morning sunshine, sitting on a wooden lakeside bench, drinking a large latte and reading the morning edition of Le Figaro. The paper was full of speculation on voter sentiment in the pending French elections and some minor gossip related to corruption by senior political figures, along with a business editorial describing the astounding economic rise of a newly formed breakaway country in North Western Argentina.

An hour later, Mathers received a brief phone call on her generic android mobile, which radically altered her plans to return to Paris that evening. Instead, she ordered a Coopérative de Taxi and, minutes later, she was heading South West through the city to Place du Bourg-de-Four in the old town of Geneva.

The black Nissan NV200 taxicab dropped Mathers at the curb, in front of a large twenty-foot diameter circular fountain that had once been the community's source of clean drinking water. This water feature was surrounded by waist-high, cast iron, black pedestrian protection posts that delineated the centre piece of the small square. The ancient meeting place was lined along its Western side with street-side cafes that sprawled out in front of a row of tall, eighteenth-century buildings.

Walking towards the Northern end of the square, opposite the local Police headquarters, Mathers approached a large, five-storied townhouse with a narrow, solid iron door set into a side road by Rue de l'Hôtel-de-Ville. Beside this ancient doorway, on its right side, was a polished brass plate that proclaimed,

"Société pour la préservation des lignages ésotériques européens."

And, underneath in smaller block capital letters, the acronym "S.P.L.E.E.".

Further up the wall, a few feet above head height, was a much older fresco, set into the eighteenth-century stonework, depicting the symbol of a feather and balance scales with the Latin date, MCCXXXIII[99].

The "Society for the Preservation of European Esoteric Lineages" is almost entirely unknown to the public and even those who profess deep expertise in esoteric secret societies, which is precisely how its selected membership prefers it. Over the centuries, this society has had many names and has spawned numerous subsidiary organisations, each reflecting some fundamental principle emerging in society at that time. But no matter what name the organisation adopted, it has always stood for specific immutable values that reflect the principles that were the

---

[99] 1233 CE

core beliefs of those who initially founded the order many centuries ago.

In more recent times, that is within living memory; it had used its network of affiliated lodges throughout the European mainland to support certain resistance groups, assist persecuted racial minorities escape from genocide and allied soldiers to avoid capture, internment and torture. As a result, the society's lodges, and their members, had suffered terrible consequences. Many historically significant meeting places that had belonged to the organisation for centuries had been razed to the ground. Throughout Europe, membership in the society and its affiliated bodies was made illegal and subject to summary execution. Still, its members had fearlessly continued their resistance to the evil ravaging Europe. Only here in neutral Switzerland could the society continue in relative normalcy. Therefore, this building in Geneva had survived as the sole remaining Lodge for the most ancient Right-Hand Path (RHP) order in the European tradition.

The order's original and most ancient name was the Meri-Maat (Beloved of Maat[100]). The society's European roots could be traced back to when Europe was just emerging from the dark ages, when a handful of adventurous people risked everything, venturing to the edges of the then known world to gain knowledge of secret arts that had been thought lost to humanity. While their contemporaries in Europe thought the peoples of these remote lands to be heretics and infidels, whose cities should be razed to the ground and their peoples exterminated by fire, these early esoteric scholars sought out adepts of an ancient sacred science that claimed a lineage back before recorded history. After decades of study, many of these scholars remained

---

[100] Maat was the ancient Egyptian goddess devoted to harmony, truth and order.

where they had studied until they died, but a few returned to their native Europe, bringing the seeds that would later become science, philosophy and, of course, magic. The early centuries of the first millennia were harsh times for anyone who questioned the dead letter interpretation of The Bible, so it was natural that these renegades, and their descendants, would group together and find stimulation in mutual discourse, to exchange ideas, techniques and understanding, with the goals of being guardians of esoteric justice and custodians of the secrets of the Great Art. So, the society was formed, dedicated to studying, preserving, and practising RHP esoteric principles.

Creation always seeks balance, so there was also an equally ancient order dedicated to opposing everything related to justice, order and truth. This rival order's ancient and original name was the Meri-Isfet (Beloved of Isfet). Their order was dedicated to the Egyptian God Apep[101], the deity of darkness and chaos (izft in Egyptian), the opponent of light and Ma'at (order/truth). Apep is portrayed in Ancient Egyptian art as a giant serpent, often with the extended hood of the cobra, fangs bared and about to strike. He was known as the "Enemy of Ra" and "The Lord of Chaos". The Abrahamic religions know him better simply as Satan, the principle of Evil.

Similarly to SPLEE, the Meri-Isfet had adapted their ancient name to something more amenable to the modern world: the "International Society for the Furtherance of Esoteric Traditions" or "ISFET" for short. Unlike the SPLEE, this dark order did not have a publicly listed address, at least not since 1945, when their Berlin headquarters was destroyed, and the society went underground, having lost its mighty patrons.

---

[101] Known in Ancient Greek as: Ἄποφις

Since then, their activities became focused exclusively on two things; encouraging the formation of LHP societies that appeal to modern tastes for superficial study, rapid progression through numerous initiations and, secondly, the global promotion of egotistical individualism. A selfish ideology that has become the ultimate modern virtue, where the aphorism, "Do What Thou Wilt, " replaces the Nazarene's injunction to "Do unto others as you would have them do unto you".

Back in Place du Bourg-de-Four, the black, cast-iron gate made a clicking noise as the lock was remotely released, and Mathers pushed open the heavy door and walked into a small brick-lined tunnel, some ten feet high and six feet wide. The gate's spring mechanism pulled itself closed and, momentarily, left the enclosed space inside the tunnel in complete darkness before another door opened and bright light streamed into the tunnel, making Mathers close her eyes. The contrast between dark and light was deliberate symbolism for the darkness in the outside world and the illumination within the lodge.

Walking forward through the illuminated doorway, Mathers found herself in a large reception area, with a heavily-worn stone floor, inlaid with a white and black square pattern, that ran off to some stairs to her left and a set of large dark oak double doors in front of her, that she knew led to the ritual meeting areas. To her right were a set of three single doors that she knew from experience led to cloakrooms, showers and lockers for the members. The long staircase on her left headed up to a floor for offices and meeting rooms and four additional floors of storage for books, manuscripts and artefacts.

This reception area was one of Mathers' favourite places in the ancient building because of the significant history that was always on display. The sides of the room were lined with glass cabinets, where the attendance registers from bygone periods were displayed in periodic circulation, so each time she visited the lodge rooms, she found different attendance logs, each filled with the signatures of those who had visited these premises at some period in the past.

Over the years she had been coming here, she had seen many famous signatures recorded as visitors consulting the library, while others had attended as guests for meetings. Then there were the members, some listed as officiating (conducting and leading the ceremonies).

Mathers had kept an informal mental list of those names that she had seen written in long dried ink in the leather-bound ledgers. The oldest she recalled dated back to the 13th and 14th centuries and were faded to the point of being almost unreadable on their dried, calf skin parchment. They included:

Ramon Llull, syncretic mystic; Roger Bacon, philosopher; Nicolas Flamel, alchemist; Roger Bolingbroke, astrologer and Albertus Magnus, who had contributed many of the earliest texts to be found in the library above the reception area.

More recent attendance records were in a much better state of preservation, and the names were much easier to decipher. Mathers recalled that she had seen the following notables from the 15th, 16th and 17th centuries:

Heinrich Cornelius Agrippa, occult philosopher and astrologer; John Dee, occult philosopher, mathematician, alchemist and Queen Elizabeth's advisor; Robert Fludd, occult philosopher and astrologer and Michel Maier, author of many famous anonymous manifestos and founder of the Rosicrucian movement.

Even more recent attendance registers read like a veritable who's who of the 18th and 19th century's esoteric revival. They included:

Louis-Claude de Saint-Martin, founder of Martinism, and famously known as the "Unknown Philosopher"; Edward Bulwer-Lytton, author of several occult novels; Eliphas Lévi, French occult author and ceremonial magician; Count Apponyi, who initiated Kenneth MacKenzie in 1850 and provided the original Cypher Manuscripts which, after editing, formed the basis for the founding of the Hermetic Order of the Golden Dawn in 1888.

And, of course, Mathers own famous forebears:

Moina Mathers, first initiate of the Hermetic Order of the Golden Dawn, Imperatrix of the Alpha et Omega and her husband, Samuel L. MacGregor Mathers, founder of the Hermetic Order of the Golden Dawn.

Above the glass cabinets that contained the attendance registers were several banners and certificates for orders and societies that were affiliated with S.P.L.E.E and who used these lodge buildings for their meetings. Many of the certificates showed numerous renewals of authority from S.P.L.E.E. to continue the respective order for a further century. Some of the oldest affiliated bodies had septennial certificates of authority hanging proudly on display.

Higher up the walls, continuing up the many levels of stairs, were paintings, sketches and, for more recent periods, photographs of the numerous previous masters, imperators and preceptors who had assumed the ceremonial leadership of a specific group for a calendar year. Mathers was proud that high up on the fifth floor was her own picture from when she was Imperatrix of S.P.L.E.E two years ago. Aside from the pomp and ceremony, she recalled the endless late-night phone calls from angry members complaining about seating arrangements at after meeting dinners and disputes about the exact wording involved in some obscure ceremony that had not been performed in living memory.

Mathers reflections about the amazing history presented here in this reception room were broken by the opening of one of the double wooden doors in front of her, which led into the lodge rooms. An older man with silver hair and a pale complexion emerged and, after carefully considering her jeans and plain white T-shirt for a few moments, tactfully enquired,

"Soror Mathers, allez-vous changer avant votre réunion avec le conseil ?"

(Will you be changing before your meeting with the board?)

Smiling at the polite reminder of the dress code expected when one was summoned to meet with the supreme RHP esoteric authority in Europe[102], she took the key from the elderly servitor for the lodge's communal lockers, located at the rear of the gentleman's changing rooms.

Eighteen minutes later, she re-emerged into the reception area wearing a close-fitting man's black, two-piece, linen, Tom Ford business suit, a white cotton dress shirt and a black silk bow tie. Her white plimsols had been replaced with a pair of highly polished dress shoes.

To complete her elegant and stunning androgynous look, she had wet her auburn hair with tap water so it stuck close to her head. The old servitor smiled,

"C'est formidable, mais..." (fantastic, but...)

He reached into his left jacket pocket and removed a small flat jewellery box, around the size of a large box of matches, with the brand De Grisogono on its lid. Opening the box, the older man removed a small, solid gold lapel pin, cast into the shape of a conjoined feather and balance scales, the symbol of Meri-Maat. He approached Mathers, pinned the small emblem on her left jacket lapel, and checked her

---

102 Once known, among occultists, as the "Secret Chiefs".

right hand for the golden initiates ring that denoted her esoteric rank. On finding it, he nodded his approval before returning through the double doors and closing them behind him.

He was gone some five minutes, during which time Mathers discovered a wall hanging of an ancient shield that she had not noticed before. The old piece of armour was heavily dented, with numerous chunks of the original metal missing. However, one could still make out the faded image of three six-sided stars of David, two above and one below, a field of blue with a yellow banner separating the three stars[103]. Before Mathers could consider the shield further, the elderly servitor re-emerged and, opening the double doors wide, announced.

"Les grands maîtres vont vous voir maintenant, Soror Mathers."

(The grandmasters will see you now, Sister Mathers)

---

103 This sounds like the heraldic device (symbol) of one Hues de Paiens delez Troies (Hugh of Payens near Troyes). Payns was a village 8 miles from Troyes, in Champagne, Eastern France. Hugues de Payens (1070-1136) is remembered by history as the co-founder and first Grand Master of the Knights Templar.

6 SMOKE

"The only rule for a gunfight is to bring a gun, preferably two." – attributed to US Military sources.

A Small Oasis, Twenty Miles West of The Gurvan Saikhen Mountains
Gobi Desert
Southern Mongolia

15:45HRS (GMT+8), 8th Sept, Present day

The dark vortex of vultures continued to circle high above the sole survivor who wandered amongst the blood-splattered bodies of the dead. Although his strength was returning, after eating a packet of dried nuts and a box of "Frosties" breakfast cereal, he still could not remember who he was, why he was here in this remote desert oasis, or what skills he had acquired in the forty-odd years he had walked the earth.

He did, however, recognise the bodies that lay around him, each one clearly having died a horrific and agonising death. When he was semi-conscious, lying among the reeds, they had pulled him from the water; he had memorised their faces as people who had offered him kindness, a rare gesture in his brutal life and one he had intended to reward.

Examining the massive haemorrhages that were in evidence on each body, the rapid nature of the disease was all too clear. Such terrifying symptoms led the surviving man to wonder what kind of disease had killed these innocent traders and, more pragmatically, if he would be the next to die. He caught himself checking his own pulse, not at the wrist, as most civilians would do, but clinically, at the throat. His blood pumped, slow and steady; fifty beats per minute, like an Olympic athlete. Somehow, he knew that he was unaffected by this terrible plague because he had an artificial immunity conferred by vaccination.

As he gathered the bodies, all covered in the same red ooze, something triggered a memory of an ancient port city and some horrifying plague coming from the sky. Again, he saw vivid images of the same beautiful, dark-haired woman. Her memory triggered the conflicted emotions of both pleasure and great fear. By means of an effort of will, he dismissed the random memories that had flooded his mind, and he continued the gruesome task of dealing with the dead.

Instinctively he knew how to organise large rocks to create the optimum burn pattern for disposing of human remains. How did he get such knowledge? Was he an undertaker? He considered this for a moment and almost instantly dismissed the idea.

As he recalled the airborne plague again, he had a memory of a terrible biological weapon. With a jolt of realisation, he understood that these poor people were victims of one of humanity's most terrible creations. Further, he had been the unwitting carrier of the disease. As a consequence, he knew that everything must be incinerated. Using the assorted perfumes and alcohol carried by the traders as accelerants and a child's magnifying glass as a focus for the sun's rays, he initiated an intense cremation of the bodies. The ferocious blaze startled the four camels, who had been grazing peacefully by the oasis and caused them to stampede from the shelter of the clearing out into the surrounding desert.

Being too exhausted to chase the animals, the hawk-faced man resumed his purging of all infected materials. He consigned all his old clothes and possessions to what was now a two-thousand-degree blazing inferno. Stripped naked, he then washed in the oasis.

The thick black smoke from the funeral pyre rose high into the clear sky, where it was picked up within milliseconds by the trillion gigapixel Zeiss image recognition systems housed in three rival surveillance satellites.

Each reconnaissance system was almost identical, primarily because two of the three were direct copies of the original, which was designed at the massive Boeing factory at Everett, Washington, USA. Floating at the height of just under 700 miles above the earth, the three systems, owned by the Chinese[104], Russians[105] and Americans, respectively, followed each other in a complex dance through space to make sure no one superpower knew anything that was not also known by the other two superpowers.

The American spy satellite[106] was a jet-black crewless spaceship, complete with a distinctive logo that depicted a sinister-looking octopus sitting astride the globe with the motto "Nothing Is Beyond Our Reach". Like its two orbiting twins, this National Reconnaissance Office system monitored every inch of the planet's surface from pole to pole and identified objects as small as a human being.

The US satellite's recognition of a smoke plume emanating from an uninhabited region of the Gobi Desert was intercepted by a secret control centre deep under a mountain near the idyllic Swiss town of Grindlewald. An analysis was completed by Maelstrom/Wolfsangel staff before the signal was forwarded to the National Reconnaissance Office[107] and from there to all the

---

[104] Yaogan 31A.

[105] Kondor No.202, developed by NPO Mashinostroyeniya.

[106] NROL-39.

[107] The National Reconnaissance Office (NRO) is the US Government's primary signals intelligence analysis unit. Similar in function to the British GCHQ.

intelligence services of America's allies. Within three hours, the data was shared with GCHQ[108] in the UK and, shortly afterwards, reached the desk of the Director-General of Her Majesty's Secret Intelligence Service[109] (SIS).

Four thousand three hundred miles North West of the Mongolian desert, a striking looking woman in her early forties, with the body of a professional athlete, lay sleeping on a small cot bed. Her flawless skin accentuated her natural beauty as she lay sleeping.

The small rectangular bedroom where this woman slept was sparsely furnished and was intended for occasional use. It was accessible through a concealed door attached to the woman's office, discreetly located in Horseferry House, SW1 and not in the brash public façade of the modern SIS buildings at Vauxhall Cross.

A sharp computerised tone broke into the woman's dreamless sleep. The alert denoted an event critical enough for her to pull the iPhone that rested on a small glass and metal bedside table towards her. Her face screwed up as she focused on the brightly illuminated text.

Whatever the notification was, it was clearly important enough for the woman to rise, pull on a blue silk dressing gown and double-check the information on the Lenovo X1 Carbon laptop that lay open on the traditional wooden desk in the main office. Minutes later, she had typed an

---

[108] Government Communications Headquarters (GCHQ) is the UK's modern successor to the famous World War Two intelligence and code breaking centre, Bletchley Park.

[109] SIS: also known as MI6 – The UK's foreign intelligence service. Not to be confused with MI5, known as the Security Service, which is the UK intelligence agency directed towards threats within and on UK soil.

encrypted email request to her supervisors to authorise the deployment of a high-resolution drone[110] to check on the source of the smoke plume in the Gobi.

Three hours later, after a session in the basement gym punishing kickboxing equipment in ways that sport-oriented martial artists would find highly disturbing, Dame Cynthia Sinclair emerged. She was dressed in an elegantly tailored black Prada business suit with a pair of matching black four-inch Prada stiletto heels. The tailoring of the classic business suit accentuated Sinclair's body so that the five security officers at the entrance to the Government building at 2 Marsham Street, London, never considered searching her for weapons. They, therefore, completely missed the tiny, five-inch, polymer, eight-round, 9mm Beretta Nano concealed in the femme fatale thigh holster between Sinclair's long legs.

The meeting was in a tasteless modern office, buried amongst other anonymous front facing floors of an ugly modern office block. Sinclair was deliberately kept waiting for twenty long minutes before being permitted to meet with two corpulent men in their sixties. These two men had purposefully selected their seating in advance so that this upstart woman, with dubious roots[111], would have to stare into the rising sunshine.

---

[110] Probably the XQ-58A Valkyrie, which has sufficient range to be deployed from a US Aircraft Carrier in the Sea of Japan. This long-range reconnaissance drone has been specifically developed by the Air Force Research Laboratory and Kratos Unmanned Aerial Systems for such covert missions.

[111] Not having the preferred Oxbridge pedigree, instead having risen through the operational ranks on merit alone. Nothing is so threatening to the corrupt and incompetent as someone with ability.

Sir Reginald Twiffers was the former UK foreign secretary who had recently been promoted to Home Secretary by Prime Minister Susan Merriweather. The other man was Lord Jeremy Kenner. He was the former party chairman, who had appointed Merriweather to become Prime Minster without party consultation. It was rumoured that as a direct result of this action, he was now Minister of Defence.

Sinclair had anticipated the "school boy" power games with the sun and negated the ploy by entering the office wearing a pair of tinted anti-glare glasses that provided the additional advantage of hiding where she was looking during the meeting.

Sitting in front of the two former public-school boys, who had never really grown up, Sinclair made a point of adjusting her skirt while crossing her smooth legs, and she got the satisfaction of noting that the eyes of both senior politicians followed her movement, like two dogs watching a squirrel. Dame Cynthia Sinclair, Director General of her Britannic Majesty's Secret Intelligence Service, smiled a knowing smile. She was the only one in the room capable of thinking with her head.

As she had anticipated, since her request for the drone deployment had been ignored, and instead, she had been summoned to this meeting, she was abruptly handed a two-line memo overruling her request to conduct a secondary follow up investigation. The smoke was just a funeral. Nothing more.

Home secretary, Sir Reginald Twiffers, was clearly enjoying this opportunity to exert his authority.

"Dame Sinclair, you must cease your obsession with this Ad-Dajjal woman and her organisations."

Lord Jeremy Kenner added, in a condescending tone, while mimicking a concerned smile,

"Yes, Cynthia, *dear girl*, you must forget the Gobi. It is over."

Sinclair thanked the two men for their opinion but was scrupulous not to indicate that she agreed with their assessment. Instead, she focused from behind her dark glasses to read the briefing papers on their desk, noticing a short, single-line message signed with the Greek letter Alpha. The note was an order to ignore the signal, written in bold upper case, as an instruction for an imbecile, which, she reflected, was not too far from the mark with these pair of upper-class twits[112].

Once the meeting was over, Sinclair left the building and walked slowly around the block. She checked she had not been followed and entered a public house called "The Barley Mow", one of many renovated pubs in central London catering to city workers. It had saw dust carefully scattered on sanded wooden floors, projecting a carefully cultivated fake "working class" setting for wealthy young people who had enjoyed a privileged upbringing but wanted to play at being connected to working-class roots.

Wooden floors and walls, covered with fake Victorian prints, crowded next to a series of wide screen TVs that provided sports coverage for city workers in the evenings but now were showing live 24 hours news coverage: Chaos in parliament; Trouble in the Middle East; Famine in developing nations due to unfavourable currency fluctuations and a series of shocking stock market runs on national pension funds.

Pulling a disposable black plastic Alcatel dumb-phone from her black Prada handbag, she selected a new sim card out of a container of prepaid anonymous sims from various telecommunications providers and inserted the card. She

---

[112] British slang: a silly annoying person who was, almost always, born to wealth.

did this in a practised manner and called a number from memory.

Sinclair's call went unanswered as an old Nokia[113] vibrated on the walnut dashboard of a meticulously restored black 1967 Mercedes 250 SE soft top, left-hand drive sports car. The old Mercedes had spent the last weeks in a bespoke classic car restoration specialist in central London. The vehicle had been riddled with over sixty 9mm and 7.65mm full metal jacket rounds. This damage had left the car a wreck on a cold dark road beside a Scottish loch and had prompted the owner to insist on the installation of Kevlar around the entire passenger compartment during the extensive restoration.

Sinclair gave up making her call with a frustrated exclamation,

"Tavish, where the hell are you?"

Turning to the one staff member working at this early hour, Sinclair ordered a double espresso from a scruffy-looking twenty-year-old behind the bar, who was more interested in the latest social media feed on his thousand-pound folding phone than anything in the real world.

Back inside the restored classic sports car, hundreds of hours of dedicated repairs had brought the classic car's bodywork back to its former glory and, after a refurbished 250 SE engine had been recovered from a similar car and fitted to replace the irrevocably damaged original, the exhausts once again made that unmistakable burble of a seven bearing, six-cylinder, 2,496cc German engine.

---

[113] An ancient Nokia 3310

Delighting in the return of his old car, the tall and well-built[114] Scottish owner made the most of the Indian summer weather and took the car for a short test drive around Southern London. He intended to return to the garage before driving it back to his home near Stirling, in Scotland, that night when the roads would be clearer.

The car still had some of the mechanic's bits and pieces left on the right-hand passenger seat. The carefully restored red leather was hidden under thick, black plastic seat covers that proudly displayed a vintage car logo with the text "Park Lane Classic Car Restoration" and phone number underneath. The tools resting on the seat included a can of Mercedes-Benz Obsidian Black (197) spray paint and a Sealey digital MOT Corrosion Assessment Hammer.

With the car roof down, the fumes from numerous car exhausts filled the air. Like so many other affluent open-top sports car enthusiasts, the owner believed that the enjoyment of having the sunshine on his face without the obstruction of a roof was worth a lungful of fumes. His intelligent grey eyes sparkled with delight as he drove his beloved car.

Heading South, down through Chelsea, past Sloane Square Station, and into the King's Road, the classic Mercedes sports car became stuck behind a red London transport number 11 Route Master bus with "Fulham Broadway" on its destination display. The experienced eyes of the sports car's driver noted, in passing, from the reflections in shop windows, that directly in front of the bus was a VIP escort: an unmarked Ford Mondeo and a black, classic Range Rover.

---

[114] Six feet, two inches tall and weighing a fit and lean, two hundred pounds. His chiselled jaw was accentuated with a cropped beard which matched his short greying hair.

Based on the weight displacement of the leading SUV, it was armoured. Probably level 2 or 3A, recent budget cuts made it unlikely the vehicle would have protection against IEDs[115] or high-velocity rifle rounds, thought the Scotsman. The subsequent reflection in a long restaurant window confirmed the suspicion, showing the famous face of a striking, dark-haired woman in her early forties. As was the fashion for "The Firm's"[116] members to appear "just like us", she was driving the SUV, with a smartly dressed male protection officer in the left-hand front seat. A young child was just visible playing in the rear seats. If it wasn't for the armed protection escorting the Range Rover, it could have been any typical mum on the school run.

The sluggish pace of the traffic became even slower than usual, and then, as they reached the junction between the King's Road, Blacklands Terrace, and Duke of York Square, in a completely unforeseen action, the London Transport Bus pulled across the road, making a classic obstruction manoeuvre. The transport driver, who was now visible as the vehicle turned dramatically, was not dressed in a London Transport uniform but instead in fully pixilated urban camouflage fatigues. The bus driver opened his passenger side door and exited, drawing what the Scotsman recognised as an American Colt AR15 semi-automatic machine gun and started opening fire at whatever was in front of the bus.

The air was then filled with the characteristic clatter of 5.56mm, semi-automatic machine gun fire, followed shortly after by several reports from what Stewart recognised as two 9mm handguns, probably Metropolitan Police Glock 17s. The crowds on the pavements responded to whatever mayhem was unfolding in front of the bus by screaming and

---

[115] Improvised Explosive Device

[116] The British royal family are known to insiders as "the Firm"

running in almost every direction, some even straight towards the gunfire.

The only person who did not panic was the middle-aged Scotsman driving the fifty-year-old black Mercedes. Instead of fear, his response was a low growl of frustration, followed by a sigh of acceptance as he patted the walnut veneer of the dashboard of his restored car fondly. He then thrust the white gear stick on the classic four-speed manual gearbox into first, turned the steering wheel sharply to the right and floored the accelerator. The newly renovated open-topped sports car mounted the right-hand side pavement, passed around the front of the bus, and drove through the panicking pedestrians, many of whom were covered in blood, their own and that of the persons next to them.

Coming around the front of the bus revealed a scene of carnage. The two men in the escorting unmarked Police Mondeo were lying in pools of blood close to their vehicle; the two front doors of the police escort vehicle remained open, peppered with ugly holes. Clearly, the RaSP[117] officers had been completely outmatched by the American-made semi-machine guns' superior firepower.

Further down the King's Road, two large blue unmarked Vauxhall Movano Babcock "bullion in transit" armoured vehicles had pushed all the cars from the morning traffic up onto the pavements and road junctions. This action effectively blocked access to the emergency services that could be heard rushing toward the scene.

Directly in the line of sight in front of the open-topped vintage sports car, the black Range Rover was surrounded by five men, dressed in identical urban camouflage military uniforms, and wearing full body armour, that the Scotsman

---

[117] Royalty and Specialist Protection (RaSP): one of the Specialist Operations directorates of London's Metropolitan Police Service.

recognised as the latest experimental US DOD specification. This state-of-the-art body armour protected the operatives' face, throat, shoulders, chest, groin, and knees. The full-face protection included the so-called "mandible", making the operatives look like some enormous insect. According to the product's marketing materials, these modifications made the wearer invulnerable to all traditional armed and unarmed, close quarter attacks.

The black bodywork of the Royal Range Rover was covered with deep indentations synonymous with high-velocity rounds. The front and side windows showed the classic spiderweb pattern of bullet impacts, and the rubber on all four run-flat tires had shredded under a sustained barrage of gunfire. The five terrorists had assumed a formation around the Range Rover so that three men faced the right-hand driver's side and the other two operatives faced the left side of the black SUV. The Scotsman recognised this formation as a classic signature of several Islamist terrorist groups. These were a set of techniques to kidnap protected VIPs perfected in war-torn Iraq and taught in the numerous covert terror training camps around the world.

The terrorist's equipment was undoubtedly sourced from the CIA, who probably assumed the weapons had been provided to US-supported militia, covertly fighting to overthrow the Syrian regime to liberate the rich oil fields for Western commercial exploitation. In reality, once these weapons left US control, they ended up in public auctions where they could be purchased by any group rich enough to outbid the competition.

Four of the terrorists carried the latest generation of Colt AR-15 semi-automatic rifles. In contrast, one, who appeared to be coordinating the operation, carried an American rocket-propelled grenade launcher[118] mounted with a classic antitank warhead[119]. The leader of the terrorists had used the grenade launcher in the early stages of the attack to dissuade the royal bodyguard inside the SUV from trying to escape the ambush.

As all five men trained their weapons toward the single RaSP bodyguard, the group leader searched through the frequencies on a universal car door remote system.

Inside the Range Rover, the dark-haired woman driver had climbed back into the rear passenger seats to comfort her terrorised child, while the RaSP bodyguard was desperately trying to use his dedicated radio to summon help. But, judging by his face, the cold realisation had dawned on him that he was dealing with professional kidnappers who had anticipated almost every eventuality, including jamming all radio and mobile transmissions.

The leader of the five kidnappers stood on the right side of the SUV, slightly behind his two colleagues. He was gesturing to the RaSP security operative to open the doors. He showed a hypodermic syringe gun, indicating that he would sedate the two hostages before removing them from the kidnapping scene. The intended getaway method became apparent moments later. A two-seater Boeing A/MH-6M Little Bird helicopter, fitted with two full-length panier medivac personnel carriers and four external standing frames[120], landed noisily in the cleared area of the Duke of York square. The kidnappers had indeed planned

---

[118] The Airtronic RPG-7USA PSRL-2: Precision Shoulder-fired Rocket Launcher

[119] The PG-7VL variant of RPG HEAT: high-explosive anti-tank warhead with a 4.5 second fuse.

[120] That permit the rapid deployment and extraction of military personnel.

extraordinarily well and had anticipated every eventuality, except for one.

As the lead operative finally found the frequency to release the remote locking mechanism on the Range Rover, causing the door locks to pop up, and the mother and child inside to scream in terror, a black classic 1967 Mercedes sports car tore around the red London Transport bus. It accelerated from the right-hand side of the street, clearing nearly fifteen feet from the pavement, before colliding straight into two of the three terrorists on the driver's right-hand side of the black SUV. The impact sent the terrorist's bodies flying before they came to rest some twenty feet further along the King's Road. They lay still, and their weapons, including the RPG and the syringe gun, lay close by them.

Simultaneously with the arrival of the black Mercedes coupe, the two, armed men on the opposite side of the SUV callously shot the surrendering RaSP officer as he opened his door. A plume of red exploded from the head of the young policeman as he fell, lifeless at the feet of the two, armed kidnappers. The woman inside the Range Rover screamed again in terror and cradled her child close to her.

The violent car impact and death of two of their team members diverted the attention of the two kidnappers from their targets. They turned, and both directed fully automatic fire at the newcomer in the open-top sports car. Heavy 5.65mm rounds thudded into the bodywork of the ancient Mercedes. The windshield shattered into numerous small fragments, scattering over the driver and car interior. Bits of tempered glass covered the thick, red blood splatter from the two terrorists that had already smeared over the protective plastic seat coverings and stained the fabric on the sleeve and lapel of the grey Ede and Ravenscroft jacket worn by the Scottish driver.

Back in the Barley Mow public house, coverage of the event began to be relayed from bystanders' mobile devices and appeared on the widescreen TVs. The charge of the fifty-year-old sports car and its success in eliminating two of the five terrorists prompted the young bartender to text furiously on his phone, sending numerous messages while pointing to the TV screen.

"Jesus! Look what that old guy just did!"

Dame Cynthia Sinclair watched the grainy mobile phone footage while she continued slowly sipping her coffee before sending a single text message[121] and turning towards the excited young man.

"Hmm, yes, this is going to get bad. Really bad."

The young bartender became more animated,

"You worried about that old dude? He is as good as dead. These caliphate gunmen are real badass, and he just took out two of their team."

Sinclair smiled knowingly,

"Keep watching, honey. That "old dude" is Sir Tavish Stewart, and they just shot up his car. He liked that car."

Back at the kidnapping scene, after brushing the glass fragments from his suit, the elegantly dressed Scotsman timed the opening of his car door perfectly. The door violently impacted into the unprotected left thigh of the one remaining gunman on the Scotsman's side of the Range Rover. This particular kidnapper had come beside the

---

[121] Her two-word message, "BBC News", went to three addresses: Clive Basildon, Director General, MI5; Brigadier Tony Green, Director, United Kingdom Special Forces (UKSF) and Alan Williams, Chief Constable of the Metropolitan Police.

sports car and raised his AR15 to make this newcomer's end especially brutal.

As the long barrel of the machine gun came into view, the elegantly dressed driver moved with blinding speed, pushing his own body to one side and bringing himself close to his attacker so he was inside the length of the weapon's barrel and out of its arc of fire. Simultaneously with his body movement, he deftly wrapped one of the black plastic seat coverings from the sports car over the head of the gunman and struck the left elbow of his attacker with the Sealey Corrosion Assessment hammer. The thunderous sideways blow with the hammer produced a low cracking noise as it shattered the unprotected bones of the humerus and radius, sending overwhelming neurological pain signals into the terrorist's central nervous system.

The Scotsman's face wrinkled in distaste at the noise, and he raised an eyebrow as the digital display on the hammer's handle read "FAILED MOT".

With the gunman distracted and disoriented, the elegant sports car owner reached the terrorist's waist and withdrew the operatives sidearm, a black titanium alloy pistol that his experienced eye recognised as a French military issue handgun[122] with a fifteen-round magazine.

Dropping the Sealy hammer, the Scotsman lifted the injured arm of the wounded terrorist. After turning off the safety, he discharged the newly acquired handgun under the armpit and towards his attacker's central body mass, avoiding the terrorist's heavy Kevlar and ceramic body protection and killing him instantly.

The Scotsman then picked up the spray can of black paint from inside the Mercedes, looking toward the two

---

[122] PAMAS G1: Based on the 9mm Beretta 92

remaining shooters on the opposite side of the Range Rover, who had temporarily ceased their gunfire to avoid shooting their teammate; Stewart lobbed the paint can high into the air so it would come down at the midpoint between the two terrorists. But, before the can of paint could complete its trajectory and land between the terrorists, it exploded from a single bullet shot fired from the French pistol that was now in the Scotsman's right hand. Using the distraction of the exploding paint can, the elegantly dressed man rapidly closed the distance between himself and the cover provided by the right-hand side of the Range Rover.

The pressurised contents of the spray can exploded into the air around and between the two gunmen, covering their bodies and masked faces in Mercedes-Benz Obsidian Black (197) paint. The more experienced of the two terrorists immediately dropped down behind the SUV as he was forced to remove his face protection. The other man was less prudent and, as a consequence, received a single, deadly accurate shot into his forehead the moment his face protection was removed.

The one remaining gunman charged around the rear of the Range Rover, his face protection removed and his AR15 machine gun pointed towards where he expected his opponent to be waiting. His attack was short-lived. The elegantly dressed Scotsman was anticipating this charge; grabbing the barrel and stock of the long weapon with both hands, he pulled it past him and then, as the shooter resisted the attempt to remove his gun, combined his strength with the strong pull of resistance from the gunman into a strike with the rifle butt. Pushing the thick rifle stock up and rapidly back towards the gunman, so it rammed violently into the shooter's unprotected face, stunning him. As the gunman dropped his hold on the AR15 so he could grasp his broken nose, the sound of a single 9mm handgun round reverberated around the deserted street.

Finally, the elegant man walked alone, slowly down the King's Road, towards the sound of the helicopter, that was, after having seen the five-person kidnap team killed within a matter of seconds, beginning an emergency take-off.

Back at The Barley Mow public house, the young bartender was transfixed watching this elegant Scotsman walk down the empty street and reach the bodies of the two men he had run over in the opening seconds of his attack. Besides the remains of the two men was the long shape of the antitank weapon.

"Does HE know how to use a bazooka?"

Sinclair finished her coffee with an ironic raise of her right eyebrow.

"What do you think?"

Rising slowly from her chair, Sinclair walked calmly behind the wooden bar and crouched down, assuming the classic crash position familiar to air travellers. Checking on the young bartender, she sighed, pulled him down behind the bar, and gestured for him to assume the crash position.

Back on the King's Road, a small smile crossed the Scotsman's face. He picked up the discarded Airtronic RPG, turned off the safety, and directed the anti-tank gun towards the escaping helicopter rising high above the London skyline.

The streak of fire and loud whooshing noise was followed by the rocket soaring upwards and embedding itself into the aircraft's fuselage. The silence down on the King's Road was broken only by a Scottish voice slowly counting from one to four as he calmly walked behind a large stone sign proclaiming "Welcome to Duke of York Square."

With each second, the helicopter rose higher above the streets of London, its pilot clearly believing that by some miracle, he would be permitted to escape.

The fireball filled the London sky, followed by an explosion that could be heard across the Thames and took out the windows in every building within a five-mile radius.

In the designer pub, Dame Cynthia Sinclair rose up from behind the bar, brushing dust and debris from her black Prada skirt and slowly walked out of the public house. Her four-inch steel stiletto heels crunched over the broken glass littered the wooden floor. She made a call on her official iPhone while looking at the TV screen that showed dozens of SCO19[123] officers surrounding the single remaining figure of the Scotsman, who was standing in the King's Road.

"Helen? Yes, I am sure he will welcome your legal advice around now."

---

[123] The Metropolitan Police's Specialist Firearms Command

7 WHEN IN ROME

"Catholic churches and private collections still overflow with hundreds of thousands of items. Included are pieces of the True Cross (enough to build a few log cabins), bones of the children slain by King Herod, the toenails and bones of St. Peter, the bones of the Three Wise Kings and of St. Stephen (as well as his complete corpse, including another complete skeleton!), jars of the Virgin Mary's milk, the bones and several entire heads and pieces thereof that were allegedly once atop John the Baptist, 16 foreskins of Christ, Mary Magdalene's entire skeleton (with two right feet), scraps of bread and fish left over from feeding the 5,000, a crust of bread from the Last Supper, and a hair from Christ's beard - not to mention a few shrouds, including the one at Turin." -
James Randi

Roman Catholic Diocese of Lausanne, Geneva and Fribourg
Episcopal See Office,
Rue Du Rhone, 4th floor,
1204 GENEVA,
Switzerland.

07:45HRS (GMT+2), 8th Sept, present day

Four hours after his encounter with the terrifying skeletal lake phantoms at the Fontaine estate, Father Thomas O'Neill found himself standing in the provincial office of the local Roman Catholic Diocese. Although he had washed and changed into rather shabby, oversized, clerical clothing provided by the nuns at the hostel, he was sure he still retained the highly distinctive smells of vomit and alcohol.

Sitting behind his large oak desk, Bishop Gerard was clearly a very unhappy man. The police report in his hand told how, after responding to an emergency call, officers found O'Neill at the Fontaine address, reeking of strong spirits and covered in his own vomit. O'Neill's vestments were torn, and he was soaking wet. Wet footprints by the lakeside strongly suggested that the inebriated priest had taken a swim in the icy waters along with a small dog that was found accompanying him. The attending police officers had found O'Neill wandering at the rear of the Fontaine Mansion, badly dishevelled and rambling incoherently about dancing skeletons and beautiful, leather-clad witches. If the Police report was not bad enough, there had also been several hostile phone messages from a very angry realtor, threatening legal action for the numerous bald patches that now afflicted the coat on his champion poodle that had been left in O'Neill's care.

The entire situation was of such severity that Gerard had immediately copied the police report to the Secretary-General of the Vatican, Cardinal Regio, in Rome. Surprisingly, for one of the most senior members of the Vatican, Regio had been awake at the early hour that the report was sent, as he responded almost immediately with an email.

In his capacity as a renowned psychiatrist, Regio felt that O'Neill's behaviour was a reoccurrence of the psychotic episode O'Neill had experienced in Mongolia. O'Neill was summarily instructed to return to Rome immediately and report to Regio at the Chief Exorcist's offices within Vatican City at 17.45HRS that evening.

Clearly, Bishop Gerard had anticipated this response from Rome, as O'Neill's belongings had been hurriedly dispatched from the lodging house. His small Adidas bag was standing outside the Bishop's Office building when O'Neill ignominiously exited to a waiting taxi that took him directly to Place de Cornavin, where he arrived at 08.07HRS.

Gare Geneva[124] was busy with morning rush-hour commuters, but, in a final humiliation, O'Neill found two, armed cantonal police officers waiting for him at the taxi rank. These two police officers briskly escorted him to the 08:00HRS train to Visp. Unusually, for a departure from Geneva, the SBB[125] had delayed the train for O'Neill. Having endured numerous hostile stares from his fellow passengers, O'Neill finally found a seat near the busy and fragrant communal toilets. Therefore, he was thankful when, two hours later he escaped the unfriendly atmosphere on the train at the town of Visp, where he transferred to the ItaliaRail Milan express.

The five-hour journey through the mountains and into the Italian countryside passed more pleasantly as O'Neill enjoyed lunch and coffee from the café in the train's central carriages. For long periods he was able to escape from the worries related to his current situation by putting in his headphones and escaping into the evocative melodies on his favourite J Edna Mae album[126]. As the train progressed South towards Rome, the weather became increasingly unsettled, turning from thick clouds to heavy rain. By the time they reached Lazio[127], the conditions had transformed into one of those heavy thunderstorms that mark the end of many humid September days in Southern Italy.

An entire Discworld novel later[128], at 16:58HRS, the train pulled into Rome's Metropolitan City station amid loud rumbles of thunder, bright flashes of sheet lightning and the

---

[124] Geneva Central Railway Station

[125] Swiss Federal Railways

[126] "Pause" (2021) by J Edna Mae Music.

[127] A region North of Rome.

[128] One of Sir Terry Pratchett's novels.

sound of heavy rain beating on the transparent glass platform roof.

The large open space of the main station foyer was crammed with commuters, hoping for a break in the weather. Sadly, O'Neill did not have the luxury of being able to wait, as his appointment with Cardinal Regio had been carefully calculated to ensure that O'Neill had no spare time and had to travel directly to Vatican City.

Instead, he had to join the queue for a taxi outside, under the enormous overhang that was not providing much protection from the sheets of heavy rain due to the gusting wind. Thankfully, O'Neill's clerical clothing influenced the taxi rank coordinator, who directed a battered, white Ford Focus full of dents and scratches to draw up beside the now drenched priest. Inside, the rear plastic seats were scuffed, and the floor was obscured by a series of ill-fitting rubber mats from a variety of different car brands. The highly distinctive smell of stale cigarettes and body odour was in no way mitigated by the "Little Tree" air freshener that was hanging from the central mirror. However, the fat, middle-aged driver showed that extraordinary ability, shared by many Mediterranean taxi drivers, of defying the laws of physics by passing through gaps in the traffic that were clearly too small for any vehicle.

After twenty minutes of traffic maneuverers that would have made Isaac Newton double-check his SUVAT equations[129], the small Ford drove along the Via di Porta Angelica and then turned left, coming to a stop in front of the red, wooden checkpoint barrier that was lowered across the

---

[129] SUVAT is an acronym of the five variables that describe a system in motion with a constant acceleration, such as an Italian taxi that never gives way or slows down. In case you wondered, the variables are: s=displacement, u=initial velocity, v=final velocity, a= acceleration, and t=time.

Sant' Anna Gate. Seeing the taxi draw up, the Swiss guard on duty waited a few moments, in case the taxi was lost and would turn away, before reluctantly exiting his wooden sentry box to brave the pouring rain. His black, plastic rain cape did little to counter the gallons of water emptying from the sky. Approaching the small taxi, he rapped on the rear passenger window and peered into O'Neill's face and checked if it matched the Vatican City identity card being presented and then the list of names typed on a soaked piece of A4 paper attached to the clipboard he carried in his right hand.

After raising the red, striped wooden barrier, he waved the small white cab through and, then closing it, gratefully returned to the small wooden hut that provided him with some refuge from the driving rain. The taxi traversed several narrow-cobbled streets within Vatican City, finally arriving at O'Neill's destination.

After paying the driver and exiting the taxi, O'Neill stood in the pouring rain outside the cream coloured, flat-roofed, two-storey, nineteen-fifties office building that formed the central hub of the Vatican's Deliverance service. The first thing O'Neill noticed was that the small brass wall plaque that had proclaimed "H. Venchencho – Capo Esorcista" had been removed. Given Venchencho's elevation to the Papacy, that was not surprising; what was a shock to O'Neill was that the other signage, for the *Deliverance Service* itself, had also been taken down. The large sign that used to grace the frontage had clearly been removed with some haste since the plastic was badly split in numerous places and, what remained, was propped against the right-side wall of the building, beside the allocated parking area.

If anything, since his arrival in Rome, the rain had intensified. O'Neill checked the time through the soaking wet, sapphire glass of his MX10 and noted that he was, unusually for him, precisely on schedule for his 17:45HRS appointment. Just as he was about to walk through the wire-framed glass doors that served as the main front entrance to the building, he noticed stacks of cardboard boxes beside the broken signage.

Walking through the large pool of rainwater that was forming in the cobbled street, he approached the containers. Upon opening a few of the soaked cardboard lids, he could see that the contents of the Deliverance Service's specialist library and Venchencho's office had been removed and stacked on the roadside for collection. Each cardboard box was labelled;

"Per l'incenerimento" (for incineration)

Alerted by a pathetic crying noise, O'Neill walked further alongside the stacked storage containers. At the far end of the row was a cardboard animal transportation box that was rapidly becoming soaking wet. Inside the box, Venchencho's beloved old Ginger tomcat, Ezekiel, was meowing pathetically; his terrified green eyes looking imploringly towards O'Neill through a cardboard patchwork of ventilation holes. O'Neill examined the top of the animal carrying box and saw it was labelled,

"Inviare a Colonia Felina di Torre Argentina: Eutanasia" (Send to Feral Feline Colonies Torre Arge: Euthanise)

Alongside these soaking cardboard containers was Venchencho's ancient, square angled Mercedes 450SEL 6.9 saloon[130]. Thick dust was caked over its once shining black bodywork where it had been neglected. There was a large, white paper sticker attached to the driver's side window instructing;

---

[130] Rather than quoting performance statistics please watch the video of Claude Lelouche's short film "C'était un rendez-vous" where the Mercedes 450SEL 6.9 is shown going through its paces through the deserted streets of Paris.

"Per la raccolta da: FB RAFFINERIA ALLUMINIO S.R.L.[131]" (For collection by: FB RAFFINERIA ALLUMINIO S.R.L.)

O'Neill reflected on the callous removal and pending destruction of the items, many of which had been highly prized possessions of the former Chief Exorcist.

After a moment's reflection, he opened the driver's door, took the keys from the ignition and then placed the cat box on the large, velour covered rear seats of the Mercedes, leaving one of the windows partially open for ventilation. He then opened the car's boot and placed all the wet cardboard storage boxes in the car's vast trunk.

His baggy vestments had become totally drenched by the time he placed his small black Adidas travel bag on the front passenger seat, locked the car and peeled off the paper sticker from the driver's side window. He crumpled the adhesive paper into one of his side pockets, along with the car key. Realizing that he was now over a quarter of an hour late, he walked quickly through the deep pool of water that had accumulated in the street, back to the building's entrance.

Opening the wired glass front door, he was immediately confronted by a female figure who was standing, deliberately out of sight from the main entrance. Once O'Neill had entered, she stepped from the shadows where she had clearly been waiting for his arrival. She was a tall woman in her mid-thirties, dressed in a quite distinctive, red coloured, full-length habit; that contrasted starkly with the close-fitting, white coloured coif and wimple that covered her neck and cheeks.

Looking pointedly at the dishevelled man who had just entered, the Sister remarked simply;

---

[131] A car scrapyard in the Province of Viterbo, Italy.

"Sei in ritardo. Seguimi." (You are late. Follow me.)

She abruptly turned and began walking rapidly along the corridor towards the stairs at the rear of the building that led to the upper floor. Her heels made a distinctive "click, clack" sound on the uncarpeted floorboards.

In contrast, O'Neill's-soaked shoes made a loud squelching noise reminding him with each step of his somewhat unkempt appearance.

At the top of the stairs, the nun stood to one side of the door to what had been Venchencho's office and announced;

"Sua eminenza è qui" (His eminence is in here)

Crossing the threshold, O'Neill was immediately struck by how different the space looked now it had been stripped of all the books, relics and pictures that had been accumulated by the Chief Exorcist during his long career. O'Neill could not help recalling how the office had been on his fateful meeting with Venchencho during his classes on demonic possession[132] before visiting the feared Sanatorium of St Michael.

A short, middle-aged man, who had been standing, looking out of the rear window at the heavy rain, turned and regarded O'Neill through a pair of steel, wire-rimmed circular glasses in the same way that a School Master looks at a disgraced pupil that he is about to discipline.

O'Neill had taken the time during his lengthy train journey to do some research on the man he was about to meet. Dr Regio's Wikipedia entry stated he was a sixty-two-year-old Italian national. Although he had married, his wife and two children had died tragically in a car accident while on holiday in Argentina ten years previously. It was this

---

[132] The post-doctoral seminar programme "Discarnate Intelligence: Theological and Historical Perspectives".

tragedy that had impelled Regio to join the Catholic Church. The first part of his Wikipedia entry was devoted to his illustrious career as a psychiatrist. He specialised in diagnosing and treating severe mental illness, especially psychotic breakdowns and their accompanying delusions. He owned several drug patents in collaboration with German and Swiss pharmaceutical companies.

The second section of the Wikipedia article focused on his conversion to the Catholic Faith. He had joined the Roman Catholic Church while on bereavement leave in Argentina, resigning from his tenured chair at Pisa University.

Once ordained, he had made extraordinarily rapid progress, becoming the Bishop of Azul, then Archbishop of Buenos Aires, before being elected to the College of Cardinals and transferring to Rome, where he had recently been appointed Secretary-General of the Governorate of Vatican City. As Secretary-General, he was in charge of the Catholic Church's day-to-day running, leaving the Pope and other dignitaries free to focus on their largely ceremonial duties. His mandate from the Governorate was to implement a comprehensive review of the Church to increase efficiency and make the Church more relevant to the modern world.

In person, Dr Regio was shorter and smaller than O'Neill had anticipated. Still, like many people of small stature, he carried himself with an air of considerable authority that would have been intimidating for many people. O'Neill reflected that it could have been this attitude and bearing that resulted in his meteoric rise through the ranks of the Church.

He had short-cropped, thinning, dyed black hair and wore rather severe, wire-framed spectacles that gave the man a very scholarly look when combined with a rather pale complexion. He wore a two-piece Gammarelli suit[133] in worsted wool, with a matching black clerical shirt and a white dog collar around his neck. On his right ring finger was an ecclesiastical ring that took the form of a large, square, golden rectangle-shaped into a classic crucifixion scene.

Cardinal Regio coughed loudly, breaking O'Neill's introspective observations and dragging him back into the here and now. Dr Regio looked pointedly at his elegant dress watch[134] before reaching out his right hand towards O'Neill, who, not regularly meeting senior Church members, was unfamiliar with the formalities associated with greeting a Cardinal. He grasped the outstretched hand with his own in a traditional handshake.

Regio reacted with disgust, pulling his hand away, exclaiming,

"Father O'Neill!! You continuously disappoint!"

Regio called out, "Sister, your presence is required." The tall, red-robed nun came rapidly into the room.

The Cardinal looked pointedly at O'Neill as he again extended his right hand,

"Let Sister Christina Mirabilis show you the proper form for greeting a Cardinal."

O'Neill could have sworn he heard a sigh pass from the Nun's lips as she dashed forward and fell to her knees before kissing the Cardinal's ring with an eagerness that verged on the inappropriate. However, O'Neill missed the full nature of the kiss as he was too preoccupied trying to

---

[133] Ditta Annibale Gammarelli (founded 1798) is the official tailor of The Pope and the most senior Catholic clerics.

[134] An 18kt yellow gold, A. Lange & Söhne, 1815 annual calendar, with a white enamel face and blue moon phase complication.

recall his Church history, as the Nun's chosen name[135] had triggered something significant in his unconscious,

"Christina Mirabilis is an unusual name. Isn't Saint Christina the Patron Saint of mental illness[136]?"

Sister Christina turned towards O'Neill, and, for the very briefest moment, the Irish American priest could have sworn that she smiled at him in a highly smug manner before resuming her sombre attitude, staring towards Cardinal Regio.

It was Regio who responded to O'Neill's question,

"I am glad to see that your many years of education have not been entirely wasted. If the Sister will permit?"

She nodded. Strangely O'Neill noted that her senses seemed totally focused on the Cardinal.

Having gained the nun's permission, Regio continued, "Sister chose the name as a reminder of her past. For you see, she was, until recently, a resident at the Sanatorium of St Michael."

O'Neill gasped, recalling the highly dangerous nature of the demonically possessed that he knew to be contained within the institution.

Regio continued,

"Yes, I believe you have been there and seen the terrible privations inflicted on the patients in the name of *treatment.* I have put an end to all of that medieval nonsense. All of the former Sanatorium *residents* are now free of those terrible confinements and are working with me to spread a more open-minded approach. You see, Father, I have

---

[135] A name that a Nun takes with her final vows.

[136] Christina Mirabilis is also known as Christina the Astonishing. She is Patroness of the mentally ill.

devoted my life to understanding the human mind and its potential. I see it as my personal mission to bring a more modern and, dare I say, enlightened approach to the Catholic Church.

To that end, I have founded my own sub order within the Church, committed to debunking all deliverance phenomena as fraud or psychological illness. I am replacing the medieval concept of exorcism with new medical and psychiatric care breakthroughs.

As part of this modernisation, I am closing down the Deliverance Unit and repurposing institutions, like the Sanatorium of Saint Michael."

O'Neill was clearly surprised by this development,

"How does this affect my role in the Deliverance Unit? Will my position be moved within this new order?"

Regio waved his hand dismissively, "Well, Father O'Neill, first we will have to see *if* you are suitable for admission to the Order of the Concealed Light[137]. Not everyone is *suitable*."

O'Neill queried, "Ordo Lucis Occultos?"

Regio smiled, "Yes." he pointed to a small, gold pin badge on Sister Christina's robe that portrayed a figure holding a flaming torch.

Sister Christina turned her still kneeling body towards O'Neill, ostensibly so he could more clearly see the badge that was proudly pinned on her right breast. However, once her body was facing directly towards him, the light from the window behind her made the fabric of Sister Christina's habit assume a semi-transparent nature, graphically highlighting the shape and outline of the nun's athletic

---

[137] Affiliated with the International Society for the Furtherance of Esoteric Traditions (ISFET).

body and emphasizing that the woman was not wearing any undergarments.

Having sensed O'Neill's observation of her body, Sister Christina remarked, in English, using a deep, husky voice,

"Your Eminence, if Father O'Neill is found *worthy* of admission to our order, perhaps I could be permitted to assist in his *preparation* for the consecration ceremony?"

O'Neill found himself being made increasingly uncomfortable by the Nun's attitude and took a step backwards.

Regio laughed,

"I do not doubt that Father O'Neill would find your *instruction* so *profound* that it would utterly alter the direction of his life, as it did to the members of the Governorate[138]. All of whom are now *devout* followers of the new order."

Regio looked pointedly at the scruffy priest who stood before him. O'Neill's borrowed clerical vestments were ill-fitting, marked by numerous darning repairs, and soaking wet. A fact emphasized by the large pool of water that had formed around his shoes.

"The question is, *are* you worthy, Father O'Neill?"

O'Neill shuffled uncomfortably as the Cardinal gestured for Sister Christina to resume her post outside the office.

"I mean, look at you!

Your appearance disgraces the Church. But if it was just your appearance, then we could make allowances. God knows we have enough shambling wrecks running local parishes. However, when we review the performance of your

---

[138] Regio is referring to the members of the Governorate of Vatican City State.

duties, then you have hardly made a positive contribution to the Mother Church, have you?

First, there was your nervous collapse after being evacuated from that temple in Iraq, followed by extended medical leave. You enrolled in highly dubious courses related to the medieval *hocus pocus* that I am committed to eradicating. That led you on a wild goose chase across the world, chasing an absurd esoteric theory and ending up in the deserts of Outer Mongolia, where you *claim* to have found a *lost civilization* and helped to *save* the world.

Not content with your delusions, you had the audacity to publish these absurd claims in the world's press."

Regio looked at O'Neill with abject pity.

"Naturally, after publishing such nonsense, you were relieved of your academic post. But, instead of dismissing you, as would have been normal practice in any other setting, the Mother Church showed infinite mercy and found you alternative duties- here in the Deliverance Section. Most people would have tried to redeem something of their reputation by settling down and doing a good job. But not you. You are sent on a simple task to examine a supposedly haunted house in Geneva. You transform it into an opera, complete with dancing skeletons, leather-clad witches, copious amounts of strong liquor, and midnight swims."

O'Neill interjected, "But you cannot dispute the reality of the human remains found at the bottom of the lake!"

Regio snorted, "They could be left over from the last Ice Age for all we know. Besides, even if they were victims of some psychopath, that is a job for Interpol, not the Roman Catholic Church!"

O'Neill was becoming increasingly irritated at the unfair way in which genuinely supernatural events were being presented as if they were signs of growing mental illness, specifically, *his* mental illness.

"Cardinal Regio, don't my eyewitness reports stand for anything? I can assure you of the reality of the phenomena I have encountered. Blaming them on mental instability is a gross injustice; after all, I am not the only witness to these occurrences."

Regio smiled, "Father O'Neill, where are these witnesses? Before holding this meeting with you, I called for character references from your former colleagues and department heads at the Pontifical Archaeology department. And I can tell you that even the most supportive of them feel your report of visiting "*The Citadel of the Djinn*" has cast doubt on you and your entire body of published work. Your former department chairs even went so far as to call you "intellectually bankrupt" and "a pseudo-intellectual".

O'Neill flinched, "You have been an academic, Regio. You know they are all two-faced backstabbers who will run down their colleagues at the first opportunity!"

Regio's sober attitude towards O'Neill lightened slightly, "I concede, Father O'Neill, there you may have a point."

Regio continued, "But you must realise that much of what you have claimed to experience sound like psychotic delusion and, more importantly, does not reflect the new role of the Church, namely to provide rational comfort, not supernatural hocus pocus!"

"Where does that leave the role of Christ in redeeming souls?" asked O'Neill, who was still feeling victimised by Regio's prejudiced assessment of his performance.

"Need I remind you, Father O'Neill, that more suffering has been inflicted under the excuse of pleasing some deity than any other cause in history. If the church is to survive, it needs to offer more than just some beneficent father figure sitting on a cloud. The starving, poor, and sick of the modern world have more need for food and medicine than for prayers and good intentions." Stated Regio.

"Do I take it then that you do not believe in God or the Immortal Soul?" Challenged O'Neill.

Regio deflected the question, "O'Neill, it does not matter what I believe. If you want to continue serving the Church, you need to adapt your behaviours radically. You must accept that the mission of Deliverance has changed. For the Mother Church to continue, it must show that it is aware that it's older doctrines are dangerous nonsense. I expect you to embrace this change of direction or stand down from your position."

O'Neill grimaced; he certainly did not want to leave the church. Based on the reaction of the academic community to his Citadel of the Djinn monographs, no reputable institution would touch him.

Regio noted O'Neil's reaction,

"From your expression, I see you wish to remain in the ministry. In that case, I will show you the future basis of the Deliverance Mission."

Regio reached into his jacket pocket and produced a small glass bottle with the label "WB" written on the side in a large blue typeface. He handed the container to O'Neill, who regarded it with some suspicion.

The Cardinal pointed to the bottle in O'Neill's left hand, "What you have in your hand is the end product of decades of my research into treating delusional states. Developed in conjunction with colleagues in Germany and Switzerland, "WB" or "Wahrnehmungsblock" is a German manufactured neuro-inhibitory drug that stops certain, specific, complex sensory and cognitive processes. It will revolutionize mental treatment for serious psychotic illnesses. I am delighted to say that the Catholic Church has the exclusive license to use the product.

"What are its primary constituents?" asked O'Neill, still looking at the bottle with considerable scepticism.

"It is a complex mix of ingredients, including tetrodotoxin."

O'Neill looked shocked, "Isn't that the puffer fish toxin? The one used in Haitian Voodoo to turn people into Zombies?"

Regio sighed,

"O'Neill, I will kindly ask you not to try and turn everything into ridiculous superstitious nonsense!

A single dose of WB promises to be more effective than a thousand exorcisms, certainly *your* kind of exorcisms." said Regio pointedly, thinking to himself that O'Neill was a prime candidate for the WB treatment himself.

"Sister Christina is currently running through every person who has been seen by the Deliverance Unit in the past ten years, consulting with their medical practitioners and providing an ongoing treatment regime of WB. I anticipate that, within twelve months, we will have provided every patient with permanent relief from supposed paranormal occurrences. The world will then be free from such supernatural nonsense, and the Church will be able to focus on more important issues.

I have decided that you will assist Sister Christina to ensure this work is done and, most importantly, that the new drug is administered to everyone who would, previously, have been offered an exorcism."

At this point, Sister Christina re-entered the room, clearly waiting for Regio to leave with her as the driver of Regio's Vatican limousine was now waiting outside for him.

"Your new duties commence immediately, and I expect you to be here, at the old Deliverance Unit, at eight AM sharp tomorrow morning to assist Sister Christina with her work.

And, Father O'Neill, this is your final chance, so do not blow it."

With that, Regio swept from the room, with Sister Christina following six paces behind him.

8 SCEPTRED ISLE

"A family with the wrong members in control - that, perhaps is as near as one can come to describing England in a phrase." - George Orwell

Home Office Building
2 Marsham Street,
Westminster, London SW1P 4DF

09.20HRS (GMT+1), 8th Sept, Present Day

After taking Cynthia Sinclair's urgent call to go to Tavish Stewart's assistance, Helen Curren joyfully left the tedious UNITY class action litigation files on her desk, picked up the distinctive trident embossed key for her beloved, red Maserati[139], only to reluctantly place it back on her desk after checking the time[140] and remembering the lack of parking in central London during the morning rush hour.

Anticipating the security checks at the entrance of the Government building, where Stewart was being held, she made sure that her professional ID card[141] was clipped securely to the lapel of the Salvatore Ferragamo jacket, before critically checking her appearance in the full-length mirror on the back of her office door. After some minor adjustments to her shoulder-length brown hair and reapplying her Dior Rouge lip stain, she went into the

---

[139] A Maserati GranTurismo Coupe. A gift from Stewart after the sad and violent demise of her previous car.

[140] On her steel Jaeger-LeCoultre Reverso.

[141] A Council of the Bar and Law Societies in Europe (CCBE) Lawyer's Professional Identity Card. Giving Curren a license to practice law throughout all the nations of Europe.

wooden panelled communal chambers office. After informing Andy, the Chambers office manager, about her absence, Curren skipped down the three flights of wooden stairs to the street below. She always relished the cases involving her favourite client, Sir Tavish Stewart, as they invariably challenged her professionally and frequently led to some of her wildest adventures.

Twenty minutes later, she arrived outside the Home Office building on Marshall Street in a black LTI TX1 London taxi cab. The grey-haired, cockney taxi driver would not come too close to the building frontage due to the extensive broken glass that littered the sidewalk.

After being signed through the strict building security, she was escorted to the Senior Home Office reception. Every floor in the building was filled with glaziers rapidly replacing the numerous broken windows from the earlier helicopter explosion.

The suites on the top floor were reserved for the elite of senior civil servants and serving cabinet ministers. The settings were opulent, and the staff had looks that could have all gained them lucrative modelling contracts. A forty-year-old secretary, whose appearance made her look like she could have stepped from a Robert Palmer video, took enormous enjoyment in informing Curren that she could not see Tavish Stewart because,

"Your client is being held on *terror*-related charges,"

She emphasized the word "terror", clearly expecting a horrified reaction from the strait-laced lawyer in front of her; instead, she heard,

"Again?"

Curren took some small satisfaction from the look on the secretary's heavily made-up face before commencing what could be a long wait to gain access to Stewart. She made herself comfortable on a white leather sofa and watched the breaking news on a large screen TV on the interior wall of the reception area. The headlines read:

"Coordinated terrorist incidents have occurred across Europe. Airports, railways, sea ports and major roads throughout the region are completely locked down. Army units are mobilised, and all police leave is cancelled."

Nearby to where Curren was sitting, Stewart was in a large, exceptionally well-ventilated reception area. The entire East side of the room, which should have provided a panoramic view over the city through tempered glass, was now an open void through which a strong breeze was flowing. Yellow safety tape provided a warning of "spillage stay clear" in an attempt to comply with health and safety rules within the stringent financial cuts enforced on most areas of the public budget.

A smartly dressed, plain clothes police detective constable guided Stewart towards the leather-covered door labelled "Home Secretary",

"Good luck, Sir. Two *very* angry VIPs in there,"

before whispering conspiratorially to the Scotsman,

"Injured from flying glass."

"Who would be stupid enough to watch an exploding anti-tank missile inside a plate glass window?"

Queried Stewart before being confronted by two senior politicians, Sir Reginald Twiffers and Lord Jeremy Kenner, their faces and hands thickly covered in sticking plasters.

Stewart mumbled something under his breath before being made to sit and listen to what promised to be a very long lecture, detailing how he would be severely punished for his irresponsible actions that morning. The Scotsman made a point of glancing at his watch[142] as he listened to the angry diatribe: how no one could help him, that his QC would never get to see him and that he imminently faced being sent to a secret detention camp on a forgotten island in the Indian Ocean, where even titled British subjects, like himself, could be made to disappear, forever.

Mercifully, at that moment, a large, red desk phone, without any dialling buttons or controls, began to ring, interrupting the seemingly endless castigation. Twiffers answered it with a harsh and angry tone.

"I told you we are *not* to be disturbed! No, I do not care *who* you are.."

Pause.

"Ah,"

The Home Secretary stood and adopted a highly submissive manner, like a small school boy discovered in some forbidden act by his House Master[143]. It was a complete transformation from his former attitude.

"Yes, yes, he is here. Right in front of me, actually, he is uninjured; yes, quite an achievement. I was telling him, yes, of course, released immediately. Yes, thank you, your Royal Highness. I trust you are in good health?"

"Your Royal Highness?

---

[142] A black resin cased Casio G Shock, which showed signs of extraordinarily hard wear on its armoured case, glass and carbon strap.

[143] A House Master is a senior teacher at English exclusive (fee paying) private boarding schools, responsible for the proper running of a residential "House" and the pupils assigned to that "House". Think Harry Potter but instead of the goal of acquiring Magical skills the goal at these schools is acquiring social influence.

Pause as the other end hung up.

"Odd must have been disconnected."

Twiffers turned to Stewart, "As I was saying, fine job you did there, Stewart, fine job."

He turned to the other senior politician, who was looking highly animated.

"Stewart saved the future King, you know."

The two senior cabinet ministers looked at each other, both clearly excited at having been contacted by The Palace. Completely forgetting the original purpose of their meeting, they became increasingly absorbed in discussions about how they would behave at The Palace, what they could wear, and, most importantly, who they could tell about their pending Royal recognition. Slowly realising their need to promote their involvement with the recent attempted kidnapping, the two men turned back to Stewart, only to find he had gone, leaving their office door wide open.

In the office entrance lobby, Stewart encountered a distraught looking Curren, who pointed to the sixty-inch TV showing the breaking news:

"Coordinated terrorist attacks, Europe in unprecedented lockdown, the heirs to every European royal family, except the UK's, abducted, ransom demands expected imminently."

The news ticker tape at the bottom of the screen ran with a sensational headline. Curren read the banner aloud to her client, clearly relishing the prospect of another epic adventure.

"Diabolical international conspiracy..."

Stewart grinned at his legal counsel, "Our favourite kind..."

To Curren's evident disappointment, Stewart thanked her for coming at short notice but told her he did not anticipate any further legal challenges that morning. Facing endless paperwork back at her desk, Curren decided she would take a detour through the upper-end boutiques in Oxford Street before finally heading on her way back to her chambers in Temple Bar.

Six hundred and forty miles to the South East of London, in a luxurious underground board room buried beneath a snow-covered peak in the Swiss Alps, Brigadier Smegget had risen from his seat at the head of the board room table. He was fuming at his assistants, who were gathered to discuss the simultaneous kidnapping of the heirs to every European monarchy.

"Sixty trillion dollars of surveillance equipment, and you had no fucking idea that Alpha was planning these kidnappings?"

Everyone around the table pointedly avoided his gaze.

Smegget then gestured to the 16K LG widescreen display replaying Stewart's encounter in the King's Road early that morning. The four minutes of footage, showing the single-handed, systematic termination of five, highly armed commandos, ended with the anti-tank missile firing and the massive explosion of the fleeing helicopter over the London skyline.

"And, while we are discussing the ineptitude of your intelligence gathering, does that look like a bloody antique dealer to you?"

Back in Central London, on Marsham Street, a sleek, black Porsche 911 soft top[144] cut through the morning traffic and

---

[144] A Porsche 911 Carrera GTS 4 - with Sinclair's tastes, what else could it be?

pulled up just as Stewart emerged from the building. A well-toned arm opened the roadside door of the sports car, and a honey-drenched Caribbean accent asked,

"Looking for an adventure, handsome?"

"Always..." answered the Scotsman as he slid into the passenger seat.

Cynthia Sinclair performed a finely timed U-turn through the heavy traffic and accelerated South down Marsham Street. Sinclair briefed Stewart as they drove,

"From what I have seen, these were exceptionally well-coordinated simultaneous kidnappings of the heirs to the twelve sovereign monarchies of Europe[145]. Their only failure was here in London."

Stewart nodded, "Maelstrom?"

"I doubt it. Five[146] informed me that there were some odd findings from examining the bodies of the kidnappers you encountered this morning; they were all active serving army personnel. 601 Commando, Argentinian Army[147]."

"Any chance of my seeing the bodies, I may notice something else."

"That is where we are heading."

They turned right at the Horseferry Road junction and pulled in on the left side, at number 65- the Westminster Coroner's Court for the Royal Borough of Kensington and

---

[145] Seven kingdoms: Denmark, Norway and Sweden and the United Kingdom of Great Britain and Northern Ireland, Netherlands, Belgium and Kingdom of Spain. Five principalities: Andorra, Liechtenstein, and Monaco and the Grand Duchy of Luxembourg.

[146] MI5 – The UK Domestic security service.

[147] AFOE: Agrupación de Fuerzas de Operaciones Especiales (Special Operations Forces Group).

Chelsea. The three-storey brick building had its double doors wide open; lying in the doorway were the bodies of two, armed police officers, both severely injured from multiple gunshot wounds. Their blood slowly spread over the grey paving stones, and their weapons lay close by their bodies.

While Stewart knelt to administer first aid, Sinclair called for an ambulance on her mobile as she entered the deserted building. However, she had to rapidly retreat as a wave of thermite charges engulfed the interior, instantly incinerating the bodies of the five terrorists and any forensic evidence.

Stewart dragged the two wounded detectives to the roadside, where, fortunately, they were tended to by some passing nurses from the nearby Millbank Medical Centre. He informed Sinclair of the descriptions he had acquired from the severely injured police officers.

"There were six, armed commandos, using two cars, a black BMW and a white Mercedes. The officer who understood Spanish overheard that they were going to Clarence House."

"The Royal residence? Isn't one of them scheduled to be visiting there today?"

At that moment, their conversation was drowned out by the sound of a helicopter passing very low and fast above them. Stewart listened carefully to the distinctive rotor noise and noted the shape of the dark silhouette of the aircraft as it passed mere feet above the roof tops above them.

"A Super Cougar[148]. Used by the French and some South American Military, but not the British, too expensive. Useful bit of kit. It carries over twenty people, is heavily armoured and has a range of weapons systems."

---

[148] An Airbus Helicopters EC 725 military transport

"So, you know your military aircraft."

"That can only be intended for the extraction of the bastards who did this!" Stewart gestured to the two injured police officers.

"Merdi!" exclaimed Sinclair in her native Creole.

Sinclair and Stewart jumped back in the black sports car, Stewart using the car phone to inform the emergency services of the description of the two target vehicles heading towards Clarence House.

As the 911 became stuck in the thick London traffic, Stewart searched the dashboard and queried,

"Do you have a turbo?"

"Something better..." quipped Sinclair as she flicked a red switch under her dashboard that caused concealed blue strobe lights hidden in the front and rear of the sports car to begin flashing and a piercing siren to be emitted from under the bonnet.

"Show off," teased Stewart, grabbing the hanging handle from the car's side door frame as Sinclair made her second U-turn of the morning. They flew through the junction from Horseferry Road into Marsham Street at sixty mph and began bullying their way through the rush hour traffic. Eventually, they saw the terrorist's two high-speed getaway cars, a wicked-looking white Mercedes[149] and, behind that, a sleek, black BMW[150].

Inside the BMW M5, the two commandos sitting in the rear seats noticed the ominous black 911 with "blues and

---

[149] Mercedes AMG E63 S

[150] BMW M5 (F90) – four wheeled drive variant.

twos[151]" relentlessly pushing its way through the heavy traffic towards them. Both men lowered their passenger windows, unfolded the stocks on small Micro Uzi submachine guns[152] and callously started spraying 9mm rounds behind them at 1,200 rounds per minute.

The windscreen in the Porsche disintegrated into an explosion of tempered glass, and a series of ugly holes appeared in the dashboard plastic. Around them, the public ran screaming in a disorganised panic. The armed police on duty outside the Home Office retreated inside and started lockdown procedures.

Stewart sighed as he calmly brushed tempered glass fragments from his Ede and Ravenscroft suit for the second time in less than three hours.

"How often have I told you the importance of bulletproofing your car?"

"Honey, what is the point of having a 911 that weighs more than a tank?"

Stewart leaned over and reached up between Cynthia's long, smooth legs.

Sinclair joked, "You certainly pick your time."

"Stop complaining. You know I am only after one thing...." Stewart quipped back as he retrieved a tiny black polymer gun that he knew Sinclair always carried in a concealed holster between her thighs. He pulled the slide mechanism

---

[151] The two-tone siren of a UK emergency vehicle responding to an official incident.

[152] The Micro Uzi is a scaled down version of the Israeli manufactured Uzi submachine gun. Adopted by Argentinian special forces.

on the small Beretta Nano and exhaled as he drew his sights on the BMW some ten yards in front of them.

Stewart's first two shots impacted into the BMW's rear tyres, but with little effect, followed by two equally ineffective rounds directed into the car's rear window.

"Bugger, they are armoured."

Cynthia gestured towards the floor.

"My Handbag."

"I am not sure I could throw it hard enough to make a difference..." Stewart retorted as he pulled up the black leather Chanel bag and located Sinclair's old Beretta "Raffica"[153].

The recent exchange of gun fire had caused the other road users to pull off onto the pavements and side roads. While the Police on duty in the Home Office building had declared a Kratos class incident[154], causing the surrounding area to be evacuated and all the streets cleared.

As the road ahead narrowed, the three cars barrelled through the junction with Great Peter Street and there was another volley of high-velocity submachine gun fire from the rear windows of the BMW in front of them.

This time it received a 1,100 round a minute response from the Porsche. Armour piercing rounds from the fifty-year-old Italian machine pistol caused substantial damage to the rear of the BMW, puncturing the right run-flat rear tyre, creating ugly holes in the rear boot and forming the classic spider web pattern on the bulletproof glass in the rear window.

---

[153] The Beretta 93 "R" (Raffica is Italian for "volley") is a machine pistol, designed and manufactured by Italian firearms manufacturer Beretta in the 1970s for counter terrorism duties.

[154] Armed terrorists at large within a populated area.

Based on the red arterial blood spray that now covered the inside rear window, at least one of the gunmen inside the BMW had also received a hit.

With the roads clear, the two escaping cars increased their speed to over 120 mph and headed straight on into Great Smith Street.

With Sinclair focused on driving, Stewart made a call on the car phone to the senior military officer responsible for the protection of the area around Buckingham Palace.

"Tim?"

"Yes, Tavish Stewart. Yes, Royal Scots."

There was a pause, as a very aristocratic voice talked about the regimental positions in a 19th-century conflict. Sighing at the irrelevance, Stewart responded patiently, "Believe you are right, Tim; the Royals were on your left flank at The Battle."

Laughter on the other end of the line as the other man recited a quote, "Twas a dreadful day and night of thunder and rain"[155].

Stewart tried again to bring the topic of conversation forward two hundred years.

"Listen, Tim, any of your lads on duty this morning?"

Pause.

"Yes, you could call it trouble."

At that moment, the two cars in front exchanged places, the damaged BMW taking the lead. At the same time, the white Mercedes slowed and opened its sunroof to reveal a gunman, who stood from the front passenger seat up through the sunroof and commenced directing fire from his

---

[155] Field quote from the Battle of Waterloo, 1815.

Micro-Uzi down on the 911 sports car that was close behind it.

Stewart and Sinclair both ducked beneath the dashboard; while Stewart returned fire with the Raffica through the sports car's broken front windshield, clearly scoring numerous hits on the figure standing in the sunroof of the vehicle in front, causing the gunman's body to visibly shake in a macabre dance, while emitting a thick spray of red arterial blood splatter over the white Mercedes' body work.

Stewart continued his phone conversation, "Open your window, Tim. You can probably hear the machine-gun fire,"

slight pause.

"Yes, fully automatic,"

Stewart glanced to his left, calmly examining one of the numerous rounds now embedded into the back of his seat rest, "Yes, pretty sure they are 9mm hollow points."

The phone speaker gave out the sound of a group of upper-class accented men calling to Tim to come back to take his turn playing a tabletop battle re-enactment.

Stewart ignored the distraction and continued,

"No, I know they did not have that kind of firepower at Waterloo. Listen, Tim; these hoodlums are heading towards The Mall, where I believe they will be extracted by helicopter."

"You don't do modern tactical games? Tim, this is not a game..."

The line went dead.

Sinclair exclaimed in exasperation, "Try Lev[156]! I know he is in London."

Stewart nodded and dialled another number, commencing a short, more positive conversation.

Colonel Timothy Tompkins adjusted his scarlet silk cummerbund and swaggered back to the group of his fellow senior officers, all similarly attired in full evening dress uniforms[157], smoking Arturo Fuente Opus X cigars and drinking a range of expensive spirits, while they gathered around a sizeable beige table, where model soldiers were arranged in 19th-century battle formations.

However, the resumption of their war game was short-lived, as all conversation was drowned out by the tremendous noise from a large grey helicopter that appeared above The Mall and commenced spraying 30mm cannon fire[158] at the surrounding buildings and security postings. As the police and military personnel on duty along The Mall scurried for cover, the assembled senior military officers playing their war game threw themselves to the floor of the officer's mess, spilling drinks, and smashing Waterford crystal decanters, as window glass, wooden window frame sections and masonry flew in all directions.

Back in the Home Office building on Marsham Street, emergency flash communications were accumulating from the civilian emergency services and the various branches of

---

[156] Lev Bachrach is a retired Russian Federation intelligence officer with pro-Western sympathies.

[157] Yes, even though it was still mid-morning.

[158] French made GIAT 30 M 781 30mm helicopter mounted machine gun.

the military, urgently requesting instructions on how to respond. All were going unattended as Sir Reginald Twiffers and Lord Jeremy Kenner had declared themselves incommunicado while they were involved in the vital work of consulting the two, full time, professional "wine butlers" hired by the Government to administer the taxpayer-funded multi-million-pound wine cellar, maintained for the enjoyment of senior civil servants and government minsters[159].

Meanwhile, the three cars flew across the empty Victoria Street and up Storey's Gate at over 140 mph.

"Four-wheel drive?" queried Stewart as they completed a series of steep corners that appeared to defy the laws of physics and slammed his large body into the fitted GTS seat.

"Yes, all three of us, unfortunately." Sinclair gestured to the screaming noise and smoke coming from the tyres on the large Mercedes saloon close in front of them. They then made a violent left turn, leading to Birdcage Walk and the two cars in front split into different directions, the white Mercedes taking off down Birdcage Walk, while the black BMW headed down Horse Guards Road.

"Any preference?" queried Sinclair as the 911 hurtled through the junction at close to 130 mph.

"The helicopter..." Stewart gestured towards the wide pedestrian entrance into St James Park, some yards ahead on their right.

The Porsche flew through the narrow park pathways and over the thin bridge. A large, grey helicopter, hovering above the green space to their right, turned and started directing 30mm cannon fire towards the black 911. Turf,

---

[159] Clearly an important Government budgetary priority.

asphalt and stone chippings flew into the air close behind the sports car, which only avoided being hit by charging through the double gates on the other side of the park onto The Mall. However, instead of gaining a respite from the onslaught of the cannon, they came under fully automatic 9mm gunfire, coming simultaneously from the white Mercedes to their left and the black BMW from the right. Both cars hurtled towards them along the deserted approach to the Royal Residence.

Less than a mile away, in an elegant oak-panelled room hidden deep within one of the more exclusive private clubs that provide refuge for London's super-rich, three men sat on a classic leather chesterfield four-seater sofa, smoking classic Cuban cigars[160]. Carefully stacked to the left side of the chesterfield sofa, near the tall sash windows, were three sets of monogrammed[161] carry-on luggage[162], complete with British Airways EZE/LHR[163] first-class "*diplomatic/customs exempt*" labels.

The central and more influential of the three figures was a sophisticatedly dressed older man, who was known to his associates simply as Alpha. His long white hair was swept back into a pony tail that draped over the rear collar of his black linen, classically tailored Brunello Cucinelli suit jacket. Instead of a silk tie, he wore a thick black threaded, leather bola tie, the two ends of which were threaded together by a silver keeper, embossed with a single strange character that was not immediately recognisable as either a letter or a

---

[160] Montecristo Linea 1935 Leyenda cigars.

[161] For its more discerning and wealthy patrons most manufacturers will personalise their products.

[162] Louis Vuitton Monogram Canvas Pegase 70 Suitcases

[163] Buenos Aires to London Heathrow.

number but was similar to the letter "Z" placed sideways with a single bar through its centre. Whatever the unfamiliar symbol was, the dark leather cord and thick silver clasp perfectly complimented his white Canali linen shirt. The man's piercing blue eyes were focused on the unfolding conflict at The Mall that was being relayed from a camera mounted on the helicopter that hovered mere feet above the tree line of St James Park.

Seated on either side of the distinguished older man, on the luxurious, mahogany coloured leather sofa, were two younger men. Both shared the same robust and aristocratic family facial characteristics but were some decades younger than the older gentleman, who could have been their grandfather. All three men were lean and powerfully built, with the deep tan and that undefinable healthy aura that only comes from prolonged, strenuous outdoor activities.

The images of the violent confrontation unfolding on The Mall were shown in real-time on the high-resolution display of a top of the range Apple laptop that rested on the polished dark teak 19th-century table. Beside the Macbook was a black metal, Bosch branded, encrypted communications system connected to the computer to provide a secure real-time video feed. In stark contrast, lying beside this 21st-century technology on the table top were some sheets of vellum parchment, covered with a strange handwritten square[164] of letters that, when translated[165], linked closely with the violent action taking place on the computer screen.

---

[164] Clearly some variant of the system of magic attributed to Rabbi Yaakov Moelin (ca. 1365–1427), a German Jewish Talmudist. The system was popularised by the 19th century occult group The Golden Dawn under the title "The Book of the Sacred Magic of Abramelin the Mage".

[165] קְרָב - Karáv (combat, military operation) and אוויר - Avír (air)

K	A	R	A	V
A	V	I	R	A
R	I	A	I	R
A	R	I	V	A
V	A	R	A	K

Meanwhile, at the St James Gate on The Mall, it looked increasingly certain that the fate of Sinclair and Stewart would be sealed by the overwhelmingly superior firepower of their opponents. They briefly kissed as they exited the 911; both then loaded fresh magazines into their respective weapons and opened fire at the speeding oncoming cars. Spent rounds littered the asphalt around them as they stood, side by side, left arms interlocked for stability, Stewart firing the tiny Beretta Nano's 9mm rounds at the armoured Mercedes accelerating towards him. His shots were aimed at the armoured windshield, not in the hope of penetrating the unbreakable glass but as a distraction to the driver. For her part, Sinclair unleashed the full power of the ancient but deadly Raffica at the black BMW M5 that, in turn, hurtled towards her.

Just as the white Mercedes was about to close into a killing distance with Stewart, an enormous black, square, ZIL-41047 stretch limousine with Russian Federation flags accelerated out of the Marlborough Road, straight into the side of the oncoming Mercedes. The acceleration from the eight-litre engine and 8,000 lb weight of the Russian diplomatic limousine piledrove the lighter Mercedes into the black iron railings of the St James Park gate. The impact pulverised the entire front of the smaller, more lightweight car instantly, without causing any noticeable damage to the ZIL.

The two surviving gunmen slowly dragged themselves from the rear windows of the smashed Mercedes and opened fire ruthlessly with their Micro-Uzi machine guns at the occupant of the ZIL. Their jacketed hollow point rounds smashed into all the exposed areas on the diplomatic vehicle but caused only superficial damage due to the ZIL's full metal armour plating. After a moment, the driver's door on the massive limousine swung slowly open, revealing a large and powerfully built man with grey hair, a distinctive broken nose, and wearing a black leather jacket.

He carried a thick, short-barrelled, wire stocked pump-action shotgun and discharged two, solid steel, 0.9-inch rounds at the gunmen firing at him. The legendary Soviet "Barricade " shots, known to disintegrate iron engine blocks at a distance of one hundred yards, literally blew the two gunmen into bloody offal that spattered over the white bodywork of the now pulverised Mercedes.

On Sinclair's side, the deadly charge by the black M5 had come under the scrutiny of a group of around twenty Grenadier guards. These soldiers had left their posts around Buckingham Palace and were kneeling in their full ceremonial uniforms under whatever cover they could find. They drew their Heckler and Koch assault rifles on the approaching car, unable to fire without first being fired upon by an aggressor.

Inside the speeding black BMW, the heavily tanned leader of the commandos, seated in the rear right passenger seat, made an insulting comment in Spanish. He gestured towards the distinctive bearskin hats exposed above the various concrete and metal objects used by the troops as cover.

"Mira, armado pero demasiado asustado para disparar. Soldados de chocolate ceremonials!" (See, armed but too scared to fire. Ceremonial chocolate soldiers!)

He then directed his Micro Uzi out of the rear car window, peppering holes into the exposed tops of the eighteen-inch-tall, bear skin hats worn by the concealed troops. Now that the Grenadiers had come under direct gunfire, their highly restrictive rules of engagement, while on ceremonial duties, finally permitted a response.

The six hundred round a minute barrage of 5.56mm armour piercing rounds, fired simultaneously by twenty highly trained combat soldiers, caused the lightly armoured BMW to disintegrate before Sinclair's eyes. By the time the car ground to a halt, some ten yards in front of Sinclair, there was no question of anyone remaining alive in the vehicle. It was just a smouldering mass of ugly bullet holes.

A few moments later, the thick cordite smoke cleared, revealing a sight that could have come straight from Colonel Timothy Tompkins' battle game. A thin row of red tunicked soldiers advanced menacingly towards the BMW with their bayonets fixed to ensure they had finished their work.

Meanwhile, as Stewart had taken the distinctive short shotgun from his Russian friend and aimed it at the helicopter's spinning rotors, a cry came out from the shattered third-floor windows of the nearby senior officers' mess.

"I say, jolly good show! Look, everyone, it's Travis, Travis Steward!"

A group of around twelve heavily inebriated men, all in somewhat dishevelled looking full mess dress uniforms, joined Colonel Timothy Tompkins, leaning out of the shattered window frame of the senior officers' mess. They all raised their champagne glasses and shouted, "Hip, Hurrah for Steward!"

Stewart's expletive-laden response was thankfully drowned out by the roar of the short-barrelled KS-23M shotgun, followed closely by the deafening noise of the military transport helicopter shedding a large section of its fuselage. This debris dropped into St James Park Lake, scattering crash debris high into the air, much of it impacting the third-floor senior officers' mess. Meanwhile, the critically damaged aircraft flew low over the barracks buildings and rapidly disappeared from view.

Back at the British Home Office building, the news coverage in the executive lounge showed the gunfight at The Mall from numerous angles, taken by camera drones flying around the scene. Two heavily inebriated cabinet ministers struggled to express themselves.

"Isn't that... that... bloody insolent Stewart fellow?"

The older of the two professional Government "Wine Butlers" looked at the TV while he put another empty vintage claret bottle in the plastic bin on the side of the steel drinks trolley.

"Yes, Home Secretary."

The Defence Secretary partially choked on his sixty-year-old port.

"Is.. is.. isn't that the second helicopty thing he has shot at today?"

"Yes, I believe it is, Sir." Replied the second wine waiter as he opened the next Sandeman Cask 33 Tawny Port bottle.

9 THE CAVE

"There are no experts in outdoor survival. There are only students..." – Dave Ganci

A Small Oasis, Twenty Miles West of The Gurvan Saikhen Mountains,
Gobi Desert,
Southern Mongolia.

20:00HRS (GMT+8), 8th Sept, Present day

Unaware that the funeral pyre for the unfortunate group of six Mongolian traders[166] had attracted the interest of the world's three superpowers, the mysterious hawk-faced man went through his few possessions before consigning them to the intense flames to avoid any risk of them spreading the deadly haemorrhagic virus.

The shattered ceramic Suunto watch no longer functioned. Still, its memory did show the last latitude and longitude coordinates it had measured through its crushed sapphire glass and fragmented LCD display. Somehow, the hawk-faced man knew instinctively that these numbers indicated a remote area of the Outer Mongolian Desert. Still, he had no idea where or when he had acquired such navigation expertise. From the date and time stamp on the watch, he could see that these location coordinates had been recorded just over three weeks earlier and he realised that he might have travelled some considerable distance. He, therefore, set himself the future goal, once he had finished his current grisly tasks, of determining his current location,

---

[166] Who had pulled his semi-drowned body from the water of the oasis.

before deciding which direction to travel or if he should stay put and anticipate some form of rescue.

He next examined the remains of his clothing. The damage patterns and odour evident on his Kevlar-reinforced Scorpion uniform, Dragon Skin body armour, and Warrior boots showed sustained attacks by multiple large marine animals that delivered extraordinarily destructive wounds with large serrated teeth or perhaps even claws[167]. Inside one of his cargo trouser pockets, he found a Luminox watch with a distinctive logo on its dial. The watch glass was smashed, and the case waterlogged. The dark spiral symbol on the dial was a source of pride, but he could not remember precisely why.

Holding the steel dagger by its damaged nine-inch blade, he found he knew the composition of the steel, along with its strengths and weaknesses in a variety of combat scenarios, just from its touch and how the metal caught the light. While momentarily lost, wondering what kind of man would carry such items, one of the giant black vultures that continued to circle above swooped down. The dark shape and sudden movement startled the hawk-faced man, causing him to instinctively duck and, simultaneously, without any conscious thought or even sight of the vulture, effortlessly throw the nine-inch blade in its direction.

Rising and slowly turning towards the source of the disturbance, he found that the thrown blade had pinned the large bird to a nearby leather saddle bag, piercing through the vulture's central body mass, killing it instantly. Walking a dozen yards to the dead creature, he freed the broken knife. He realised, as he did, that his throw had automatically compensated for the altered balance of the weapon due to its blade damage and that, even in its

---

[167] Technically, they were pincers called chelae, but that is unknown to the hawk-faced man.

broken state, it would be perfect in sixteen of the dozens of knife throwing techniques he retained in his deep muscle memory. Although a part of him felt discomfort at the realisation that he had some unusually well-honed skills devoted to the most efficient ways to terminate life, another, more practical side of his nature welcomed the realisation since it might help him get out of this desperate situation alive.

He temporarily dismissed these concerns as he focused on searching through the numerous items that had been carried for trade on the camel caravan. It quickly became apparent that there was nothing of real value, just lots of cheap plastic and metal trinkets, mass-produced in Asian sweatshops for a quick profit. There was around four hundred thousand Mongolian Tögrög in cash. He had no idea of its value[168], so he placed the colourful bank notes in a plastic wallet covered with unlicensed Disney character images.

He did find two-litre plastic water bottles decorated with children's cartoon characters that he filled with boiled water, using the cooking pot that the Mongolian traders had used to prepare their coffee. Searching through the clothing containers, he found a white polyester cotton mix full-length tunic and a blue sleeveless body warmer, with the image of a galloping pony and the text "Rolf Lorine" embroidered over its exterior surfaces. The selection of shoes was equally disappointing; after searching through dozens of fake Nike trainers in tiny sizes, he used a pair of simple white lace-up canvas plimsols.

After having burnt all his possessions and outfitting himself as best he could from the items from the caravan, he set himself to the task of confirming his location. Taking a wooden tent pole, he broke it into two sections and tied

---

[168] Around 150 USD.

them together with some white synthetic cord, and he sat and waited patiently for the sun to set. Once the sky was dark enough, he located Polaris[169], which was dimly visible at the extreme edge of the horizon, to determine his bearing to North. He marked the direction with lines in the rough sand and also with rows of rocks, so he would have a lasting record of the direction once daylight returned.

After a tough and gamey tasting meal of cooked vulture, he enjoyed a good night's sleep, waking an hour before sunrise to create a simple sundial with a five-foot-tall wooden tent pole that he buried into a vertical position at the highest point beside the oasis. He did this so he could mark points in the rocky dirt around the pole periodically between sunrise and sunset, in conjunction with a cheap quartz "call to prayer" clock that he had found among the goods transported by the traders. Somehow, he knew that this clock was set to the time in Mecca[170].

In between marking the location of the cast shadow from the sundial's gnomon during four[171] of the five adhan (calls to prayer), he used children's chalk crayons to mark the angle of the sun to the horizon on a simple sextant he had created, using two sections of wood tied together.

After a full day of careful monitoring and recording, he determined his latitude (based on the sun's angle to the horizon) and his longitude, using the rough approximation of each hour being one time zone and each time zone as roughly fifteen degrees. He estimated seventeen nautical

---

[169] Polaris, the North Star. The brightest star in the constellation of Ursa Minor.

[170] Lat. 21.4225° N, Long. 39.8262° E. A set of coordinates which the hawk-faced man found he already knew.

[171] Dawn, Midday, Afternoon and Sunset, respectively.

miles[172] further West from the last position recorded on the Suunto watch. But he again had to pause to wonder what kind of man knew numerous deadly knife throwing techniques and could determine his location within a few yards using sticks and chalk.

His instincts told him that he was thousands of miles off the main flight paths and that there was little point in waiting for a rescue. As he settled down to sleep, with a meal of cold vulture meat, he decided that the first thing the following morning, he would have to walk out through some of the most hostile terrains in the world.

An hour before dawn, he gathered two full water bottles and placed them, along with the body warmer, into a plain black fifteen-litre nylon mesh backpack before walking towards the highest point in his immediate vicinity. Using his thumb to measure the rough height of the mountain, he estimated it was around ten thousand feet high and would provide him with an excellent vantage point to see the nearest habitation if there was any.

His progress walking towards the peak was slow; the ground was formed of numerous highly polished mica and quartz rocks of various sizes, making the surface uneven and treacherous in his simple white canvas plimsols. Eventually, after six hours of walking up a gradually increasing incline, he faced a one-thousand-foot-high sheer rock face. He wondered, momentarily, if his skill sets included free climbing. He was not surprised to discover that he rapidly and effortlessly ascended the sheer rock face, going from one overhang to the next, like it was something he did every day. He intuitively utilised fist holds and finger pull-ups while using the crushed powder from the children's chalk crayons to dry his grip. The only evidence that the climb was taking a toll on the lone climber was the small blood

---

[172] Approximately twenty statutory miles.

stain that appeared on the midriff of the white polycotton tunic, as a deep wound that had only partially healed began to weep.

After four hours of concentrated effort, he heard voices, some of which he recognised as speaking with an American accent. Other group members talked in a mix of European inflexions; all conversed in English. His early memories of how his family and his beloved Egypt suffered under US interference and his indoctrination while serving with Soviet intelligence caused an instinctively negative emotional response to all things Western.

There were, his intuition estimated, around seventeen people gathered above the summit of the sheer rockface to his immediate right. Although exactly how he could be so sure of the approximate size of the group or their location in relation to his position was a mystery to him. He could hear the sounds of them queuing in order to have their photographs taken in a posed position, to make it look like they had just completed what the authoritative voice of their guide proclaimed to be the only V 5.15e graded climb[173] currently officially recognised in the world.

As the hawk-faced man emerged over the top of the sheer rock face, the group of adventure tourists had moved some twenty feet, facing away from him. They all stood next to a brand-new Bell 525 "Relentless" transport helicopter with a bright blue livery that proclaimed "Xtreme Tours – creating the definitive selfie record of the world's ultimate adventures".

Standing at the top of the thousand-foot precipice, the lone hawk-faced man caught his breath and coldly evaluated the group before him, coming to his assessment within the blink

---

[173] The most severe rating for a free solo climb under the Yosemite Decimal System of climbing difficulty.

of an eye. The two guides were armed with what he recognised as fourth-generation polymer Glock 17 pistols, with stock, seventeen round magazines, chambered for the standard 9mm parabellum round. Both guns and holsters showed the steady wear patterns associated with regular practice and proper maintenance.

Six of the remaining fifteen men and women carried survival, boot and neck knives. Judging from their pristine condition, most of these weapons had never seen any serious use or practice. The lone man's instincts told him that, due to his current severely weakened physical condition and lack of weapons, he had a sixty-two per cent likelihood of sustaining serious injury if he attempted to overpower the entire group. So, although he looked at the Bell Relentless with undisguised longing, he knew he would have to build his strength and wait for when another opportunity presented itself.

The entire group of seventeen people were so totally absorbed in the act of posing for pictures by the helicopter that they failed to notice as the lone figure, dressed in a single white polycotton robe and a pair of canvas plimsols, walked around the gathering of adventure junkies, all of whom were outfitted in this season's bespoke equipment. Each item the tourists wore was ostentatiously branded to show that it had cost its owner thousands of dollars.

The lone, hawk-faced figure ignored the crowd; he only paused next to a long folding table set up with refreshments to pick up a bright red, aluminium can of a caffeine energy drink that he cast to one side after a single taste. He preferred to continue sipping from his own dirty plastic water bottle. This hawk-faced stranger rapidly passed out of sight through a break in the hillside that led into a narrow chasm.

Following what looked like a dried-up stream, the lone, hawk-faced man found some odd carvings deep in the bedrock that resembled stylised winged middle eastern djinn[174]. Their shape triggered some recent memories repressed since his emergence from the oasis. He experienced recollections of leading an elite group of special forces troops to the Gobi, entering into a lost underground city in search of a single man, a man who had been the cause of considerable personal and professional loss. In a blinding flash, he recalled the man, what he looked like and most importantly, his name. Tavish Stewart, a Scotsman who he had sworn to kill, but a simple death was no longer enough, not after all of this.... The hawk-faced man considered his wounds, illness, his current desolate state. He decided not only would he survive, but he would also rise again to lead a team of elite warriors and bring unimaginable suffering to this accursed Tavish Stewart.

After this epiphany, he found himself filled with new optimism and energy. However, this euphoria was short-lived, as a clump of dried white sticks that had randomly formed into the shape of a crab on the dried river bed caused him to experience an unexpected panic attack. He gathered himself and continued walking, eventually finding himself in a long flat valley with high sand-covered cliffs. Numerous giant vultures circled in the thermals formed by the air currents rising from the valley floor.

Back at the helicopter, the loud voices continued their endless complaints. These included but were not limited to: the lack of a phone signal on the mountain, that many of their excursions lasted longer than the battery life of their designer smart "sport adventure" watches, the inability to get a decent low fat, decaf mochaccino and the monotony

---

[174] Supernatural entities, mentioned in pre-Islamic and Islamic mythology and theology.

of having to tolerate poor service when travelling outside the mainland US or Europe. Meanwhile, the two guides separated themselves from the group in preparation for getting the tour back on board the aircraft. They discussed which of the females on the tour were likely to be the most energetic lovers.

As the lone, hawk-faced man progressed further along the flat valley floor, he noticed two large metal objects protruding from the steep valley side to his left. As he got closer, he identified them as the fuselage remains from a passenger aircraft[175], decorated with a large tiger's face on the nose section and the distinctive dark grey paint from a military transport plane[176]. Some enormous force had clearly moved both aircraft before dumping them into the steep side of this valley. More evidence of some recent cataclysmic event was provided by some thirty-foot square sections of rock that had cascaded down the right cliffside wall and gathered in a pile of debris on the valley floor.

On approaching this massive obstruction, the hawk-faced man could see the debris trail left by the rocks as they had descended the steep cliff side, and, far up on the cliff face, he noticed something metallic glittering in the midday sunshine.

Before advancing up the steep, sandy incline, he encountered two human skeletons pinned under some of the smaller rocks that had cascaded down to the valley floor. The rock fall had occurred in the early phases of some

---

[175] A Boeing 747-446 EI-XLD

[176] An Airbus A400M Atlas

enormous storm and had sheltered the human remains from any further disturbance.

Examining the smaller of the two skeletons, who was probably a youth, he could clearly see the neck had been efficiently broken. In contrast, the larger adult skeleton had a bullet through its left temple and based on the position of the two sets of bones, it looked as though the two people had perished simultaneously.

Momentarily wondering what caused the violent demise of these two individuals, the hawk-faced man began the sharp ascent up the steep cliffside towards the glinting object. His white canvas sneakers sunk deep into the fine sand, making his progress both slow and arduous. Eventually, after around five minutes of hard climbing, he came up to a cave entrance, clearly only recently revealed after a massive movement of sand and rock, possibly associated with the same storm that had so spectacularly deposited the two aircraft, further back along the valley. The walls of the cave entrance showed evidence of being carved out of the bedrock by some unknown human agency. More stylised effigies of middle eastern djinn were carved into the walls at eye level, alongside some unintelligible ancient text and an arrow that pointed in the opposite direction to that the lone man had been walking.

Cautiously entering the dark cave, it took some moments for his eyes to accommodate from the bright sunlight of the sand-covered valley to the total blackness inside the cave opening. Only as he accustomed himself to the gloom deep inside did he notice he was not alone. A group of three badly decayed human remains, dressed in classic expedition clothing, were posed, sitting in a circle of wooden chairs. Near the feet of each skeleton lay a small square of greaseproof paper embossed with a large IG Farben logo. Reaching down around the leather boots of one of the bodies, the lone man found dozens of unopened paper packets with the same symbol. Inside the wrapping, he found a small, oval-shaped glass vial covered with a thin brown rubber coating[177] that he recognised as old-fashioned potassium cyanide (KCN) based suicide pill[178]. More modern versions used Saxitoxin (STX), but many of the older Soviet intelligence agencies had issued similar cyanide-based last resorts to elite operatives in case of capture and interrogation. Gathering the unused KCN suicide ampoules, he placed them in his jacket pockets.

Viewing the bodies with renewed respect, he realised these were fellow elite warriors who had decided to take their own lives after being buried without hope of rescue inside the cave's darkness. The hawk-faced man began to explore what equipment these men carried before they became trapped.

Pulling the heavy canvas rucksacks nearer to the light, he began a systematic search through their contents. In the first, he found the expedition's supplies of spare clothing. Although the sizes available were not an exact fit, he quickly exchanged his bloodstained, full-length polycotton smock for a matching, classic khaki fabric shirt, cargo trousers and multi-pocket jacket, all with Hugo Boss labels[179].

Moving on to the next bag, he found it partially empty, as it originally contained a radio set. He emptied its remaining contents onto the floor. He found a pistol, carefully wrapped in an oiled fabric sheet. He carefully and expertly tested the mechanism on the old weapon. He loaded eight 9mm

---

[177] These thin-walled glass ampoules are covered in a layer of thin brown rubber to minimize the risk of accidental breakage. Breaking the glass and swallowing the cyanide caused collapse and brain death within seconds.

[178] Known as an "L-pill" or lethal pill by secret agent operatives.

[179] Hugo Boss were the proud suppliers to the Waffen SS.

bullets, taken from a small cardboard box marked with an old Böhmische Waffenfabrik factory logo, into the magazine. The classic Walther p.38 still functioned perfectly. Taking the leather belt holsters from one seated body, the hawk-faced man made a few practice draws with his new weapon before putting it inside the holster and resuming his search through the supply bags. They proved to contain nothing more of value beyond some tins of corned beef that were well beyond their perishable date.

He then proceeded to search the decayed bodies. The penetration of decomposition fluids had damaged most of the items they had carried, but, on the body of the leader of the group, he found an iron-cased Laco[180]-Sport watch that started to run after he wound the mechanism a few times. He also found a magnificent long steel, double-edged dagger with a highly distinctive skull[181] and Sonnenrad[182] symbol embossed into the hilt, along with the text "Wewelsburg. Zentrum der neuen Welt[183]" and the date, 23rd April 1943.

All the items worn by the leader were old but of exceptionally high quality. The hawk-faced man examined a dusty old log book clasped tight in the skeletal fingers of the dead man. The linen-bound book had a highly distinctive decoration on its cover: a sword with an intertwining ribbon flowing on both sides of the long blade.

---

[180] Laco watches were issued time pieces for Nazi forces.

[181] Deaths Head symbol adopted by the SS.

[182] The dark sun symbol adopted by the inner circle of the SS.

[183] The address of Wewelsburg castle, the ideological headquarters of the SS.

A border of runic characters surrounded the sword and ribbon, which ran right around the central motif[184].

The left ring finger had a silver ring with the same skull and dark sun logos shown on the steel dagger. Both the ring and the blade had been presented to the leader of this group during the height of the second world war, somewhere in Germany. The hawk-faced man took the log book and placed it in one of the canvas rucksacks he had emptied during his search. He also pulled the distinctive silver skull ring from the dead man's digit and placed it on his own ring finger. Finally, he removed the dead man's leather boots which, although badly stained from decomposition fluids, fitted reasonably well and were a distinct improvement from the canvas plimsols.

After a few more hours of searching through the items in the cave, the hawk-faced man had acquired a highly detailed paper survey map of the area, a compass, and a pair of dark NEOPHAN branded desert sunglasses.

As he began to exit the cave, he found a paper note amongst the dust on the floor; it was a proposed radio transmission written in German and signed by someone called von-Gustoff, presumably the name of one of the decomposed bodies that sat in the wooden chairs.

"Wie geplant haben Führer beendet, um den Standort der Zitadelle zu erhalten. Ein massiver Sturm stoppte den Fortschritt. Habe zwei Tage vor dem Zielort in der Höhle Zuflucht gesucht. Wird beraten, wenn der Fortschritt fortgesetzt wird. Halt."

(As scheduled have terminated guides to preserve location of citadel. Massive storm halted progress. Have taken

---

[184] The logo of the Ahnenerbe. A specialist occult research group for the SS.

shelter in cave two days march from target location. Will advise when resume progress. Stop.)

So, the hawk-faced man surmised, these men had been searching for the lost city, that he now remembered he had visited himself and they had killed their guides, which must account for the two bodies he had found at the base of the cliff.

Leaving the dark cave, the hawk-faced man consulted the map and compass before heading over the lip at the top of the cliffside. He then headed down a steep rocky incline towards the South, where, according to his old paper map, there lay a track that headed West and, after some twenty miles, led to a small habitation. His pace improved considerably now that he had proper hiking boots and could follow an established track. After five and a half hours, he saw that the group of houses marked on his map had transformed into a small settlement, with dozens of two-storey buildings and a petrol station, all connected by a series of small rock paved roads and pavements.

One of the more significant buildings was a hostel of some kind. On entering the reception, he was instantly reminded, by the startled looks of the staff, of how dishevelled he looked after so many days separated from civilisation. He had no idea of the value of the Mongolian currency that he carried, so he had to trust the receptionist's honesty in taking the appropriate number of colourful currency notes from his outstretched hands for three nights' room and board.

Two hours later, he had acquired the luxury of a private room, where he washed, shaved and had superficial medical care from a local nurse for the laceration wounds he had accumulated on his arms and legs. However, these were minor compared to a deep wound in his stomach that looked like it had already been treated only to be savagely reopened.

The nurse, who was called, Badma, was a thirty-year-old Mongolian woman with round metal glasses and short black hair that framed her face. She had received her medical training in Russia, so she could converse while she cleaned the wounds and stitched up the stab injury in his stomach. From her, he discovered that this settlement was related to some open face mining operations nearby, and thankfully, like all the other transient mining workers at the accommodation, she had been immunised against the "Red Death". She also revealed there was a single internet café in the town, located at the rear of the gasoline filling station.

Next morning at dawn, the hawk-faced man queued alongside the other thirty residents of the hostel, who were almost entirely mining workers, for a highly malodourous breakfast buffet in the hostel lobby. The scent of fried mutton fat, boiled mutton fat and braised mutton fat permeated every room in the building and impregnated every clothing fibre for days afterwards. The only thing that could be said in favour of the aroma was that it helped obscure the mine workers' body odours, which, if bottled, could have been used to replace water cannon as a crowd dispersant.

The selection of food at the buffet centred exclusively around sheep, with mutton kebabs and thick mutton and noodle soup that the hawk-faced man learnt was called "Guriltai Shol". These meat courses were accompanied by a dried cheese biscuit called "Aaruul" and a thick horse's milk called "Airag".

The hawk-faced man made his way to the gas station after consuming the meal, which was hardly gourmet but was a welcome change from his more recent culinary delight of the roasted vulture. Surrendering some more of his precious supply of bank notes, he found himself seated in front of a grey Hyundai branded Windows XP desktop computer. The system comprised a base unit, a cathode ray twelve-inch monitor, and an old Logitech web camera stuck on its top with duct tape and a keyboard that looked like it had been dipped in the Guriltai Shol mutton soup.

After an agonisingly sluggish series of searches, due to the slow internet connection, he found some China news articles related to the recovery, by a Russian search and rescue helicopter, of four Westerners. After one of the most severe storms in living memory, these Westerners were stranded on the top of one of the Gurvan Saikhen Mountains.

Having found the names of these four survivors, he was rapidly able to determine their current locations and status. Dr Thomas O'Neill was now an exorcist with the Deliverance section at the Vatican, Father Chin Kwon was a junior administrative secretary for the Pope, while the British lawyer Helen Curren was leading a class action case for former UNITY members who had surrendered their entire wealth to the movement under duress. After the death of the UNITY leader, ownership of the fund, which was estimated at several trillion US dollars, had been taken over by the governments of the Western nations, who were now refusing to discuss the return of the money, leaving nearly a billion displaced persons in refugee camps in various locations around Tel Megiddo, near Haifa in Israel. Finally, Sir Tavish Stewart was reportedly semi-retired from his business interests and was focusing on supervising the extensive repairs to his estate in the Highlands of Scotland.

As the hawk-faced man followed the trails of information associated with the UNITY law case, he came across mentions of the sinking of the Tiamat[185], of the death of the beautiful Dr Nissa Ad-Dajjal and her associate, an international terrorist, Issac bin Abdul Issuin, who was the

---

[185] One of the world's largest and most luxurious private yachts.

leader of a discredited international private intelligence provider, Maelstrom.

The hawk-faced man paused, his mind reeling; first from the pictures of Dr Ad-Dajjal, who was the mysterious, beautiful, dark-haired woman who played such an important part in his disjointed memories and second, by the recognition of his own identity as the terrorist Issac bin Abdul Issuin. These two combined revelations acted as a catalyst, resetting his consciousness so that he had recovered complete recollection of his life and situation within moments.

Returning to his room to gather his thoughts, he lay on his bed and, for a distraction, he began to read the log book that he had taken from the hands of the decaying body in the cave. It was written in rather old-fashioned German. The entries mentioned an ancient esoteric map leading to a legendary lost city. They mentioned ten kilos of gold carried by the expedition to buy their way out of any problems. The hawk-faced man smiled for the first time in weeks as he thought how hundreds of thousand dollars' worth of gold would help him buy his way out of his problems as well.

Meanwhile, his recent internet searches and secretly recorded web cam images triggered various automated monitoring systems in the Kremlin and Beijing. Unknown to most Western analysts, there is extremely close cooperation between the Russian SVR RF[186] and the Chinese MSS[187] intelligence agencies, extending to shared covert operations. So, while the hawk-faced man planned how to use his newly found wealth, three Harbin Z-20

---

[186] Foreign Intelligence Service of the Russian Federation (SVR RF), which replaced the KGB in 1991.

[187] Ministry of State Security (MSS).

Helicopters[188], containing members of the PLA[189]'s elite Chengdu Special Forces Unit "Falcon", were dispatched from Bayannur airbase, near the Chinese/Mongolian border. Their mission was to investigate the re-emergence of the world's most feared international terror mastermind, Issac bin Abdul Issuin.

---

[188] A reverse engineered copy of the US Blackhawk helicopter, taken from the wreckage of a crashed Blackhawk in Pakistan during the raid on Osama bin Laden's compound, in May 2011.

[189] Chinese People's Liberation Army (PLA).

10 PRESUMED INNOCENCE

"It is legal because I wish it." – Louis XIV.

42, The Mall,
Opposite St James Park,
London SW1A 2BJ

11.20HRS (GMT+1), 8th Sept, Present Day

Thick, acrid clouds of cordite smoke drifted over the now deserted parade way. They mixed with the potent odours of aviation fuel and a faint scent reminiscent of overcooked pork chops. The cacophony of gunfire, high-performance engines, screaming car tyres and helicopter rotors that had so recently pierced through the London morning rush hour had abruptly ceased, leaving an eerie silence.

Apart from the chatter from the group of Grenadier guards, who were now busy joking and passing around cigarettes nearby to what remained of the BMW M5, the only sound was that of Sinclair urgently issuing a series of instructions into her encrypted phone. She spoke to the duty officer at Thames House[190] to relay a request to NATS[191] to track and trace a damaged military transport helicopter that was currently flying low over central London in a North Westerly direction from the point of origin in the Mall. Having completed the short phone call, she walked towards where Stewart was standing next to the bullet-ridden remains of what had been her own personal, two-seater sports car.

The distinctive clicking sound of Sinclair's four-inch stilettos echoed over the open space as she approached, stepping

---

[190] MI5 Headquarters in London. (12, Milbank, Westminster, SW1P 4QE – in case you need it.)

[191] NATS is the UK, National Air Traffic Services

over the shards of broken safety glass that littered the tarmac.

"Any luck?" The tall Scotsman queried.

"Too soon to tell, the Met have alerted their spotter aircraft, and NATS have started a thorough scan of all matching air traffic moving over central London. All we can do is wait."

Stewart nodded towards the wreckage, "Looks like we will need a lift...."

Sinclair surveyed what was left of her beloved Porsche. It was now a sad reflection of its former glory. All four tyres were flat, shredded by countless high-velocity rounds, and the carbon fibre bodywork showed patterns of closely targeted small and large calibre gunfire. The leather interior had not faired any better, showing the same ruthless patterning from a sustained firefight.

"Jezi Kri[192]" (Jesus), She muttered under her breath.

Stewart patted her shoulder and pointed to the remains of the pursuing Mercedes and BMW that were both now literally formless wrecks of steaming, bent metal.

"Don't forget how we left the other guys...."

She looked at the two cars that their mysterious attackers had driven and then at the burning remains of the undercarriage from the military transport helicopter that was still raising a thick smoke cloud high into the London skyline from the nearby St James Park.

---

[192] Creole, or more accurately, Jamaican Patois, known locally as Patois (Patwa or Patwah) is Dame Sinclair's native tongue, to which she tends to revert in emotional moments. Although in this case Sinclair seems to be adopting the more explicit Haitian version of creole, perhaps because of the cost of the damage to her beloved car.

THE NEW REPUBLIC

Recognizing she was lucky to have escaped with just the loss of a car, she embraced the Scotsman. When she finally pulled away from Stewart, she wiped some of the numerous smoke and carbon stains that were smeared across his face and then, recognising that it was a lost cause, settled on straightening the lapels on what remained of Stewart's Ede and Ravenscroft jacket.

Their shared moment of intimacy was broken by a comment made in a thick Russian accent.

"Two Helicopters in one day, T, not bad, even by Russian standards."

Stewart grinned mischievously as he glanced at the time on his friend's large Fortis Cosmonaut watch, remarking,

"And it is not even noon yet."

On hearing numerous sirens approaching, Sinclair quickly retrieved the torn remains of her black, leather Chanel handbag from the driver's seat of her Porsche and put the ancient "Raffica" machine pistol inside one of the bags custom side pockets, along with the tiny Beretta Nano that she took from a reluctant Stewart, who had become attached to the small but deadly weapon. Lev Bachrach, meanwhile, strode back to the massive ZIL limousine to return his distinctive shotgun to a storage compartment hidden in one of the numerous recesses located inside the diplomatic vehicle.

Once they had concealed their weapons, Bachrach remained beside his car while Stewart and Sinclair made a point of standing near the Princess Diana memorial gates, well away from the Porsche, in an attempt to look more like passing bystanders.

While the ordinary police established a cordon two hundred yards around the entire area, specialised officers arrived in three BMW 5 series ARV[193]s that contained a total of six, armed AFO[194]s who, now the danger was over, strutted fearlessly around the scene, issuing cautions to everyone, while asking for full cooperation with their "colleagues". The aforementioned "colleagues" arrived in two black short wheelbase Ford Transit minibuses with dark tinted glass and a distinctive livery based on the classic image of the scales of justice and the brand name "Presumed Innocence[195]".

These vans contained a dozen men and women in their early to mid-twenties, dressed in identical, smart off the peg black business suits and carrying Apple tablet computers to document the scene.

After completing their footage of the car wrecks and the downed helicopter fragments, they waited until the police had completed cautioning the soldiers before commencing their interview process. Their process clearly emphasised leading questions to trick the soldiers into admitting to a lack of legal justification for opening fire on the BMW. The video interviews focused on the number of rounds fired, what warnings had been issued, when the soldiers had commenced their attack and what had prompted them to cease firing.

Stewart became increasingly curious about the ongoing process and so approached close enough to become under the scrutiny of one of the "Presumed Innocence" team

---

[193] ARV – Armed Response Vehicle

[194] AFO – Authorised Firearms Officers

[195] "Presumed Innocence" is an initiative from the Home Secretary, Sir Reginald Twiffers, to bring in private legal expertise (Twiffers was one of the founding directors) into the early stages of the criminal justice system, supposedly to help identify miscarriages of justice and, of course, to maximise the profit to be derived from massive tax payer funded compensation payments.

leaders[196]. This young woman had short blonde hair and a somewhat naive looking face, set behind a set of expensive, thick-framed, black designer glasses[197]. She beamed a two-hundred-watt smile at the somewhat dishevelled man who appeared to have come from St James Park.

She directed a barrage of questions at Stewart related to what the Scotsman might have seen regarding the merciless killing of the innocent victims in the Mercedes, BMW and the damage to the helicopter. She introduced herself as "Ms Smyth", and she wanted to know if any of the "victims" from this terrible incident might have survived, as, if they did, they needed urgent help and supportive understanding[198].

Ms Smyth did not give Stewart a chance to reply before she continued a well-rehearsed speech that indicated that the car drivers and helicopter crews were a victimized minority group, with no other avenues available to express their frustration.

Stewart nodded as though he sympathised and asked,

"You sound like you know who they are?"

Ms Smyth gushed on, obviously proud of the detailed knowledge of her would-be client in this "unlawful killing" compensation case. She explained that although "Presumed Innocence" had initially offered to provide its services to the Argentinian Government, Argentina had

---

[196] As proclaimed on a large, white enamel badge worn on her left lapel which stated "Ms Smyth – team leader, initial screening team C."

[197] The type of glasses that try too hard to look like 1960s free national health prescription frames, while still screaming that they cost way more than you or I could ever afford.

[198] The kind of specialised help and understanding that only a compensation lawyer can provide.

strenuously denied any connection with the events in London or the Royal kidnappings in other European nations. Instead, Argentina asserted that the actions had been made by a former Argentinian territory that was now an independent state.

"And you believe them?" Queried Stewart.

Ms Smyth looked quizzically at Stewart like he was a simpleton. She then clarified that no one would ever deny their connection if they were involved since, as victims, they would stand to make billions in compensation from the British taxpayer for the brutal massacre that occurred in Chelsea earlier that morning and the events here at The Mall.

Stewart nodded, again feigning supportive agreement and, encouraged by having found an interested listener, the ever-keen Ms Smyth continued to detail what she knew. She had been briefed that morning that Presumed Innocence had been retained by activists from a small nation, recently formed in the extreme North of Argentina, just South of the borders of Paraguay and Bolivia.

The government of this breakaway state, called "La cuarta república", had a bold new agenda; to overcome decades of prejudice and persecution from the rest of the world towards its people, their beliefs, their right to existence and self-governance.   They claimed their people had been kidnapped, tortured and unlawfully executed for too long, and now they had determined to make a stand to gain global recognition of what they believed to be their legitimate birth rights.

These activists had confirmed that they had undertaken the coordinated kidnappings of European royalty and that they were agreeable to exclusively using the services of Presumed Innocence to represent them legally and to lead any negotiations that would be forthcoming.

By this time, Ms Smyth had come to the end of her well-prepared notes and was beginning to view Stewart and his two companions with increasing suspicion. She suddenly noticed that the Scotsman reminded her of someone mentioned in her briefing. He was the smartly dressed middle-aged man who had single-handedly dealt with the attempted Royal kidnapping in Chelsea that morning. During that encounter, he exhibited extraordinarily ruthless efficiency in dealing with multiple armed kidnappers, who had been representatives of her new clients. Now here was the same man at the scene of another violent event, where more of her clients had been unlawfully killed with the same clinical efficiency. Ms Smyth quickly decided that this strange man and his female accomplice were perfect targets for sustained high profile civil and criminal prosecutions. Such a project would undoubtedly please her new clients by highlighting the brutal and unlawful killing of their members and prove highly lucrative for her company.

Just as she was about to call over the armed police officers to detain Stewart, a very large, black, square-shaped limousine drove slowly past. The car approached so closely that it caused Ms Smyth to take an involuntary step backwards while completely obstructing her view of the Scotsman. After the massive car moved, The Mall was empty; both the man and woman standing in front of her had disappeared.

Inside the heavily insulated, sumptuous cocoon that was the rear of the ZIL limousine, the floor, seats and even the door frames were all upholstered in a thick, black velour that was so popular in the 1970s.

Stewart and Sinclair exchanged glances as they sank deeply into the two extraordinarily soft rear seats. Sinclair rubbed her hand over the velour door covering as though she could not quite believe what she was seeing.

Bachrach anticipated their comment,

"Say what you want about the ZIL; at least it does not dissolve into a smouldering wreck at the first sign of gunfire."

The Russian emphasized his point by effortlessly accelerating the massive limousine through the improvised police cordon at the end of The Mall. Stewart and Sinclair could only watch the row of startled faces exhibited by the six police officers manning the road block, all of whom looked like they had only recently graduated from the Peel Centre[199] in Hendon.

The recent high-intensity car chase combined with the numerous exchanges of high and low-velocity gunfire had taken their toll on the bespoke tailoring worn by both Sinclair and Stewart. The Scotsman's Ede and Ravenscroft suit was not only torn by numerous close misses but also sported an array of stains from smoke, carbon, and, of course, cordite[200].

The damage to Stewart's suit made him look like he had been sleeping rough for some weeks. In contrast, the tears and rips to Sinclair's fitted Prada business suit only accentuated the intensity of her fitness regime and the quality of her diet. The recent exertions from pushing the 911 to its limits through the streets of central London, followed by a life-or-death gunfight, had left a light sheen of perspiration on her body that only served to highlight the perfection of her smooth skin.

As Sinclair's attempts to cover her exposed long legs, using only the ribbon-like shreds that remained of her pencil skirt, proved impossible, Stewart leaned forward through the

---

[199] The Police Training Centre of the Metropolitan Police.

[200] Cordite may, in fact, have to replace Hermes Orange Verity as Stewart's signature fragrance.

separating screen between the opulent passenger seats and the more spartan driver's compartment and was in the process of providing his Russian friend with the address of Horseferry House, when Bachrach responded,

"Relax, T. We are already on the way to Sinclair's London address, and after that, I will drop you at your showroom off New Bond Street before returning "black beauty" back to Kensington Palace Gardens[201]."

The Russian's strong, calloused hands affectionately patted the dashboard of the thirty-year-old limousine. Stewart nodded his appreciation before leaning back into the passenger seat to begin briefing his two friends about what he had discovered from Ms Smyth about the new clients of Presumed Innocence. When he had concluded describing the sparse facts related to the fledging South American Nation, who had admitted responsibility for the recent Royal kidnappings and the aborted helicopter attack they had just thwarted in The Mall, there was a moment of silence in the car.

Then the thick voice of the Russian interjected,

"I don't know about you two, but such a callous disregard for humanity, kidnapping and then endangering public safety with armed attacks during rush hour reveals a ruthless nature I instinctively dislike."

Sinclair and Stewart indicated their agreement with the distaste expressed by their Russian friend before Stewart suggested that they should investigate all leads related to these instigators of the Europe wide kidnappings and the armed attacks in London. As a result, all three agreed to use their combined contacts to learn what they could and share

---

[201] Embassy of the Russian Federation.

their intelligence that afternoon, by phone or in person at Stewart's New Bond Street offices.

By this time, the Russian embassy car had arrived outside the entrance to Horseferry House, and, after a brief goodbye kiss for Stewart, Sinclair emerged from the back of the limousine and strode purposefully across the pavement and through the building's partially open wooden double doors. The revealing nature of what remained of her Prada business suit triggered some minor car collisions directly outside Horseferry House.

Bachrach made the most of the ensuing traffic delays to rapidly turn the limousine and begin heading towards the showroom in New Bond Street.

Less than a mile and a half from the minor traffic disturbances in Dean Ryle Street, in an elegant brick, fronted Edwardian townhouse in St James Square, the Home Secretary, Sir Reginald Twiffers, was seated in a supremely comfortable, large, brown leather, two-seater chesterfield sofa. Twiffers was waiting in one of the private meeting rooms available to members of one of London's more exclusive gentleman's clubs[202]. The early afternoon sunshine flooded onto the polished, dark, elm wood floor from two tall, wooden sash windows.

Even through the mild buzz that remained from his lunchtime drinking session, Twiffers could appreciate the quality of his surroundings. He smelt the aroma of rich leather mixed with beeswax from the highly polished woodwork and the sounds of the London traffic moderated

---

[202] Possibly the Sliver Club. One of London's exclusive, private gentlemen's clubs, it was founded in 1900. The club is for those with close links to Argentina and other Latin American countries.

184

by the slow, sonorous ticking of a nineteenth-century grandfather clock that stood near the single entrance door.

The high walls of the room were panelled with classic stained oak, tastefully decorated with a series of oil paintings depicting high mountain ranges, fine thoroughbred horses and rough-looking cowhands sitting by camp fires. His drink, a deep red Malbec[203], had been presented in a Bohemia cut crystal wine glass on a Sterling silver platter, which now graced the mahogany side table conveniently located within easy reach.

Even the high-backed sofa where he was sitting was of extraordinary quality; under the fine Aniline leather, three layers of high-quality horse padding made for supreme comfort. Twiffers noted that he would have to make an effort not to succumb to the combined soporific influences of such luxury, silence and the copious amounts of alcohol flowing through his veins[204].

Twiffer's introspection was interrupted by the arrival of his host, who was announced by one of the club's servitors as "Senor Cortez". Cortez was a tall, elegant man in his late middle age. He strode confidently into the private meeting room and smiled as he noted that Twiffers had already been provided with a suitable refreshment.

A powerful and confident voice with a slight Spanish accent intoned,

---

[203] A 2011 Vina Cobos 'Cobos' Marchiori Estate Malbec, from Perdriel, Argentina.

[204] Fortunately, many years of high government office had, at extraordinary taxpayers' expense, hardened him against the soporific effects of high alcohol consumption and extreme comfort.

"Sir Reginald, I am pleased you could make time during your busy schedule."

Twiffers stood, and the two men shook hands before the elegant newcomer gestured for the Home Secretary to sit. The distinguished older man waived away the offer of a drink from the servitor, and, once the door was firmly closed, he sat in the tall Chesterfield chair opposite Twiffers. Even in the act of sitting, Cortez's actions exuded an undefinable air of authority and style; a true Alpha reflected Twiffers.

Cortez's long white hair was swept back from his face in a ponytail that emphasized a classic profile and the deep, penetrating blue eyes that, Twiffers noted, were impossible to meet directly. As Twiffers took in the details of his host, he noted that the man's hand-tailored Brioni suit fitted him perfectly and highlighted a lean and muscular physique crafted by arduous exercise. He looked in his late fifties, but he could have been a decade older.

It was not often that Twiffers felt that his own Saville Row tailor had let him down, but the cut of the fabric[205] on Cortez's grey Brunico two-piece suit induced feelings of inferiority that Twiffers also recalled feeling at their previous meeting two weeks before.

Yes, something was disturbing about Senor Cortez, like sitting close to an over coiled spring that could explode into unpredictable violence at any moment. Still, there was nothing wrong with the ten thousand Euros[206] that appeared in his Credit Swiss numbered account after

---

[205] Brioni's own Super 160's wool fabric.

[206] It is surprising how small the amounts of money are that can sway the actions of the unscrupulous and amoral.

providing the information Cortez had requested at their last meeting[207].

"This morning was a...." the older man paused, trying to find the appropriate English word, "disappointment to us."

It was a simple statement from the older man that carried no emotion. Twiffers had expected some anger after the failed operation to kidnap the Royal and the subsequent thwarted attempt to destroy the bodies of the terrorists. After all, there must have been considerable planning and a significant allocation of resources to launch such daring attacks. Twiffers reminded himself that attacks had succeeded in all the other European nations and would have undoubtedly had similar success in the UK but for the million to one chance intervention.

"The loss of your highly trained operatives must be a harsh blow," Stated Twiffers, hoping to appease and gain favour with his host.

Cortez was unmoved,

"If they had been more efficient, they would have succeeded. Their failure will be minutely analysed to ensure future operations succeed."

"Indeed, but no amount of planning could have anticipated the intervention of such a highly skilled bystander." Added the Home Secretary.

"Untrue. The truly superior warrior thrives on the unexpected." Retorted Cortez, directing his piercing blue eyes at his guest in a flash of anger before instantly drawing himself back into control and continuing, coldly,

---

[207] To people like Twiffers, providing information which directly caused the violent and untimely deaths of the two Royal close protection officers is of little consequence.

"We have our ways to make an example of such a "have a go hero", as you will see, in due course."

The ominous threat filled the air, and Twiffers wondered if he should leave before he was also threatened. Maybe this whole thing was a bad idea.

Cortez sensed the change and modified his tone,

"But, my dear Sir Reginald, we are more concerned about the intervention this morning by one of your senior intelligence operatives. We know of her from her previous operations in our region[208]. She is intelligent, resourceful and persistent. With legitimate access to official resources. We have determined she is the real threat to our plans."

"You mean Dame Cynthia Sinclair? But,"

Twiffers stammered nervously before continuing,

"She is the Director-General of MI6. One cannot just fire her, especially when she was on the national news this morning, risking her life single-handedly defending this country against foreign aggression on British soil."

Twiffers reddened in the face as he suddenly realized he was speaking to the person who had initiated the very action he had just called foreign aggression.

Cortez smiled, "To a strong leader, such obstacles are easy to overcome. Sir Reginald, to be frank, we had thought you were the sort of man who was strong enough to master any situation. Strong enough to be a future Prime Minister, in fact. Are you such a man? Or have we misjudged you?"

Twiffers' eyes widened, "A future Prime Minster?"

"With our help, of course. A Prime Minster needs strong friends, and trust me, we are *very* good to our friends."

---

[208] Sinclair worked against the drug cartels in South America.

Twiffers smiled nervously.

"But what about Merriweather[209]?"

"Play your part, and we will take care of the rest. We have been helping Mrs Merriweather cultivate some," He paused and smiled evilly, "Unhealthy habits."

Back in the luxurious Russian limousine, Stewart sat back and admired how his old friend fully exploited the diplomatic status and enormous size of the ZIL to cut his way through the busy London mid-day traffic ruthlessly. It was only a matter of minutes before they entered Oxford Street, crossed numerous lanes of heavy traffic and entered New Bond Street, where the massive vehicle conspicuously and, Stewart suspected, deliberately mounted the pavement directly opposite a pair of traffic wardens. The wardens could only look on in helpless frustration as Stewart thanked his friend and exited the car. He emerged in front of the exclusive two-story central London address that was Stewart's Antiquarians.

The large and immaculately clean plate glass window at the front of the showroom gleamed in the midday sunshine. It reflected the image of a tall and powerful man with close-cropped hair and beard who, although no longer in the prime of youth, was still filled with the joys and vigour of life.

Stewart's Ede and Ravenscroft suit was severely torn. His face was smeared with dirt and blood from the numerous minor cuts he had accumulated from broken windscreen glass and the metal shards that had flown from the damaged helicopter fuselage. However, he still strode with

---

[209] The Right Honourable Susan Merriweather, MP, Prime Minster of the United Kingdom and Northern Ireland.

the powerful, unassuming manner typical of natural leaders. As he turned his striking grey eyes towards the window, it was not to see his reflection[210]; instead, he focused on the items that made up the display, prompting him to reflect on how much everything had changed over the past few weeks.

The showroom had once been filled with rare and often priceless artefacts from around the globe. Indeed, many London guide books included the showroom alongside other notable commercial premises worthy of a discerning tourist's time visiting the British capital. However, times had radically changed.

Dr Nissa Ad-Dajjal's plot to assume control of the world, through the insidious machinations of Maelstrom and UNITY, had come terrifyingly close to taking over all the world's governments. As evidenced by the ubiquitous presence of UNITY barcodes on the underside of almost every person's forearm, Ad-Dajjal had successfully enslaved over half of humanity through the release of the 'Red Death' virus and her exclusive control of the only effective vaccine, which she only permitted to be administered in return for absolute submission to her rule. A submission marked, so pointedly, by tattooing the infamous UNITY Barcode on the supplicant's body.

Ad-Dajjal's Satanic[211] plan had been thwarted[212], but the world would never be the same. Jeffery Sonnet retained his position managing the London showroom, but the Italian branch remained closed after the brutal torture and murder

---

[210] Thankfully Stewart was spared the preoccupation of vanity that affects so many in the modern world.

[211] Quite literally.

[212] Largely through the direct actions of Tavish Stewart, although he would have been the last person to have acknowledged or sought such recognition.

of Stewart's friend, Mario Donne, inside the Rome showroom. The Istanbul showroom was also no longer trading, as it had to be rebuilt[213] after its destruction at the hands of Maelstrom head, Issac bin Abdul Issuin.

The closure of these two international showrooms had severe financial implications for Stewart. It was true that he had acquired[214] some sound investments over his lifetime, but he was currently nowhere near as financially secure as he had been before the Ad-Dajjal affair.

The UK Government had never returned the assets that they had confiscated from Stewart, based on the false accusations made by the now-discredited Brinkwater[215] Government of being a global terrorist mastermind. Stewart had been wholly acquitted of these charges and had been promised his seized assets would be promptly returned; however, this had never materialised. Every enquiry on the refund's progress received some vague bureaucratic excuse, which implied that there would be considerable further delays.

Unfortunately, the loss of income from the closure of the Rome and Istanbul showrooms meant that Stewart lacked sufficient funds to take the Government to the High Court over their non-payment. The Scotsman had developed a lack of confidence in the impartiality of the UK's justice system based on hearing the frustrations of Helen Curren, as she tried to lead the class action lawsuit to obtain refunds from various Governments for the billions of people who

---

[213] By Mohammed Sek and his extended family but funded by Stewart.

[214] Entirely through his own hard work and prudent investment.

[215] The previous British Prime Minister, Simon Brinkwater, who, allegedly, took his own life in the Downing Street upper floor confidential office.

had their life savings extorted by Ad-Dajjal's UNITY movement. Everyone knew that someone had acquired the enormous sums held in the UNITY movement's bank accounts. The problem was everyone denied it was them.

Stewart was also unable to rebuild his home in the Highlands after it had been razed to the ground by Maelstrom since, as the destruction had been ruled an act of terrorism, the damage was not covered by insurance. This ruling left Stewart with the prospect of considerable expenditure if he ever hoped to rebuild his ancestral home. For this reason, he was currently living in improvised accommodation whenever he travelled.

Therefore, Stewart's London showroom was all that remained of his business empire and was now his sole source of income. The substantial reduction in cash flow meant that Stewart could no longer afford to speculate on acquiring rare and unusual antiquities, which was once his business's cornerstone.

The fifteen-foot wide and five-foot-high reinforced Hammerglass window that Stewart's intelligent grey eyes carefully regarded no longer exhibited the magnificence that it had once enjoyed. Instead, the business focused on the recent world catastrophe. It utilized Stewart's privileged access to memorabilia linked with UNITY, Maelstrom and, of course, the epic journey to the legendary "Citadel of the Djinn".

The large window display was decorated with a backdrop formed by a red and gold "Cübbe" traditional Turkish robe that covered the wooden backdrop's fifteen-foot width and three-foot height that acted as a partition from the window into the showroom proper. This low barrier afforded passers-by a view of the window contents and a view of the shop interior. To the right side of the display was a dressers mannikin wearing a dark grey Ede and Ravenscroft three-piece suit that exhibited large tears on the sleeves and some heavy staining[216].

Just in front of the distressed suit was a detailed model of a Boeing 747-400 passenger jet[217] that was dwarfed next to an identically scaled model of a very futuristic looking mega yacht, decked in blue grey paint, UNITY livery and bearing the distinctive name "Tiamat" on its bows. The vessel was so large that it had a marina located at its rear, and the ship's upper deck, behind the bridge, housed a helicopter landing pad. A small red two-person helicopter[218]was shown on the model as about to take off from the vessel.

The very centre of the window display space was flanked, on either side, by a resin replica of a nine-inch-long Obsidian Dagger[219], a large, antique wooden, single-barrelled shotgun[220], complete with a single, enormous, circular, brass shell casing, an opened packet of Turkish Royal cigarettes and a battered Ronson lighter.

The far left of the display contained a fragment of blue glazed ceramic in Arabic, with an English translation typed on a small sign, saying,

"اختبئ في الاوكار وفي صخور الجبال .وقل للجبال والصخور اسقط علينا واخفينا
لانه اليوم جاء الموت نفسه ولن يقدر احد ان يقف تحت السماء وينجو".

---

[216] Probably a mix of smoke, blood, aviation fuel and, on this one occasion, reindeer urine.

[217] This Russian passenger jet was decorated with a highly distinctive tiger themed livery.

[218] A Robinson R22 Marine model.

[219] With a seven-inch blade section, that would have been carved from the single section of black obsidian, if such an object ever existed.

[220] Sir Samuel White Baker's "Jenna-El-Mootfah – a legendary 2 bore shotgun, named "son of a cannon".

(Hide yourself in the dens and in the rocks of the mountains; and say unto the mountains and rocks, fall on us, and hide us for today death itself is come and none shall be able to stand under the sky and survive.)

The far right-hand of the window, nearest to the shop entrance, had a reproduction of a fifth-century Byzantine religious icon, portraying an enormous six-winged creature with long razor-thin talons where its fingers and toes should have been. The entity's entire body was covered in dark shapes that could have been feathers or scales and everywhere, seemingly on every part of its body, were enormous predatory eyes[221]. Stewart's face broke into a knowing smile, as though he was privy to a private joke, as he looked at this image.

In the centre of the window space, pride of place was given to a large and exquisitely bound paperback book with a highly distinctive red themed cover, highlighting the unmistakable green, hypnotic eyes of Nissa Ad-Dajjal, dominating the skyline of the Scottish Capital city, Edinburgh. This book was the fictionalised description of Stewart's adventure, written by Father Thomas O'Neill, under the pseudonym of KRM Morgan[222], with the title "Bridge of Souls. Ancient Prophecy, Ultimate Evil". Although the book had been well received internationally and was widely available[223], Stewart's was the only venue that could provide copies signed by the entire team who were allegedly, involved in the epic adventure.

As Stewart looked beyond the window display, over the four-foot-high back partition and into the shop showroom,

---

[221] A Hexapterygon – otherwise known as a Sephiroth. One of the most powerful of the Angelic hierarchy.

[222] To avoid further censure from the Vatican.

[223] Through the specialist publisher, MadBagus books.

he could see a group of customers browsing through the merchandise in the different themed sections within the premises. Close to the main sales counter, at the front of the shop, to the far left of the entrance, there was a large and powerfully built, middle-aged man with a dense beard. He was dressed in a red Gortex Northface hiking fleece, smart black Gant branded jeans, and well-worn, black leather Merrell hiking shoes. On his head, he wore a blue cloth baseball cap, embroidered with the text "Haukeland Universitetssjukehus" on its sides and adorned with an owl logo on the cap's front[224].

He talked to Julie, one of the salesroom staff, as he examined items from the large glass display case reserved for genuine Maelstrom goods. Specifically, this man's interest was in the equipment that bore the distinctive whirlpool logo and had been issued to the covert organisation's most elite operatives.

To the right of this bearded man was an attractive, middle-aged woman with collar length, honey blonde hair, who was also examining some of the recovered Maelstorm equipment. She was interested in a grey metal container, around the size of a shoebox, retrieved from the UNITY headquarters in Grindelwald, Switzerland.

This unit provided Ad-Dajjal and her staff with the ability to analyse and process vast amounts of data gathered on every living person. The dedicated data analysis hardware and software contained in the unit had been acquired by Maelstrom. It was, allegedly, able to rapidly process unimaginably large data sets using methods and techniques that were decades beyond the industry's current state of the art. The woman customer was talking animatedly to John, another of the sales assistants.

---

[224] The University of Bergen's teaching hospital, in Bergen, Norway.

Behind and beyond this front counter, the showroom was segregated into themed areas:

On the shop's ground floor, the first and largest area was devoted to Ad-Dajjal, her life and her interests. The entrance to this zone was marked by a large framed publicity poster of Dr Ad-Dajjal, that the UNITY foundation had produced. It showed a smiling Ad-Dajjal, dressed in one of her signature white Chanel trouser suits, Christian Louboutin "Very Prive 120" heels, and her magnificent gold Rolex GMT Master watch. She was standing diagonally with folded arms at a forty-five-degree angle from the camera. Behind her was the entrance to the UNITY headquarters in Grindelwald.

Beyond the poster, copies of which sold in surprising numbers, were small sections that covered her life interests, with locked glass cabinets for the more valuable items. Next to these labelled cabinets were shelves with books covering everything from the theory of Magog generators, the history of UNITY and Maelstrom, to a series of biographies, each with different perspectives of Ad-Dajjal's life. Finally, after a cabinet filled with scale models of the Tiamat and a replica of a massive weaponised robot[225], some cabinets contained a range of items that reflected Ad-Dajjal's study and operationalisation of Magick[226]. The sub-

---

[225] Replica of the Mobile, Intelligent, Nuclear powered, Outdoor-all Terrain, Automated, unTethered, Robot, or "Minotaur". This was a nuclear powered, autonomous (self-directed by Artificial Intelligence), eight-foot tall, bipedal humanoid robotic weapon. The parts forming the original MINOTAUR robot are, allegedly, now dispersed over a wide area of Crete (and probably other neighbouring countries).

[226] The spelling of Magic as Magick is to try and differentiate occult study from performance magic and in this context Magick was defined by Magus Aleister Crowley as "the Science and Art of causing Change to occur in conformity with Will".

section, devoted to Ad-Dajjal's interests in Buddhist and Western forms of the Black Arts, was one of the busiest sections of the shop. It always seemed occupied by solitary and furtive customers, invariably dressed in black and covered in diverse rings and amulets. These customers either tried to disguise their purchases or made a point of loudly correcting every supposed mispronunciation made by the shop staff of any obscure[227] Magical terms and concepts.

Several rare Tarot decks were beyond the racks of esoteric books, including facsimile copies of Ad-Dajjal's own Visconti di Modrone Tarot deck. This deck was one of the top-selling items in the section, coming a close second to the Magickal diaries and grimoires, purported to have been found in Ad-Dajjal's private temple in the lowest level of the UNITY Grindelwald complex.

The final part of the Ad-Dajjal section included her favourite personal products, including Dark MAC eyeshadow, Givenchy Le Rouge Rose lipstick and a newly released cologne called "Evil", which was a close copy of her Armatigie signature perfume[228].

Standing in this restricted showroom area was a young woman, around five feet seven inches tall, dressed in a superbly cut, black linen Camilla Hosbjerg jacket, matching pencil skirt and flat-heeled Stine Goya shoes. The woman had her light brown hair stylishly cut in a bob, and her piercing blue eyes gazed out through a pair of Samsøe & Samsøe tortoiseshell rimmed glasses. She was reading one of the showroom's rarest and most expensive items from

---

[227] To the truly dedicated esoteric student *everything* can be made to sound obscure. Rather like academics.

[228] An intoxicating musky scent from the rare Ghost flower of the Mojave Desert, distilled exclusively for Ad-Dajjal by the Sultan of Oman's own perfume house, Amouage.

Ad-Dajjal's personal esoteric library; a handwritten copy of the 12th-century, "Ghâyat al-Hakîm fi'l-sihr", the infamous Arabic grimoire devoted to astral magic.

Directly next to the section devoted to Ad-Dajjal was the partition dedicated to Stewart's involvement with the adventure. In addition to copies of the fictionalised account of the epic story were sets of brass compasses, replicas of the Fra Mauro map (from Venice), diagrams of Marco Polo's mirror and the map concealed in its design. The middle section of shelving in this section was devoted to the Elizabethan scholar Dr John Dee and his system of Enochian Magic, along with numerous facsimiles of original texts related to apocalyptic prophecy. The final display unit in this section included some collectable items and souvenirs that were, allegedly, accurate replicas of the Emerald Tablets, the Silver Folio that housed them and, of course, numerous sinister-looking Djinn statues.

Given her devotion to evil, it was surprising that the section devoted to Ad-Dajjal was the most popular with visitors to the showroom. Over eighty per cent of the shop's regular income came from sales of Ad-Dajjal's Magickal works, replicas of her ritual equipment and accessories. Signed copies of O'Neill's account of the adventure and the related publicity materials, such as t-shirts and merchandise, also helped cover some of the running costs of Stewart's showroom.

Stewart completed his observation of the window display, pulled open the ornately decorated oak door and entered his premises, brushing, as he did so, past a tall, clean-shaven, dark-haired male figure. This individual was wearing a jet-black, linen, oriental style jacket and trouser suit, similar to the outfit made famous by Joseph Wiseman when he played Dr Julius No in the first Bond film. The left breast of this customer's jacket was embroidered in fine red silk with the letter Z, lying sideways with a single line passing through its centre. Stewart noted the symbol and the oriental style dress without any further thought. It was clear that the young man had finished making a significant purchase since he was clutching a badly damaged ship's life belt, with the word "Tiamat" just visible on its side, through various deep scratches and dark burn marks on its orange surface. As an original item that once graced Ad-Dajjal's vessel, this artefact had been one of the showroom's more expensive items since Ad-Dajjal devotees highly coveted it.

As Stewart let this strange figure hurry past him out through the open door, he looked down the sales counter. He could now see that the woman interested in the Maelstrom data analysis unit wore dark-framed glasses, which highlighted a pair of hazel-coloured eyes. She spoke in a gentle Canadian accent that hinted at Scandinavian inflexion as she inquired, discretely, if the units were "guaranteed as genuine". Customers frequently asked this question as John, the sales assistant, pointed to a large sign above the counter that announced "all goods sold as seen".

At the furthest end of the counter, Stewart could see that the powerful man in the baseball cap had completed his examination of the Maelstrom memorabilia and produced a Norwegian medical identity card that permitted him to examine one of the shop's most restricted items. A long thin glass cylinder covered in Maelstrom whirlpool logos and the international biohazard symbol. Even though the cylinder was certified as deactivated[229], Julie, the sales assistant assisting him, looked nervous when handling the item. She became even more anxious as the customer took it and began his examination of a fragile glass object that once killed billions of people and brought the human race close to extinction. Thankfully, after his curiosity had been sated, the big man carefully handed the thin glass cylinder back to

---

[229] With a 98% confidence.

Julie and decided to purchase an XXL sized T-shirt with the distinctive Maelstrom logo, to the great relief of all the shop staff.

Just as the Norwegian Surgeon took his T-Shirt, the midday news began on a forty-inch, wall-mounted Samsung TV set above the counter space. The coverage led with a report on the morning's kidnapping of the heirs to various European thrones and described how a group of armed terrorists had also attempted to kidnap the youngest member of the UK Royal family.

The reporting described how the kidnappers had targeted the British Royal party as they passed through Chelsea. The female news reporter stated that a group of terrorists had killed the Royal protection officers and would have succeeded in abducting the young Royal were they not stopped by a quick-thinking and decisive passerby. The news switched to drone footage showing the mysterious saviour of the British Royals, along with a ticker-tape at the bottom of the screen identifying the man as a decorated military veteran, Sir Tavish Stewart.

At that moment, the showroom door closed loudly. The noise caused the two customers at the counter to turn and look into a tall Scotsman's smiling, good-natured face. He was dressed in the same immaculately tailored Ede and Ravenscroft suit worn by the man shown on the slow-motion news coverage. The Scotsman's clothing sported long tears from numerous near misses from high-velocity rounds[230], was severely stained and smelt strongly of cordite and aviation fuel.

After carefully double-checking the TV image against the tall and powerful man standing before them, both customers requested to add a "Stewart's Antiquarians"

---

[230] 9mm, probably.

themed T-shirt to their orders. Stewart winked at the two customers and walked towards a stairway at the rear of the showroom.

11 SECRET CHIEFS

"Behind the veil of all the hieratic and mystical allegories of ancient doctrines, behind the darkness and strange ordeals of all initiations, under the seal of all sacred writings, in the ruins of Nineveh or Thebes, on the crumbling stones of old temples and on the blackened visage of the Assyrian or Egyptian sphinx, in the monstrous or marvellous paintings which interpret to the faithful of India the inspired pages of the Vedas, in the cryptic emblems of our old books on alchemy, in the ceremonies practiced at reception by all secret societies, there are found indications of a doctrine which is everywhere the same and everywhere carefully concealed." - Eliphas Lévi, Transcendental Magic, 1854

Société pour la préservation des lignages ésotériques européens, (S.P.L.E.E.)
Place du Bourg-de-Four
1204 Genève, Switzerland

11:30HRS (GMT+2), 8th Sept, Present day

The elderly servitor, who had assisted Mather's preparations, opened the double wooden doors before standing to one side and gesturing for the French adept to step forward through the entrance. The two open doors revealed a set of ten inlaid brass steps leading down to a much more massive second set of dark oak doors. The brass inserts on each step were engraved with Latin and Hebrew characters naming one of the ten Sephiroth[231] of the Kabbalistic "Tree of Life"

---

[231] The Sephiroth (סְפִירוֹת) (emanations) are the ten attributes through which the unknowable (Ein Sof) reveals itself. Listed by 16th century Kabbalist Moses ben Jacob Cordovero as: Keter (Crown), Chokhmah (Wisdom), Binah (Understanding), Chesed (Kindness), Gevurah (Discipline), Tiferet (Beauty), Netzach (Victory), Hod (Splendour), Yesod (Foundation) and Malkuth (Kingship).

that forms the basis of so much of the Western Esoteric Tradition.

As Mathers began descending the steps, the two large doors behind her were closed and locked, making a resounding noise that echoed through the small stairway and lowered the light level considerably. The only remaining illumination came from ten spotlights placed at ground level on each step, clearly intended to help avoid missteps for those wearing the full-length gowns and robes that were so often required in more traditional rituals.

At the bottom of the steps, a small red-carpeted space of around twelve square feet led to a cast iron door frame containing two massive hobnailed oak doors with a smaller, sub door inset into its right side.

This entrance was guarded by Frater Léon, an older, white-haired man in his late seventies, who was well known to Mathers, having served for decades as the secretary for many of the societies that met in these ancient rooms. However, today he was looking uncharacteristically stern and serious. He stood at the bottom of the stairway carrying a seventeenth-century short-bladed rapier[232] in his right hand and bearing a primed and cocked flintlock pistol[233] in his leather waist band. Having acted as the lodge guard herself on numerous occasions, Mathers knew that he was also carrying a more modern nine-millimetre automatic[234].

---

[232] The rapier (*espada ropera*) is a sword with a thin and sharply-pointed two-edged blade. It was popular in Western Europe for civilian and military use in the 16th and 17th centuries.

[233] This 18th century .45 calibre pistol had been in the lodge's possession since 1772 and bore the makers mark "F. Ulrich, Bern".

[234] A Sphinx 2000 Series with a ten-round magazine, that was standard issue to members of the territorial army in Switzerland.

Léon pointed the rapier's needle-like point directly at Mathers' heart and demanded the password. He smiled as he received a vowel rich, four-syllable word before striking the wooden door seven times with the hilt of his sword. Four knocks then emanated from the other side of the entrance. Moments later, the smaller inset door was unbolted and opened, allowing Mathers to step over the raised door sill into a pleasant smelling and much warmer environment.

On the other side of the small entrance, Mathers was greeted by an older woman called Soror Joanne, who, after locking the door, embraced the French adept and whispered,

"Ravi de vous voir, Madeleine. Cette fois, j'espère qu'ils décideront d'agir plutôt que de tergiverser." (Nice to see you, Madeleine. This time I hope they decide to act, rather than prevaricate.)

Mathers nodded and handed the woman the five-inch, spring action folding knife[235] that usually resided on Mather's right ankle[236] before continuing down some more heavily worn stone stairs to what was once the original level of the city of Geneva. At the bottom of these final steps, Mathers entered a long room with high vaulted ceilings, a flagged stone floor, and stone walls showing successive construction layers[237]. The orientation, shape and

---

This Swiss made firearm is very similar to the CZ 75 made by Czech firearm manufacturer ČZUB.

[235] A Fontenille Pataud Corsican Vendetta folding knife – actually 4.7 inches long but, as they say, that is *sufficient,* if you know what you are doing.

[236] Weapons are surrendered upon entering the temple as they carry negative and destructive energies.

[237] The lowest level of the walls inside the temple date back to the second century BCE, when this area of Geneva become part of the

dimensions of the room had been designed to amplify and enhance the vibratory frequencies of specific sacred vowel sounds; so as to maximise the effect of a famous Brocken-Rennes ley line that ran through the building on its way from Brocken peak[238] in Germany's Harz Mountains in the North East, before continuing in a South Westerly direction through key European sites to Rennes-le-Château in Southern France.

There were rows of oak pews arranged along both sides of the stone walls, like an old-fashioned church choir, so that around seventy-five people could once have been seated in them. However, sadly, in more recent times, they were more often filled with guests who just attended to say that they had been in the ancient temple.

The room's only illumination was from a few candles attached along the length of the pews. The environment in the temple had a wonderful dry warmth due to the under-floor heating from an original Roman hypocaust, which was an essential provision so that rituals could be performed barefoot in comfort that would otherwise have been impossible in the Swiss city. The dry air in the hall was permeated with the distinctive scent of a special incense that was prepared from roses grown on the premises[239] and was based on a formula that had remained a closely guarded secret of the order for over a thousand years.

Pax Romana ("Roman Peace"). A 200-year period of prosperity for Geneva.

[238] Brocken peak has always had strong links to the supernatural. Johann von Goethe set portions of his play, Faust, there including the infamous Walpurgisnacht scene where Mephistopheles led Faust around the Brocken to observe the Witches sabbat.

[239] The order's lore told that the rose seeds were originally from ancient Greek roses from Bulgaria and brought back to Switzerland by some of the founders of the Geneva temple.

As Mather's proceeded along the length of the hall, towards a small wooden trestle table set up in the centre of the room, she passed heavily worn Latin engravings carved into the walls on either side of the hall. These detailed the many orders that had met in this location over the centuries, along with their most notable past members whose names and dates of service were carved into the stone under each of the order's crests. The many layers of construction evident in the walls showed numerous building foundations built one on top of the other, leading to the current level that was constructed in the thirteenth century, complete with domed high vaulted stone ceilings.

The old room was familiar to the French adept in its role as a temple, but today the space had been transformed into a meeting room. Three people were seated around an old wooden bench at the Northern end of the lodge and were clearly arguing about something; as their voices were raised, however, it was not possible to catch what was being said as they abruptly ceased their discussion as Mathers approached them.

At the head of the table, furthest away from Mathers, was her mentor, Frater Gabriel, an older man in his early 90s with more than a passing resemblance to the actor Morgan Freeman. Gabriel was dressed in a light-coloured tweed jacket and matching trousers. In front of him, on the table were some maps of various regions of Europe that had been heavily annotated with green ink in Gabriel's distinctive handwriting, which was so familiar to Mathers from the numerous corrections and comments he used to add to her magical diaries as she progressed through her studies in the order. Beside the maps were some traditional genealogical charts and a stack of photocopied documents, organised into four neat piles.

Seated to his right, taking notes with an old fountain pen, was a striking-looking woman called Soror Emmilia. She was in her late 80s with high cheek bones and thick, long, white hair flowing down over her shoulders. She was wearing a handmade, full-length, blue cotton dress embroidered with alpine flowers and some Romany symbols that Mathers recognised as being devoted to healing and prophecy. Her fingers were adorned with numerous rings, many of which, Mathers knew, had been passed down through many generations. Beside her on the table were numerous hand-drawn astrological charts[240] and several thick, handwritten notebooks. Some of the notebooks were opened on pages that showed hand-drawn representations of Tarot card readings and two hand palm prints that Mathers recognised as ones Emmilia had taken of Mathers' palms some ten years earlier on the occasion of Mathers gaining the rank of Adeptus Minor[241].

To the left of Gabriel, seated opposite Emmilia, was a thick-set man with thinning grey hair and a matching goatee beard. His name was Frater Aron, and his area of the table top was stacked high with old books and moth-eaten scrolls of vellum parchment that stood rather incongruously next to a sleek, brushed aluminium Dell Linux laptop. Mathers recognised some of the Hebrew text visible on one of the scrolls, but the others were covered in some unknown cypher unique to each Master Alchemist.

The three adepts rose unsteadily from their seats, and each embraced Mathers in turn, greeting her with a familiarity that spoke of a long and deep association. Eventually, they

---

[240] These charts would be quite unfamiliar to modern students of Astrology since they are square diagrams with a smaller square inset inside a larger square. The twelve houses are shown in a clockwise direction in a series of small triangles that progress around the inner square. They also make use of the Alchabitius Houses, Essential Dignities, Moiety and Quadruplicities.

[241] The fifth degree of the order.

resumed their places around the wooden table, and Gabriel gestured to Mathers to sit in the vacant seat at the end facing him.

"Soror Mathers, please join us. For some time, there has been discussion and debate about how we should respond to the increasing strength of the Meri-Isfet."

"And our own, comparative enfeeblement." Interjected the gruff voice of Aron through his grey beard.

"Yes, and our dwindling numbers." Admitted Gabriel, "There has been considerable pressure, especially from the more junior members, to reduce the difficulty and duration of our studies."

"Dumbing it down and opening progress to the three higher degrees, you mean!" retorted Emmilia, clearly thinking the proposal completely indefensible.

Gabriel sighed, "There has been some disagreement. I will not deny it. Some of us," Gabriel looked at Emmilia to his right, "think we should ignore the threat of the Meri-Isfet as we have too few resources now to risk our only remaining young Adeptus Exemptus. That is, you, of course, Soror Mathers."

Emmilia nodded and smiled at Mathers. "Our hopes for the future."

Gabriel remained pensive and looked to Aron on his left. Both men turned to Mathers with deadly seriousness.

"Others, myself included, think we must act as our forebears would have done and confront the enemy." Aron nodded but remained silent.

Gabriel continued by opening one of the maps in front of him and passed it over the table to Mathers.

"Aron has followed your investigation reports and agrees with you that there appears to be a pattern of activity that always aligns along the ancient Euro Asian ley lines[242] that converge on a location close to the village of Godinje, near the Montenegrin and Albanian border."

Aron added, "Yes, and I have also used the pendulum,"

he picked up a pear-shaped brass object, around the size of small fruit, from the table top beside him. The brass surface of the object was covered in dense cuneiform[243] engravings, and a frayed, white silk cord was appended to one end.

"to assess changes in the vicinity, we believe the Meri-Isfet have made substantial renovations to an old island stronghold on Lake Skadar."

Emmilia interjected, pointedly looking at the two men, "And? Tell our Soror the rest!"

Aron nodded, "Yes, well, the pendulum and our scrying[244] also indicate physical and astral threats emanating from the island fortress."

Emmilia added, "These two old men are tactfully trying to avoid saying that we are sending you, our only remaining vigorous senior adept, directly into harm's way; to face numerous advanced LHP adepts of your own or even more advanced rank. Some of them have even crossed over the

---

[242] Lines that link ancient sites and are believed to transmit unseen energies for healing or more maleficent purposes.

[243] Dating the pendulum would be extremely difficult but the order's own lore asserts it to be from the Sumerian city of Uruk dating from the third millennia BCE.

[244] Scrying is a traditional form of clairvoyance that uses reflective surfaces to enable the magician to "see" and "sense" places, objects or people who are distant in terms of geography or time. In modern times the techniques have been renamed as "remote viewing".

abyss![245] Even *we* have no clear idea what such advanced adepts may be capable of doing to anyone who stands in their way."

"We believe there are *only* four members of the Meri-Isfet who have claimed such illustrious advancement. And only three of those remain, now *she* has gone." Clarified Aron.

Gabriel coughed loudly and looked at both his elderly colleagues. He wanted to deescalate what was rapidly becoming an open argument that threatened to undo weeks of tense negotiation between the three members of the council.

"Madeleine, there is no hiding that this will be a perilous mission. We believe we are sending you to what is probably the headquarters of the Meri-Isfet. Of course, you can decline, and none of us would think the worse of you."

"Certainly, I would applaud such a decision." Added Emmilia.

Mathers nodded at Emmilia, "I understand, and I am thankful for your concern. But I happen to agree with Gabriel and Aron. We must take some kind of action, or we may as well transform the order into a reference library."

"If you are killed, that is exactly what will happen!" Sighed Emmilia in frustration before continuing,

"While Aron consulted his pendulum, I cast the chart for the Meri-Isfet over the next twelve months."

She pulled over one of the large, hand-drawn paper charts spread out on the table beside her and passed it to Mathers.

"It is a period when their Ascendants, Essential Dignities and Moiety all show it to be time for them to rise and renew, as

---

[245] *Crossing the abyss* is a euphemism within esoteric orders for reaching one of the three highest grades in the Western Esoteric Tradition, the 8th, 9th and 10th degrees respectively.

a powerful new general will emerge from the West to lead them. Perhaps as they did during the middle of the last century[246], they may even attempt to repeat their ancient folly from the time before when Osireh brought light to humanity[247]."

Mathers carefully scrutinized the chart and pulled a black roller ball pen[248] from her inside jacket pocket along with a small notebook[249]. She then made a few notes using a mix of astrological symbols and numbers before remarking,

"It's bleak, I agree. But not entirely without hope. I just wonder who this person is who will be universally hated before being imprisoned by the combined forces of the material world, as they appear to be the only hope of blocking the powerful ascendants and conjunctions that are assisting the rise of the Meri-Isfet."

Emmilia nodded her agreement with Mathers' astrological assessment before passing another large, hand-drawn astrological chart over to the younger adept. "Madeleine, before you make any final decisions, you should also see your own chart for the same period."

Mathers' face became darker as she examined a chart filled with negative influences and planetary squares that intimated numerous mortal challenges. "Thanks. Clearly, I will have to be especially careful."

At this moment, Aron turned his laptop screen around to face Mathers, who leant forward and scrolled the touch

---

[246] The rise of the Third Reich.

[247] A myth related to the wise ones who supposedly founded the Ancient Egyptian civilization after fleeing a massive global cataclysm.

[248] A modern classic Montblanc M rollerball pen.

[249] A small black Moleskine Classic Ruled Paper Notebook.

screen to scan through sets of communication summaries covering the past six months.

"This will help put some of Emmilia's darker fears to rest. Based on my monitoring of email, phone and text communications, we have good grounds to believe that the Meri-Isfet has lost the most important of the esoteric materials that they gathered during the war[250]. Furthermore, there has been no evidence that they have access to any of the terrible devices needed to repeat their ancient *folly*."

Emmilia sighed, clearly unimpressed by modern technology, "Before we all grow complacent, the aspects show that a time is coming when these secrets could re-emerge unless the current trends can be stopped."

"Exactly why Soror Mathers should investigate!" asserted Aron forcefully.

Gabriel seized the opportunity to interrupt the evident tension brewing between Aron and Emmilia. "On a different topic, I take it you have all seen this morning's headlines?"

Aron and Emmilia indicated that they had, while Mathers queried, "The Royal abductions?"

Gabriel nodded,

"Obviously, it is too early to know if there is a link between these acts and the Meri-Isfet's plans, but just in case, I gathered these materials so that Madeleine can be aware of the possible esoteric applications for such Royal abductions."

Gabriel passed around the genealogical charts that had been in front of him, along with copies of papers that, based

---

[250] The second World War.

on their distinctive[251] logo and dates, came from Berlin during the Third Reich. Additional acquisition stamps showed that the documents had been assimilated into a restricted collection in an Eastern European Nation's government archive after the war. The papers were written in German and related to secret occult rites to derive power from Royal bloodlines and ancient relics.

"Fascinating, you really think they would kill these abducted Royals?" queried Aron as he finished skim reading through the papers.

"In the blink of an eye, if they thought it would bring them power." Answered Gabriel.

"They will need relics associated with each of the blood lines. That is something they most certainly do not have." Said Mathers.

"Yet! We can only hope that you are wrong about this, Gabriel." Added Aron.

"One final thing," interjected Gabriel,

"The area where you are going is being led by an advanced adept. Our scrying has determined from his aura and the residual energies left behind after his rituals that he practices the darkest forms of Chaos Magick."

Mathers nodded, "I will be careful."

"Please do. And remember that he and his associates will not be bound by the Paris Council of 1682. Therefore, it is imperative that if you encounter any magical opposition, you should not, under any circumstances, respond in kind."

---

[251] Ahnenerbe Research Unit logo was a sword with an intertwining ribbon, flowing on both sides of the long blade. The sword and ribbon were surrounded by a border of runic characters, that ran right around central motif.

Mathers could swear that Gabriel's old face broke into a momentary wink as he made the meeting's final instruction.

12 QUESTIONS IN THE HOUSE

"Politics have no relation to morals." - Niccolò Machiavelli

1st floor, Stewart's Antiquarians,
18a, New Bond St,
Mayfair,
London W1S 2RB

12.40HRS (GMT+1), 8th Sept, Present Day

Upstairs, above the spacious showroom, Stewart strode purposefully from the top of a single narrow flight of wooden stairs and past an external doorway that stood to the right of a small landing that provided alternative access from the showroom offices down to New Bond Street below. Above this exterior door was an illuminated fire exit sign. As if to emphasise the door's important safety role, directly at the top of the stairs were a pair of red, pressurised fire extinguishers[252].

Ignoring the fire exit, Stewart turned left. He entered a spacious but artificially narrow[253], first-floor office area, complete with three desks and the associated computers, phones, printers and piles of paperwork typical of any ongoing modern business premises. Leading out from the right side of this office space was another narrow corridor that led towards the rear of the 19th-century property that had once been a fine Regency townhouse. Looking at the

---

[252] One marked as powder and the other as liquid spray.

[253] The upper floor of Stewart's premises is narrower than the ground floor showroom, but this is only noticeable to a very well-trained eye. Allegedly, there is a concealed safe room located behind a heavily armoured partition, that runs alongside the innocent looking office space. How one accesses this secret location is known only to a very select few.

ornate plaster ceilings, one could see where modern partition walls had been erected, obstructing the smooth flow of some delicate ceiling decorations and some original heavy-duty chandelier fittings.

Stewart headed purposefully down this passage, passing on his left a modern kitchenette and a small but tastefully decorated lounge where his staff could sit, eat and plan. Temporarily ignoring the urge to prepare himself a well-deserved meal, Stewart continued down the long, narrow, natural wood-floored corridor. The tall magnolia coloured walls were decorated with a series of black and white lithographs depicting various scenes from sites of antiquity before they had become the crowded tourist destinations so familiar today. Alongside these classic historical scenes were a series of framed stone rubbings traced by Stewart from some of the standing stones on his estate[254]. The original, sanded, and varnished wooden floorboards contrasted starkly against the painted white skirting boards. In several places, the white glossed skirting and magnolia walls showed evidence of scuffing, where heavy objects had collided with the sides of the passageway as they were transported down this walkway. This twenty-five-foot-long passageway led past the small office washroom on the left side and continued towards a single, unmarked white wooden door that signalled the corridor's end.

When Stewart opened this final door, he entered a small storage area, around thirty feet square, illuminated by a single fluorescent light with no windows. The flickering of the light filament settled, revealing a clean and orderly room that continued the theme of the magnolia-coloured

---

[254] Stewart had placed these stone rubbings periodically around all the walls of the upper floor, as he found the strange Neolithic symbols to be a compelling reminder of his ancestral home and its long history.

walls and sanded, wooden floorboards in evidence throughout the entire first floor.

The room contained rows of metal storage racks with various items that formed the consumables for running a busy business office in central London. However, some of these racks had been moved to make space for a khaki coloured metal-framed folding bed[255] that was immaculately made, with crisp sheets and blankets that tightly[256] fitted together. A well-used leather Gladstone bag[257] covered in numerous labels from various travels over the past thirty years had been placed at the foot of the camp bed on the wooden floor. Inside this open case, the exposed clothes were rolled and folded perfectly in a manner that would make any regimental sergeant major proud.

After removing his dirty shoes[258] and placing them on the floor beside the foot of his bed for later cleaning, the Scotsman reached over and removed a blue, cotton, Uniqlo oxford shirt[259], a pair of stone-coloured, Dockers chinos, some grey silk socks, Sunspel Egyptian cotton boxer underwear, Musto classic deck shoes and, finally, a red

---

[255] A standard BCB International camp bed (general issue to British Army).

[256] Easily tight enough to bounce a ten pence coin, or quarter, if you prefer US minted.

[257] A bespoke larger version of the classic Gladstone bag by Mackenzie Leather of Edinburgh, Scotland.

[258] Cheaney Romney, Grain Leather, Brogues.

[259] An off the peg, classic OCBD (Oxford cloth button-down). Due to his budgetary constraints, he was no longer having his shirts bespoke made by Ede and Ravenscroft.

leather Dunhill toiletry bag[260]. He then walked barefooted to the office washroom, to emerge some ten minutes later, looking immaculate and filling the air around him with the distinctive, citrus aroma of Hermes Eau D'Orange Verte.

Having placed his discarded clothes within the kitchen's front-loading AEG washing machine, Stewart commenced searching through the contents of the large, brushed metal Bosch fridge. He began preparing a communal meal for the staff, who gradually started to come in through the connecting double doors from the office and congregate in the kitchen after closing the downstairs showroom for lunch. When Sonnet came upstairs, he saw their boss searching the fridge and instinctively began laying four table places and loading a series of heaped table spoons of a dark, rich Sumatra coffee into a Smeg[261].

While the smell of freshly brewed coffee began to fill the air, Stewart located a couple of magnificent fresh salmon that he had caught the previous day before heading down to London by train from Waverly Station in Edinburgh. The Scotsman reverently removed the two large fish, took a sharp knife[262] and began preparing them.

His trip to town was initially intended to be a personal celebration, to mark being reunited with his beloved 1967 classic, open-topped Mercedes, which had been lovingly restored after being riddled with bullets during an intense gunfight beside Loch Chon, near his ancestral home. He

---

[260] Embossed with the Edinburgh Balmoral Hotel livery, which had been given to Stewart as a gift.

[261] Climpson and Sons, Sumatra Wahana blend coffee in a Smeg, DCF02 Drip Filter Machine. All purchased in more prosperous times.

[262] A well-used, Victorinox Grand Maître Chef model, in case you were wondering.

could currently ill afford the expensive restoration work but had commissioned the repairs when he had anticipated a prompter return of his assets by the Government. After the events of the morning, what remained of Stewart's beloved vehicle was now impounded by the Metropolitan police, pending a thorough forensic examination and would not be able to be returned for an attempted second restoration for some weeks, that is, if, Stewart's finances ever permitted.

Within a few minutes, the air inside the small kitchen was filled with the delicious aroma of fresh Salmon poached with a freshly made Salsa Verde, scrambled eggs on whole-wheat bread, cooked with virgin olive oil and, as an accompaniment, some delicious green club sandwiches.

The staff sat silently around the wooden, Ercol kitchen table, appreciating the perfectly prepared meal. At the same time, they listened to their boss fill in the details about the morning's adventures that had been missing from the news coverage. After Stewart informed them of his curious meeting with Ms Smyth and the new clients of Presumed Innocence, the staff began to exhibit their typical curiosity. They were delighted when Stewart indicated that "La cuarta república" would now be their primary focus, with a preliminary summary of progress meeting later that afternoon. Without further prompting, each team member began to volunteer leads and contacts that they would follow up to research the unknown Argentinean breakaway nation. They all agreed to extend the shop lunch closure for what remained of the day, and each member headed off to pursue their lines of research so that they would be prepared for the planned meeting.

While Sonnet and Stewart cleaned up after the meal, they made a joint speaker phone call to Mohammed Sek in Istanbul, using Sonnet's Samsung phone on the round, beechwood table. At the same time, Stewart and Sonnet placed the dirty plates and cutlery in a Bosch dishwasher and wiped down the kitchen surfaces. Sek's booming baritone voice filled the small meeting room with his larger-than-life energy. After ascertaining that Stewart was unharmed, he immediately offered to use his contacts from the Turkish government. Stewart had no doubt Sek would also explore his unofficial sources to investigate the mysterious South Americans who had emerged with such unexpected violence onto the global scene.

Meanwhile, less than a mile away, Cynthia Sinclair had showered and emerged from the small bathroom attached to her Horseferry House office. She was wearing a matching set of grey Guia La Bruna lingerie that was only partially concealed under a full length, blue Prada silk dressing gown. Sinclair filled the air with a sophisticated aroma[263] as she strode over her small office's grey wool Wilton carpeting towards her sleek, Astoria desk and sat in a black leather Serta executive chair, her bare toes flexing as they luxuriated in the thick wool pile.

Pausing for a moment's thought, she scrolled through the numerous contacts on her official, encrypted mobile phone, selected one name from her favourites sub list, set the phone on speaker and left it on her desk as it connected. While listening for the other end to pick up, she walked to the right side of her small office, towards a set of tall, dark, full length, double cabinet doors that, when opened, revealed a small kitchenette, complete with a matching set of Miele kitchen appliances. Opening the brushed metal fridge door, she removed a litre sized blue blender glass, removed the sealed top and slowly stirred the contents with a long white paper straw. After this preparation, she began

---

[263] Maison Francis Kurkdjian, Baccarat Rouge 540 Eau de Parfum.

sipping the chilled smoothie[264] as she strode slowly back to her desk area and waited for her call to be answered. Standing behind her desk, she gazed through the slightly distorted tinted glass[265] of her window down to the busy lunchtime London traffic passing through Horseferry Road.

Moments later, Sinclair's call was connected to an efficient sounding female voice, who announced that Sinclair had reached,

"Room 306."

Sinclair smiled at the Foreign and Commonwealth Office (FCO) protocol, which precluded mentioning anything specific, and asked for "Sir Richards".

After establishing with the highly protective receptionist that Dame Sinclair's unexpected call would be accepted, Sinclair sat in her comfortable desk chair and listened to a smooth, cultured voice, expressing genuine pleasure at taking her call.

"Sin! What a rare pleasure!

Saw you on the BBC lunch coverage, firing that bloody splendid machine pistol of yours! Causing all sorts of fuss throughout the whole of Whitehall. MI6 operating on UK soil and all that. Better prepare yourself to answer some endless questions from those idiots Tweedledee and Tweedledum[266]."

---

[264] Sinclair's usual lunch time smoothie recipe includes Optimum Nutrition Gold protein powder, almond milk, a banana, a whole egg in its shell, and a tart cherry juice for improved muscle recovery.

[265] British Standard BS 5051 standard bullet and explosive resistance impairs optical clarity.

[266] Sir Reginald Twiffers and Lord Jeremy Kenner, Home Secretary and Defence Secretary, respectively.

Sir Richards made an aside that was only just audible on the phone,

"Dum being the operative word."

The comment caused Sinclair to smile as she fondly pictured the noble face of one of her oldest friends. A man who had acted as her mentor during her long career in the intelligence community.

Sir Fredrick Richards, the former principal private secretary (PPS) for the Foreign and Commonwealth Office (and, in preparation for his impending retirement, mentor to the current FCO PPS), was a career civil servant in his mid-sixties who had successfully managed[267] numerous foreign secretaries from various political parties. Having just completed his lunch of seafood linguine[268], carefully prepared by the FCO's resident chef[269], along with some delicious chilled white wine[270], he was feeling fully at peace with the world and intrigued by the unexpected call from

---

[267] Contrary to popular belief it is the civil service and their vast army of administrators who actually control and run the nation (any nation). The elected politicians get the limelight and think they make decisions but, in reality, it is the faceless, unaccountable, bureaucrats who decide on the items that will be included on any important agenda, the order in which they will be presented, what information gets presented (and what gets mysteriously omitted), what time the meeting takes place (so some people are unable to attend) and, after the meeting ends, it is they who record the decisions, write up the minutes and then also act (or often mysteriously do not act) to implement decisions.

[268] Indulgently delicious seared scallops and king prawns with linguine pasta. Served with roasted cherry tomatoes and fresh pea shoots.

[269] Michelin starred, former head chef at Arpège in Paris.

[270] A three-year-old, Nals Margreid Punggl Pinot Grigio, from a south facing vineyard in Trentino-Alto Adige, Italy.

the head of SIS. He knew from personal experience that Sinclair was a popular and efficient leader and a competent field operative. She was also someone who he looked upon with considerable fondness, almost like his own daughter, having mentored her throughout her career—beginning when he was just a lowly executive officer, responsible for liaison between British Overseas Territories (BOTs) and the US state department's Drug Enforcement Agency (DEA). Here, he had first encountered Sinclair as a rookie operative in the joint Caribbean drugs taskforce. As Richards' career had progressed through the byzantine structures of the British Civil Service, finally reaching the heady level of Senior Civil Service (SCS) and finally PPS[271], he had observed Sinclair also progressing through periods with the British Military[272] and finally to a series of positions within the FCO's own foreign intelligence branch.

Taking a final sip from his wine glass, he glanced at his Longines[273] and returned his attention to Sinclair.

"Anyway, Sin. Enough of my senile ramblings; what can I do for you? Something exciting and questionably illegal, I hope!"

Sinclair briefly updated Richards about the arrival of Presumed Innocence at The Mall, almost immediately after

---

[271] Senior Civil Service (SCS) grades include directors, and principal private secretaries, who assist (run) all government.

[272] Including periods of service in Northern Ireland with the Special Reconnaissance Unit, also known as the 14 Field Security and Intelligence Company or "DET".

[273] A white faced, gold filled (plated), Longines, conquest automatic, worn on a plain, brown leather strap. Originally purchased by Richards to commemorate his 21st birthday at the duty-free price of sixty-two dollars (nearly two month's salary for a junior civil servant in the seventies) at the Bijoux jewellery store in Kingston, Jamaica.

the departure of the damaged helicopter, and their disclosure to Stewart that they were representing the organisation that had accepted responsibility for the royal kidnappings in Europe and the two attacks on London that morning.

"Sadly, I am not surprised that Twiffers' company would misuse taxpayers' money to willingly represent those who would do us[274] harm. It is typical of an amoral attitude that is sadly so common these days." Reflected Richards, in an aside, before urging Sinclair to continue.

Sinclair smiled at her mentor's evident devotion towards the country before she continued to explain that, according to the representative from Presumed Innocence, these aggressors, who had launched the two attacks in London that morning, were from a breakaway South American movement called "La Cuarta República"; who had recently formed a small independent republic in the extreme North of Argentina, just South of the borders of Paraguay and Bolivia.

"La Cuarta República?" Mused Richards, before translating from Spanish, "The Fourth Republic. An intriguing choice for a name. I will happily make enquires about them, Sin, but be aware, my dear, that my sources may be more limited than they once were as, officially, I no longer hold any role within Government. Since I am on the way out, anyone who feels inclined to be unhelpful due to imagined past injustices[275] or current allegiances can insist that my

---

[274] Sir Richards was one of dwindling breed who still held to the ideal that people had a duty of loyalty towards, and for, the shared interests of their nation.

[275] Everyone who has had their promotion rejected within the civil service imagines that a deep personal injustice has been inflicted upon them by every member who ever served on or might have influenced their promotion panel.

requests for information be first approved by our beloved Home Secretary, and, as you know, there is no love lost there, so such requests would probably take months only finally to be refused."

Sinclair indicated her understanding and thanked Richards before informing him that she, and her colleagues at Stewart's Antiquarians, were planning a group briefing that same afternoon to share everything each had been able to ascertain about the mysterious "La Cuarta República".

Richards chuckled, "I see. So, you would appreciate it if I could check my sources as quickly as possible? I will see what can be done and call you back at 13.30 hrs. If that is acceptable?"

"Highly acceptable, and again, thank you." Responded Sinclair.

"Not a problem, my dear. Chat again soon."

With the conversation ended, Sinclair rose and noted that her desk phone, which she had muted before commencing her call to Richards, had accumulated over a dozen voice messages over the last five minutes, as indicated on the flashing LCD display. She began to play them while she walked back into her adjoining bedroom and dressed.

The first two phone messages were from her own personal secretary, Julian, warning her that the Home Secretary was raising questions in the House[276] about unauthorised and illegal direct action by a senior serving FCO officer on UK soil.

"Typical petty interdepartmental jealousy."

---

[276] House of Commons.

Sinclair muttered to herself as she realised that this could only refer to Sinclair's engagement with the "La Cuarta República" terrorists that morning.

There were also phone messages from the PPS for the Home Office and the Defence Ministry. These calls demanded that Sinclair call them back immediately and come to a preliminary internal inquiry meeting, scheduled for 10:00 HRS, the following morning at conference room C in the Marshall Street building[277] to explain her actions.

Sinclair ignored the implied urgency in the Home Office and Defence Ministry messages and took her time before emerging from her small bedroom wearing a grey, silk, Prada trouser business suit with matching kitten heels. After placing the now empty smoothie glass into the dishwasher, she slowly walked back to her desk and called her secretary, Julian, on the desk phone to reassure him that she would deal with the supposed crisis. Ignoring the messages related to the impending inquiry, she counted the few remaining minutes on her Cartier's blued minute hand and waited. Promptly, her mobile vibrated at the agreed 13.30 HRS, and Sinclair immediately took the call on speaker.

Unusually for Richards, his voice sounded noticeably stressed.

"Sin, I am the bearer of disappointing news. I could not find anyone within our own Government who was willing to admit knowing anything much about this new state. Other, that is, than the unofficial insight that they were extraordinarily wealthy and unusually generous to their allies. These two factors have made them extremely well regarded by certain members of the current Government."

"Twiffers?" mused Sinclair.

---

[277] The Home Office

"And our beloved PM[278]." Chuckled Richards before he continued.

"Thankfully, my contacts at the Argentinian embassy were more forthcoming but clearly VERY nervous about making any statements on an open phone line. They insisted on calling me back via one of my burner numbers. Always feels such a bloody nuisance to use one of those prepaid, one time SIM cards."

Sinclair made a sympathetic noise.

Richards continued, "Anyway, according to the first secretary, these newcomers are extremely close to and highly influential with the most senior members of the Argentinian government. Hence the lack of any protest when they formed a breakaway republic on what was Argentinian soil. Anyone who publicly opposed the new breakaway republic found family members abducted. If they refused to surrender to such blackmail tactics, they were themselves found dead, in various mysterious and very convenient circumstances, that were all ruled suicide or a freak accident by the government-approved authorities."

"Does not surprise me," mused Sinclair, "It closely matches how they behaved in London this morning. I would not put it past Twiffers to have come to some devious financial arrangement with them about the planned kidnapping of this morning."

"Indeed, that thought had crossed my mind as well. The terrorists seemed too well briefed about the Royal's planned route and the protective detail. They must have had considerable inside assistance. Damned lucky for the occupants of the Royal car that Stewart was on the scene, but you and he both need to be extra careful with these

---

[278] The Right Honourable Susan Merriweather, MP.

characters. They are some extremely unpleasant people, even by your standards."

"Thanks. I will warn Tavish."

"Indeed. And Sin? Please take some extra precautions yourself."

Sinclair made a mental note to up her own security awareness. Maybe even begin to use Kevlar, as Stewart was always urging, at least until the situation with this new group was resolved, but she hated the way the padding spoilt the cut of her clothing. She returned to her conversation with Richards.

"Did you discover anything about the group's origins or history?"

"No, nothing definite. Vague rumours that they are remnants of some former "Gran Republica" who were forced to hide from persecution by spreading themselves out over vast South and Latin America regions. However, within the last five years, they sold those interests and began to consolidate into one location. They systematically purchased enormous tracts of grazing land in and around the area they had declared their autonomous zone. Through unprecedented investments in roads and infrastructure, they converted open grasslands, interspersed by small ranches, into a series of major conurbations that includes a magnificent capital city and some massive industrial manufacturing and processing complexes. These rival the best facilities in the US and Europe. Must have cost a fortune."

"All with a focus on agriculture and beef production? It must be part of some very long-term plans, as it inevitably takes decades to establish serious R&D[279] endeavours." Sinclair queried.

"No, that is the strange bit. Although they have only just opened these new facilities, their capabilities indicate that they are already highly respected, with high-profile international subcontracts with world-leading companies in medicine, aerospace and even groundbreaking propulsion systems. Another oddity that indicates some longer-term existence for this group is that they hold the balance on hundred-year leases, initially taken out in the late 1940s, for two extensive facilities.

One, high in the Andes, near the border with Chile, for astronomical research and the other, far down near Rio Gallegos, on the Southern tip of the continent, for marine and oceanographic research. All legit, apparently, and staffed by the most qualified scientists, recruited worldwide."

"Does not sound like the kind of people who would suddenly decide to become kidnappers. Any clues about the motivation for why they would want to kidnap the heirs to the European royal lines?"

"No, except that the reputation for how they dealt with any form of opposition when they declared independence does not preclude anything, so it is well within their capabilities and ruthless nature. But, no, no one I spoke to had seen any warning indications about what this group allegedly did in Europe this morning, nor could they speculate as to why the group would suddenly undertake such provocative and high-profile actions outside of Argentina. Until now, they have focused all their attention exclusively on activities within South America."

---

[279] Research and development.

Sinclair was silent for a moment, thinking, and then responded.

"Agreed, it is all very curious. Thank you for giving up your lunch hour at short notice, Freddie. As always, you have come up trumps."

"You are most welcome, my dear. Take care of yourself if you go after these people. They have potent allies in the highest places, so watch your back."

Sinclair agreed, and, ending the call, she checked her mobile was fully charged and placed the phone in her left outer jacket pocket. She then opened the upper, right-side drawer on her desk and removed a bespoke, grey leather gun-holster[280] that blended perfectly with the colour of her Prada business suit. Sinclair then expertly fitted the finely stitched leather gun holder inside her waist band, on the left side, using the two dark plastic spring grips that were discreetly integrated into the holster's grey leather work. Unlocking the lower desk drawer, she opened a finely grained, mahogany wooden box. She took out a Walther PPS[281] that she fitted into the holster after making some trial gun draws to check with her right hand for any potential snagging. A spare magazine clip went into her right-hand side jacket pocket. Sinclair carefully checked her profile in a full-length mirror on the back of her office door to check that there were no tell tail signs of her armament and, satisfied, she left her apartment.

Having written off her 911, Sinclair had already phoned ahead to the central Whitehall car pool to arrange for

---

[280] An Alexandra Inside-the-Waistband, Tuckable Leather Holster

[281] A thinner, more discrete, version of the full-sized Walther PPQ, designed specifically for concealed carry. Sinclair's version had a 3.5-inch barrel and was chambered for .40 SW JHP (jacketed hollow point) rounds.

transport. When she exited the front of Horseferry House, she was not surprised to see an unmarked white Ford Mondeo pulling up on the curb. She was not, however, expecting to see three occupants. Two men and one woman, all under thirty and all dressed in dark polyester, off the peg, two-piece business attire.

As all three occupants exited the car and approached Sinclair, she noted that, up close, their clothes looked in need of a dry clean and press, as though they had been worn for too long in confined spaces, where they had consumed take away meals and slept in their vehicles as and when they could. Sinclair's experienced eyes took in the classic tell tail signs of long-term surveillance work, which she knew only too well from her personal experience. They were either Special Branch or, more likely, MI5.

Moments later, the female agent confirmed Sinclair's supposition by showing a laminated security service (MI5) identity card for a "Ms J. Malone" and a signed piece of A4 paper that was a warrant to search Sinclair's apartment and seize any firearms. Sinclair took the warrant and read it carefully.

Malone smiled as she rapidly and efficiently frisked Sinclair, taking the Walther and the spare magazine, making a big show to her colleagues of placing the weapon in a plastic tamper-proof evidence bag. Malone checked the time on her smart watch, pulled a plastic biro from her jacket's inner pocket and scribbled some text on the evidence bag. She seemed very pleased with herself, and all three young operatives exchanged knowing smiles. While they were distracted by their self-congratulation, Sinclair momentarily considered dealing with all three of them with "prejudice[282]"

---

[282] Without the normal health and safety restrictions governing restraining law enforcement officials who are interfering with a case related to a threat to national security.

but decided, on reflection, to see where this farce would lead.

"Dame Sinclair, I must caution you under the firearms act 1968...."

Sinclair interrupted her, "I am fully aware of the firearms act, Ms Malone, and its numerous amendments. Just as you are fully aware, I am exempt from the acts as a serving member of the intelligence services."

The woman smiled again, "You don't know? How sad. Clearly, you are well past your peak intelligence-gathering days."

A cynical smirk crossed the female agent's face. Sinclair reflected, to herself, that this woman was enjoying her moment of power over the Director of the British Secret Intelligence Service (SIS) and had no idea of the violence Sinclair was capable of inflicting. Again, Malone exchanged a knowing glance with the other young MI5 agents before clearing her throat and declaring,

"Dame Sinclair, as of noon today, the eighth of September, the Defence Secretary, in conjunction with the Foreign Secretary, have formally revoked your exemptions with respect to owning and carrying any form of calibrated weapon. Further, they have suspended you from your role as Director SIS and all active duty, on and off British soil. Pending the outcome of the formal enquiry into your unauthorised actions on UK soil, you will remain under house arrest. Now kindly accompany us into your flat, where we will continue searching for firearms."

13 THE TETHERED GOAT

"Hunting is not a sport. In a sport, both sides should know they're in the game." - Paul Rodriguez

Top (Sixth) floor Apartment
Horseferry House
Horseferry Road, London, SW1

13.45HRS (GMT+1), 8th Sept, Present Day

Once Sinclair had decided to allow herself to be detained, she had been briskly escorted from the pavement and into the building's foyer, where the three agents made a dramatic performance for the building's security officer, Henri Ducal. Always smartly dressed, polite and efficient, Ducal was a tall and distinguished-looking man whose thick, white, receding hair was only disturbed by the black elasticated straps from the eye patch that covered his right eye.

The three agents perpetrated a cruel joke as they deliberately presented their identity cards and the court warrant, authorising them to search Sinclair's apartment on Ducal's blind side, forcing him to apologise for having to move around before reading the presented documents.

If they had known that Ducal was a former Jamaican Police Detective[283], who had worked alongside Sinclair in the Caribbean task force going against the drug cartels, they would have realised he was unimpressed by their theatrics. He was more intent on looking for any subtle signals from

---

[283] A former detective sergeant in the Jamaica Constabulary Force (JCF) based in Kingston. Ducal was forced to take early retirement after receiving serious injuries during an undercover operation that went wrong in Columbia.

Sinclair that she required assistance. Based on a single, subtle nod from her, the moment the four figures had vanished into the elevator, Ducal picked up the reception's phone and made a single call.

The progress towards Sinclair's apartment started a string of security errors that highlighted the three MI5 agents' lack of training or, more likely, their complete lack of interest in their assignment.

Where they should have sent one of their team ahead to check that the way was clear and that no unpleasant surprises awaited them in the apartment; instead, they all rode up in the elevator together.

Inside the confined space of the lift, apart from the canned classical music, Sinclair realised that at least one of them had recently enjoyed a meal laced with garlic. Therefore, it was a considerable relief when the elevator reached the sixth floor, and the doors opened.

As the agents led Sinclair down the corridor to her office, she deliberately tested their discipline by walking slowly and feigning the odd stumble that resulted in her being pushed and receiving a series of age and race-related derogatory comments. Seeking to confirm their discriminatory biases, Sinclair exaggerated her supposed physical weakness so she would have the advantage of surprise when she needed to act. She had a good idea of how the rest of the process would unfold since the agents were undisciplined and filled with an exceptionally high opinion of their abilities. They also had a predisposition to dismiss the skills of others, especially, from what Sinclair could hear, anyone over the age of thirty-five or from a different ethnic or social background. Unfortunately, Sinclair fitted every single one of their preconceived prejudices.

Once in her apartment, Sinclair sat patiently in her black leather office chair. She had hung her grey Prada suit jacket carefully, on the back of the Serta, before occupying the seat and cautiously watching the activities of the three MI5 agents who had arrested her. Sinclair's full-length, grey trousers covered her long legs that stretched out luxuriously beside her desk at a ninety-degree angle. Her leg placement looked casual but was, in fact, carefully calculated, so her body would not be encumbered by the desk, should, and when she needed to move quickly.

Right from the outset of the arrest, it had been clear to Sinclair that this detention was a preliminary diversion for some more devious plan. Her two unanswered questions were, for what purpose was she detained and by whom? The only way to find out these answers was to play along. She was thankful for her foresight in wearing a trouser suit as it provided fewer restrictions for when, and she had no doubt there would be a when the main event began. For the time being, she focused her energy and prepared herself as best she could.

What Sinclair was uncertain about was, did these three operatives have any idea of what was to happen next? Based on their relaxed attitude Sinclair suspected they were simply unwitting stooges for a more sinister operation designed to keep Sinclair at a known location and, more importantly, to make sure she was unarmed. If she was correct, the next stage would take place after the weapons had been removed. Sinclair feigned disinterest and kicked off her grey, leather, low heeled Prada shoes, taking care to push them well under her desk, where they posed no future impediment to her movement.

She watched the three young agents perform an exceptionally poor and superficial search of her office, kitchen, adjoining bedroom and bathroom. Even they could not fail to find the large, black steel weapons safe[284] in

---

[284] A Burg Wachter, Ranger N5E - 5 Gun Safe.

Sinclair's bedroom. Predictably, they made another big show of placing the Raffica[285], Nano[286] and their associated spare magazines into standard Met[287] tamper safe, evidence bags.

Sinclair's professional eye noted that the agents' concentration was seldom focused on their assigned tasks. They preferred, instead, to joke with each other and pass loud, pointed comments about how unfair it was that a fellow government operative, Sinclair, who was just a pen-pushing senior manager, should be provided with such an expensive and luxurious apartment at tax payers expense[288]. While passing these comments, they performed the unnecessary task of pulling off all of Sinclair's wardrobe from their hangers and posing for selfies while holding some of the more recognisable branded items. When they reached Sinclair's exotic lingerie[289], they proclaimed that such things were wasted on older people, who could barely walk, let alone perform energetically at anything.

These diversions, combined with the endless series of alert sounds that issued from their oversized phones and smart

---

[285] A Beretta 93R, a 9mm, selective-fire machine pistol, much beloved by Sinclair. Its ferocious firepower having saved her from deadly situations on numerous occasions.

[286] Sinclair's preferred concealed carry weapon, usually worn in a can-can concealment, classic, garter holster. This 5-inch-long, polymer framed, 9mm Beretta micro pistol carries an 8 round magazine but weighs only 19 ounces (half a kilo).

[287] Common abbreviation of London's Metropolitan Police.

[288] An unfair accusation, since Sinclair insisted on paying for the apartment's luxurious outfitting and furnishings herself, along with the exorbitant annual service charges.

[289] I would describe them in detail, but this is not that kind of story. Suffice to say, none of us could afford them, or look anywhere as good in them, as Sinclair.

watches, meant their search pattern was inconsistent. As a consequence, they missed the numerous concealed locations for the variety of weapons that Sinclair, like all experienced operatives, had strategically placed around her dwelling.

More critically, they had also missed the presence of a sleek, black Porsche SUV[290] parked across Horseferry Road when the arrest took place. This high-performance off-roader was fitted with exceptionally dark tinted windows that had just been partially lowered to get a better line of sight on the entrance to the building. The lowering of the vehicle's windows permitted Sinclair a view of the occupants. She could see that seated inside the Porsche were four young males, all of whom had identical short-cropped, crew cut hairstyles and were dressed in matching, black, roll-neck shirts. Either they had attractive bulk discounts with both hairdressers and tailors, or these were military or paramilitary operatives with requirements for a standardised appearance. They gave off an unmistakable impression of professionalism that was absent from the three MI5 agents, who were, Sinclair, noted, taking selfies as they posed with her designer labelled belongings. In contrast, the occupants of the SUV were remarkably clean-cut. They were also exhibiting perfect trade craft[291] in their focused interest in the top floor and the entrance of Horseferry House.

Back in Sinclair's apartment, the endless round of selfies ended. The MI5 team decided they had found everything of interest since they entered the details of the three weapons[292] they had acquired during their detention of

---

[290] A Porsche Cayenne Turbo.

[291] The techniques used by operatives during covert operations.

[292] Including the Walther PPS taken from Sinclair at the street level.

Sinclair into an app on the female agent Malone's iPhone. Then, following their protocol, the two male agents took the three evidence bags down to their car, leaving Malone with Sinclair. Once the agents had left, Malone walked over to the window and stood next to Sinclair, watching the street below for her colleagues to emerge from the building's ground floor lobby.

"Will the other agents be joining us?"

Enquired Sinclair as she indicated the sleek black, rented[293] Porsche SUV parked on double yellow lines across the street.

Malone laughed cynically,

"Don't flatter yourself, thinking you warranted a second team. I don't even know why the section head assigned three of us to bring in a geriatric has been, like you."

Sinclair ignored the caustic put down and began to prepare herself for whatever main event had been planned for the pretence of her detention. She did not have to wait long.

Simultaneously, as the two male MI5 agents reached their Mondeo, and placed the three evidence bags in the car's boot, three of the well-groomed men emerged from the black Porsche SUV and rapidly crossed over to the rear of the Mondeo in a well-coordinated, fluid movement. Their arrival was so silent that the two MI5 agents were unaware of their presence. Then, one of the well-groomed men withdrew a black handgun from a concealed holster on his waist and fired four rapid shots - two rounds into the centre mass of each of the two MI5 agents, killing them instantly.

---

[293] Sinclair had observed the Avis hang tag on the SUV's rear-view mirror. Presumably the car had been picked up from Heathrow.

The sounds of the four shots were muted by an odd-looking, square-shaped suppressor[294] fitted to the handguns, so the only sound a passerby might have heard were four muted clicks, which were lost in the general London traffic noise. The other two smartly dressed men from the SUV had clearly anticipated these brutal executions. They caught the two dead bodies before they fell and rapidly bundled them into the Mondeo's boot without anyone on the street noticing. Closing the boot, the three smartly dressed men then separated. Two men headed towards Horseferry House, while the third, who had now holstered his gun, used his mobile phone to remotely start the Mondeo[295], which he then promptly drove off.

Sinclair had calmly watched the immaculate implementation of an operation that had ensured that all weapons and dead bodies were accounted for and there would be no unpleasant surprises. It was nicely done, reflected Sinclair. The mark of pros.

Meanwhile, the remaining MI5 agent, Malone, was staring in complete disbelief at what she had just seen down on the street below them. Sinclair watched as the cognitive processes of the young woman took in the full implications of what she had just seen.

"They, they, just killed my partners!"

Sinclair nodded and added in a completely calm voice,

"And they are coming up here, honey, so we are next on the menu."

---

[294] Which Sinclair recognized as a German designed, Fischer Development, FD917 model.

[295] Using a modified FordPass app on the phone. Isn't technology wonderful?

Malone stared at Sinclair with a growing terror, the colour noticeably draining from her face and her breathing becoming shallow and rapid.

"Two hit men are coming... Do you think they will have guns?" She demanded in a hysterical tone to Sinclair.

Sinclair looked at the young woman with a raised eyebrow,

"Most do, honey. Most do."

"Oh, God... Oh, God..." Malone began to hyperventilate.

Sinclair's senses were assaulted by the unique aroma and sounds associated with involuntary emesis as Malone bent over double and the apartment's thick Wilton carpet acquired a new pattern.

Reflecting that blood would, almost certainly, soon join the vomit, Sinclair decided she would ignore the revolting mess on the floor and instead begin to take some active role in the unfolding events. She gently queried,

"Do you have a gun, honey?"

"Not, not... departmental policy. We.... police by consent..." gasped Malone.

"Politically commendable, but tactically disastrous[296]."

Commented Sinclair as she rapidly assessed where she could place the MI5 operative, so she did not get in the way and had some chance of survival. The two assassins would undoubtedly have split, one using the stairs and the other the elevator, so getting Malone out of the building was not an option.

Sinclair gently guided the now sobbing Malone through the bedroom, grabbing some of the Kevlar vests that the MI5 agents had left on the bed after emptying her wardrobe;

---

[296] Real life violence is not compatible with many modern ideals.

she placed one around Malone's chest and, once in the small bathroom, told Malone to lie in the bathtub.

"Keep still and quiet, and they may miss you. Since they have come for me, you may survive."

Sinclair then walked back to her office space, gathering just one additional item from the discarded pile of clothing on the bed and unlocking and partially opening her apartment door[297]. She then put on her grey Prada jacket from the back of her chair and carefully posed herself behind her desk, with her back to the door. She looked down at the street below with an icy calm and waited.

Down at the street level, in the sleek, black Porsche SUV, the remaining smartly dressed agent was seated in the driver's seat, talking into a throat microphone attached to a small, black polymer, tactical shortwave radio[298]. This unit was broadcasting through a dedicated encrypted channel to the earphones worn by the two other smartly dressed agents, who were coming up in the elevator and staircase to Sinclair's apartment on the sixth floor.

The smartly dressed agent in the SUV consulted the minute timer, which was running on an unbranded[299] but highly distinctive, brushed steel tactical chronograph, that he was wearing and announced,

"transcurrieron tres minutos." (three minutes elapsed)

---

[297] It saves on damage to the locks and hinges when one is expecting forced entry.

[298] AN/PRC-126 model, rebranded under licence by Bosch.

[299] Genuine special forces issued watches are without any branding that might identify the home nation of the operative.

Less than a mile from where the action was unfolding at Horseferry House, in the luxury of an oak-panelled room within the inner sanctum of one of London's more exclusive private clubs, the distinguished older man, who was simply referred to as "Alpha" by his associates, again sat with his two younger companions on a luxurious, rich brown, leather Chesterfield sofa.

The two younger men were keenly leaning forward, engrossed, partially listening to the audio feed broadcast from the smartly dressed agent in the expensive SUV outside Horseferry House. The older man was sitting back, exhibiting a more relaxed attitude. He slowly inhaled from a sizeable Cuban cigar[300] and then, after relishing the moment, exhaled the thick, fragrant smoke up and towards the ornate ceiling, some six feet above them. A growing pile of ash was being deposited on the highly polished wooden floor beside the seated men. Still, it was clear that they did not care, or more likely, were totally beyond repercussions for any damages they might cause to the premises.

In front of the three men and directly beside the Bosch shortwave radio speaker was an older woman seated on a small wooden stool. She was dressed in a full length, black, high-necked dress, once popular in the 19th century, with a severe cap that made her look like she had escaped from a strict religious community. Her face was deeply wrinkled and heavily tanned; her eyes were dull and covered with thick cataracts, causing her to squint at sets of small, white objects that she had recently cast onto the highly polished wooden table before her.

The older woman's fingers were bent and badly misshapen with arthritis, and her palms were deeply lacerated by self-inflicted knife wounds caused by a six-inch, black-handled,

---

[300] A Montecristo, Linea 1935 Maltes.

thin ritual blade[301]. Having completed its task, the knife now rested beside the woman and awaited a lengthy ritual cleansing that would have to follow this ceremonial reading.

The palms of the older woman's hands copiously leaked her blood. She deliberately spread the dark red liquid over each small white object that she pulled from a tanned leather bag after shaking the bag vigorously. While performing this strange operation, she sang in an unknown tongue filled with harsh, biting, guttural sounds.

Her hands shook the bag once more and withdrew another white object that she covered with her blood before casting it to the table top, where it settled amongst the others. Up close, one could see that the small, white, blood-covered items were bones, each carved with strange ancient symbols from an obscure alphabet[302].

The men looked expectantly at her as she pulled another bone from the leather bag, which, now it was in her bloody palm, could be seen to have a close resemblance to the size and shape of her own fingers[303]. After rubbing more of her blood onto the bone, the older woman examined the symbol carved on it before casting it over the scattering of similar bloody bones that filled the centre of the mahogany table before them.

The older woman looked at the three men and announced,

---

[301] The classical Magical bladed weapon is called the Athame, but in modern Magic the ritual blade is seldom used to draw blood or cut flesh. This runic divination is clearly derived from a much older ceremonial form of magic with more blood thirsty inclinations.

[302] These cryptic symbols look similar to the Elder Futhark runes, first used around 150 AD,

[303] These blood runes are, traditionally made from the finger bones of previous seers (magical practitioners) who performed the same ceremony in ages past.

"Tiwaz. Extreme violence."

The older man sighed,

"Yes, but with what outcome?"

The old woman shook the leather bag and pulled another rune before announcing,

"Todesrune. Death."

But, after casting the blood-soaked human finger bone to the table top, she gasped and looked shocked.

At her exclamation, the three men leaned further forward and demanded to know what she had seen, but the older woman was afraid of the men's reaction. She simply stated,

"Wolfsangel. A ferocious wolf is about to take its prey."

The three men looked amused,

"Yes, we know, there are two such... wolves approaching their prey."

Back at Horseferry House, Sinclair's wait was over. The unlocked door burst open, and two men thrust their way into the room, armed with the same black, metal, full-framed pistols fitted with the odd-looking square suppressors (silencers) that Sinclair had seen used efficiently down at the street below. Then there were two loud clicks, and Sinclair felt a violent and overwhelming blow to the centre of her back, between her shoulder blades, followed almost instantly by excruciating pain as she was thrown forwards to the floor. Her body, partially hidden behind her desk, was motionless. The silence in the room was only broken by the sounds of sobbing from the nearby bathroom. The gunman who had shot Sinclair declared,

"Despejado." (Clear)

into his throat microphone.

Back in the oak-panelled private room located in the luxurious gentleman's club, the older man had now joined the two younger ones by moving forward and sitting on the edge of the rich brown leather chesterfield. He motioned for the younger man to his left to hand him the microphone from the Bosch radio receiver. Once it was in his hand, he barked a command,

"Confirmar fallecida" (confirm deceased).

The gunman nodded and, holstering his gun, removed a smaller iPhone and walked around Sinclair's desk to take photographic proof that the hit[304] had been successfully completed. The second gun man, who continued to hold his gun ready in preparation for use, moved silently into Sinclair's bedroom to locate the source of the sobbing that continued unabated.

---

[304] A professional assassination is often termed a "hit".

14 CONGREGATA DE ANIMA CONDEMNABITUR

(Gathering of a damned soul)

"Beware of false prophets, who come to you in sheep's clothing, but inwardly they are ravenous wolves." - Matthew 7:15, New King James Version (NKJV) Bible.

Upper Floor,
Former Deliverance Unit Building,
Via del Pellegrino,
00120 Città del Vaticano, Vatican City.
Rome.

18:21HRS (GMT+2), 8th Sept, Present day

Moments after Cardinal Regio had descended to the ground floor, accompanied by Sister Christina and his official Vatican driver, Father Thomas O'Neill exited from Venchencho's old office. With his soaked shoes marking each step with a distinctive slopping sound, he turned left and walked along the narrow upper floor landing to the single glazed, cast iron, white framed, double window that faced out over the del Pellegrino access road.

As the rain lashed against the glass panes, O'Neill watched the Vatican driver open an LV[305] branded umbrella and escort Regio to a large black seven series BMW limousine that had been left parked in Via del Pellegrino with its headlights on, its windscreen wipers and engine running. It was noticeable that Sister Christina precisely matched the Cardinal's slow pace, following six paces behind Regio, even in the torrential rain, like some figure from feudal Japan.

After the Cardinal had entered the luxurious rear of the vehicle, the driver placed the now soaking umbrella in the

---

[305] Louis Vuitton

car's boot while Sister Christina walked to the front passenger door. Before entering, it was noticeable that she looked up directly at O'Neill and gave a knowing smile before getting into the front seat.

Immediately after the large BMW had driven away, towards the main thoroughfare of Via Sant' Anna, O'Neill hurried down the stairs and out of the building, over to Venchencho's ancient black Mercedes. Thanks to the heavy rain over the past hour, the old car had lost much of the accumulated dust and grime on its bodywork.

On entering the driver's seat, O'Neill was greeted by a muffled meow from the wet cardboard box that rested on the thick velour covered rear seats. Thankfully, the fifty-year-old car started the first time. O'Neill cranked the ventilation up to try and overcome the pungent smell of stale Turkish Cigarettes that permeated every surface of the old car's interior. Even if the ventilation failed to remove the odour, it did, at least, quickly clear the condensation that had formed on the front and side windows. The two enormous windscreen wipers made easy work of the heavy rain. Thanks to the large windows in the old car and the excellent street lighting within Vatican City, O'Neill followed Regio's BMW without turning on his headlights and risking giving away his position.

As he thought about Regio's outright dismissal of everything related to supernatural phenomena and the role of Christ in salvation, O'Neill grew more convinced that something did not quite add up. But he wanted to see what Regio and Christina were up to before deciding what he should do next.

The cat gave a soft chirping noise that sounded for all the world like he agreed with what O'Neill was silently thinking.

"Well, Ezekiel, given what they had in mind for you, it's only natural you would think they are up to no good." O'Neill chuckled and then went quiet as he realised he had started talking to the cat.

O'Neill focused on the task of following the BMW's tail lights some ten yards ahead of him; exiting Via del Pellegrino, he turned right and followed the BMW along Via Sant' Anna, through some high arches in the Lapidary Gallery building before entering a large central courtyard to the South of the Vatican Library. The square, which was usually full of parked cars, was almost empty, as most staff and visitors had hurried home early to escape the worst of the storm that was now raging over the Italian Capital.

Regio's BMW passed beside Fontana del Cortile del Belvedere in the centre of the courtyard, and, following the glow of Regio's brake lights, O'Neill turned left onto Via delle Fondamenta. He kept some ten yards behind, still with his headlights turned off, before coming to a sudden halt as he saw Regio's BMW had stopped outside the Church of Saint Stephen of the Abyssinians. Regio's driver quickly obtained the umbrella from the boot and assisted the Cardinal in meeting a group of clerics who had gathered outside waiting for him. According to the sign displayed beside the road, Regio was due to deliver a Mass at the Church that evening. O'Neill continued to observe if Sister Christina joined the Cardinal, but she remained in the car, clearly anticipating being driven to another destination that evening.

Once the Cardinal had entered the Church, the driver returned to the BMW and drove past the Piazza Santa Marta, continuing in the same direction until it exited through Porta del Perugino at the Southern extreme of the Vatican City walls.

Once outside the relative calm of the Holy See's tiny streets, O'Neill became increasingly concerned that his lack of experience following another vehicle might quickly lead to him losing his quarry.

Deciding it was too late to give up his pursuit now, he turned on his headlights and picked up his pace so he could keep within one or two car lengths from the big BMW. Thankfully, the heavy Rome traffic meant that progress was slow enough for even the most incompetent amateur detective, like O'Neill, to keep up.

The BMW headed East until it arrived at a large open area, where a set of six identical portacabins had been erected in the Coach Parking Janiculum, just off the Rampa del Sangallo. Beside the portacabins were a series of covered folding tables set up as a feeding station for the numerous homeless people who frequent central Rome around Vatican City. The flimsy tarpaulins erected above the food tables offered scant protection from the heavy rain driven by the gusting wind. Three nuns, dressed in black religious habits, were getting soaking wet as they ladled hot food onto paper plates for the long queue of young and old who were seeking a warm meal on this rotten night.

Regio's big BMW drew up beside the row of portacabins, stopping in front of the one furthest away from the food kitchen. Sister Christina exited, waved to some of the homeless who knew her, and walked briskly towards the shelter of the portacabin and entered it.

O'Neill parked the old Mercedes some twenty yards away from the soup kitchen and reflected on what he had seen to his only passenger, who regarded him impassively with a pair of large green eyes from within the cardboard container.

"Well, Ezekiel, I misjudged the two of them. Regio is delivering Mass, and Sister Christina is volunteering at a soup kitchen for the poor and the homeless. You cannot get much more worthwhile than that!"

Unusually, for what was a highly vocal cat, Ezekiel remained silent.

O'Neill was about to restart the Merc and head for his apartment on Vicolo del Giglio when suddenly Ezekiel gave a loud, deep growl that was so intense that it made his box shake on the rear seat.

Looking from the rain-streaked side window of the old Merc, O'Neill could see that a woman had emerged from the same portacabin where Sister Christina had entered a few minutes earlier. But this looked like a radically different person, two inches taller than Christina, with a less angular face and more symmetrical features[306] that made her look like a fashion model.

This newcomer was wearing a plain, grey coloured head scarf and a clear plastic rain coat that revealed that the woman was wearing a knee-length, low cut, black cocktail dress and a matching pair of black high heels with ankle straps that accentuated the shape of her legs.

The unknown figure approached within five yards of the parked Mercedes, prompting Ezekiel to issue a rasping hiss of anger that made O'Neill grateful that the animal was inside the carrying container. As the woman continued walking, the cat's furious outburst eased until it ceased entirely as the figure stood some ten yards away under one of the coach park's numerous flood lights, clearly waiting for someone. Now the stranger was better illuminated, O'Neill could see a strong resemblance between this unknown figure and Sister Christina.

"Yes, it could be her." Admitted O'Neill, before suffering a momentary embarrassment, realising he had started talking with the cat again.

---

[306] According to the ancient Hebrew Book of Enoch the fallen angel named Gader'el taught human females the art of cosmetics. People have been transforming their appearance ever since.

To add to O'Neill's feeling of discomfort, Ezekiel issued an "Mmm" sound as though agreeing.

The woman remained standing in one of the many empty coach parking bays as a red Alfa Romeo Giulia GTA entered the coach park and headed directly for where the unknown female figure was standing. The driver exited the vehicle, revealing that he was a tall, lean male who looked to be in his thirties. He carried himself with that air of supreme arrogance that is so often the hallmark of the "successful" modern businessman.

He was wearing an expensive and well-cut[307], cream coloured linen suit, polarized driving glasses, and leather driving gloves, even though it was an extremely dark and stormy evening. The driver was relieved to see that it was a woman who was waiting to meet him; he loudly exclaimed,

"Che piacere! Sei una bella donna!" (What a delight! You are a beautiful woman!")

He walked around the front of the red sports saloon to the front passenger door and opened it, clearly expecting the woman to accept the implicit invitation. It was too far away for O'Neill to be able to hear what the woman said in response. But it became apparent that this strange woman did not want to be a passive passenger, as she surprised the man, pulling off her headscarf, revealing a mane of cascading, thick, long, blonde hair that reached right to the bottom of her back. The strange woman used the headscarf to wrap around the man's neck, pulling him close to her; then, while laughing, pushed him down into the right-hand front passenger seat and slammed the door. She then strode confidently around to the driver's side, removed her raincoat, cast it to the ground beside the car and hoisted up her cocktail dress, revealing long legs in sheer, black silk

---

[307] Armani

stockings held up with a suspender belt, as she entered the vehicle. If these actions were intended to entice and provoke the driver, it worked; O'Neill could hear him loudly laughing as he exclaimed through the partially open front passenger side window.

"Non avrei mai immaginato che saresti stato così! Adoro gli stiletti!" (Never imagined you would look like this! I love stilettoes!)

Unseen by O'Neill, inside the Alfa, the woman buckled up the man's safety belt while leaving her belt unfastened. She then laughed as she spoke for the first time, using perfect Oxford accented[308] English.

"As do I!"

She raised her skirt to show a thin, double-edged, steel dagger in her stocking top.

The man snickered like a naughty school boy before exclaiming in Italian accented English.

"I am so relieved, I thought this meeting would be filled with terror, but I can see now that we will instead have an evening of sublime pleasures."

He reached towards the woman's exposed right thigh, but instead of caressing silky-smooth skin, he found that the woman had firmly grasped his hand and deliberately dragged his flesh against the razor-sharp blade.

As he felt the acute, stinging pain from the deep cut into the flesh on his palm, he pulled his left hand away and started to feel his rage growing, but that anger stopped when he heard the stunning woman beside him exclaim in a highly sensual, teasing tone,

"Tut... Tut.... No touching..."

---

[308] Also called Received Pronunciation.

His anger dispelled; he smiled before sucking the blood from his hand, thinking again that this was another sign of the potential for an exotic, pleasure-filled evening ahead. These thoughts prompted him to enquire,

"What should I call you?"

She ignored the question; instead, she turned the rotating engine mode selector to Dynamic, put the gearbox[309] into drive and placed her right foot hard down on the accelerator.

From where O'Neill was sitting inside the old Merc, he saw the Alfa's low profile, twenty-inch rear wheels spin before the car accelerated away from where it was standing. For a full two minutes, the high-performance[310] vehicle careered around the coach park in a series of wild, high-speed manoeuvres that highlighted the extraordinary skill of the driver in keeping control of the astounding acceleration of the car on the soaking wet tarmac.

Inside the Alfa, the man kept looking nervously at the RPM dial on the dashboard buried well in the red warning zone and repeatedly glanced sideways at the laughing woman beside him as she delighted in exploring the car's ability in the confined space of the coach park. Eventually, he grew concerned about the screaming sound coming from the engine and the growing smell of burning rubber and oil permeating the cabin.

---

[309] An eight-speed ZF automatic transmission.

[310] The enhanced Alfa 2.9 Litre V6 Bi-Turbo engine develops 540 HP, can accelerate from 0 to 60 mph in 3.6 secs and can achieve a top speed of 191 miles per hour.

"Mind the..." He stopped in mid-sentence as he realised that the woman beside him had been deliberately provoking him again.

The woman grinned wickedly, "It will be much easier if you just relax, Luigi. It is not as though you have any alternative."

The man nodded and relaxed back into his seat as the Alfa sped out of the coach park, back onto a small ring road and headed in a Westerly direction.

In the Mercedes, O'Neill started the engine and headed after the red Alfa, making a small prayer as he did,

"God, please keep her below the speed limit. The last thing I need is to be stopped by the Police, driving a stolen car."

The cat made a short mewing sound. But it was unclear if the vocalisation was related to O'Neill's prayer or if the car had started moving again.

Back inside the red Alfa, the striking woman continued to tease her passenger,

"Investment bankers get some nice toys; what else do you have?"

She reached over and grabbed his left wrist and glanced away from the road to see what kind of watch the man was wearing

"No Rolex? Did you get a bad bonus this year or something?" She asked.

The man pulled back his left sleeve and stated proudly,

"It's a *solid gold* Apple watch. A prototype model direct from Cupertino, filled with next year's tech. It monitors my heart and everything. Better than *any* Rolex." The man scrolled his right finger across the tiny watch screen, and the device began to monitor his vitals. When the car came to the next traffic light, the small screen displayed 92 BPM (beats per minute) and a BP (blood pressure) of 125/78[311].

The woman glanced at the display and nodded, "Pulse seems a little elevated." She raised her eyebrows, "Don't tell me you are nervous."

The man nodded, "To be honest, I never thought this day would come. The ten years have passed so quickly."

The woman glanced at the man, "You had everything you desired."

"Yeah, but I never thought. I was young when I agreed. Who thinks that this kind of thing is real."

"It was real." She said firmly, "as you are about to find out."

The man sighed, "Yeah, but it could all just have been chance... you never really know if it's luck or...."

She sounded firm again. "Luigi, let's not play games. Your career went from nowhere to CEO of one of the world's largest investment banks.

You enjoyed the perks! The women especially and beating the odds on your trades. Let's not forget ruining your competitors."

The man smiled, "Yeah, it was good. But surely, I mean, it can go on, can't it?

I did do whatever was asked of me by.... your associates."

She laughed deliciously and provocatively. Her laugh promised unimaginable delights and that anything was possible.

---

[311] The first number is called systolic pressure and is measured after the heart contracts. The second number is called diastolic pressure and is measured before the heart contracts.

Emboldened by her attitude, he said, "The arms shipments, hedge bets against aid investments, forcing the ending of medical care during the Ebola outbreak."

She interjected, "Mmm. Funding those cluster bombs.... even when you knew they would be used on school kids in Yemen. I think that was your high point."

He reacted angrily, "They could have been used for legitimate self-defence!"

She laughed, "Whatever you have to tell yourself to sleep at night."

He turned to the woman and tried appealing to her, "The suffering that I caused must count for something?"

She had little sympathy, "You profited well from every deal."

The man relaxed back into his seat, "Yeah, I suppose. Surely, you can offer an extension? Even just another year? You really don't look like someone who comes to collect when the time is due."

She sighed, "If you are going to prattle on like this, we will have to find something to distract you."

At that moment, the Alfa was stationary, waiting in another of Rome's long, slow-moving queues of traffic. The woman let go of the steering wheel, reached over and appeared to kiss the man seated beside her passionately. Several other motorists in the queued traffic around them approved as they all beeped their horns loudly.

These observers could not see that the man began to convulse in his seat after the embrace, and his breathing became erratic. His eyes glazed over, and blood began to flow from his mouth and nose. His gold smart watch beeped, showing an alert, as his pulse raced to over 160 BMP and his blood pressure reached 178/42.

While the man continued to convulse beside her, the woman began to drive the red Alfa more aggressively, skipping ahead of queues and cutting up other vehicles at junctions.

Up until that moment, O'Neill had been quite successful following the red car, keeping around two car lengths behind and blending into the dense traffic. However, O'Neill was struggling now that they had moved from the Via Aurelia onto the A90, and the Alfa had begun to drive more aggressively. At a major intersection, the red Alfa pulled away, running a red light and causing several cars to execute evasive manoeuvres that were unusual, even for an Italian rush hour.

O'Neill was directly behind the Alfa when it ran the red light, and with great reluctance, he braked and started to come to a halt, mentally accepting that he would have to give up his pursuit. However, instead of stopping behind the red stop light, the old Mercedes engine roared, lurching forward and accelerating rapidly through the intersection, cutting up the other traffic. A police camera flashed, but the wind gusted at that precise moment. The freak gust forced copious amounts of the heavy rain over the flash and into the speed camera lens, hopelessly obscuring what would have been an image of a terrified priest screaming as he sat behind the steering wheel of an old car.

With his dramatically increased speed, O'Neill quickly caught up with the red Alfa and resumed his position some two car lengths behind it. As the old Merc slowed, the engine noise reduced, and O'Neill could hear the VDO branded dashboard clock ticking and a gentle and calming, purring sound emanating from somewhere behind him.

O'Neill settled back into the discipline of following the red sports saloon, and soon they passed signs announcing that they were joining the Circonvallazione Occidentale. This large circular motorway surrounds the metropolitan area of

Rome. Moments later, they passed warning signs reminding drivers that the GRA (Grande Raccordo Anulare) speed limit was 130 kilometres per hour, which was around 79 miles per hour by O'Neill's rough estimation.

Meanwhile, in the red Alfa, the woman was distracted from the road by a persistent electronic buzzing noise that she soon determined was coming from the man's smart watch. She pulled his left arm towards her to read the display.

The heart rate reading fluctuated between 45 and 177 BPM, the blood pressure was 205/120, while the lower portion of the watch's display showed a flashing "AF[312]" alarm.

She let go of the wheel and pulled the man towards her, breathing into his face while exclaiming, "No! No! No! You don't escape *that* easily.... Not yet anyway."

The man's vital signs calmed, and the woman casually let his body collapse back down into his seat. She resumed her focus on driving through the relentlessly heavy rain that caused her windscreen wiper to flash rapidly back and fore. The man's condition must have been a cause for urgency as the woman began to drive even more aggressively, taking the red Alfa to 130MPH.

Back in the following Mercedes, O'Neill looked on in dismay as the taillights of the red Alfa began to move away into the distance, and he was left cruising at the 80MPH speed limit.

A white Fiat 124 Spider sports car streamed past him through the thick waves of surface water on the road, increasing O'Neill's feelings of disillusionment about the injustices of life for those who follow the rules. O'Neill glanced through his left side window and saw that inside the Fiat Spider were two young men wearing Kappa

---

[312] Suggestive of atrial fibrillation (AF).

branded designer tracksuits and Nike baseball caps[313]. The two men had seen the accelerating Alfa and decided it was an ideal opportunity for them to race the red sports saloon.

As they passed O'Neill, the two men laughed and gestured that they thought the priest in the old Merc was a loser by forming the letter L with their hands on their foreheads. O'Neill noted that they had several mounted cameras on their dashboard. Two cams were facing the forward direction of travel, while the other two were directed sideways and back at the two young drivers. The combined video feeds showing their insults to O'Neill were posted to their social media with the hashtags #Stunad[314] #Merc #SadLoser, while their ongoing pursuit of the red sports saloon car was streamed with the hashtag #OwntheAlfa

The white Fiat soon pulled alongside the red Alfa, and the two young men grinned inanely at the beautiful blonde they could see driving beside them. Their feed posted #Bellissimo #Ciccio[315] #Babe alongside blurred images of the woman across the soaking carriageway.

Inside the red Alfa, the woman glanced sideways, waived dismissively with her left hand at the two grinning faces and floored her accelerator, rapidly taking the Alfa to over 150mph. The 140-horsepower engine in the white Fiat was already working at its limit, so the two young men were left venting their frustration to their social media followers with the hashtag #Cheated.

Meanwhile, visibility in the old Mercedes had radically deteriorated with the additional spray being thrown up by having two cars in front. For the second time that evening,

---

[313] Worn backwards, naturally.

[314] Stupid

[315] Honey or Sweet – used in flirting.

O'Neill accepted that he would have to give up his attempt at following the mysterious Sister Christina.

However, at that moment, O'Neill saw a flashing blue and yellow light and heard an emergency siren's distinctive high pitched sound. From a concealed layby, a blue and white police Lamborghini Aventador Polizia[316] launched itself on the highway and started in pursuit of the red Alfa.

In the speeding white Fiat, the two young men reacted with horror, posting the hashtag #Sbirro[317] as their live video stream showed the Lamborghini streak past them.

Inside the police car, the officer who was not driving picked up the two-way radio,

"Alla ricerca di un'Alfa Romeo Giulia GTA rossa" (In pursuit of a red Alfa Romeo Giulia GTA)

Sister Christina glanced in her rear-view mirror in the speeding red car, and calmy noted the flashing lights rapidly gaining on her, even though she continued her acceleration to well over 180MPH. Her eyes reflected the light in some bizarre optical phenomena, like those of a night predator.

She took one hand off the steering wheel and placed her right finger against the razor-sharp blade on her right thigh. As a thin stream of red bubbles of blood emerged from her fingertip, she first inscribed a circle on the car's dark leather dashboard, then added the letters "B" "A" "E" "L" around the circumference. After completing these letters, she drew what looked like an insect in the centre of the circle, with

---

[316] The police version of the super sports car used by the Italian Highway Patrol in Rome. Designed to cope with the problem of speeders in high performance vehicles escaping from police pursuit. The 720HP vehicle can accelerate from 0 to 60 in under 3 seconds and has a theoretical top speed of just under 220MPH.

[317] Pigs – insult about cops or police.

four spindly legs, two below and two above the body. The head of the insect was at the lower part of a segmented body, and the thorax was in the upper part. The two legs above the body had strange feet that looked like the "clubs" symbol from a deck of playing cards, while the lower two legs ended in small transparent circles[318].

Having completed this sigil in her blood, she took a deep breath and began speaking in a rasping inhuman voice that vibrated throughout the entire structure of the car. The sound was so disturbing that even the semi-comatose man beside her moaned in terror and evident discomfort.

"Dominus opem ferre de tenebris servum tuum, abscondere a inimicos suos." (Lord of darkness aid your servant, hide her from her enemies[319])

As she completed this strange evocation, the sky filled with a brilliant flash of lightning, and the air shook with the sound of a monumental clap of thunder that made the Alfa's windows rattle.

During the flash of lightning, the image of Sister Christina reflected in the car mirror was momentarily transformed into an inhuman, scale-covered face with slitted, reptilian eyes. The image only lasted for the lightning flash duration and was instantly replaced by the woman's flawless complexion and high cheek bones.

---

[318] The classic grimoire, the Lesser Key of Solomon (Lemegeton) lists this symbol as the Sigil or summoning sign for the demonic King Bael (Baal), who rules over numerous legions of demons (The Lemegeton says sixty-six while the Sloane MS 3824 mentions 250) and among the many gifts that Baal's can bestow is the ability to evade detection.

[319] From Johann Weyer's (1516–1588) heretical Grimoire, "Principes inferni detractos".

261

After the deafening thunder, the rain intensified, making the spray from the road worse. Even with the Alfa's wipers working at top speed, visibility was less than five yards. Even under these conditions, the woman continued to push the car to its limits, driving with some uncanny awareness or remarkable luck that somehow kept the Alfa within the narrow marked central lane. On the car's instrument panel, the rev meter showed over 7500 rpm, buried well inside the engine's red zone, and the speedometer quivered at 302KPH (188MPH).

Close behind the speeding red Alfa, the blue and white police Lamborghini Aventador suddenly began to aquaplane. Losing traction from its enormous tyres, it began to spin uncontrollably and careered off the carriageway, over the hard shoulder and ended up burying itself in the dense foliage of olive trees planted along the decorative verge on the left side of the motorway.

15 THE EYE OF EXPERIENCE

"Old age and treachery will always beat youth and exuberance." - David Mamet

Top (Sixth) floor Apartment
Horseferry House
Horseferry Road, London, SW1

13.55HRS (GMT+1), 8th Sept, Present Day

Back in Cynthia Sinclair's apartment, the smartly dressed agent continued his progress across the floor, over to where Sinclair's inert body lay behind her elegant, black office desk. The camera app on the agent's phone was ready to confirm his target's identity and mark the culmination of another successful operation for the powerful men, who he knew were listening, coldly evaluating every action.

Prompted by an urgent phone call from Henri Ducal, the doorman at Sinclair's apartment block, Tavish Stewart and Jeffery Sonnet had just completed a hurried search through some locked cabinets. They had placed the two items they had recovered into a small, grey canvas duffel bag[320]. Both men then hurried from the store room, through Stewart's showroom and out into the busy street, towards the Q-Park, underground parking area, nearby.

Less than a mile from where Stewart and Sonnet were hurrying along New Bond Street, the old woman looked again at the blood-soaked runes on the table in front of her. She then examined the faces of the three men who sat

---

320 A Filson duffle bag.

eagerly before her. The arrogance and blood lust was unmistakable in their faces as they anticipated the confirmation of cold-blooded murder.

The older woman feared angering these men. She knew from her own experience that they were cruel and ruthless when they did not get their way or were delivered information that displeased them, which is what she was about to do. But she had a duty to the runes, a responsibility that these men would never understand. It was a duty linked to the ritual spilling of her blood with the runes, making her, in a very literal way, linked to the ancient sacred symbols for eternity.

The older woman looked again at the runes before her before slowly shaking her wrinkled face,

"No, my Lords, the stones see but one predator, and it is clear that it is a manifestation of Lupa[321]; the female Wolf Goddess herself!"

Back in the top floor apartment of Horseferry House, the smartly dressed assassin reached down and pulled Sinclair's body around so that he could photograph her face. The massive holes in the rear of the woman's grey Prada jacket told of the deadly efficiency of the black hand gun that he had recently holstered.

As Sinclair's body was lifted to be rolled onto her back, she suddenly burst into a blur of motion that caught the smartly dressed agent entirely by surprise. Using the existing movement of her body being rotated around, Sinclair's left hand lunged sideways and plunged the long blade from her

---

[321] Lupa, the female Wolf Goddess, who was associated by the Germanic tribes with being responsible for the martial training of the legendary 12th Legion of Rome (Legio duodecima Fulminata - "Thunderbolt Twelfth Legion")

silver, Carrs Georgian letter opener deep under the right knee cap[322] of the man standing above her. Making the most of the instant distraction caused by the pain inflicted by this wound, Sinclair grabbed her attacker's shoulders. She pulled him down to his knees and, moving her body weight, prepared to ram the rear of the man's neck into the metal edge of her desk, intending to cause critical damage to the assassin's spine.

The pain from the unexpected stabbing had momentarily distracted the man. Sadly for Sinclair, the distraction was short-lived, for as Sinclair moved to grab the man's shoulders with both her hands, her guard was dropped, and the agent delivered a rapid, left, right, combination of punches to Sinclair's face. The final, right hook punch impacted cleanly against Sinclair's jaw, temporarily stunning her. As Sinclair shook her head and tried to recover her senses, her would-be assassin searched around on the desktop and, finding the land line phone, dragged it from the desk and wrapped the long plastic cord around Sinclair's throat. Trapping her left wrist in his right hand as he did so, he then began to choke the life from her. Sinclair struggled to break her left hand free and, after a futile attempt to get the fingers of her right hand under the tightening cord around her neck, she searched wildly for anything that could break her from the deadly garotte. She knew this technique would kill her within seconds unless she could take some immediate action.

Searching her attackers' body, she found his waist band and, finally, his gun, which she pulled free and, aiming into the man's groin, pulled the trigger, but nothing happened. She tried again—still nothing.

---

[322] The patella, which protects the anterior articular surface of the knee joint.

Her attacker looked into her puzzled face and smiled.

"Autenticación biométrica." (Biometric recognition)

His words sounded strange, booming, distorted, filling the room, and, Sinclair noticed, the edges of her vision had begun to fade to an indistinct grey. A feeling of profound relaxation began to flow through her. It would have been so easy to surrender to its deadly seduction.

The man cruelly smiled as he could see the life fading from his victim. Finally, relaxing his grip on Sinclair's left wrist, he used both his hands to finish the strangulation of his victim.

Sinclair's world was rapidly fading out of her consciousness, but not enough for her to fail to recognise that her left hand was no longer restrained. Gathering her last reserves of willpower and physical strength, she delivered a simultaneous, double-handed fist strike, with her knuckles, against her attacker's left and right temples[323]. The effect was instantaneous and dramatic; a massive cerebral haemorrhage caused copious blood to flow from her attacker's eyes, nose, ears, and mouth. The strength quickly vanished from his body, leaving him slumped like some grotesque puppet whose strings had suddenly been cut. The man was dead.

Sinclair pulled the tight plastic phone cord from her neck and took some controlled, deep breaths, inhaling each time until her stomach rose before forcing all the air from her lungs with each exhalation. Her vision and senses slowly returned, but she was only too aware that it had been a close call. She reflected that these bastards, whoever they were, were very good. Not many operatives would have continued to fight after receiving such an agonizing knife

---

[323] The vital points known as "Kasumi" in Japanese martial arts.

wound, deep into the knee joint, but this man did and very nearly succeeded.

After the heavy bullet impacts, strangulation and the two brutal blows to her face, Sinclair would have, ideally, taken a few minutes to recuperate. However, she was only too aware of the second armed agent, who was still at large within her apartment and could return at any moment. She needed to move now, to keep any hope of surprise.

Sinclair began a systematic search of the body of her dead assailant to see if there were any weapons that she could make use of when she confronted the other assassin. After wiping most of the excess blood from the earpiece in the dead agent's left ear, Sinclair removed the rest of the wireless throat communication. After quickly wiping the rest of the cable, so it was no longer so bloody, she placed it around her own throat and inserted the earpiece so that she would be aware of any communications. Thankfully the airwaves were silent.

Continuing her search, Sinclair raised her eyebrows as she handled the unusual gun. She could now see a series of flashing optical readers on its grip, uniquely linking it to one user[324]. Unusually, there were no makers marks or serial numbers on the weapon, just an odd symbol that looked like the letter Z placed sideways and with a small line through its middle.

She discovered a quick-release sheath for a knife by the dead man's right ankle. Having depressed a small plastic release tab, she took out a distinctive, black dagger with a

---

[324] An operational technology in guns for situations where it is thought likely that close quarter combat or capture might result in a weapon being used against the operatives or other members of the public.

wicked-looking, seven-inch-long, Japanese style Tanto[325] blade and a composite, high grip handle.

Discarding the strange but useless gun, Sinclair held the knife in a reverse grip, with the long blade concealed up the back of her right arm. She rose silently, steadying herself with her left hand as she stepped around her desk. Her body was noticeably weak after the shock of being hit by the two high-velocity rounds. If that was not bad enough, she also had the trauma of being nearly strangled by the telephone cable. As she reflected on her close brush with death, Sinclair decided she would never dismiss the merits of Kevlar again.

Less than a mile away, in a Southerly direction, a small and somewhat battered, light blue Fiat Fiorino Cargo Van, decorated with Stewart's Antiquarians livery, rapidly emerged from the Cavendish Square underground parking exit, just off Oxford Street. As the small van pushed its way into the heavy traffic that was practically stationary due to the lunchtime rush, Stewart consulted the running timer on his G Shock, clearly frustrated by the urgency of reaching Sinclair and the snail-like pace of the traffic. After less than a minute, it became clear that they would never get to Horseferry House within a reasonable time, even with Sonnet's aggressive driving. Stewart opened his passenger side door and emerged from the small van, searching the two lanes full of traffic. He suddenly smiled as he saw an

---

[325] A Tanto blade has a sharply angled tip that resembles a chisel point. Such blades have little up-sweep (belly) in the main edge and are primarily designed for armour piercing stab attacks, although the straight blade is usually also razor sharp, derived as it is from the design of the classic Japanese Katana sword.

imposing, red motorcycle[326] weaving rapidly through the gaps between the numerous vehicles crammed into Oxford Street. Noting the probable path of the crimson Husqvarna bike, Stewart walked directly in front of it and proceeded to wave the vehicle down, much to the young rider's annoyance. However, what started as a heated exchange, rapidly transformed into something more constructive as the young male courier listened to what Stewart said. Within moments, the leather-clad rider had taken Stewart's G Shock Rangeman and, in return, passed over the still running motorcycle to the Scotsman. Ignoring the offer of the rider's helmet, Stewart immediately mounted the borrowed bike. He drove off at considerable speed in a Westerly direction, weaving expertly between the stationary vehicles. He left the bike's original driver gazing at the rapidly disappearing motorcycle and then at his newly acquired watch. The despatch rider then walked over to the somewhat battered blue delivery van. He sat in the front passenger seat next to Sonnet, anticipating the moment he would be reunited with the courier company's bike.

Meanwhile, a mile away (as the crow flies[327]), in the top floor apartment of Horseferry House, Sinclair's body coordination began to return as she stepped slowly and silently across the carpeted office space and very carefully entered the adjoining bedroom. The apartment's sleeping area was empty, but loud sobbing continued to emanate from the

---

[326] A courier favourite, the Husqvarna Nuda 900. A remodelled parallel twin-cylinder BMW F800 with an additional 100cc engine capacity. This particular machine was adorned with numerous adverts promoting the company who provided the bike to its couriers.

[327] Or a high-speed courier bike ridden with a liberal interpretation of the British highway code.

bathroom. Malone was still alive but not following Sinclair's advice of remaining silent. However, her crying continued to divert the attention of the second assassin, so it was an asset to Sinclair, provided it did not result in the unnecessary death of the female MI5 agent.

Sinclair mentally prepared herself as she slowly approached the entrance to the small bathroom. She could see the form of Malone, lying under a layer of Kevlar in the bath where Sinclair had left her, but there was no sign of the assassin. It was not until Sinclair had entered the bathroom that she saw her attacker in one of the bathroom's wall mirrors. The assassin had concealed himself behind the door and anticipated shooting Sinclair as she entered the enclosed space. The combined length of the seven-inch gun frame and its long, square suppressor provided Sinclair with a large enough target to permit her to execute a powerful, sweeping, reverse blocking kick[328]with her right leg that knocked the gun cleanly from the assassin's hands. The weapon flew into one of the bathroom walls, smashing the patterned ceramic tiles and discharging a round that ricocheted wildly around the small space. The noise caused Malone, who had sat up in the bathtub, to issue a loud whimper and instantly throw herself back down, cowering under her Kevlar coverings.

Sinclair followed up the advantage of her reverse kick and the current motion of her opponent's body as he reached down towards his ankle for his knife, with an upward thrust with the KM2000 blade in her right hand, directed towards the throat of the assassin. However, the deadly trajectory of Sinclair's blade was unexpectedly interrupted by the assassin's right hand, which had adopted one of Okinawan karate's[329] more extreme knife counters—grasping the

---

[328] A variant of Ura Ushiro Mawashi Geri Karate kick.

[329] Kyokushin (極真) Karate.

incoming blade within the palm, ignoring the resulting injury from the weapon's sharp edges.

Sinclair was momentarily surprised by this unusual counter. Looking at the copious blood flowing from the assassin's hand, she became so distracted that she almost failed to see the deadly knife swipe directed towards her throat by her opponent, who, by this time, had drawn his own KM2000. Sinclair had to quickly abandon her own blade so she could pull away and avoid the assassin's knife stroke. As she backed out of the bathroom, Sinclair's bare feet began to slip on the tiled floor that had become slick from the growing pool of blood flowing from the assassin's badly cut hand. Knowing that her smaller physical size, combined with an increasingly slippery floor, would put her at a disadvantage facing a larger opponent in the confined space of the bathroom, Sinclair retreated into the bedroom.

As she ran towards her bed, her feet left a bloody trail of footprints on the grey Wilton carpet. Looking through the mass of clothes that had been casually discarded on the bed by the MI5 agents during their search of her possessions, she grabbed two thin, metal chain belts, one black and the other silver. The belts were designed as evening wear accessories to compliment some of the many cocktail dresses that were part of the dress code required for the numerous formal FCO[330] evening events, but today they would serve a different purpose.

Sinclair's attacker pursued her into the bedroom, now armed with two of the wicked KM2000 blades, one in each hand, although, Sinclair noted, that the assassin's right hand was still copiously bleeding. Sinclair reflected that the wound would be compromising his grip on the knife and probably his dexterity in that hand. Noting this weakness,

---

[330] FCO = Foreign and Commonwealth Office. The UK's diplomatic service.

Sinclair advanced toward her attacker, using the belt buckles on the two chain belts as grips, one in each hand. She started to swing the belts in rapid, circular motions derived from a traditional Japanese knife defence[331]. One chain was rotated horizontally above her head and the other vertically by her right side.

As Sinclair approached even closer, she increased the speed with which she was rotating the belts until the chains were blurs of motion and began to make a sound, not unlike the beating wings of numerous angry insects[332]. Both the assassin and Sinclair seemed frozen in time as they each assessed the other for a brief moment. Then, in a blur of motion that was too fast for the eye to follow, they attacked simultaneously.

The assassin lunged forward with his left leg and swung both his knife blades, held in his left and right hands, in two simultaneous sweeping diagonal slashing motions from the left and right. These moves would have inflicted two deep, deadly cuts to Sinclair's throat. If either stroke had been successful, it would have partially decapitated Sinclair.

For her part, Sinclair engaged with her two rotating chains, so they made contact with and wrapped themselves repeatedly around the assassin's two weapons, exactly where the KM2000 knife hilt was located, between the end of the seven-inch blade and the composite grip handle. Then, before the two chains had completed their motion of wrapping themselves around the hilts, Sinclair pulled the two tightly entangled chains violently outwards with her left and right hands, abruptly halting the assassin's intended

---

[331] Kusari-fundo – a type of metal chain (kusari) normally used with a heavy iron weight (fundo). The adaptation, of using a chain without the heavy weight, being improvised by Sinclair, is part of the curricula from Koga Ha Kurokawa Ryū Heiho Ninjutsu.

[332] Called "Mushi no hane" (insect wings)

knife strokes. Sinclair completed her attack with a loud shout[333] that coincided with her executing a blindingly fast, forward-thrusting kick[334] with her right leg, which buried her right heel into her attacker's solar plexus, just under the assassin's sternum.

The force of the kick caused the assassin's body to bend forward and be lifted bodily off the floor, flying backwards through the bathroom entrance framed behind the killer and, simultaneously, pulled both knife blades violently free from the man's left and right hands. The kick's momentum caused the assassin to impact heavily into the tiled bathroom wall and caused the two knife blades, still wrapped in the belt chains that Sinclair had just released, to fly wildly through the bedroom, smashing into the full-length mirrors in Sinclair's bedroom. The deafening noise of Sinclair's martial shout, combined with the sound of bathroom tiles breaking and the wall mirror shattering, caused the terrified MI5 agent, Malone, to issue a scream before some semblance of silence returned to the apartment.

This exchange took less than a second but left Sinclair breathing heavily and thinking about how best to handle this formidable opponent. Even though he no longer had any weapons, he was younger, taller and stronger than her and would; she had no doubt, be highly skilled in unarmed combat.

Sinclair's momentary martial contemplation was interrupted by the return of the assassin, who strode through the bathroom door with a disconcerting vigour, given the open

---

[333] The shout issued during a Karate technique is called the Kiai (気合). It focuses the mind and spiritual force of the Karate practitioner into the single focus of the technique being executed. The sound can also serve to distract and intimidate the opponent.

[334] Mae Geri Kekomi – thrusting forward kick.

wound on his right hand and the bathroom tile fragments that were now clearly embedded into his shoulders.

At that precise moment, a male voice, with a gentle Edinburgh accent, announced over the wireless communication earpiece in Sinclair's left ear,

"For those listening, your planned ride home is cancelled. Indefinitely."

The sound of the familiar voice gave Sinclair a badly needed morale boost but clearly, Stewart's announcement had the opposite effect on the assassin, as he narrowed his eyes and looked contemptuously towards Sinclair, tearing off his throat microphone and earpiece. He snarled, in a thickly accented English, that exhibited a strong South African dialect instead of the smoother Spanish inflexion that Sinclair had been expecting.

"It will be a great pleasure to klap a fokken gham[335]. When I have finished with you, kaffir bitch, you will finally learn your proper place."

Sinclair did not fully understand all the Afrikaans colloquialisms, but the tone of the voice and the final sentence told her the insulting, racist intent of the message. Good, she reflected, it was always an advantage when an opponent became emotionally distracted from what should be their primary focus. She decided to goad the man further,

"Is that so, and what IS my proper place?"

The man snarled, gestured towards his groin,

---

[335] The assassin is threating to deliver a physical beating (klap) and is making a deeply offensive insult (fokken gham), that is both racist and sexist.

"Just before I finish you, I will show you. Once I am between your thighs, you will see who is Boss!"

Sinclair backed away into the larger space of the main office, remarking as she did,

"Be careful what you wish for, Honey. Be careful what you wish for."

Once in the relatively larger space of the office, Sinclair's body began to move in a series of smooth, flowing motions, almost as if she was warming up for a vigorous dance routine. Her long legs were bent, keeping her body close to the floor. Her movements were a series of swaying motions, back and fore and sideways, across the floor space, her upper body bent forwards, facing towards her attacker, her arms swaying in exaggerated movements[336].

In contrast, the assassin, who had followed Sinclair into the office area, moved very linearly. He headed towards wherever Sinclair was standing and directed a ferocious series of classic Karate punches, kicks and leg sweeps, any one of which would have ended the fight if they had connected with Sinclair. The man was a very skilled martial arts practitioner because his techniques were so fast that they became a single blur of movement that would have required a slow-motion camera to appreciate properly.

Fortunately, for the moment at least, every strike, kick and sweep attempted by the assassin missed Sinclair, as her circular body movements effortlessly evaded the linear motions of her attacker[337]. So far, she had not tried to block any of the numerous attacks directed toward her. Instead, she focused on continuing her strange rhythmic dance,

---

[336] In Brazilian Portuguese such a rocking back and forth technique is called ginga.

[337] Such evasions are called esquivas.

which grew in intensity, as she performed a sideways cartwheel and a full backward body flip. Her movements looked more and more like a gymnastic display.

The assassin noted her athletic exhibition and grunted,

"Fokking backflips won't help you, kaffir. This is a fokking stryd (fight), not a bloody acrobatic display."

Sinclair was breathless from her exertions but grinned as she spun around. She came close to her opponent, flipping her body as she did so, her right knee making violent contact with the assassin's stomach[338], knocking the breath out of him and physically striking his body backwards, so he staggered. The killer immediately responded with several punches, but Sinclair had already moved away, continuing her strange, swaying dance of the Capoeira martial art. Once she was two body lengths away, she responded,

"But honey, I thought you would enjoy a little slave dance[339]... Before we find out who is Boss."

Infuriated by Sinclair's comment and her apparent refusal to engage in what the assassin regarded as proper combat, he launched into a series of wild, swinging, roundhouse kicks aimed at Sinclair's mid-body. The wild and uncoordinated attack brought the assassin much closer to Sinclair. Sinclair moved beside her attacker in a blur of circular motion, her legs, driven by her whole-body motion, violently sweeping her opponent to the floor[340]. The movement of Sinclair's body naturally carried her over the fallen assassin, so she ended up seated on his chest, her legs instantly wrapping around her attacker's neck.

---

[338] Tesouras (knee strike).

[339] Capoeira is a martial art, developed by African slaves in Brazil in the 16th century. It combines dance, acrobatics, and music.

[340] Rasteiras (leg sweep).

The assassin's eyes went wide in shock as Sinclair gripped the man's neck between her powerful thighs, raising the assailant's skull from his neck, pulling the C1 and C2 vertebras apart. Then, looking coldly into the terrified eyes of the assassin, Sinclair pushed with her right thigh upwards and towards the left. The momentary terror in the assassin's eyes faded as a loud click issued from his neck. His body twitched, went limp and the air became filled with the distasteful aroma of the dead man's evacuated bowels.

Sinclair pulled herself up and off the dead man's body, breathing heavily from her exertions over the past minutes. She wiped her forehead with her jacket sleeve and surveyed the room around her.

Malone, the MI5 agent, was standing in the doorway to the bedroom, stunned. Having watched how Sinclair had dealt with the armed assassin, her voice filled with newfound respect,

"As Fuck!"

Meanwhile, Sinclair had caught sight of her reflection in the full-length mirror behind her apartment's front door and noticed the massive gashes on the back of her grey Prada jacket. She misinterpreted the reason for Malone's exclamation.

"Yeah, the jacket has had it."

Glancing at her Cartier to note the time, Sinclair saw her beloved timepiece had not fared well during the violence of the last few minutes. The glass was shattered, crystal fragments were embedded into the dial, and the hands had become dislodged, presumably now lying on the floor of the apartment. Raising her eyes to Malone, Sinclair saw the dishevelled state of the young MI5 agent. The front of the young woman's shirt was heavily stained with the remains of her breakfast, and her makeup had run badly, tear stains marking her cheeks.

Sinclair walked over to her office drinks cabinet. She took out three cut crystal glasses and a dark bottle adorned with a label showing the picture of a Cockerel[341] standing on an oak barrel. The label read, "St Clair[342], Classic 140 proof, Gold award-winning 170-year-old heritage Jamaican Rum". Sinclair poured three generous measures into the three glasses and handed one to Malone, who took a sip and began coughing loudly.

After the initial shock, Malone noted the subtle tastes of dried apricot, fresh peach and a slight hint of sweet molasses, followed by a deep warmth and relaxation. As Sinclair sipped appreciatively from the second glass, a tall and powerful male figure with short-cropped greying hair and a handsome profile pushed open the apartment's front door.

Sinclair turned to find Stewart carrying an old British Military issued sidearm[343] in his right hand. The Scotsman was breathing rapidly from taking the twelve flights of stairs at considerable speed, but his gun hand was, Sinclair, noted rock steady.

Sinclair remarked to the still shell-shocked Malone,

"Typical man turns up when the work is done,"

---

[341] The emblem of the Sinclair family.

[342] The Sinclair family business in Jamaica.

[343] A Browning Hi-Power, known within the British forces as 'Pistol No 2 Mk 1', it was issued to the Special Operations Executive (SOE), known to its friends as the "Ministry of Ungentlemanly Warfare", during WWII. The weapon is a single-action, semi-automatic handgun, most frequently available to British forces in its 9mm format, it carried a 13-round magazine at a time when most other handguns carried only 8, hence the term, Hi Power.

Before walking over to the Scotsman. She handed him the third glass of rum she had prepared while pulling him close in a tight embrace and whispering,

"Thanks for coming."

After a few long moments, she broke free and gestured towards Malone,

"Does she need to call this in, or are they already downstairs?"

Stewart shook his head while he sipped the strong rum, clearly appreciating the liquor, even if it wasn't his preferred single malt whiskey[344].

"The Met and Five[345] will be up once we confirm this area is clear.[346]"

Stewart looked at the mayhem in the small apartment and then, with concern at the numerous bruises rapidly emerging on Sinclair's face, wiped some of the congealed blood from Sinclair's cheek.

"Not mine," Sinclair said reassuringly and then queried,

"What about the remaining bastard in the black SUV across the street?"

Stewart grimaced,

---

[344] Glenfiddich is Stewart's preferred single Malt, although he has been known to indulge in other brands when times were tough.

[345] MI5. The UK's Security Service.

[346] They were probably conducting a detailed risk assessment.

"Dead, from self-administered poison. SOCO[347] suspect he had a false molar implant modified to contain a lethal dose of cyanide."

Sinclair raised an eyebrow,

"Pity, it would have been good to talk with the bastard. Taking a suicide pill means they must be hiding something big."

"Or they were too proud to permit their capture,"

added Stewart as he knelt beside the body of the dead assassin that lay, spread-eagled, in the centre of the living space.

"We should make the most of being able to search these bodies to find our clues before this place becomes a designated crime scene and we lose access."

Stewart commenced a detailed and expert search of the assassin's body. The trouser pockets were empty, but the dead man's jacket pockets revealed a leather wallet[348] containing over a thousand South African Rand, mostly in 200-Rand notes and a folded piece of thick card that Stewart handed to Sinclair while he continued his search of the body.

The only other item was a black dialled, tactical chronograph with a bead blasted hardened steel case and a rotating aluminium elapsed time bezel. Unusually, the winder and chronograph buttons of the watch were all

---

[347] Scene of Crime Officer, who performs a detailed forensic examination and analysis of a scene of crime.

[348] Carrying any identifying or personal items is a serious breach of operating procedures. Clearly this was an undisciplined member of whatever service he represented.

located on the left side of the case. The stopwatch was still running and showed twelve minutes elapsed.

Stewart removed the watch and looked carefully at the dial and case back,

"Sterile, no branding whatsoever, only a single character, printed on the dial and etched on the case back."

Sinclair nodded,

"Yes, I noticed the same symbol on their weapons, knife and the gun. It looks like a sideways letter Z with a bar through the centre[349]."

Stewart nodded and placed the curious watch in his shirt pocket,

"At least we have something to help trace them."

Sinclair unfolded the piece of cardboard that had been inside the man's wallet. It was a gilt-edged invitation with deeply embossed gold text, admitting the holder, and one guest, to an event at seven pm that evening at the Wigmore Hall in London.

Sinclair showed the fancy invitation to Stewart, who looked at the dead body beside him and remarked,

"Guess they won't be going to the ball," then he grinned mischievously at Sinclair, "but I know someone who will...."

---

[349] The ancient Germanic rune, Wolfsangel or Wolfhook.

16 SEARCHING FOR CLUES

"It is a capital mistake to theorize before one has data. Insensibly one begins to twist facts to suit theories, instead of theories to suit facts." — Arthur Conan Doyle, A Scandal in Bohemia.

Stewart's Antiquarians,
18a, New Bond St, Mayfair,
London W1S 2RB

15.00HRS (GMT+1), 8th Sept, Present day

What had started as a perfect summer's day, with clear blue skies, turned increasingly cloudy by mid-afternoon. The light blue firmament transformed to a miserable slate grey, and a fine, penetrating drizzle started to cascade from the London sky. After the excitement at Horseferry House, Stewart made sure the dispatch rider was safely reunited with his beloved Husqvarna before he and Sinclair crammed into the wide bench seat in the front of the old Fiat Fiorino. With Sonnet at the wheel, they slowly worked their way through the thick afternoon traffic to return to Stewart's showroom in New Bond Street.

Later, in the upstairs office, Sinclair updated the assembled friends[350] with the information she had acquired about "La Cuarta República" from her mentor, Fredrick Richards, at the FCO earlier that morning. At the end of her expert summary

---

[350] Tavish Stewart, Jeffery Sonnet and Cynthia Sinclair were physically in the office kitchen, while Helen Curren sat in her office and Mohammed Sek in his villa in Istanbul. Both participated via a large black Betron speaker that was placed strategically on the office kitchen table, while John and Julie, who had been working in the showroom that morning, resumed running the business downstairs.

of the group's takeover of sections of the South American nation, Mohammed Sek's booming baritone came over the speakerphone.

"Interesting, Sin. I know something of influencing governments...."

Sinclair, Sonnet and Stewart smiled at their friend's understatement. Sek was a larger-than-life character who usually ran the Istanbul showroom and routinely used his extraordinary political and social influence to acquire rare antiquities that would be utterly unobtainable to anyone else.

"... it would take more than just vast sums of money to buy a section of a sovereign nation and declare it as your independent republic. We are talking about combinations of close social ties with important key players and, more importantly, fear. Considerable amounts of fear."

Sinclair nodded her agreement, "Yes, and such fear is almost always associated with demonstrations of force combined with unusual degrees of violence."

Helen Curren was less convinced,

"But what kind of power could a small breakaway republic possess that would frighten the Argentinian government and its people? The Argentinian army is hardly a pushover."

Stewart intervened, "Well, there were some pretty ruthless characters at Horseferry House this morning, and I don't think they were visiting by accident. The whole incident looked extremely well planned." Stewart nodded towards Sinclair. "As Cynthia can attest."

With her usual modesty, Sinclair downplayed her handling of the well-coordinated assassination attempt that had caused Stewart and Sonnet to abandon their plans for an afternoon of information gathering and instead rush across London to Horseferry House.

Therefore, it was Stewart who provided the group with a detailed assessment of the meticulous planning that must have gone into the attempted assassination. After Stewart had finished, Sonnet was becoming increasingly angry.

"The bastards who planned this must have had the active collaboration of the Security Services[351]!"

"Yes, again, that brings us back to the considerable influence possessed by this group. But what links could a small group from South America have with the highest levels of the British Government?" Queried Sek, whose booming voice dominated the conversation even from the small speakerphone in the centre of the wooden kitchen table.

Sonnet had already assigned blame,

"It has to be that slimy bastard Twiffers[352]! He complained about Cynthia's action against the attempted attack on The Palace[353] in The House[354] this morning, and only he would have sufficient political clout to have Five[355] arrest Cynthia!"

"Suspend, detain and disarm were the exact orders." Clarified Curren over the speakerphone from her office at The Temple[356]. "And for such a directive to be actioned

---

[351] The British domestic intelligence and security service, MI5.

[352] Home Secretary, Sir Reginald Twiffers.

[353] Buckingham Palace.

[354] The Houses of Parliament.

[355] Another reference to the Security Service, MI5.

[356] The Temple refers to an area of central London located near Temple Church. It is one of the main legal districts for English Law.

against the head of SIS, the order would have been sanctioned by Number 10[357]."

"The intent was the same," responded Sonnet, "But what influence could these people have on Twiffers or Susan Merriweather?"

Sinclair smiled, "Well, rumour has it that our beloved PM has developed quite a fondness for a certain Argentinean Polo player, Edwardo Salvador,"

Curren sighed loudly over the speakerphone, clearly indicating her approval of Merriweather's choice of lover and causing Stewart and Sinclair to smile. However, the humour was not shared by Sonnet. He clearly preferred Curren to keep her romantic attentions focused elsewhere[358].

"... and with other "products" from South America."

"Nose Candy?" Asked Sek.

"Indeed, her habit is for "Columbian pure"[359], by all accounts," clarified Sinclair, "A habit, incidentally, shared by most of the rich and powerful in London. Why do you think there have been such massive reductions in police numbers and an increase in the illegal drug supply and consumption?"

---

[357] The Prime Minister's office, at 10 Downing Street.

[358] Sonnet and Curren have had an on/off relationship ever since they shared captivity in Crete.

[359] The term "Columbian pure" does not, in fact denote 100% uncut cocaine, as such purity is impractical for mass production and would cause too much mortality among users. It is more profitable to sell weaker products that encourage increased and prolonged consumption.

"You are telling me the entire government are controlled by their drug habit?" Curren asked incredulously.

Sinclair laughed. "No, but the best-kept secret within the intelligence community is that, after the whammies of the subprime banking crisis, the COVID pandemic, the Russian invasion and, most recently, Ad-Dajjal's global blackmail, we came close to the collapse of our Western way of life.

We came so close to the complete collapse of capitalism[360] that, in utter desperation, governments worldwide accepted lines of credit from the largest organised crime syndicates, including the major drug cartels, many of whom originate in or around our suspiciously powerful New Republic. It occurs to me that this might be part of the answer to how such a small group could weald such immense influence."

"That and having teams of highly-trained killers." Added Sek, darkly.

"Yes, we can all attest to that, with the commando-style kidnappings across Europe, the attacks on London's streets this morning and the Horseferry House assassination attempt. But that still begs the question, why would such a powerful group want to kidnap the heirs to the European Royal houses?" Stewart's question brought the group's discussion to the most relevant key issue.

"Are there any clues from the physical evidence left after the attack on Cynthia this morning?" asked Sek, his voice again booming from the speaker.

Stewart briefly described the items he and Sinclair had discovered on the dead bodies of the assassins. Namely, the wallet contents linking at least one of the men to South Africa, the false molar cyanide suicide pill, the mysterious

---

[360] Fiat currency, consumerism and the principle that economic growth is the only acceptable measure for a society to be judged a success.

symbol engraved on many of the items of equipment used by the assassins and, finally, the folded gilt embossed, formal invitation to an event, scheduled for that evening at the Wigmore Hall.

Sonnet picked up the knife that Sinclair had brought with her and scanned a picture of the dagger and the mysterious symbol etched on the distinctive black, seven-inch blade on his phone, sending it to Sek's and Curren's mobile numbers. The sounds of the texts arriving echoed from the speaker in the centre of the kitchen table.

Sek's voice immediately responded upon seeing the picture, "That blade is a customised variant of the KM2000[361] combat knife," After a long pause, he added, "But I am sorry to say that the symbol is completely unknown to me."

Not to be outdone, Sonnet decided to add his expert insight based on his well-known love of wristwatches. "I am also at a loss concerning the symbol, but I think I recognise the watch. It is a modified version of a military mission timer[362], manufactured by Sinn of Frankfurt."

Sonnet handled the chronograph, testing the two left-sided pusher buttons, setting the sweeping red-tipped seconds hand running before stopping the mechanism and resetting it.

---

[361] The NATO approved KM2000 is a Military tactical dagger with a 6.7 Inch blade and a weight of 11 ounces. The KM stands for Kampfmesser or "combat knife". It is manufactured in Germany by Eickhorn-Solingen.

[362] A custom-made variant of the Sinn EZM 1 (Einsatzzeitmesser means "mission timer" in German), designed specifically for use by elite commando units within the German federal forces. The watch has also been widely adopted by other special forces units around the world.

"A very nice piece of kit. Better than the cheap watches issued to our troops. Clearly, no expense was spared when equipping these murderous bastards."

Stewart chipped in, "I can continue, what is becoming a theme regarding where their equipment was sourced. These assassins' pistols were highly modified Glocks[363], complete with a very fancy biometric recognition system, built into the grip."

Curren laughed. "While you boys were appreciating the assassin's toys, I tried a reverse image google search on my phone that showed that the mysterious symbol is a Viking rune, called "Wolfhook" or "Wolfsangel". Wikipedia says its meaning is Liberty and Independence."

There was a long pause while everyone thought about the implications. It was Sek who responded first.

"Vikings? In South America? What kind of nonsense is this?"

"Maybe not that far-fetched, Mohammed," countered Stewart, "One group springs to mind, who were renowned for suicide pills, superlative equipment for their operatives and an obsession with runic symbols."

"Neo-Nazis? Surely you are joking!" Sonnet looked incredulous.

Sinclair looked at Stewart, "Actually, I thought the same, T. I was just reluctant to propose it. But why would Neo Nazis want to kidnap the heirs to the European royal lines?"

In the background, Sek could be heard remarking, "At least they will make a change from that bloody insidious Maelstrom and all that occult mumbo jumbo."

---

[363] A highly modified variant of the Glock 17, a full framed handgun designed by the Austrian manufacturer, Glock Ges.

Although everyone ignored Sek's comment, they all shared the sentiment, especially Stewart, who, since the recent adventure, had been predicting Maelstrom's return with a regularity bordering on the obsessive.

"Well," Sonnet speculated, "The original Nazis were fixated about blood lines. Maybe the Royal blood lines are something they want?"

"Maybe." Stewart did not sound convinced, "The only way we will find out for sure is to use this fancy invitation." Picking up the gold embossed card that they had recovered from the dead assassin at Sinclair's apartment, he read out the bottom line "Dress code: Black tie or mess dress uniform for gentlemen and gowns for Ladies." Looking at Sinclair, who was wearing a well-worn sweat top and bottoms adorned with a large, blue Pelican[364], he announced, "I think it is time we both visited Selfridges and explored their formal attire rental service."

One thousand one hundred miles to the South East of Stewart's London showroom, two glistening glass and steel wonders of modern technology[365] flew, almost silently, in a close formation together, like two giant dragonflies. They flew across the sloping Montenegrin hillside, leading to Lake Skadar's sparkling blue waters.

As the two aircraft reached closer to the lake's edge, they swooped down, accelerating to over 170 knots, skimming

---

[364] The University of the West Indies (UWI), whose mascot is a pelican.

[365] Two AS365 DAUPHIN N2 Airbus Helicopters. Their twin Turbomeca Arriel 1C2 turboshaft engines make these amongst the quietest executive class helicopters. They can carry 8 passengers in extraordinary comfort and carry extensive luggage, or in this situation, assorted ritual paraphernalia.

just yards above fields of lush, toad green foliage that formed the region's best vineyards, famous for their dry, red, Vranac wine.

Inside the two speeding aircraft, apart from the pilots, were ten excited men and women of various ages and ethnicities. Their only shared characteristic was a deep interest in matters of an esoteric nature. They had passed a stringent global selection process from thousands of applicants who had a proven, serious, long-term interest in the occult, its alleged secret powers and hidden mysteries.

They had been recruited from online esoteric groups and various physical societies devoted to spiritual and metaphysical studies around the world, all affiliated in some way or another with the International Society for the Furtherance of Esoteric Traditions (ISFET). At the termination of a brief, but fierce competition, involving examinations based on occult theory and metaphysical lore, were face to face interviews in their respective nation's capital cities. This selection culminated in these select few being mentored by the most respected initiates available at their respective Nation's premier lodges devoted to the Western Esoteric Tradition (WET). Such was the influence of those who had organised this highly unusual competition that the successful candidates embarked on a highly accelerated schedule through the numerous initiations[366] required to make them amongst the highest ranked adepts. This process made them eligible to receive, as was promised in the selection advertisement, "some special mark of recognition on their progress".

---

[366] Including the five Outer Order grades, from Neophyte to Philosophus and then through the three grades of the second order, Adeptus Minor, Adeptus Major, through to the exalted rank of Adeptus Exemptus.

Those who completed this extraordinarily accelerated initiatory process had first-class transportation from their homes to an exclusive resort in Switzerland's Bernese Alps, which was the central collection hub for these extraordinary individuals. Once they had assembled and one of the planners who had coordinated the initiative arrived, the combined group of eleven moved to a nearby Swiss airport[367]. At noon, two executive helicopters had taken the group up, over the snow-capped Alps and in a South Easterly direction for a six-hour flight, requiring no less than three refuelling stops, before finally approaching their long-awaited, secret destination.

For each of the ten newly created, high-ranking initiates, this flight was the culmination of a lifetime's search that promised to fulfil an enduring desire. At midnight, on the thirteenth of September, which would be precisely one week before the autumnal equinox, they had been promised to be shown the real inner secrets of the mysteries in a ceremony performed by three of the highest-grade initiates of the Western Esoteric Tradition. The event was promoted as providing a revelation that would answer any doubts about the objective reality of so-called hidden powers and would change them forever.

In light of these promised outcomes, the applicants had been told that their existence would be so radically transformed that they would not be able to return to their former lives. Therefore, each of them had made arrangements to settle their affairs and had signed a strict non-disclosure agreement about the selection procedure and the secret esoteric order to which they would henceforth dedicate their lives.

---

[367] Flughafen Zürich (Zurich Airport: ZRH)

In the cockpits of the two aircraft, the pilots checked their instruments, including their Sinn navigator timepieces[368], before announcing over the aircraft's speakers that they were approaching their final destination. The ten successful applicants immediately stopped their chatter and began to gather their belongings, preparing themselves for whatever excitement would come next.

In contrast, the one other passenger, seated in the lead helicopter's rearmost seat, exuded an icy calm that befitted his status as one of the three highest initiates in one of the world's oldest, continuously operating, esoteric orders. This mysterious master of the magickal arts was a young man in his late twenties who cultivated an image of muscular, physical dominance. He was wearing a long-sleeved leather tunic and matching leather trousers, both handcrafted to resemble traditional warrior dress from eighth or ninth century Scandinavia, but with suitable adjustments for the modern world[369]. This historical theme continued to the thick, black, hand-sewn, hide boots that covered his ankles and feet. This muscular, tattooed man's face was decorated with a long goatee beard waxed into two points and adorned with beads and odd, discarded globules of chewing tobacco. He called himself Magister "Oskar IronHeart", although he had been christened Oscar Pedersen in Kristiansand Cathedral some twenty-eight years earlier in Southern Norway. Magister Ironheart's clothing precluded tie or lapel badges. Instead, mixed amongst the

---

[368] EZM 10 Pilot Chronograph by Sinn Specialist Watches (Sinn Spezialuhren), Frankfurt, Germany.

[369] Such as pockets for essentials such as a knife, chewing tobacco and of course an automatic pistol.

numerous tattoos and piercings[370] that covered his face, arms and torso was a pattern of thick scar tissue, deliberately burnt into the skin of his right hand, depicting a stylised, striking snake with exposed fangs.

Down in the lush green vineyard, beneath the two speeding Eurocopters, stood a large, heavily tanned, middle-aged man, who looked up with some irritation at the two passing aircraft that caused a disturbance to his precious crops, with the violent downdraft from their rotor blades. Pavel Ivanović had invested his life in these fields and their precious vines, protecting them during the harsh winters and ensuring they were watered during the blisteringly dry summer months, as had his father before him.

Ivanović had little time for the "аристократия"[371], who flew in and out from their retreat on the small island in Lake Skadar with annoying regularity. Like all the locals, he tolerated them for the money that they brought into the village economy and, in return, turned a blind eye to their odd behaviour, wild parties, strange hours, and their obsession with privacy.

But these wealthy outsiders were undoubtedly up to something special tonight, with twelve helicopters coming in and out through the day. Ivanović had little doubt that there would be lights and strange noises coming across the lake for the rest of the coming night, as there was so often when large numbers came to visit. He sighed as he walked slowly back to his ancient, two-storey stone farmhouse, with

---

[370] Magister Ironheart had avoided body modifications, such as tongue splitting, as it would interfere with his pronunciation of various esoteric evocations.

[371] Aristocrats or Burzhuaziya (буржуазия) bourgeoisie - Wealthy elite.

its red terracotta roof tiles, located at the vineyard's edge. He braced himself for the terrified reaction of his superstitious wife when he told her to prepare for another sleepless night from "The Castle", as the locals called the small Ottoman fortress on Grmozur Island, just off the coast.

After leaving the lush green of the sloping vineyards of Godinje (Годиње) the two aircraft flew on a North Easterly bearing for around one mile. Their intended destination was finally highlighted by the rays of the setting sun behind them, illuminating the glistening waters of Lake Skadar, around the small island fortress. Having completed their approach, the two Eurocopters circled once around Grmozur Island before coming to a perfect landing on a small floating promontory constructed as a helipad near the Southern end of the island. As twilight descended, the landing site became highlighted by intense lights that made the facility capable of servicing four simultaneous helicopter landings at any time of the day or night.

A group of ten smartly dressed men and women had assembled to meet the helicopters and escort the passengers from the Eurocopters to the stone structure that the vineyard owner, Ivanović, knew as "The Castle" but was known to its residents and guests as "The Temple of the First Light".

The main stone structure, complete with its tower and stone ramparts, had initially been constructed by the Ottomans in the middle of the nineteenth century as a defence to protect one of the most remote edges of their empire. After the decline of the Ottomans in the early twentieth century, its medieval-looking stone towers, halls and walls had rapidly fallen into ruin, as the local community had pillaged the stone works for their building projects. Around ten years ago, a wealthy Swedish national purchased the island from the impoverished regional government as a "spiritual retreat". They began an extensive renovation and reconstruction project, which went on for nearly five years, providing considerable investment in the local economy, which was most welcome in the aftermath of the numerous regional conflicts.

Since that building work finished, the structure had acquired a permanent resident staff of around twenty young men and women recruited through affiliated esoteric organisations from various nations, but notably never from the local regions. It was assumed that this recruitment policy was to ensure the strict privacy of the numerous visitors that came to stay at Grmozur Island and participate in whatever spiritual study was undertaken there. Given the considerable, regular payments the island's owners made to the regional government and law enforcement, no one queried their employment preferences or their somewhat obsessive desire for privacy.

Although, at first sight, the ten people who had assembled near the landing strip appeared very similar, all dressed in oriental style, two-piece, black linen, trouser suits, in fact two distinct groups had gathered to meet the helicopter. Seven of them, who guided the newcomers from the helicopters and helped carry their numerous bags to the nearby fortress gates, had the symbol of a striking snake's head finely embroidered on the left breast of their jackets.

The remaining three operatives wore, what looked at a casual glance, like identical uniforms, except, instead of a striking snake, they had a sideways Z symbol with a bar through its centre embroidered on the left breast of their black linen tunics. These three, one man and two women, stood well apart from each other[372] and appeared, ostensibly, to be focused on observing the perimeter of the landing zone, watching for any movement on the still waters

---

[372] To minimise their vulnerability to an attack.

of the lake. Those with the requisite experience to notice such things would see these three operatives were, in fact, carefully observing the behaviour of the newcomers who were disembarking from the two helicopters. An even more skilled observer would have noticed that these three agents were heavily armed[373]. However, their weapons were discretely obscured from any of the disembarking guests by their body positioning, combined with the carefully planned direction of the lighting around the helicopter landing pads.

While the ten guests were escorted from the floating helipads to the fortress gates, the three, armed operatives waited for the high initiate to disembark from the rear of the lead Eurocopter. These three Wolfsangel agents bowed with considerable deference to the high initiate and then carefully removed three separate magickal items; a gold and jewel-encrusted wand, a long silver knife and a simple gold headband, from inside a special, lead and silk lined storage space behind the rearmost seat of the helicopter. The three magical items were handled with extraordinary care; each wrapped in long reams of newly sewn, red silk before being placed into lined, cedarwood boxes shaped to match each of the three items so closely that they must have been made specifically to contain them.

Once the three precious magical ritual items had been successfully packed into the boxes, Magister "Oskar IronHeart" led the way along a narrow walkway to a large gateway shaped into an extended Cobra's hood. Each of the three, armed guards carried one of the cedar boxes and walked slowly behind their leader into the fortress. Once all four people were inside, two cast iron doors closed, fitting precisely into the gateway's Cobra hood shape and

---

[373] Heckler & Koch UMP - Universale Maschinenpistole (German for "Universal Machine Pistol"). Chambered in a large calibre (.45 ACP) these weapons are regarded as "man stoppers".

revealing two large, highly polished, metal door handles embedded into the gate's ironwork. These two handles, either by design or fortuitous accident, caught the lights from the helipad floodlights and, in the growing twilight, made the entrance look like the head of a venomous snake with glowing eyes.

17 GIVING THE DEVIL HIS DUE

"Hell is empty, all the devils are here." - William
Shakespeare

Circonvallazione Occidentale
(A90, Rome's Circular Highway)
South of Rome,
Italy.

20:04HRS (GMT+2), 8th Sept, Present day

More than two miles behind the crashed police car and
some three miles behind the speeding Alfa, O'Neill
encountered his own problems. Not only had Ezekiel
started making the most dreadful noises, but the headlights
on the old Mercedes had also, inexplicably[374], dimmed some
moments before, dangerously reducing what was already
appalling visibility due to the weather.

Hoping to turn on the old car's fog lights, O'Neill flipped
some of the unlabelled switches that did not match the
other controls on the dashboard. Venchencho had added
these switches[375] over the many years that the old Merc had
served as the Chief Exorcist's official transportation. The
moment that O'Neill flipped the switches, three things
occurred simultaneously. The first was that Ezekiel's terrible
howl of despair abruptly stopped and was replaced by a low
whistling sound that began to be emitted from the engine
and grew in intensity. The second noticeable thing was a
dramatic increase in the car's velocity that violently pushed

---

[374] O'Neill was unaware of the demonic evocation made by Sister
Christina in the speeding red Alfa some miles ahead of him.

[375] Progressively added by Mercedes-AMG over the past decades
at the tuning specialist's headquarters in Affalterbach, Germany.

O'Neill back into the well-worn velour driver's seat. The third was that a small, red AMG[376] symbol illuminated on the car's dashboard.

Whatever enhancements had been made to the Chief Exorcist's vehicle extended to adaptive suspension as the car became noticeably closer to the ground. Simultaneously, discrete active spoilers emerged at the front and rear of the old vehicle, reducing its aerodynamic profile and pushing the car down to increase traction. The whistling sound grew in intensity as the heavily modified, twin-charged[377] seven-litre V8 engine reached 3,500 RPM. At that point, O'Neill suddenly experienced a second violent push back into his seat as bright flames illuminated the road behind the old black Mercedes for some five yards.

The road in front of O'Neill began to blur on either side as his speed continued to increase. The speedometer needle on the VDO dashboard rapidly moved past the highest indicated speed of 260KPH (161MPH) and continued right round the bottom of the dial and up again, finally bouncing against the white plastic tab located at 20KPH that stopped the needle when the car was stationary.

O'Neill's reaction was blind terror, leaving him praying while grasping the large steering wheel so hard that his knuckles became white. Despite O'Neill's terror, the old car seemed quite comfortable at whatever speed it had finally achieved. The rev counter showed 5,500, which was just below the red zone, and the engine temperature hovered below 120 centigrade, again just below the red zone. The only gauge that could eventually become a concern was the fuel

---

[376] "AMG" stands for Aufrecht, Melcher and Großaspach. They are the performance modification division of Mercedes.

[377] Includes both a turbo charger and supercharger on the same engine.

indicator which showed a remarkable gasoline consumption rate.

Ezekiel began to purr loudly as the old Mercedes flew past the two young men in their Fiat Spider, making them feel like they were travelling in the opposite direction at some considerable speed. As the two young men looked in disbelief at the flames spurting from the twin exhausts of the old car, their dash-mounted speed detector flashed "ERR 675 – radar tracking error".

Meanwhile, in the central Rome Polizia Stradale[378] control room, four miles North from where O'Neill was experiencing the enhancements made by AMG to Venchencho's old Mercedes, were two Police officers, dressed in shirt sleeves, seated in front of a bank of large, high definition, radar speed monitors. These screens showed the section of the Circonvallazione Occidentale[379] where the Police Lamborghini had recently announced that it was in pursuit of the red Alfa sports saloon before mysteriously losing control.

The radar screens were currently showing two extraordinarily fast targets[380]. The leading radar signature was being tracked at 190MPH and was assumed to be the red Alfa Romeo, while a second signature had just appeared and had, within seconds, caught up to the speeding Alfa.

The more junior of the two Police officers turned to his superior,

---

[378] Specialist Highway Patrol Police

[379] Rome's ring road motorway, the A90.

[380] In what would have been a #Disappointment to the two attention seeking men in the Fiat Spider they did not warrant interest from the Polizia Stradale.

"Che cazzo è quello?" (What the fuck is that?)

pointing to the second radar signature.

The older, more experienced officer looked closely at the tracking history of the second target before dismissing the query.

"Ignoralo, probabilmente uno di quei caccia Typhoon che volano bassi per far scattare deliberatamente il nostro radar" (Ignore it, probably one of those Typhoon fighters[381] flying low to set off our radar deliberately.)

Six miles[382] South of the Police traffic control room, O'Neill could finally see the rear tail lights from the Alfa. It was slowing down and clearly about to leave the GRA. After watching the Alfa's red brakes lights come on, O'Neill turned off the mysterious switches that had transformed the performance of the old Mercedes. As Sister Christina turned right onto an exit road, O'Neill signalled, using his car's indicators and followed close behind onto the Via della Pisana and then headed East.

Since he was unfamiliar with the area, O'Neill fumbled in his pocket and placed his soaking wet iPhone on a small sill that protruded from under the dashboard and enabled Apple Maps. Although the phone's screen was misted up from O'Neill's recent soaking, it continued to function well enough for O'Neill to find where Sister Christina might be heading.

Once the AMG modifications had been turned off, the old black Mercedes rapidly returned to its former stately pace.

---

[381] The Aeronautica Militare (Italian Air Force) F-2000A Typhoon is a twin-engine, canard delta wing, multirole fighter aircraft.

[382] Yes, well spotted. The Police Radar station *was* four miles away, but that was a few seconds ago.

O'Neill settled back into keeping a reasonable distance behind the red Alfa as it turned right off the main Via della Pisana road and headed South along the tree-lined Vialone di Somaini.

The iPhone showed that they were on the Western edge of the "Riserva Naturale della Tenuta dei Massimi" (The Tenuta dei Massimi Nature Reserve). From the little that O'Neill could see in the darkness of the rain storm, the area was a mix of agricultural land and small coppices of trees and vegetation that had grown alongside the ancient drainage work in the old flood plain for the Tiber River.

There were no street lights or other traffic, so O'Neill turned off his headlights to avoid alerting Sister Christina that he was following her. The darkness under the leafy canopy, combined with the torrential rain, slowed his progress considerably as he struggled to see through the downpour that beat against his windscreen with an intensity that made a mockery of the two enormous windscreen wipers. As O'Neill continued, he frequently lost sight of the tail lights from the red Alfa as it became obscured by thickets of oak and cork trees that littered the edge of the narrow track. After around two miles, the red Alfa turned left, heading deeper into the nature reserve and, a few moments later, O'Neill followed.

As they headed East, the road surface transformed into a rough unmade track that the rain had, in places, transformed into a thick muddy bog, interspersed with large rocky outcrops that were barely passable. Sister Christina drove through all these obstacles with a reckless abandon, indicating she had no interest in preserving the expensive car she was driving. Thankfully, the old Merc had a manually adjustable suspension[383], providing an extra four

---

[383] The adaptive suspension was not an AMG enhancement but came as standard on this S Class.

inches of ground clearance that saved O'Neill from damaging the underside of Venchencho's beloved fifty-year-old car.

After six minutes of slow, torturous driving that was made worse by the pouring rain, the track ahead was illuminated in the red glow of the Alfa's brake lights. O'Neill pulled to a halt some five yards behind, hoping to hide the black Mercedes in the dense shadow cast by a thick oak tree that overhung the narrow track.

He could see inside the red Alfa ahead of him, as the interior lights had gone on, when Sister Christina opened her side door. Aware that the Merc's dashboard might cast some residual light, O'Neill quickly turned off the engine, casting the interior into total darkness only broken by the tritium vials on his MX10 and a glowing pair of eyes peering out from the cat carrying box.

Back at the red Alfa, Sister Christina had exited the car, walked around to the passenger door and, after opening it, lifted out the passenger with an ease that made O'Neill ponder at the Sister's strength. The male passenger appeared to be unconscious as his head lay to one side and his arms and legs swayed as Christina carried him like a rag doll in her arms to a small earthwork. This natural feature comprised five distinctive ridges, each around six feet high, that lay some ten feet to the right from the track where the Alfa had been parked, with its two front doors still open, spilling light over the small track ahead.

O'Neill covered the screen on his iPhone to obscure any cast light and shuddered as he saw that Apple Maps described the area where Christina was depositing the man as "Le dita di Satana" (Satan's Fingers). A web search later, and O'Neill was scanning an article by a local historian titled "*Siti del Sabbat delle streghe in giro per Roma*" (Witches Sabbat sites around Rome). This article claimed this location had hosted the most notorious of the Italian witch sabbats during the sixteenth century[384]. The location had been frequently cited during the witch trials in Val Camonica[385]. During these trials, many of the accused had confessed that Le dita di Satana was a site of pilgrimage for those practising the dark arts throughout Europe and was where they had summoned their Dark Lord to physical manifestation to perform the Osculum Infame[386].

Some twenty feet away, Christina was standing with her arms outstretched above her head, chanting. O'Neill quietly wound down his window but could only catch odd phrases,

"Wə-La taʕel lan lə-nisyon. Wa-Švuq lan ḥovenan. Piṭṭan də-ṣoraḵ hav lan yoməden. Tehəwe raʕuṭaḵ."

What he could hear was deeply disturbing. If O'Neill was correct, he was listening to fragments of the original Lord's prayer in Galilean Aramaic[387], but the prayer was reversed into that blasphemous dark parody that forms part of the black mass.

Behind him, Ezekiel began to hiss loudly, like most cats do when confronted with something they find threatening. O'Neill tried to comfort him before the noise risked attracting Christina's attention,

---

[384] In fact, the location has a much older history, having been a significant site of what were described as "harmful acts of magic" (which were strictly forbidden under the Twelve Tables of Roman Law) mentioned in trials held before Spurius Albinus in 157 BCE and Cornelius Hispanus in 139 BCE.

[385] These witch trials took place in Val Camonica in Eastern Lombardy, Italy, between 1505–1510 and 1518–1521. In total, 110 people were found guilty of witchcraft and executed.

[386] The name of the ritual greeting upon physically meeting with the Dark Lord. The name means The Shameful Kiss, or The Kiss of Shame and involved kissing the anus.

[387] The dialect spoken in the region of Galilee at the time of Christ.

"Shhh, puss. It will be alright. Oh God, if only I could see what she is doing to that poor man."

At the precise moment, Christina ceased her blasphemous sacrament, the storm unleased one of its most violent lightning flashes yet, causing a blinding discharge to fly from the heavens and strike one of the taller oak trees some ten yards ahead of where O'Neill was parked.

As the surrounding area vibrated from the accompanying thunder, the Mercedes suddenly lurched to one side as one of the many small stones under the massive tires settled. The violent motion caused the passenger's side glove compartment to fall open, revealing a packet of Turkish Royal Cigarettes, an old Ronson lighter and a pair of low light field glasses.

O'Neill gazed up, towards the sky, with a silent thanks as he reached for the small Nikon binoculars. A sudden clearing of the clouds caused a break in the heavy rain and allowed O'Neill to see the scene clearly for the first time. Looking through the light intensifying lenses, he could see that Sister Christina had ceased her chanting and was now kneeling on the ground beside the man's prone body. Her low backed, black cocktail dress revealed a lean but well-defined torso with a beautifully detailed tattoo of a hooded snake centred between her shoulder blades. At some point, Christina had removed the long, blonde wig she was wearing and now could be seen to have close-cropped, black hair that was military in its severity and styling.

She had her hands joined together above her head and held a thin, classically shaped dagger whose blade glinted in the moonlight. As O'Neill watched, she loudly shouted the phrase[388],

---

[388] An incantation from the Ephesia Grammata (Ἐφέσια Γράμματα), a collection of fourth century BCE Greek magical formulas.

"Το σκοτάδι απαιτεί αποπληρωμή !" (The darkness demands repayment!)

took the blade in her left hand and inflicted two deep wounds on her right forearm before switching hands to hold the blade in her right hand and inflicting two similar wounds on her left arm. She then dropped the dagger and stood astride the man's prone body and allowed her blood to flow over him.

The silence of this surreal scene was abruptly broken by a piercing scream issued by the man lying beneath Christina. He was clearly in great distress based on the volume of his outcry and the urgency with which he struggled. His escape attempts were forcibly prevented by Sister Christina, who stood astride him, holding her bare right foot onto his chest.

Both figures were suddenly engulfed in flames that entirely consumed the man but left the figure of Sister Christina unscathed. Instead, her image appeared grossly distorted, growing much taller, her limbs becoming more protracted and thinner, ending in misshapen claw-like hands. Her jaw became elongated, almost reptilian, full of long serrated fangs, and her unblinking eyes glowed a malevolent red.

Christina's transformation seemed to be linked, in some uncanny way, to the storm that continued to rage around them. At the moment of her transformation, there was another violent flash of lightning, this time striking directly onto the parked Alfa, causing the red sports saloon to burst into bright flames that brilliantly illuminated the track in all directions, including where the old Merc was parked.

The repeated lightning strikes had also caused the atmosphere to become so supercharged with electrical potential that O'Neill noticed the hairs on his arms and neck rise. Realising that the blaze from the Alfa would reveal his location, O'Neill repeatedly tried to start his engine to make a rapid escape, but the old car was unresponsive. To emphasise O'Neill's desperate situation, Ezekiel started to emit a long and melancholy sounding meow.

O'Neill ignored the cat. Instead, he prepared to open the car door and run for it, but presumably, due to the recent freak electrical surges, the Mercedes' two headlights unexpectedly came on full beam, and its horn sounded. The Merc's twin beam headlights were pointed towards "Le dita di Satana", brilliantly illuminating the unnaturally tall figure standing in flames. At the same time, the old car's horn broke the relative silence of the nature reserve with a deafeningly loud noise.

The hideous figure turned slowly to look at the old Mercedes and strode towards O'Neill, who was paralysed with fear, sitting in the driver's seat. As it got closer, O'Neill could see that the thing towered over the Merc. At first glance, its long arms appeared to be enclosed in loose-fitting sleeves attached to its torso, but, as it approached, O'Neill could see that they were not sleeves. They were thin membranes of skin. The rest of the thing was covered in scales that shimmered beneath thin rippling flames that rose from all over its body.

O'Neill tried again to start the car, but it still refused. Instead, the interior light illuminated the vehicle's interior, showing O'Neill's terrified face peering through the windshield and praying in desperation.

The advancing figure recognised O'Neill and began a series of disgusting noises that were its form of laughter. It stopped its enormous striding walk and placed its claw-like hands on its hips regarding O'Neill and the black Mercedes. After a pause, it addressed him with a deep, rasping, inhuman voice straight from a nightmare.

"Father Thomas O'Neill, still playing at being an exorcist, I see. Well, it is time for you to end that pathetic vocation."

O'Neill tried again to turn the ignition as the figure resumed its slow, menacing approach towards him,

"You've stolen Venchencho's old wreck. Shame it will not start for you...."

With long, three-fingered, claw-like hands, the monster reached down and grabbed the bonnet's front.

"Here, let me help..."

The thing that had once been Sister Christina laughed as it violently rocked the old Mercedes, making O'Neill have to steady himself and causing the cardboard cat container to fall off the rear seat onto the floor, the impact splitting the soaked cardboard. Once the cat pushed his way free from the box, it rushed through the front seats and jumped up on the dashboard.

"Saved that old fur ball as well, I see...." The monstrosity laughed,

The ancient cat's fearless green eyes looked directly at the tall, flaming figure shaking the car. It hackled up its fur and began growling at the top of its small voice, spreading its spit over the inside of the glass as it issued a massive hiss that surprised O'Neill with its intensity.

Unexpectedly, the demon stopped laughing and stepped backwards, looking at its claw-like fingers that were damaged from where it had touched the car. Remembering something that Venchencho had once said to him on their long drive from Rome to Venice, O'Neill whispered,

"Imbued with the Holy Spirit," and patted the old car's steering wheel.

Unfortunately, the hideous creature's retreat was short-lived. It came back to the front of the car but noticeably did not resume touching the bonnet. Instead, it leaned forward and roared back at the hissing cat.

While the old ginger tomcat and massive demon confronted each other in the most unfair contest, Thomas frantically searched inside every storage container in the old car. Opening one of the central compartments by the gear stick, he found Venchencho's green exorcism stole[389], an aspergillum[390] and two bottles, one containing water[391] and the other salt[392].

Having only just left a meeting where his incompetence at exorcism had been highlighted by one of the most senior members of the Church, he ignored these items and instead tried the car's ignition one final time. His enthusiasm to violently turn the key to start the engine made him accidentally nudge one of the door controls with his left elbow, causing the side door to swing open. The demonic creature noticed the error and, stopping its confrontation with Ezekiel, reached its long, spindly right arm over the car, grabbing the door rim firmly with its three claws, keeping it jammed open. Realising that this accident exposed him and the cat to the full wrath of the demon, O'Neill turned towards his fearless companion, who had now turned to face O'Neill with what was a sad expression.

"Sorry, puss. You did well, but I let us down."

The demonic entity began to edge around the car while resisting O'Neill's frantic attempts to close the door again. Sadly, the thing was just too physically strong, and the car door remained open and inviting. As the unholy abomination got closer, the smell of its breath and body became overwhelming. It was a mixture of sulphur and

---

[389] An item of clothing that is derived from the scarf that was used as a symbol of authority by officials of the Roman Empire.

[390] A liturgical implement used to sprinkle holy water.

[391] The Water will have been blessed.

[392] The Salt will have been blessed and exorcised.

decay that was so overpowering that O'Neill began to feel so faint and nauseous that the car's interior felt like it was spinning around. Realising that he had to do something urgently to overcome this foul miasma or he would have no chance of escape, O'Neill's eyes fell upon the packet of Turkish Royal cigarettes. Lighting one with the old Ronson, he inhaled and momentarily found his eyes watering and lungs convulsing before blowing the thick tar laden smoke out into the car.

"Smoking one of Daddy's ciggies in the hope it will make you a man?" Jibed the rough rasping voice before continuing, "Time to beg for that pathetic soul, Thomas. A failure at the end as you were throughout your entire, sad, little life."

O'Neill's anger had been quietly brewing all evening. Outrage had prompted him to intervene and save Venchencho's belongings. It was also anger that prompted him to act entirely out of character and follow Regio and Christina tonight after their meeting.

Sitting, waiting for a hideous death and the prospect of an eternity of damnation while smoking a disgusting cigarette, listening to the insults from an unclean monstrosity, made the simmering anger grow into a burning rage.

It grew stronger with each passing second as he remembered all the negative comments and events he had endured over the past weeks. His loss of reputation. The *ridicule* of his peers. The humiliation of being *dismissed* from the university. The hate letters from former *friends* and even complete strangers. The reaction of the Police to his call at the Fontaine mansion. Being *escorted* onto the delayed train at Geneva. His soaked shabby clothes and, finally, the comments from Cardinal Regio tonight. It was so unfair to endure these humiliations after a life devoted to *always* doing the right things but *always* getting unfair outcomes.

Suddenly, Father Thomas O'Neill, PhD, was filled with a single, focused rage[393]. He picked up Venchencho's green stole along with the other exorcism accoutrements, stormed out of the open car door, and walked towards the hideous demonic creation. Using the thick smoke from the Turkish Royal cigarette to help him cope with the intense stench from the thing's breath, O'Neill was quite *literally* a different man. Taken by surprise by the sudden appearance of the soaking wet priest coming outside the protection of the old Mercedes, the entity took a step backwards before continuing its stream of insults.

"Ah, look at you... Seriously, Father O'Neill, how can any self-respecting devil be expected to show deference to someone who looks as pathetic as you?"

O'Neill put on the green stole and crossed himself. The demon continued,

"Dressing up in borrowed clothes won't help you...."

O'Neill prayed, "Lord God almighty, have mercy on me."

There was a sudden breeze through the trees. The rain stopped, and the clouds cleared, bathing the tree-lined track in the moonlight.

The demon looked more closely at O'Neill, clearly wondering if the change in the weather was related to O'Neill's petition to God. Given O'Neill's reputation, the demon decided it must have been a coincidence and continued undermining the exorcism.

---

[393] Something that his new friend, Madeleine Mathers would have called his *True Will.*

"You don't even have the book[394], do you? You cannot do the sacrament without the right words.... Give up and accept your pathetic fate."

O'Neill thought back to the advice of his Jesuit tutor, Father Simons, at the Georgetown seminary,

"The litany is just a set of phrases... it is the *intent* that God listens to, not fine words."

Still filled with his overpowering rage, O'Neill decided he had nothing to lose by ignoring his preferred Latin rite. Instead, he would improvise.

"O Saint Joseph, whose protection is so great, so strong, so prompt before the throne of God, I place in you all my interests and desires."

O'Neill then directed his attention to the hideous thing that was towering over him,

I, Thomas O'Neill, minister of Christ and the Holy Church, in the name of Jesus Christ, command you, unclean spirit, if you lie hid in the body of this woman created by God, or if you vex her in any way, that immediately you give me some manifest sign of the certainty of your presence in possessing this woman... which in my absence you have been able to accomplish in your accustomed manner."

The monstrosity laughed, gesturing to it's enormous form that made the priest look tiny before it, "If you doubt my reality, then you are a fool."

In a move that surprised the being since it took a step backwards, O'Neill advanced towards the creature, drawing on his foul-tasting cigarette and holding the bottle of salt in his right hand, clearly preparing to scatter the contents towards the demonic form standing directly before him.

---

[394] Rite of Exorcism: The Roman Ritual

The being tilted its hideous head and looked closely at the priest,

"Something about you *has* changed, O'Neill...."

Just then, a small ginger ball of fur rushed out from the Mercedes, assuming the classic, arched sideways attacking stance typical to angry felines the world over. It hissed and spat as it charged straight towards the monstrous form that stood before O'Neill. Unfortunately, the uneven ground caused a deviation in its planned trajectory. The cat collided with O'Neill's left leg when O'Neill was moving his right arm to cast the salt. The exorcised salt flew into the air and landed all over Ezekiel's ginger body. Since some of the salt went into the animal's face, it reacted by abandoning its charge. Instead, the cat shook itself and rolled on the ground around O'Neill. The antics of the animal were the cause of considerable hilarity for the demonic figure, which issued a rasping laugh,

"Even the cat is a liability... Give up. You are both *utterly* pathetic."

O'Neill looked at the cat and suddenly realised that the animal had spread the holy salt in a semi-circular pattern around where O'Neill was standing. He nodded approval of what was an effective wall of protection from the monster he was facing down.

Remarking to himself, "Maybe not such a liability," before addressing the demonic form,

"Why not surrender the body of Sister Christina and leave while you can!"

The creature laughed, more deeply this time,

"You really do not understand anything, do you?"

The thing pointed to a deep knife blade mark on it's chest.

"This woman offered her body and soul freely to us. There is no soul to return."

O'Neill pulled the bottle of holy water from his jacket pocket, where he had deposited it while he was exiting the car, and resumed his improvised exorcism.

"Lord, have mercy. Christ, have mercy. God, the Holy Spirit, have mercy on me.

The hideous voice of the entity screamed, "Stop wasting your fucking time and stop hiding behind that pathetic wall of salt. Come Here!" It pointed to the ground directly in front of it. O'Neill suddenly felt an irrational compulsion to obey.... to walk over and surrender.

O'Neill shook his head,

"I have a better idea. I adjure thee, most evil spirit, by Almighty God, to depart.

In the name of Lord Jesus Christ...."

The monster twisted in what must have been pain before it continued to taunt O'Neill.

"You know you are not a good exorcist. Thankfully, you are the last pathetic one!"

In a move that clearly shocked the monstrosity, as it started to retreat backwards, O'Neill stepped across the protective barrier of salt, remarking as he did.

"Yes, I am the last one. So, think upon this.... Who else would God trust to cast you back to hell?"

O'Neill continued to advance, matching each backward step from the monster with an advance of his own. Not taking his eyes off the abomination, he pulled another Turkish Royal from the packet in his left trouser pocket and lit it to help counter the stench that flowed from the creature. He continued his improvised ritual while smoking.

"I command you, unclean spirit, by the mysteries of the incarnation, passion, resurrection, and ascension of our Lord Jesus Christ, by the descent of the Holy Spirit, by the coming of our Lord for judgment, to obey me to the letter, I who am a minister of God despite my unworthiness. Depart this place and return to your abode for all eternity."

The creature winced again before continuing its attempt to undermine O'Neill.

"You don't even have a candle...."

O'Neill clicked the old Ronson lighter and held it aloft. Some freak, random breeze caught the flame and made it flicker much higher than it had before. In response, the creature hissed in anger. O'Neill continued his advance towards the monstrosity and noticed that Ezekiel was arched up again and advancing sideways beside him, matching O'Neill's pace exactly.

The eight-foot-tall monster before O'Neill had now retreated to where the man's body had been burnt. The demon was now standing within the five earthworks that O'Neill could see closely resembled an outstretched hand.

Pulling out the aspergillum, O'Neill soaked the brush head with the holy water.

The creature saw what O'Neill intended,

"You know the exorcist must bless their own holy water. It is not effective if another has blessed it. Don't waste your time with these ridiculous *toys*."

O'Neill nodded, "That is true, unless...."

He cast the aspergillum, so that drops of water flew in a horizontal path over the monstrosity's body from its left shoulder, over its face, across its chest to the right shoulder. O'Neill then followed up with a second vertical stroke with the soaked brush from the top of the monster's head to its feet, forming the shape of the cross. The thing's body convulsed in agony, and deep burns appeared where the water had made contact.

O'Neill finished his sentence, "Unless... Christ's representative on Earth has blessed it."

At that moment, the storm that had cleared suddenly returned, as there was another bright lightning flash, followed by a clap of thunder that was so powerful that it made the ground feel like it was shaking.

O'Neill continued his improvised ceremony.

"By the power of the Holy Mother of God, depart you foul abomination!"

The shimmering flames surrounding the creature's body suddenly flared, and clearly, the monster could feel them as it convulsed and gasped in pain.

Sensing that the epic struggle was close to its climax, O'Neill pressed on with his improvised ritual.

"By the sword of St. Michael, I command that your infernal master accepts you back into the bottomless pit until the great final day of judgement!"

Suddenly the clear sky above them was darkened by an enormous shadow that fell right over the creature, which looked up and evidently could see something terrible as it screamed and fell quivering to the floor. The darkness created by the shadow in the sky became so intense that it formed an impenetrable black that lingered for a few seconds before clearing. The moon resumed illuminating the area and revealing only a bare patch of burnt soil where the man's charred remains had lain, and the hideous entity had been cowering.

The profound silence that followed was abruptly broken by a large car engine starting. Clearly, the Mercedes' electrical systems had recovered enough residual charge to finally respond to O'Neill's repeated attempts to start the vehicle.

Standing in the empty clearing, O'Neill noticed that his hands were shaking from the excess adrenaline that flowed through his veins. To help calm himself, he lit another Turkish Royal, picked up the purring ball of ginger fur that was wrapping itself around his legs and slowly walked back to the waiting car.

18 ONLY THE STRONGEST

"We do not subscribe to the view that one should feed the hungry, give drink to the thirsty, or clothe the naked... Our objectives are entirely different: We must have a healthy people in order to prevail in the world." — Joseph Goebbels. Reich Minister of Propaganda of Nazi Germany 1933 to 1945.

Wigmore Hall,
36 Wigmore Street,
Marylebone, London W1U 2BP

19:30HRS (GMT+1), 8th Sept, Present day

The fine drizzle that had started in the mid-afternoon had, by evening, become a thick, almost impenetrable fog that obscured visibility down to just a few yards. The sparse lighting along Wigmore Street did little to improve visibility. The brakes and headlights from the slow-moving traffic became reflected into the thick, airborne water vapour, making a mix of blurry reds, whites and bright yellows in the fog. The traffic, which seldom moves rapidly in central London at the best of times, had, this evening, slowed to a snail's pace as a convoy of unimaginably expensive limousines queued from Marylebone Lane onto the A5204[395] to let the great and the good exit from their respective vehicles. The blinding flashes of the cameras from the assembled paparazzi who had gathered around the entrance to the Wigmore Hall, were bright pinpricks of light.

Sandwiched in between the gleaming, waxed splendour of a Maybach S class and a Rolls Royce, Phantom Extended, a humble and, rather grimy, black TX4 London Cab pulled up

---

[395] Known to its friends and locals as Wigmore Street.

outside the floodlit entrance to the world-famous recital hall. The photographers paused from their usual blitz of flash photography as they assessed if the cab had simply lost its way or if it contained some celebrity who had let his chauffeur off for the night. Seeing someone was emerging from the rear of the cab, they fired off some shots, just in case, as a handsome, tall, and healthy-looking middle-aged male emerged from the taxi's rear. This man wore a well fitted, but clearly off the peg, Tom Ford[396], black, Windsor-fit, wool/mohair-blend tuxedo suit over a white cotton dress shirt that complimented his black, Thai silk, bow-tie. He gallantly held the cab door open for his companion, a tall, athletic woman dressed in a full-length, black silk Versace gown, with matching black high heels, scarf and oversized, dark glasses[397].

As the couple walked from the curb, along the length of red carpet towards the entrance of Wigmore Hall, they encountered two, heavily armed security guards. These guards were both dressed in black, oriental style, linen suits, with a distinctive, embroidered symbol made from red silk on the left side of their jackets: a sideways Z character with a bar through its centre. Stewart and Sinclair both noted the symbol and looked pointedly at each other.

"That turns up in the oddest places." Whispered Sinclair as she handed over their invitation and the compulsory inoculation passports required to enter all public gatherings.

---

[396] Stewart's finances prohibited wearing bespoke clothing from his usual and preferred tailor, Ede and Ravenscroft of Chancery Lane, London.

[397] Sinclair wore this unusually modest outfit in order to help hide her bruises from the violence perpetrated against her that morning at her apartment, especially around her neck and her badly swollen, black eye.

"Yes, maybe this will not be a wasted evening after all,"

replied Stewart as he raised his arms and allowed a metal detector wand operated by the security guard nearest to him to be passed over his body. The device emitted a very loud buzz when it passed over Stewart's left wrist.

The security officer gestured for Stewart to raise his sleeve and was surprised to see the customised mission timer recovered from the dead assassin that morning with its distinctive Wolfsangel symbol.

"Let these VIP guests through!"

Shouted the guard to his colleagues. He nodded deferentially to Stewart and Sinclair as he escorted them past the long queue of elegantly dressed people. All were patiently waiting to gain entry into a reception party that was underway inside the hall's foyer.

At first, Stewart and Sinclair thought that the shocked looks from the other guests were because they had skipped the queue. However, as they began to overhear some of the comments, they quickly realised that Sinclair was the source of the people's angry looks and spiteful asides.

An elderly woman, who was wearing a dress with more glitter than a Christmas tree and was showing more wrinkled flesh than a plucked chicken, remarked,

"What are they doing letting someone like *her* into this event?"

Her companion, an elderly gentleman, who was wearing an elaborate array of large, golden coloured medals on the left breast of his mess dress naval uniform, answered,

"Relax, Gertrude. It must be one of the catering staff or some kind of *exotic* entertainer."

As the woman sighed something about falling standards, Sinclair had had enough, stopping abruptly and turning to face the elderly couple.

Stewart quickly stepped up closer and intervened,

"Come on, Sin. They are not worth it. You will not change their prejudice, and don't forget why we are here."

Now that both Sinclair and Stewart were facing directly in front of the elderly couple, the older male companion looked closely at Sinclair, evidently noting the extensive bruising on her arms, neck, and a black eye. These injuries had been less visible while Sinclair faced away from him. He remarked, in a conspiratorial tone, and with an exaggerated wink, to Stewart,

"Good to see you are keeping *her* in check, my man!"

Stewart was about to respond when Sinclair stopped him, saying in an exaggerated accent that came from the rural deep South of the United States.

"You are right, Mister Stewart, Sir. There are so many *superior* people here."

Stewart looked momentarily aghast at the comment, then nodded, realising the intended irony. Taking Sinclair's arm, he turned back to follow the security guard leading them past the waiting queue and towards the reception party.

A small ensemble of musicians located near the stairwell played melodies by Bach and Mozart. Around them were white marble statues of Julius Caesar, Scipio Africanus and Pompeius Magnus and, somewhat incongruously next to them, twentieth-century German military leaders, including Rommel, von Schlieffen and Keitel.

Stewart spent a moment observing the statues. Then he briefly entered the auditorium to appreciate its world-famous decoration in a rich, renaissance style, with marble and alabaster walls and Moira's famous dome, above the stage depicting the Soul of Music. Back in the reception area, beyond the musicians, Sinclair and Stewart were left by the security guard beside a bar area serving a very exclusive selection of drinks. After declining a flute of champagne, poured from an ostentatiously labelled[398] Nebuchadnezzar, Sinclair opted for a speciality cocktail, The Sazerac[399], served by a waiter wearing a badge denoting that he was on loan from the "American Bar at the Savoy". Stewart opted for a speciality single malt whiskey[400], which he sipped appreciatively from a crystal glass as the pair began to explore the event further and mix with the other guests.

Next to the bar were a series of indoor market stalls, each offering speciality snacks from the world's finest eateries and chefs, including St. Erik's Potato chips[401], Dolicious Donut's Donutopia[402] and Berco's Billion Dollar Popcorn[403]. There were some of the world's most exotic desserts for

---

[398] Krug Clos d'Ambonnay, 1995.

[399] A version of an "Old Fashioned" made from the classic brandy Sazerac de Forge from 1857, Pernod Absinthe from the mid twentieth century and bitters from the early twentieth century.

[400] Glenfiddich Janet Sheed Roberts Reserve, 1955.

[401] Created by Swedish chef Pi Le, these handmade potato chips are made from the rarest Nordic ingredients: matsutake mushrooms, truffled seaweed, India Pale Ale wort, crown dill, Leksand onion, and Ammärnas-region almond potatoes.

[402] Sourced from Donutopia in Melbourne, Australia. These donuts boast gold flakes and edible "diamonds".

[403] Sourced from Berco's in Chicago, IL. USA, and made with edible "real gold" popcorn.

those guests with an even sweeter tooth, including Golden Opulence[404] sundaes and Golden Phoenix cupcakes[405].

"There is a shed load of money spent here, T!" Mumbled Sinclair as she consumed some of the golden popcorn. Stewart nodded his agreement at the extravagant displays but declined to sample any of the culinary delights, wanting instead to focus on their information gathering. Stewart nudged the reluctant Sinclair to accompany him as he started towards a group of four people who were standing nearby. All four were dressed in distinctive regional costumes and were deeply engrossed with some shared interest.

"Come on, let's mingle and find out what people discuss."

The Scotsman declared as he walked towards the group of four people who had attracted his curiosity. The first and nearest person in the group was a woman in her fifties, dressed in a blood-red silk Sari[406] that revealed numerous roles of fat around her midsection. The second person in this group was an elderly Tibetan monk dressed in orange robes, and he was wearing a very distinctive red hat[407] over

---

[404] From NYC's Serendipity 3. This treat uses Tahitian vanilla bean ice cream infused with Madagascar vanilla and covered in 23k edible gold leaf.

[405] (with more edible gold) from Bloomsbury's Cupcakes in Dubai.

[406] An Aghoris Shaktis. A Priestess from a little-known tantric sect, called the tama, dedicated to darkness, chaos and destruction. The sect's temple is located within ancient ruins, hidden within the dense forests along the Brahmaputra River, near the town of Mayong, in North Eastern India. A region that is known throughout India as "The Land of Black Magic".

[407] Called a Dugpa (Tibetan 'brug pa) this monk is from the Kagyupa school of Tibetan Buddhism. Early Theosophists referred to this sect as "Brothers of the Shadow" and accused them of practicing some of the darker aspects of Tibetan theurgy.

the top of his shaved head. The third person was a skeletal, middle-aged man in the traditional dress of a Japanese Shinto Priest[408]. The final figure in the group of four was a younger male, dressed in a loose-fitting, full-length tunic woven in a mix of vibrant blues, yellows and greens. This last man had a thick necklace of long, white bones[409] around his neck and wore a leather cowboy hat decorated with long, multicoloured feathers[410] on his head.

As Stewart came closer to the group, he overheard the woman talking to the other three,

"I have missed her presence in my rituals since her passing on the 14[th.]...."

"Truly, a terrible loss to us all." said the South American shaman, shaking his head in a motion that made the feathers in his headpiece wave like a peacock's tail.

"Yes, but in my moments of meditation, I can feel that she has not fully passed..." countered the Shinto priest. He was clearly regarded with respect by the other three in the group, as they immediately deferred to his opinion.

"Then she will still be in bardo[411] and could theoretically return under the correct circumstances." Stated the Monk.

---

[408] Called a Kannushi (神主, "god master"), or shinshoku (神職, "god's employee") this priest/shaman is from the Jishu-Jinja Shrine, in Kyoto. A holy site renowned for the practice of some of Japan's darker spiritual pursuits.

[409] These are usually Pig rib bones. But in this particular case, given the apparent dark nature of the Magickal practitioners gathered here, they could be ribs from another species, one that walks on two legs and has an unusually high opinion of itself.

[410] A South American "Brujo" or Shaman.

[411] Bardo (Tibetan: བར་དོ), antarābhava (Sanskrit), or chūu (Japanese: 中有) is an intermediate state between death and rebirth.

"My sources tell me that the high initiates have tried once and failed. So, Brothers and Sister of ISFET, until they try a second time, we must continue our Great Work without her." The Shinto priest added in a superior tone. The others nodded while the woman queried,

"Speaking of our Great Work, it is soon the dark lunar cycle. Ideal conditions to break open the Ten Gates, so, I understand?" The woman looked to the others to confirm she had correctly calculated the moon's cycle. Getting the confirmation from them, she continued,

"I heard that the masters will use the seal of Caffriel[412] at the Temple of the First Light, so we can all better serve the grand purpose."

The Shinto priest nodded, "Yes, little sister, it must be attempted exactly one week before the equinox and during a dark lunar phase, on the Jewish Sabbath day, in the hour of Saturn, while we are in the sign of Capricorn. A perfect alignment, if they are to successfully summon Dumah[413] and open the ten Qliphothic gates[414]."

"Where would they find ten seventh-degree adepts prepared to stand and open each gate of the Tree of Death?" Asked the young woman, clearly shocked by the prospect of the ceremony.

"Not found... created..." corrected the Shinto priest with a sly expression and then, noticing Stewart, who was by now

---

[412] Caffriel, the angel or intelligence assigned to the planet Saturn in the Heptameron of Pietro d'Abano and the Sepher Razielis

[413] Dumah (Heb. דּוּמָה) is the angel or intelligence with authority over the "wicked dead", in both Rabbinical and Islamic literature.

[414] "The Tree of Death" is the realm of evil termed "Sitra Achra" the "Other Side". The opposite of the holiness and divine balance depicted in the Kabbalah's Tree of Life.

standing close beside them, appeared somewhat startled as he repeatedly looked around the edge of the Scotsman's shoulders and head before remarking,

"Brother, your aura is one of the most unusual I have ever encountered, similar to those who have crossed the abyss[415], but I do not see any initiatory sigils[416]. I sense a mighty entity has recently worked closely with you."

At that precise moment, a loud gong sounded and a male voice issued from several speakers around the reception area, asking the assembled crowds to move into the auditorium. As the four adepts moved away from the Scotsman and towards the 550-seat hall, Stewart replied to the Shinto priest's observation, "You have no idea...."

Meanwhile, Sinclair had had much less luck than Stewart eavesdropping on the various conversations. Every time she approached a group or an individual, they turned away, unwilling to make eye contact with her.

"Snooty buggers would not even acknowledge I existed!" Exclaimed the exasperated Sinclair as she came alongside Stewart, and the pair sauntered towards the auditorium.

---

[415] The initiatory process that takes an Adeptus Exemptus (7th degree adept) through the proposed grade of "Babe of the Abyss" to the most exalted degrees of the inner order; Magister Templi, Magus and Ipsissimus. Traditionally, that is prior to the modern era, such exalted progression was not thought to be possible while still living on the material plane. Modern esoteric orders however take a more liberal view and award these higher degrees with considerable freedom.

[416] A sigil is a symbol used in ritual magic. Traditionally, the term referred to a type of pictorial signature of a nonphysical entity, or, in the case of esoteric orders, the pictorial totem that is, in many ways, a manifestation of that groups "esprit de corps" and linkage to proposed nonphysical hierarchies.

Stewart nodded, "Have you noticed that only certain racial groups are represented amongst these *fine* individuals?" The Scotsman emphasized the word *fine* with considerable irony.

"Yeah, no kidding. It feels like they could all start putting on Klan outfits at any moment! Anyway, I saw you with your group. What did you learn?"

Stewart grimaced, "Remember Mohammed's remark this afternoon about not having more Hocus Pocus? Well, I think he spoke too soon. This lot is batshit crazy about the occult."

"Kwon[417] all over again?" Queried Sinclair.

"They make Kwon look positively normal," Stewart corrected himself, "relatively normal."

When Sinclair and Stewart reached the entrance to the auditorium, they took seats near the twin doors at the very rear of the hall. Upon the stage, there was a small podium on the left side of a long table, where three men sat consulting papers and conferring with each other. Noticing that the auditorium was full of people, the most senior of the three men stood and walked over to the podium. He was a distinguished-looking older man with long silver hair tied in a ponytail. He wore an elegant dark suit that looked to Stewart's experienced eye to exemplify some of Italy's most refined tailoring. This man nodded to an unseen attendant, and a projected image appeared on a screen, set up behind the table on the stage.

The first screen showed that tonight's speaker was also the host of the evening's event, Senor Cortez, who was,

---

[417] Father Kwon is a Roman Catholic priest who was subject to what the Church calls "Extraordinary Influence". This is more popularly known as "demonic possession", although Kwon's case was far more complex.

according to the opening slide, simply "a concerned citizen of the world".

Before beginning his address, Cortez looked around the auditorium, smiling at a few select individuals[418].

"I see so many familiar faces that I am emboldened to omit the usual opening formalities and address you all as friends. Friends, who, I am sure, have noticed the same global decline in standards as I have and will, I hope, share my concerns enough to work with me towards the solution.

What are those concerns, you ask?

Tonight, I want to raise your awareness of a sickness afflicting our global society.

We can all agree that there has been a gradual decline in the standards of the Western Democracies over the past decades.

Crime, productivity, health, and educational standards are worse than they were twenty or thirty years ago.

We have all noticed dramatic increases in violent and antisocial behaviour, combined with a loss of direction and morals in a growing percentage of the population."

There were murmurs of agreement from most of the audience. Cortez continued,

"What is the cause, you may ask?

I propose that it is a consequence of changes in social policy over the past eighty years.

What started as a public good, intended to protect the population from rare moments of misfortune, through ill health, accident or unforeseen circumstances, has slowly

---

[418] It must be noted that the views expressed by Cortez do not represent those of the author.

transformed into something radically different. Successive governments have sought to buy themselves into power by increasing promises of government support and assistance."

There must have been a more neoliberal politician seated in the front row, as there were a few sounds of protest.

Cortez raised his right hand to quell the objections.

"We are among friends, so let's speak plainly. Over the past decades, our leaders have transformed, from statesmen and women, who sought public office to improve society, to career politicians, who seek only the goal of re-election to use their office for their advancement."

There were some more sounds of protest from the front row, but this time Cortez ignored them and continued.

"Politicians quickly realised that the easiest way to win votes was not through well thought out policies that would advance society but through offering incentives. Incentives that would provide such immediate, clear benefits to potential voters that they would vote for whichever party promised the best deal. Such a system rapidly transformed politics so that political parties ceased to have the substantial ideological differences that once prompted them to be formed. The only deciding factor in each successive election was the generosity of payments and support promised by the politicians. This situation rapidly led to ever-increasing numbers of people being financially supported by the State.

A situation with continuously increasing needs for welfare, social care, and health care quickly leads to unsustainable levels of government spending. Such levels of spending mean ever-increasing taxation for an ever-decreasing number of taxpayers because, as voters are actively encouraged to move from productive contribution to passive consumption, there are, by implication, fewer and fewer people paying taxes.

This change soon becomes a vicious cycle. As more and more people base their lifestyle on welfare support, the fewer remaining taxpayers end up paying more and more every year for less and less in terms of service. This outcome is inevitable because the bulk of the tax has to be spent on the ever-growing welfare payments for the majority of the population who no longer contribute.

Public goods, such as libraries, schools, hospitals and centres of higher learning, decline through lack of investment. Roads and infrastructure are allowed to fall into disrepair as there is never enough funding for the endlessly increasing social and welfare care costs."

There were more murmurs of agreement from the audience. Cortez nodded and then increased the pace of his speech, and his arm and body movements became more powerful as he began to whip up the emotions of his audience deliberately.

"Once you start rewarding people for being unproductive, they become more unproductive!

Once you start rewarding people for having children, they produce more children, not because they love them but because they are a source of income.

And, most critically for a society,"

Cortez paused for a more significant impact.

"Once you reward people for being unhealthy, they and their offspring rapidly become increasingly unhealthy!"

There were cheers of agreement from the crowd, who were becoming more and more involved with Cortez's oratory skills.

"This is a process which, within two or three generations, produces a population explosion of weak, unhealthy and helpless individuals, who are, literally, no longer able to think, act or respond without increasing support from the State. They cease to take responsibility for themselves or the consequences of their own decisions.

They make no provision for their own welfare because they no longer have to do so.

They have no ambition for self-development because they no longer have to do so.

They become obsessed with their social rights without considering their corresponding social responsibilities."

There were more cheers of agreement from the audience. Cortez gestured for them to let him continue.

"Some might think such a population are ideal, as they sound easy to control. However, the reality is that such people have lost the ability to perform any useful function since they have lost the motivation and capacity for self-improvement essential for productive, healthy individuals and, more importantly, a healthy society.

Planned or not, the end effect is the same as the eugenics programs that are so politically incorrect to mention now, except these new policies have inverted the goal of improving the species. Instead, they increase weakness, dependence and infirmity."

Shouts of agreement came from around the hall. Some in the crowd shouted, "Alpha!"

Cortez acknowledged the support,

"But this cycle of self-destruction is not unique to our modern civilization. It has happened before with previously developed societies, such as Rome.

When a society reaches a particular stage of affluence, it becomes preoccupied with the concept of increasing fairness, with the promise of social reforms to bring greater prosperity to the majority of people who had been poor.

But what appears to be a just and morally sound policy holds the seeds of the eventual demise of that society.

The reason?"

Cortez paused for dramatic effect.

Now he could see that his oratory had captured his audience's imagination and complete attention; he continued in a loud voice.

"It violates the fundamental laws of nature!

There will always be some who are stronger, faster, and cleverer, and there will always be those who are less able and less gifted.

To try and create equality is to try and obscure and violate the most fundamental principle of nature. There will always be those who are superior and those who are inferior."

A woman near the front of the audience made another protest. However, her outburst was short-lived as she was briskly escorted from the hall. She was accompanied by a single, smartly dressed man, who was some form of bodyguard. He strongly resisted the attempts by three attendants to hold him by his arms and shoulders as he was forcibly escorted from the auditorium.

As the protesting woman, and her bodyguard, passed Stewart and Sinclair at the rear of the hall, Sinclair whispered loudly to Stewart, "That's Merriweather! And I know, the guy, that's Johnston. Head of her security detail."

Sinclair's comment garnered disapproving looks from those sitting nearby. Back on the podium, Cortez waited until the British Prime Minister had left the hall and then continued,

"I am not advocating harsh or vindictive punishments on those who cannot defend themselves. Instead, I propose that we acknowledge a natural law; that forcing equality is misguided. Instead, we should reward ability and discourage irresponsibility.

Fortunately, Britain has leaders who share this vision!"

Cortez gestured to two men, who were seated in the front row. The crowd applauded as the two figures stood and turned towards the audience.

"Twiffers and the opposition leader!" exclaimed Sinclair as she turned to Stewart.

"Yes, it figures that they would be attracted by limitless money and the promise of absolute power." Commented Stewart.

"Traitors..." Sinclair's string of expletives was, thankfully, drowned out by the audience, who had now risen to their feet, applauding and cheering loudly.

Stewart leaned towards Sinclair and gestured towards the door,

"Come on, time to get out of here. Soon, Cortez will have this crowd wearing brown shirts[419] and demanding the implementation of his version of the natural order, where he and his supposedly "genetically superior" followers run things."

Sinclair nodded her agreement. As she walked with Stewart quickly through the nearby doors out of the auditorium, still carrying her unfinished cocktail, she remarked,

---

[419] Stewart is making reference to the Sturmabteilung (SA), literally "Storm Detachment", who were the Nazi Party's original paramilitary wing (before the formation of the Schutzstaffel or SS). The SA were colloquially called Brownshirts (Braunhemden) because of the colour of their uniform's shirts.

"I am just surprised there are no stereotypical representatives of the Aryan Brotherhood[420] wandering around here tonight."

Coming round the right-hand side of the auditorium's doors, Sinclair and Stewart came face to face with two powerfully built men. Both were at least six feet five inches tall, with extremely short, almost white, blond hair, either of whom could have served as body doubles for the nineteen eighties actor and martial artist Dolph Lundgren. These two striking-looking men wore jet black mess dress cavalry uniforms that sported thick, gold braids on their shoulders and numerous, ostentatious, gleaming, golden medals, on their jacket's left breasts. The other distinguishing characteristics of these men were almost identical, deep, duelling scars on their left cheeks.

The two, Nordic-looking giants smiled cruelly at Stewart and Sinclair. They pointed the business ends of two silenced, modified Glock 17s at them[421], gesturing towards an open side exit that led from the foyer and into a small courtyard beside the main length of the auditorium.

As Sinclair and Stewart raised their hands in surrender, Stewart remarked casually to the two Nordic henchmen in front of them.

"We were just wondering how long before you lot showed up."

The two blonde giants ignored Stewart's statement and, instead, gestured again for them to make their way towards the side exit door that led from the foyer area. Stewart increased his pace to close the two-metre distance between

---

[420] A white supremacist movement.

[421] With a biometric recognition system built into the hand grip.

him and the gunmen, but the two operatives were aware of his intentions.

"Keep your distance, both of you. None of your Judo[422] bullshit, or we will drop you both right here!"

Stewart slowed his pace and drew back alongside Sinclair. The pair went through the side door and emerged into a small open space between the buildings, which had been left open to the sky. The two gunmen followed behind them.

Two sizeable black polythene sheets had been placed over the courtyard paving stones, and two bodies were lying, motionless on them. Blood still pulsed, rhythmically and copiously, from large, ugly bullet wounds in the rear of their skulls. Susan Merriweather's sightless eyes stared upwards, her face locked in an expression of shock and surprise, while the face of Johnston, the RaSP[423] bodyguard, was fixed in a grimace of anger and frustration.

As Sinclair and Stewart approached the two bodies, Stewart noted that the gateway, leading from the Northern end of the courtyard through the rear of the Wigmore Hall and out onto Wellbeck Way, was wide open. Out in Wellbeck Way, Stewart could see a large, white Mercedes van[424] was waiting, its headlights on and engine running, clearly ready to clear away the plastic sheeting and its incriminating contents once this final elimination was complete.

Stewart and Sinclair turned towards the two gunmen, and Stewart decided they looked like a "right pair of

---

[422] Stewart's eastern martial practice is, in fact, more closely aligned to Daitō-ryū Aiki-jūjutsu and Kashima Shinden Jikishinkage-ryū than the Olympic sport of Judo.

[423] Royalty and Specialist Protection Command (RaSP).

[424] Mercedes Sprinter 314 L2 AUTO CURTAINSIDE.

muppets[425]", dressed in their flashy uniforms, with golden fringed shoulders and numerous, large gold medals. Stewart decided to name them accordingly; in the Scotsman's imagination, the gunman in front of Sinclair became "Gonzo", while he was blessed by the attention of "Kermit".

Kermit, the blond giant immediately in front of the Scotsman, broke the silence by proclaiming,

"Well, you two old birds have been busy today, but you should have stayed home and had a mug of hot cocoa rather than coming here tonight."

Gonzo, the blond standing in front of Sinclair, interjected.

"Yeah, coming here was a deadly mistake." His redundant comment immediately indicated to both Stewart and Sinclair that he was definitely not the duo's brains.

Kermit sighed at his colleague's rather inept comment and added while pointing with his non-gun hand at Sinclair,

"That bitch is going first as some retribution for our brothers who were murdered at Horseferry House today in that balls up planned by those MI5 operatives. I knew MI5 could never be trusted, but we will repay them in due course. And, as for this old fool of an antique dealer, he has sold his last item of fake Maelstrom memorabilia."

He pointed his weapon directly towards Stewart's forehead,

"You should have minded your own business, old-timer."

Sinclair picked up on one aspect of Kermit's statement,

"Brothers? The corpses on my living room floor did not look very Nordic to me."

---

[425] A colloquial slang term indicating that someone is an idiot.

As Sinclair had anticipated, the man's ego became roused, and he pointed to the now-familiar runic symbol of the Wolfsangel embossed on one of his numerous medals,

"The Brotherhood of the Wolf, bitch."

"Which reminds me," Kermit turned to Stewart, "Throw down the invitation card and that wristwatch you stole from our brother. We don't want to leave such obvious links to our organisation on your bodies when they are discovered in the waste landfill tomorrow."

Stewart made a rapid movement towards his tuxedo jacket pocket but was stopped by the gunman,

"SLOW. Don't get any ideas. Throw them both over there, well away from us." Kermit pointed his non-gun hand to his far right.

The Scotsman slowly removed the gilt invitation card, casting it away and then took off the mission timer watch. It made a distinctive and very expensive sounding noise as it impacted with the stone paving, two metres away from anyone.

Sinclair decided it was time to try another attempt at distraction and pray that these two made a mistake soon.

She looked at Gonzo's face, "Nasty scars, a disappointed lover perhaps?"

"Signs of Valour", said Gonzo proudly.

"Or it shows you could not get out of the way of the blade rapidly enough." Added Stewart, quickly taking up Sinclair's lead.

Kermit snarled, "A simple infantry soldier could never understand the discipline of a true officer's pursuit, such as Mensur[426]. These scars are signs of bravery, just like these,"

He pointed to the mass of large gold medals hanging ostentatiously from his left breast.

"But a stupid foot soldier would not know anything of bravery. I note you do not wear any medals."

Kermit looked pointedly at the empty left side of Stewart's jacket. Stewart played along.

"Alas, my humble bronze cross[427] would look out of place before such ostentatious splendour. What did you get your medals for, by the way? Kidnapping small children, like your Wolf brothers tried to do this morning?"

Gonzo, who had remained silent throughout this exchange, went red with anger. He was clearly about to react and give Sinclair and Stewart the opportunity they had waited for, but, unfortunately, Kermit took the initiative.

"Enough of this time-wasting! We will not give you two the chance to delay your death. Kneel on the edge of the cover, bitch, and join your late Prime Minster...."

Sinclair looked desperately at Stewart, who shrugged,

"Everyone has to go some time, Sin. Can I at least try some of that amazing cocktail you have been raving about all night before it's my turn to face the grim reaper?"

---

[426] Mensur is a formalised duel with the sabre called Akademisches Fechten (Academic fencing). The scars were recognition signs of status and bravery between elite German cavalry officers in the early part of the twentieth century.

[427] If he had worn it, Stewart's medal would have been a very simple Bronze Cross pattée with Crown and Lion Superimposed, with the two-word motto: "For Valour". With medals less is more.

Sinclair looked stunned but regained her composure, saying, "Sure, baby." Before taking a sip herself and handing the now almost empty glass to Stewart. Sinclair then appeared to accept her fate, slowly kneeling on the plastic sheeting near Merriweather so her body would fall beside the dead premier.

Behind her, she heard Stewart, clearly toasting his executioner before taking the last drink.

"Here's blood in your eye!"

Kermit's voice sounded irritated as he responded to the Scotsman, "It's *mud*, you stupid old fool!"

Sinclair mentally prepared herself for the imminent impact of the 9mm round from Gonzo's Glock. It was not how she had imagined her end, but at least it would be quick. There was a sound of breaking glass behind her. Stewart must have cast his finished cocktail to one side. Then the muffled crump of a silenced 9mm round fired from a large calibre pistol filled the small courtyard.

19 THE ENEMY OF MY ENEMY

"The king who is situated anywhere immediately on the circumference of the conqueror's territory is termed the enemy. The king who is likewise situated close to the enemy, but separated from the conqueror only by the enemy, is termed the friend (of the conqueror)." — Kautilya, Arthasastra, 4th century BCE.

Wigmore Hall,
36 Wigmore Street,
Marylebone, London W1U 2BP

21.15HRS (GMT+1), 8th Sept, Present day

Sinclair waited for the violent impact at the rear of her skull that would mark the end of her world. Instead, she felt a powerful, warm blast of air fly past her face, followed by the dreaded sound of the FD917[428] silencer and then, unexpectedly, a mass of hot blood and grey matter that violently sprayed over the plastic sheeting beside her. As Sinclair noted the strong smell of cordite and the classic, metallic, iron smell of human blood filling her nostrils, Gonzo's inert body slumped onto the soaked, black plastic sheeting beside her. There was a small hole at the rear of his skull and a much larger one at the front, which had removed half his face. Sinclair quickly surmised that the gunman had died from a single, point-blank, 9mm hollow-point round to the rear of his head.

Before Sinclair could turn to see what had happened to transform her fortunes, Kermit's dead body fell forward to join Gonzo's. The stem of a broken cocktail glass protruded from his left eye, causing vitreous humour and copious amounts of blood to pulse rhythmically from the deeply

---

[428] Fischer Development FD917 silencer.

impaled prefrontal cortex, joining the already soaked remains of the grey neocortex and skull bone fragments from Gonzo.

Sinclair then heard Stewart's gentle Edinburgh accent casually remark as he leant beside her to examine Kermit's mortal wound,

"No, that is definitely *blood* in your eye."

In the stress of the situation, Sinclair could not help but laugh at the Scotsman's gallows humour as she accepted his assistance to extricate herself from the mass of dead bodies that now lay around her, the relief causing her to issue some rare praise for the Scotsman,

"Even Bond never did that with a martini glass!"

Then, having decided that she did not want to praise Stewart too much, in mock annoyance, she rebuked him.

"But you cut it too bloody fine this time."

Stewart looked at her in mock offence,

"When was the last time you tried to aim a pistol while keeping a dead man's hand on the grip?"

Sinclair embraced Stewart, "Only this morning, baby. But admittedly, you did have the added difficulty of aiming to avoid hitting me!"

Then Sinclair, who was looking more carefully at the ballistic angles that must have been involved in the shot that had killed Gonzo, pulled back and looked into Stewart's face,

"You did *aim* to miss me, didn't you?"

Stewart teased her back, "Sort of.... Anyway, now is not the time for a full mission debriefing. We still need to get the hell out of here before more goosestepping goons appear."

Sinclair nodded and gestured towards the white, canvas sided van that was still visible through the open exit at the North of the small courtyard.

"But there are almost certainly more of them, waiting in that Merc van outside."

Considering their distinct lack of weaponry, Sinclair looked critically at the Glock that still remained in Kermit's dead hand, "We cannot exactly cut off his hand to use the pistol."

"Agreed," said Stewart, adding, now without a smile, as he removed the dagger from the ankle sheath concealed beneath Kermit's right trouser leg and placed the blade in his right jacket pocket,

"It would take too much time, even with the excellent blade on the KM2000. Besides, I would not be surprised if those Biosensors only recognised warm, living tissue. Our best bet will be to get outside and then do what we do best, improvise."

Sinclair nodded her agreement and knelt to search Gonzo's prone body to recover his blade, which she then held in a reverse grip in her right hand, with the black, razor-sharp, seven-inch blade almost entirely concealed by her forearm but ready for use in an instant.

Now they were both armed, they hugged the Eastern side wall of the courtyard[429], moving along its entire length towards the exposed doorway at the North Eastern end of the enclosed space. Having reached the open doors, Stewart leant over and gently removed Sinclair's oversized sunglasses. Using them as a mirror, he checked around the edge of the door frame to view inside the passageway at the rear of the Wigmore Hall building. They were lucky that the corridor was empty. No one was on duty at the

---

[429] To minimise their visibility to any observers looking into the courtyard from the surrounding buildings.

reception desk; presumably, the regular duty staff had been posted elsewhere, so they would not see the "wet team[430]" removing bodies.

Moments later, Sinclair and Stewart emerged through the Wigmore Hall artists' entrance, out into the thick, damp night air on Welbeck Way, at the rear of the world-famous auditorium. The pavement and road glistened from the persistent rain, and the air had a mix of three primary smells, engine oil, stale beer and half-smoked cigarettes discarded by staff who had been taking their breaks at the rear of the building.

Underneath the warm, yellow glow of the sodium street lighting, in the parking bay beside the open entrance, were two young men dressed in grey, City of Westminster, waste collection overalls. Both men held the Glock 17 handguns that Sinclair and Stewart were so familiar with from their previous encounters. However, the pistols were not directed at the Scotsman or Sinclair. Instead, the Glocks were aimed towards two dark figures, positioned on either side of the bonnet of a large saloon car, which was parked so that its full-beam headlights illuminated the two Wolfsangel gunmen and hindered their vision.

While standing outside the artists' entrance, it was challenging to make out much detail about these two silhouetted figures, as the light from the full beams forced even Sinclair, with her darkened sunglasses, to half close her eyes. However, what was visible were the two unmistakable outlines of UZI PROs[431] that were more than a sufficient

---

[430] An intelligence service euphemism used to describe the bloody work of assassination and murder.

[431] UZI PRO Sub-Machine Gun (SMG) manufactured by Elbit Systems Land (formerly Israel Military Industries). Originally in service in 1956, the UZI was adopted as a Close Quarters Battle (CQB) weapon by the Israeli Defense Forces (IDF).

deterrent to halt the planned actions of the two Wolfsangel gunmen, who had been waiting to load Sinclair and Stewart's dead bodies into the rear of the waiting van.

As the Mexican standoff[432] continued, a large, black Volvo 960 stretch limousine pulled alongside the two Uzi carrying figures. The Volvo's rear passenger door opened, causing the car's interior light to spill out over the wet tarmac towards Stewart and Sinclair.

There was a long moment where no one moved or spoke, and then a heavily accented but disembodied voice called out from inside the car,

"You two can join me inside here or inside that waste van, the choice is yours, but it is eminently more comfortable in here."

Stewart looked at Sinclair, "I think he means us two, and I don't know about you, but I prefer a limo to a plastic bin bag on the way to Hackney tip."

Sinclair nodded, and the pair walked slowly and gingerly over to the waiting car, hoping with every step that a firefight did not suddenly erupt. As Stewart got closer to the Volvo, he memorised the registration plate, "186 D 101[433]", hoping that he could trace the vehicle, that is, if they survived the ride in the car.

Upon entering through the wide, rear-facing "suicide" door, the first impression was of the brightness of the vehicle's interior in comparison to the dull street lights. Then, a fresh and spicy aroma reminded Stewart of the luxurious shaves he had enjoyed in the famous Grand Bazaar barber's shop in Istanbul.

---

[432] A Mexican standoff refers to a confrontation among two or more sides that no side can win.

[433] Israeli Embassy Diplomatic Plate in the UK.

Once seated inside the plush leather interior, Stewart got his first glimpse of their host. Facing him, across an expanse of light blue thick, piled carpet, was a genial looking, balding, grey-haired man, who was wearing a dark, navy blue, pinstriped suit that gave Stewart's expert eye, evident signs of Middle Eastern tailoring[434]. The man's jacket was unbuttoned, and either intentionally or unintentionally, the open coat revealed a large brushed titanium Desert Eagle[435] handgun. The pistol was carried under the stranger's left armpit in a well-worn, chamois leather holster that Stewart recognised as a "Berns Martin Triple-draw". Also exposed, from under the stranger's jacket sleeve, was a large, steel Eterna[436] dive watch on a steel "beads of rice" bracelet. The watch had encountered decades of heavy wear since it had a badly scuffed rotating bezel and faded luminous, tritium dial markers.

Sinclair clearly knew their host, "Hello Mark, did you just happen to be passing by the Wigmore?"

The grey-haired man smiled, "Hardly, Dame Sinclair, hardly."

Stewart looked questioningly towards Sinclair, who was seated beside him. She rapidly made the introductions,

---

[434] Slightly wider lapels, and more generous fit to the thighs and upper arms.

[435] The Desert Eagle, Mark XIX, is available with six- and ten-inch barrels and can be chambered for the largest centerfire cartridges of any magazine-fed, self-loading pistol. They were originally manufactured by Israel Military Industries (IMI) which later become Israel Weapon Industries.

[436] The Eterna-Matic KonTiki Super was issued to the Shayetet 13 (S13), the elite Naval Commando unit of the IDF (Israeli Defense Forces).

"Tavish Stewart, this is Major Mark Katz, a..." Sinclair paused, looking for the appropriate description, "representative of the Israeli government."

Mark Katz interrupted, "I prefer diplomat."

Stewart nodded to the Desert Eagle gun visible inside Katz's jacket,

"A highly persuasive diplomat, I suspect, given your choice of weapon. Chambered for .50 AE?"

Katz smiled at Stewart's appreciation, "I prefer to use the .429 DE[437]".

Stewart grimaced as he imagined the effects of such a round on a human body[438], "Does Mossad[439] have a problem with rogue elephants?"

Katz stopped smiling, "Sadly, too many. You just encountered one of the worst of them tonight."

---

[437] The .429 DE cartridge, designed specifically for the Desert Eagle, is a modified .50 AE with a 25% increase in velocity and 45% increase of energy when compared to a standard 240-grain, .44 Magnum.

[438] For example, a 210-grain hollow point .429 DE round, fired from the six-inch barrel variant of a Desert Eagle, reaches 1700 feet per second and delivers 1347-foot pounds of energy, which would be devastating to any biological organism, even the rogue elephants cited by Stewart.

[439] Mossad (HaMossad leModi'in uleTafkidim Meyuḥadim) Institute for Intelligence and Special Operations is the national intelligence agency for the state of Israel. Unlike many other national intelligence agencies, it is exempt from the laws of the State of Israel. It is therefore a classic 'deep state' operation, free from political oversight.

"You monitored the event?" Asked Sinclair, clearly showing her professional interest, "Until this morning, Six[440] were not even aware of the Fourth Republic."

Katz nodded, "Yes, we had electronic eyes and ears inside the Wigmore tonight, as we always do with their meetings."

"Really? Why such interest in an emerging Argentinian neo-Nazi group?" The Scotsman enquired.

Katz looked genuinely concerned by Stewart's question.

"Because, Sir Stewart, they are neither Argentinian nor new. We have been following this organisation, under its various guises, for some considerable time. Indeed, some would say before 1948 and the founding of the State of Israel."

Sinclair looked stunned, while Stewart's eyes narrowed as he queried, "You mean Mossad subscribes to the Urban Legends that key members of the Third Reich escaped the fall of Berlin and set up in South America?"

Katz looked directly at the Scotsman, "Perhaps I need to cover some lesser-known events from twentieth-century history? But first," Katz nodded to the concealed knife in Sinclair's hand, "I would appreciate it if you could keep that blade well away from the leather upholstery to save the taxpayers of Israel unnecessary expense."

Sinclair smiled and placed the KM2000 on the light blue, thick pile, carpeted floor of the limousine n front of her and then nodded for Katz to continue,

"All our history books agree that on the eighth of May 1945, the Allies[441] accepted Germany's unconditional surrender. This event was about one week after Adolf Hitler had supposedly committed suicide in Berlin.

---

[440] MI6 – The British Secret Intelligence Service (SIS).

[441] Soviet Union, United States, United Kingdom and Free French.

It is also acknowledged that the Nazis developed some amazing technology years ahead of anything that the Allies possessed. Both the Americans and the Soviets immediately commenced covert programs to take these secret technologies back to their home nations and the leading scientists and military officers managing them.

Sinclair nodded, "Operation Paperclip."

Katz acknowledged Sinclair's comment and continued,

"The Soviet equivalent to Paperclip was called "Alsos". The Russian army had so-called trophy brigades[442] advancing with their military forces, whose sole purpose was to seize secret weapons to be taken back on special railroad trucks to military labs deep within the Soviet Union. One such classified operation, called "Osoaviakhim", seized workers and technologies related to the V2[443] rockets and moved them at gunpoint to Russia.

Each side took these secret Nazi technologies and personnel back to their home territory and established their own programs in atomic weapons, rockets, pharmaceuticals, medicine, genetics, bioweapons, chemical weapons and aeronautics.

The Nazis had also established an outstanding secret intelligence network. Unknown to the general public, this network was left intact and continued to operate at the war's end. It was run simultaneously by both the Soviets and the Americans. Both sides believed this sophisticated intelligence network served them exclusively. The reality was that the Nazi intelligence service played both sides against

---

[442] Трофейные бригады

[443] V-2 or Vergeltungswaffe 2 (Retribution Weapon 2) was also known by its inventory name Aggregat 4 (A4). It was the world's first long-range, supersonic, guided ballistic missile and the first artificial object to travel into space.

each other while they served their own agenda. Code named Vortex or "der Malstrom" by the Nazi chiefs, it was known as the "Gehlen Org[444]" by the CIA.

Stewart noticeably tensed at the mention of Maelstrom,

"Sorry, did you just say this covert Nazi intelligence network was code-named Maelstrom?"

Katz nodded, "Yes, Sir Stewart, your old friends were, at least originally, a Nazi funded covert operation intended to infiltrate the world's leading intelligence agencies. There is even some evidence that Ad-Dajjal was regarded as a rising star within the parent organisation to Maelstrom called Wolfsangel. However, Ad-Dajjal had her own personal ambition for global domination..."

Katz paused, "Well, you know the story better than anyone.

The OSS[445], which later became the CIA[446] and the MGB[447], which later became the KGB[448], both believed they were using the former Nazi intelligence networks to spy on each other. Instead, they were infiltrated to serve Nazi interests, keeping the West and East de-stabilised for decades by false information to promote massive spending on an unnecessary cold war that benefitted the Military-Industrial Complex.

---

[444] Named after the head of the organisation, Reinhard Gehlen, head of Nazi military intelligence.

[445] Office of Strategic Services (OSS)

[446] Central Intelligence Agency (CIA)

[447] Ministry of State Security (MGB).

[448] Komitet Gosudarstvennoy Bezopasnosti - Committee for State Security, foreign intelligence and domestic security agency of the Soviet Union (KGB).

Sinclair interrupted, "Mark, it sounds a brilliant, if evil plan, but how exactly would a prolonged cold war help the Nazis?"

Katz continued, "Let me explain, Cynthia. Once America and the Soviets had assimilated large numbers of supposedly reformed Nazi experts into every strategic industry, they became entirely reliant on the former Nazi intelligence service. The two most influential members of the former Allies then became unwittingly guided into an endless series of wars. These constant conflicts weakened both the USA and USSR while serving the long-term objectives of a hidden group that amassed enormous financial and political influence that was completely unseen by anyone.

However, this was not the worst part of the situation. After the war, Israeli intelligence made a disturbing discovery. Although the Americans and Russians had taken scientists and technologies from the remains of the Nazi war machine, they did not find the best. These individuals were exfiltrated from right under the noses of the Americans and Russians by the very same intelligence network that the West and East thought were serving them. Over ten thousand Nazis were extracted from Germany through Vortex[449] operatives, using so-called "rat runs[450]" through undercover support networks in Italy, Spain and Portugal, before being transported across the Atlantic[451]. Several high-level figures

---

[449] Vortex or "der Malstrom" : the remains of the Nazi secret intelligence network, left in place by both the Russians and Americans.

[450] Code named Odessa by the CIA.

[451] They included Josef Mengele, Auschwitz's Angel of Death, and Adolf Eichmann, the architect of the Holocaust. Many (including numerous US intelligence reports, Nazi hunters and even Joseph Stalin) believed Hitler faked his suicide and lived out his life in an Argentinian town near Bariloche where there was a recreation of the Berchtesgaden, Hitler's holiday home. The town also had a

in the Roman Catholic Church were known to support the escaping Nazis and have issued Red Cross passports[452] with false identities that permitted Nazis to pass unhindered and unsuspected through allied checkpoints.

Stewart interrupted, "Mark, why on earth would the Catholic Church support the Nazis after the atrocities they perpetrated?"

Katz grimaced, "Some were believers, others were misguided into believing that the Nazis were essential to prevent the spread of communism, that was vehemently atheist and would have signalled the end of the Church. But, getting back to our potted history, these rat runs were also used to transport the Nazi's more portable secret technologies."

Sinclair commented, "The supposed Wunderwaffe[453]?

I thought they were just a propaganda exercise by the Nazis during the closing part of the war?"

Katz shook his head, "That is the cover story issued by the Allies. The reality is that as the Allies swept across Europe, they discovered evidence that the Nazis had developed technologies beyond anything previously imagined. That prompted operations like Paperclip and Alsos but neither the Russians nor the Americans discovered these ultra-secret technologies. All they found instead were tantalizing descriptions in partially destroyed documents. The actual weapons had been cleverly hidden or removed.

---

scenic restaurant, The Berghof, named after Hitler's Bavarian Mountain retreat.

[452] Supposed to be issued to genuine displaced refugees. Such passports provided an ideal way to create a new alternative identity.

[453] Wonder weapons.

Smaller "Wonder Weapons[454]" were transported via trucks and railroads across Europe under cover of essential Red Cross supplies and then from the coast via air and submarine. The larger Wonder Weapons were left in secret underground complexes within Eastern Europe."

Katz paused to let the full implications of what he had just revealed sink in before continuing his alternative history lesson.

"Sir Stewart, as you had noticed tonight, this group retains an unhealthy fascination with everything related to supposedly hidden supernatural powers."

Stewart nodded his agreement, "Yes, the meeting was full of whackos of every description."

Katz laughed at the Scotsman's language, "They would probably prefer the term practitioner, but this fascination with the occult is long-standing. During the war, the Nazis systematically gathered esoteric materials from around the globe while, at the same time, brutally oppressing anyone or any organisation that might hold such secrets themselves. Clearly, the Nazis wanted to have exclusive ownership of this hidden knowledge.

At the end of the war, numerous art treasures were recovered, but even the most rigorous searches never recovered any of these priceless esoteric texts, relics and artefacts. However, some intriguing statements emerged during interrogations of low-ranking SS officers. These SS officers claimed that these esoteric treasures had been systematically catalogued by officers from a branch of the

---

[454] Wunderwaffe literally "Miracle weapons", were ground breaking weapons that were, supposedly, decades ahead of any known existing technologies.

SS[455], formed to focus on mastery of hidden powers, before being transported to vast hidden repositories within Europe.

Sinclair interrupted, "But Mark, weren't all the senior Nazis tried at Nuremberg after the war? Surely, they would have escaped if there was a coordinated plan to exfiltrate the leaders?"

Katz nodded, "Yes, a few figureheads were given show trials to appease the public who had just suffered through the war and demanded some form of revenge. But this ignores the reality that many of the operational leaders escaped to avoid any form of legal justice."

Stewart interjected, "Even if these people did escape, they would be long dead now. The pace of technological advancement will have rendered their weapons less than wonderful, compared to what we have today."

Katz shook his head, "Sir Stewart, almost all of our modern weapons are derived entirely from those the Nazis were actively using at the end of the second world war. In contrast, what we know about their Wonder Weapons would indicate that, if even half of them were operational today, they would be hard to defeat.

Their research into biological[456] warfare produced some horrors, similar to the red death[457], that so recently threatened humanity. In terms of chemical weapons, the

---

[455] The Ahnenerbe (ancestral heritage) formed at Hitler's express command under the control of Heinrich Himmler, Reichsführer of the Schutzstaffel (SS). Also known as the Research and Teaching Community of the Ancestral Heritage (Forschungs- und Lehrgemeinschaft des Ahnenerbe).

[456] At the infamous Dachau institute.

[457] A triple agent biological weapon developed by the United States and deployed by Ad-Dajjal during her attempt at world domination.

Nazis developed the nerve agents that remain the basis of our existing chemical arsenals: tabun, sarin and soman. They even designed and developed specialised delivery systems for such chemical warheads. Thankfully, when the Allies approached Berlin, Hitler's own experiences with mustard gas in the first world war made him decide against their use.

Stewart interjected again, "Thank God! And even more critically, they could not successfully produce a working atomic weapon."

Katz frowned, "There, you are wrong, Sir Stewart. There are independently verified accounts in the US[458] and Soviet secret archives that report on numerous successful nuclear weapons tests[459], and at least one operational use of a nuclear weapon on the Eastern front with Russia, in 1944."

Sinclair shook her head, "I have heard these rumours, but radiological tests have shown only normal background levels of radiation in the soil at these sites."

Katz smiled, "True, but the lack of residual radiation is because the Nazis were not developing a nuclear fission weapon. They focused on a grander prize, a fusion weapon, which we are still struggling to develop today."

Sinclair frowned and looked to Stewart and Katz for clarification, "A fusion weapon?"

---

[458] File APO 696 from the National Archives in Washington describes a successful nuclear weapon detonation on October 1944 at the nuclear test station near Ludwigslust.

[459] Two devices were set off on March 4, 1945 and March 12, 1945, respectively in the German state of Thuringia near the town of Ohrdruf, reportedly killing hundreds of Prisoners of War, who were used as test guinea pigs for judging the effect of the weapon.

Katz explained that before Stewart could respond, "Our current nuclear weapons release considerable amounts of energy by splitting the atomic structure[460].

In contrast, nuclear fusion combines two small atomic structures into a single, larger nuclear structure. This fusion process releases enormous amounts of energy. Such fusion reactions typically require high temperatures and high pressures to initiate the process."

Sinclair frowned, "When you say *enormous amounts of energy*, what would a fusion weapon look like?"

Katz shrugged, "Well, with our current technologies, it would be large, probably too large to be integrated into a traditional missile delivery system but, to be honest, we don't know."

Sinclair continued her line of enquiry, "So it's not likely to be easily hidden. Would it have a comparable explosive yield to our existing nuclear weapons?"

Katz laughed nervously, "The size of the yield from a fusion device is hard to estimate as it would depend on the design. But theoretically, it could be unimaginably destructive."

Sinclair looked pointedly at Stewart and then Katz, "You both know I hate vague descriptions, especially when talking about possible threats. How destructive could this

---

[460] This atomic splitting is activated within an unstable enriched material, usually uranium 235. The enriched uranium is bombarded by high-speed neutrons, as a detonation mechanism. These additional neutrons combine with the nucleus of the enriched uranium, making it so unstable that the nucleus splits, causing a fission reaction, which produces more neutrons that in turn make other nearby isotopes become unstable and so on in a nuclear chain reaction. The by-products of such nuclear fission include highly radioactive materials at the site where the fission occurred.

hypothetical wonder weapon be in an absolute worst-case scenario?"

Katz returned Sinclair's gaze, "Cynthia, theoretically[461], we are talking about nothing less than a doomsday weapon."

Stewart nodded, "But, if Major Katz is correct, these bastards baulked at using the nerve gas stockpiles they had supposedly amassed when the Russians were storming Berlin. Apart from a few ideologically flawed crackpots, no one would knowingly launch a weapon that would also destroy themselves."

Katz looked at Stewart, "Sadly, Sir Stewart, I know of no better description for the Nazis than ideologically flawed crackpots."

Sinclair sighed, "Isn't that the truth. But, if this weapon ever existed, it would have been buried in some godforsaken underground facility somewhere in Eastern Europe for over half a century. It probably would have rusted away. The same goes for any other of these supposed wonder weapons."

Stewart agreed, "Yes, and if these are the Nazis, why have they waited so long to re-emerge and what would be their motivation for kidnapping the heirs to the few remaining European monarchies?"

Katz shook his head again, "Despite our best efforts, we simply don't know. Maybe they were waiting for the global political situation to become sufficiently unstable. Or for the general public to become disillusioned with democracy and

---

[461] Katz must be envisioning (or describing) a weapon design with a fusion reaction that triggered nucleosynthesis for a sequential hydrostatic reaction of helium, then carbon, then oxygen, and then silicon, in which the by-products of one nuclear fusion become the fuel for subsequent fusion reactions. In effect, an artificial supernova.

vulnerable to their promise of a strong society under a stable, single leader. As for the kidnapping, that is something odd, even by their bizarre rule book."

Stewart noticed the car was slowing. Their journey was ending, so he extended his hand to Katz, "Thanks for the history lesson, Major Katz. It was interesting to hear, even if I hope you are wrong."

Katz returned the firm, dry handshake of the Scotsman. "Yes, for everyone's sake, let's hope I am. But, in case I am right, be careful," He looked at Sinclair, "both of you. You are now known to them, and I would not rule out anything from them."

With that, the limousine pulled to a halt and, on opening the door, Sinclair and Stewart found themselves outside Stewart's New Bond Street showroom. Once they had disembarked, the Volvo 960 headed away to an unknown destination[462].

---

[462] Presumably to Palace Green, Kensington, London. The Israeli embassy.

20 VENGEFUL SPIRITS

"It is only the practitioner of black magic who compels the presence, by the powerful incantations of necromancy, of the tainted souls..." – Isis Unveiled, Vol 1, p321. H.P. Blavatsky, 1877.

Wigmore Hall,
36 Wigmore Street,
Marylebone, London W1U 2BP

21:46HRS (GMT+1), 8th Sept, Present day

While Stewart and Sinclair were ascending the side stairs from the street that led to the offices above the New Bond Street showroom, less than a mile away, a small group of men had gathered in the courtyard inside the Wigmore Hall. These men were standing around a collection of four dead bodies that lay on blood-soaked plastic tarps.

Having been interrupted from his presentation, Senor Cortez stood in the centre of three other men, two of whom wore grey city of Westminster waste collection overalls. Cortez was angry at having been called away from making his speech. With each passing moment, his fists became more tightly clenched by his side as he struggled to maintain his self-control. He listened to the two Wolfsangel operatives who had waited in the Mercedes van outside the hall. They described how a highly organised team with vastly superior firepower had taken Stewart and Sinclair away in a large stretch limousine with Israeli diplomatic plates.

"What!? The Israelis intervened to rescue that Scotsman and his whore!? At least that explains how they could kill two of my best people and escape."

Cortez's fury with the two men became tempered, after thinking that his greatest enemy had entered the Wigmore while he was giving his speech and killed the two blond giants.

Cortez curtly dismissed the two overalled operatives, sending them to wait back in the Mercedes van outside the rear of the hall. He then turned to the smartly dressed aide beside him and barked a command, not in his usual smooth Spanish or flawless English, but in a much more guttural and harsh tongue.

"Bring die ISFET Adepten!" (Bring the ISFET adepts!)

In response, the smartly dressed assistant marched quickly away. Almost immediately, he returned with a group of four people, three men and one woman, each dressed in highly distinctive regional clothing, that identified not only their home locale but also their chosen spiritual discipline. An interested observer would notice that these were the same group that Stewart had encountered earlier that evening during the reception party.

The middle-aged man, dressed in the traditional robes of a Shinto Priest, approached closer. For his part, Cortez was noticeably more respectful towards the Shinto priest and his associates than he had been to the other operatives he had just addressed.

Taking an A4 sized, glossy photograph and a target address[463] from his smartly dressed aide, Cortez passed the Shinto priest a grainy, video freeze-frame shot of Stewart and Sinclair entering the Wigmore Hall earlier that evening.

Cortez tapped the picture,

---

[463] Obtained from the immunisation passport scan completed before entry to the reception.

"I want these two to die. *Badly.* And I want it done so that there is no way to prove our involvement. Is that possible? I mean, is that within your combined," Cortez paused, clearly looking for an appropriate term that would not insult these people, "powers?"

The Shinto priest smiled, clearly sensing the nervousness of his host,

"Hai!" Then, realising that Cortez was expecting a response in English, he continued,

"Yes, Alpha, that is most certainly possible and *well* within our... powers."

With that, the Shinto priest took the large glossy picture from Cortez, turned and, pointing to the A4 photograph of Stewart and Sinclair, began a whispered discussion with his colleagues.

Cortez could not hear what was said but could make out some words that were specific esoteric terms from the respective magical disciplines represented amongst the four adepts. These terms included Gualichu[464], Onryō[465], Kṛṣṇabandhu[466] and Raakshas[467], although Cortez did not understand the esoteric meaning of the words.

At the end of the discussion, there was a consensus among the magicians that the woman would conduct whatever

---

[464] Gualichu is a demonic entity in traditional Argentinian (Mapuche and Tehuelche) cultures.

[465] Onryō (怨霊) is a "vengeful spirit" in traditional Japanese belief.

[466] Kṛṣṇabandhu (कृष्णाबन्धु) is the term for a demonic entity (friend of darkness) in Tibetan.

[467] Raakshas (राक्षस) is the term for a demonic entity in Hinduism.

ceremony would take place as her sect[468] specialised in such necromantic[469] practices.

Ignoring the dead bodies of the Prime Minister and her bodyguard, the Priestess spent some minutes standing above the bodies of the two blond men killed by Stewart. She lost herself, looking at what remained of their faces until, at some unseen signal, she abruptly turned and stepped a few paces away. She began the next stage of her preparations by sitting, cross-legged, in a half-lotus position, facing the dead bodies and then slowly bent herself forwards until her torso rested on her legs, her forehead touching the paving stones.

The Tibetan monk came alongside Cortez and explained that the Priestess had first to familiarise herself with the dead before placing herself in a profoundly altered state of consciousness by oxygen starvation. Minutes passed, and then the Shinto priest walked abruptly over to the prone figure and pulled her upright by the long-braided hair that trailed down behind to her waist, holding her up into a sitting position until her eyes opened and she regained her awareness. The Priestess nodded her appreciation to the Shinto priest. She rose slowly, as she was still suffering from considerable oxygen deprivation and walked over to where the two dead men lay and sat down beside their bodies.

The Tibetan monk continued to explain the unfolding process, informing Cortez about the next stage in the ritual,

"Senor, in order to completely control the astral forms, she must first reanimate the bodies into what we in Tibet call Ro-langs."

---

[468] Aghoris Shaktis are focused on forms of tantric worship dedicated to chaos and destruction.

[469] Magic related to interactions with the dead or their remains.

The Shinto priest, who had joined Cortez and the monk, nodded, adding,

"Yes, she will bind their immortal spirits to serve her will as an onryō[470]. Or as she would probably term it, Vizasati Sattva[471]."

The Shinto priest then looked at the deep breathing techniques that the Priestess had begun, which had already started to make her perspire. The Shinto priest suddenly looked concerned, as if he had just remembered something vital. He added,

"Senor Cortez, you should leave now. The next stage in this process should be avoided by the uninitiated."

Cortez looked quizzically, prompting the Shinto priest to add,

"The tantric techniques required to entice the deceased back into their physical shells will, by necessity, cast off an influence that will both disturb and imperil."

Cortez was unconvinced. He looked at the other three adepts, "Will you and your colleagues be leaving?"

The Shinto priest shook his head, "Senor, we are... trained for such influences."

Cortez was unimpressed, "I assure you, I can handle anything that you can!"

"As you wish, Senor. Do not say we did not warn you."

---

[470] Onryō - 怨霊 - "vengeful spirit"

[471] In ancient Vedic left hand path sutras, the Vizasati Sattva is mentioned as a violent reanimated essence sent to inflict harm on a specific living person or persons. Taken from the Sanskrit terms "Vizasati" - विशसति – (violent, cutting, destructive, harmful) and "Sattva" - सत्त्व – (spirit, ghost, reanimated essence).

The Shinto priest then returned his attention to the tantric Priestess. She was soaked through from perspiration as she chanted what Cortez thought were incomprehensible sounds. These strange evocations were extraordinarily ancient Rigvedic sutras devoted to the God of death, Yamarāja[472].

The Priestess chanted while vigorously performing an ancient form of cardiopulmonary resuscitation. Alternating between the two dead men, she sat behind each body, manipulating the dead men's shoulders to raise and lower their chests. She deflated and then inflated their lungs while her right knee massaged their hearts from behind. After some minutes of this activity, the Priestess pulled each of the men's heads up and back to open their airways. She exhaled forcibly into the dead men's mouths while vibrating a deep, vowel laden resonance[473]. This technique caused the dead men's chests to shudder. Then an awful, wet, rasping, crackling sound began emerging from the two men's lungs as the semblance of life had returned to the two formerly dead bodies.

As the Priestess rose from her seated position, she raised her two arms above her. Either by coincidence or some unseen influence, the temperature in the courtyard became noticeably colder, and the lighting became significantly dimmer. A breeze stirred up from somewhere and the air in the confined space, which had been heavy with the aroma of the faeces and blood, became filled with the distinctive scent of musk and ammonia.

---

[472] Yamaraja is the Rigvedic deity of death, justice and vengeance. Responsible for the punishment of the dead in Yamaloka; a hell like location, called the Naraka (नरक).

[473] A mantra (मन्त्र) is a sacred utterance in Sanskrit, believed by practitioners to have properties beyond the known limits of physics.

Looking at the two gasping and twitching bodies, Cortez turned to the Shinto priest, demanding,

"I don't want them alive! Look at their wounds. They will not be of any use like that!"

The Shinto priest looked at Cortez with sympathy at his lack of understanding.

"It is not resuscitation, Senor, at least not as you would understand it."

"It's necromancy?" queried Cortez,

"No, Senor, that is when the dead communicate through ritual or need. This technique is much darker and older. It is where the very soul of the recently deceased is used as a weapon against the living."

Back with the two reanimated men, the Priestess was treating each of them tenderly, like one would treat a lover. She gently lay each of them down, so their backs were resting on the paving stones, some six feet in front of the blood-soaked tarpaulins. She then sat down on each man in turn, straddling their pelvis, then raising them by their shoulders so they were sitting upright, and, as she tenderly held what remained of their faces, she intoned another series of deep, rich, vowel sounds.

As the Priestess evoked her mantra, one could see the heat rising in the air around her, causing what looked like a shimmer of energy to form about her profile. This haze obscured the Priestess like a soft-focus lens and made her skin glow with a strange light that cast no shadows but brightly illuminated her body. Strange characters[474] and symbols[475] formed on her flesh, becoming more substantial

---

[474] Such Sanskrit syllables are empowered thought forms.

[475] Yantra (यन्त्र) are mystical diagrams that are imbued with non-physical, preternatural influences.

with each passing moment, until they looked like tattoos that covered every inch of her body.

Whatever process was occurring, it radically transformed the appearance of the Priestess. The deep wrinkles and loose skin that had been in evidence on her face and neck became transformed into the taut and toned visage of youth and vitality. Elsewhere on the Priestess's body, the flaccidness and cellulite dimples that had been so noticeable on the skin of her upper arms and legs disappeared. Even her hooked, beaklike nose and narrow, mean-looking eyes became softer and more evenly proportioned. The combined effect was to make the Priestess glow, as her whole being became possessed with irresistible, preternatural energy.

Cortez suddenly felt an overwhelming desire for this woman. When he had first seen her earlier that evening, and more recently, when she entered the courtyard, he had hardly noticed her. He had definitely not regarded her as attractive, with her large frame and excess weight, but something about her had radically changed. He felt, no, he *knew* that he must have this woman. All his other concerns became minor besides this growing, irresistible need. Dealing with that meddling Stewart and his bitch could wait; he reflected. *He* was in charge here. He would interrupt this ceremony and dismiss the three other men so that he could be alone with the Priestess. The fact that she was soaked in sweat and her hands were covered in the thick plasma and gore that oozed copiously from the faces of the two reanimated bodies went unnoticed in his obsessive fixation.

Cortez started towards the Priestess, his breathing becoming increasingly shallow and his heart rate rapid as his entire being became exclusively focused on his only desire. Then, unexpectedly, his forward progress became obstructed by the Shinto priest, who called to the Tibetan monk to approach closer,

"The Senor has fallen victim to the Qliphothic thrall[476]!"

The monk nodded with sympathy and understanding. He approached behind Cortez, closed his eyes in meditation, inhaled deeply and placed his right hand at the base of the Senor's spine[477].

Cortez initially protested, trying to continue his approach towards the ongoing ritual. However, within a few moments, he became less agitated and, finally, regained his former, objective composure to continue watching this utterly macabre ritual.

While Cortez was undergoing his exposure to the darker energies projected by the ceremony, the Priestess had continued her ministrations on the two bodies that had now become more animated. They were still far from possessing normal human consciousness. However, their physical bodies had successfully pulled their immortal principles[478] back, which was the objective of this stage of the ancient, tantric Yamarāja ritual.

---

[476] It would be an error to assume that the Qliphothic thrall is exclusively sexual. It involves every aspect of physical incarnation, the desires and attractions of pleasure, power, possessions and knowledge. This pull towards material existence is, supposedly, so irresistible that even Angels are unable to resist it. According to Abrahamic religious traditions, included in such texts as Genesis and the Books of Enoch, it caused the Angels sent by God to watch over humanity, to notice "the beauty of the daughters of men" and commence an unnatural union with them, causing the "fall" of the Angels and the creation of the Nephilim.

[477] Stabilising the Muladhara (root) chakra.

[478] Within esoteric doctrine the immortal principle is more complex than is implied by the term Soul, but for convenience and space considerations we will use the term soul, spirit and immortal principal interchangeably.

The Tibetan monk leaned forward and explained that the next stage of the ceremony involved ritually binding the two souls to the will of the Priestess so that she could focus their energies against their selected targets.

The Priestess began a series of deep breathing exercises, combined with the resonation of a series of mantras. Then, she withdrew a sharp, curved dagger[479] from the folds of her soaked sari, with numerous strange symbols carved on its black obsidian blade and finely carved bone[480] hilt.

She then gently cut away the fabric of the men's clothes until she exposed the flesh on their chests, arms and legs. Smiling, she cut into the basilic vein in the men's forearms. Then, taking the deep red semi congealed blood that began to flow slowly from these vicious wounds, she used the tip of the curved blade as a form of pen nib and began writing in a script from a pre-Sanskrit language over the entire bodies of the two men. After over an hour of painstaking work, during which the Priestess continued her chanting, the bodies of the two men were covered in the strange symbols.

Once the Priestess had finished this phase of the ritual, she gently placed the bodies of the two men on their backs so they faced up towards the exposed night sky above them. She then stood, bowed slightly and took three measured and deliberate steps backwards before standing, looking at the two prone bodies before her, clearly waiting for something to begin.

---

[479] Yamarāja-Khanjar ("Death energy dagger").

[480] This specific Yamarāja-Khanjar's hilt is carved from the thigh bone of renowned holy man, Swami Matha (स्वामी मठ) who, according to the legend associated with this ancient blade, was sacrificed during an infamous Yamarāja ritual performed near the Brahmaputra River, during the Gupta Empire in the third century CE.

Moments passed, and Cortez wondered where to look since he did not know what to expect.

Then it began. Slowly at first. The two bodies began to twitch, almost imperceivably, but then the odd, jerky movements gradually increased in frequency and severity. The arms, torso and legs moved in a series of uncoordinated gestures. These movements initially looked within the normal ranges of motion but gradually changed into more distorted gesticulations that bent joints in unnatural directions. Then a low gurgling sound started issuing from the throats of the two bodies.

At first, Cortez thought this was just a variation of the rasping, wet sounds the two bodies had made since they were first reanimated. However, the hideous noises became louder and more distinct. They transformed from watery rasping sighs and gasps into what were attempts at making the syllables of speech. What was most disturbing was that both bodies were making almost identical sounds simultaneously as if they were reciting some fixed series of phrases in a harsh vocalisation that quickly evolved into a hideous screeching that made even the hardened Cortez flinch. Then, as these terrifying pronunciations grew in pitch and volume, both bodies suddenly jerked themselves up into a sitting position. The change in position was so rapid and unexpected, like a jack in a box springing from its container, that Cortez jumped, bumping back into the Tibetan Monk, who was still holding his hand over the lower energy centre of Cortez's spine. The two reanimated bodies continued their hideous attempts at speech. Their vocal cords, throats and mouths expelled mucus and blood along with the terrifying, rasping dialogue.

The Tibetan monk leaned closer to Cortez and translated what the two bodies were repeating.

"I have left Yamaloka[481] to reap the life from the living, to bring them terror and, upon their death, to drag their souls to my infernal abode!"

While the Monk translated this for Cortez, the Priestess nodded to the Shinto priest and the Shaman. They both began to systematically shut and lock all the doorways to the courtyard and then extinguish the electric lights set into the walls that surrounded them and illuminated the paved area.

Once the yard was in semi-darkness, the four adepts opened a small, wooden box covered in deeply carved images of Vedic demons. The South American Shaman had brought this ornate box into the courtyard while the Priestess had written over the bodies of the two dead operatives.

The four magicians removed four, six-inch tall, dark brown candles and four-inch square cubes of a black incense[482] in each cardinal direction. Each adept took their place at one of the compass points and, at a signal from the Shinto priest, lit the candles and incense, one by one, starting in the South[483], then the East, North and finally the West (so that the candles and incense were lit in a counter-clockwise direction[484]).

---

[481] The realm of the dead and dammed.

[482] Candles for Yamarāja rituals have to be specially prepared from the concentrated fats gathered from the cremation of suicides, while the incense has to be formed from dried and pulverised human organs mixed with Hyoscyamus niger (black henbane) and opium.

[483] South is dedicated to Yamarāja and his death related rituals.

[484] Widdershins is movement that is opposite to the apparent motion of the sun viewed from the Northern Hemisphere. When

As the candles and incense burnt, a foul miasma began to permeate the courtyard, of such a disgusting nature that Cortez had to pull a white, linen Gucci handkerchief from his left jacket pocket and hold it to his face. Then, as he continued to watch gradually, almost imperceptibly, two dark shapes coalesced from the burnt smoke. First into two narrow columns, around four feet high and one foot wide, and then, finally, into the unmistakable shapes of two human outlines, that resembled the size and proportions of the two dead bodies that were now lying prostrated on the paving stones. The ritual phase where the bodies had sat up and recited the Vizasati Sattva Sutra had ended.

The two smoke figures stood before the Priestess in the South. As these figures bowed before her, in a clear sign of supplication, the Priestess smiled cruelly. The Priestess then turned and walked towards the North of the courtyard and the exit onto Welbeck way, where the Mercedes van waited. Following closely behind her were two swirling columns of incense smoke that looked like the small whirlwinds that often play with fallen leaves on windy autumn days.

Following the exit of the Priestess and her two whirlwind escorts, the three remaining adepts began the process of transporting the physical bodies of the two dead operatives that the Priestess had reanimated. The two more elderly magicians, the Tibetan Monk and the Shinto priest, carried one body. The monk took the shoulders and the Shinto priest the feet. The younger and more vigorous, South American Shaman picked up the remaining body and heaved it over his left shoulder in a classic fireman's lift. Following the other two adepts, he headed towards the Northern exit from the courtyard.

---

done with ritual intent it is used to raise a cone of negative psychic energy. It is also associated with the Left-Hand Path.

"Should I come too?" Enquired Cortez as he watched the group heading towards the exit.

Without turning back, the South American replied,

"Quédese aquí señor, solo estamos colocando los cuerpos en la camioneta. Deben estar lo más cerca posible de sus objetivos previstos. Luego continuará la Shaktis, con la parte más gratificante del ritual." (Stay here Senor, we are just placing the bodies in the van. They must be as close as possible to their intended targets. Then the Shaktis (Priestess) will continue, with what is the most rewarding part of the ritual.)

The Shaman indicated his anticipation of the pending, horrific demises of the Scotsman and Sinclair with a wide grin. This grin revealed the Shaman's teeth were hideous filed spikes. Cortez knew from his Argentinean background that this indicated the Shaman practised that most gruesome taboo, cannibalistic sacrifice.

As the four adepts left Cortez standing alone in the dark, smoke-filled courtyard, he found himself shivering, involuntarily, not from the damp chill of the night but from the dark nature of these four individuals and the significance of the ceremony he had commissioned.

Moments later, Cortez's grim contemplation was interrupted as the four adepts returned to the courtyard and resumed their positions at the respective points of the compass, each standing next to one of the still-smoking candles and incense blocks.

Outside, in Welbeck Way, the two dead bodies had been placed in the rear storage section of the white Mercedes van. Once loaded with its gruesome cargo, the van headed down Wimpole Street, through Oxford Street, directly to Mayfair, finally stopping opposite Stewart's Showroom in

New Bond Street. The two drivers, still dressed in their City of Westminster overalls, quickly exited the cab of the Mercedes van. They climbed straight into the rear of a black BMW 5 saloon car which drove off at speed, turning into Brook Street and stopping momentarily at number sixty-five[485]. The two overalled men disembarked before the BMW headed off at considerable speed.

Back at New Bond Street, the road outside Stewart's Antiquarians was utterly silent. No lights were showing from the floors above the showroom, and all was quiet. The only movement on the street was from an old, empty MacDonald's brown paper bag caught by a momentary gust of wind, so it became propelled along the pavement. As the bag scuttled past the City of Westminster waste collection van, two small shadows suddenly appeared on the road's surface. Any rational observer would have concluded that these strange shadows were cast from a light source in the van's rear cargo space, although no such light was visible.

These patches of darkness gradually spilt further and further over the road's asphalt on the side of the van that faced Stewart's Showroom. No other shadows were visible on the street due to the thick fog that still hung in the air, but, strangely, these two dark shapes grew in both density and length, extending further and further from the waste collection van across the width of New Bond Street. Eventually, they reached the doorway of the Antiquarian showroom where, no doubt due to some optical illusion, they appeared to pass right under the entrance and promptly vanished from the street. Once these shadows had disappeared, the only thing to disturb the stillness of the night was a slight tremor in the door's tempered glass,

---

[485] The Argentinean Embassy.

as if something had caught under the entrance as it slid underneath.

21 THINGS THAT GO BUMP

"I shall not commit the fashionable stupidity of regarding everything I cannot explain as a fraud. - C.G. Jung

1st-floor kitchen area,
Stewart's Antiquarians,
18a, New Bond St, Mayfair,
London W1S 2RB

03:33HRS (GMT+1), 9th Sept, Present day.

Upstairs, above the silent and dark showroom, two figures lay, sleeping soundly beside each other, under a light grey coloured duvet, on the extended double sofa bed[486] in the communal kitchen.

Unlike the movies[487], the numerous aches and wounds acquired by Sinclair and Stewart through the arduous adventures of the long day had taken their inevitable toll, and both now slept deeply alongside each other. Sinclair dreamed about her home's warm, relaxing sunshine in Jamaica, while Stewart's dreams were of his beloved home in Scotland.

In his dream, Stewart's brick and stone-built ancestral dwelling was still intact[488]. A roaring fire of Scots pine was burning in the hearth, with three high backed leather chairs gathered around the blazing logs. Stewart occupied one seat, his dead father another and seated alongside the two

---

[486] A Sansa, 3-seater sofa bed in dark grey, fabric upholstery.

[487] Where the heroes invariably indulge in passionate lovemaking after taxing fight and action scenes.

[488] Sadly, the historic structure had been demolished by a series of thermite explosions planted by Maelstrom operatives under the direction of terror mastermind, Issac bin Abdul Issuin.

of them was John "Jock" Inness, the former RSM[489] from Stewart's old regiment[490], The Royal Scots[491].

All three men were enjoying a glass of single malt whisky[492] by candlelight on a harsh winter's night, listening to the haunting refrain of "Ailein Duinn[493]" sung by the ethereal voice of Caitlin Grey[494]. The three men discussed the sad decline of Scotland and how the wealth from the oil fields in the North Sea had funded the wasteful lifestyles of the "elites" in London.

The discussion had then moved to the perennial complaint[495] shared between Stewart and Inness. That the only reason their beloved "Royals" had merged with the King's Own Scottish Borderers in 2006 was to allow a rival

---

[489] Regimental sergeant major (RSM) is the most senior non-commissioned rank (warrant officers class 1, WO1) in the British Army.

[490] Stewart served as Colonel and operational head of the regiment.

[491] The Royal Scots (The Royal Regiment), once known as the Royal Regiment of Foot, was the oldest and most senior infantry regiment of the British Army, having been founded by Charles the 1st in 1633.

[492] A twelve-year-old Glenfiddich.

[493] "Dark-haired Alan" is a traditional Scottish lament for solo female voice.

[494] Ms Caitlin Grey is an award-winning mezzo-soprano singer/songwriter with a passion for the Celtic tradition.

[495] A grievance that caused both Stewart and Inness to resign their positions from the regiment and leave the British Army. Stewart started his Antiquarian business and Inness become the head of security at one of the prestigious university colleges of London.

regiment[496] to take over from the "Royals" as the most senior (oldest) foot regiment in the British Army.

Just as Inness began an expletive-laden diatribe, related to the unfairness of the merger, a sudden, icy-cold draught of air replaced the delightfully dry warmth and the scent of burning pine that had concentrated around the blazing hearth. This freezing blast interrupted the three men's discussion, gutted the candles, and extinguished the well-stocked fire. The room was instantly plunged into brutal cold and complete darkness.

The old, wooden-framed door that was sealed against the raging winter storm suddenly burst open, revealing a small figure, dressed in a full-length red, hooded robe, standing outside the farmstead's main entrance.

Inness, assuming that he was witnessing a manifestation of the Stewart family banshee[497], dropped his whisky glass on the floor, spilling the precious amber liquid over the ancient flagstones.

Stewart's father sat bolt upright in his high-backed leather chair while Stewart rose and moved towards the strange figure.

At that very moment, before Stewart could approach closer, a sudden, blinding flash of lightning illuminated the ground immediately outside the homestead, revealing that the visage of the hooded woman had mysteriously vanished.

---

[496] The Coldstream Guards were established in 1650, nearly twenty years later than the founding of the "Royals" in 1633.

[497] The "weeper" or "caoineag" is a female spirit in Scottish folklore and a type of Highland banshee. The appearance of this spirit is believed to foretell the death or pending mortal danger of a member of an ancient family of pure highland descent.

Stewart turned to discuss this mysterious occurrence with his father and Innes, only to find himself alone, standing within the ruins of his ancestral home during an exceptionally harsh winter storm. Thick, driving rain poured down around him, soaking his hair, face and clothing and bouncing back up from the exposed cobblestone floor of the living room.

Adding to the discomfort was a gusting, icy wind that increased the chilling effect of the heavy rain and without any light from the nearby buildings, it was almost pitch black. As Stewart scanned the immediate area, looking for somewhere he could, perhaps, gain some shelter from the storm, he noticed some tiny pinpricks of light that appeared to be moving up on the high ground, located some hundred yards from his homestead. Hoping that these lights indicated some human activity, Stewart began walking towards them. His route took him through thick heather and long grass beside the old family cemetery, where his mother and father rested within the large Stewart family vault that was as old as the house in which the Stewarts had always resided. The thick undergrowth through which Stewart was walking soaked through his twill trousers, and he felt the icy, cold winter's rain penetrating deep into his leather brogues, chilling his feet and toes, emphasizing his urgent need to find some shelter for the night.

Approaching closer to the strange lights, Stewart could see that they emanated from the Neolithic stone circle that he had spent the previous summer renovating. He recalled the back-breaking work, clearing away where soil had accumulated and uprighting some of the standing stones that had fallen over during the past millennia. Wondering who could be so active up on this high, Neolithic mound in the dead of night during such a harsh winters storm, he began to ascend the sloping hill that would bring him up to the standing circle. However, his progress was cut short by a familiar voice calling to him.

"Tavish! Don't go up there!"

Stewart turned to see his mother, Caroline Stewart, standing at the cemetery gates, gesturing for him to turn back and come to her. She wore the same long white linen shroud in which Stewart had buried her four years earlier. Standing beside her was a large, dark mass of long fur and muscle that stood as high as his mother's shoulders. It was Bella, his beloved Irish Wolfhound, who had been cruelly killed earlier that summer while bravely defending the house from Maelstrom terrorists.

As Stewart descended the grassy slope towards the cemetery gates, Bella proceeded to bound effortlessly towards him. Stewart knelt and fussed over his old canine companion before he walked to where his mother stood waiting. She immediately embraced Stewart with a long and powerful hug that lasted several minutes. Finally, she pulled herself away, with what was clearly considerable effort and addressed her son.

"You must not go up there. You did a good deed fixing the two fallen warriors[498]. The Sìthichean[499] celebrate that they stand proud once more, but no good ever comes from mixing with the Daoine Sìth[500]. Especially on a night like this one. When they *dance*."

---

[498] Standing stones are often referred to, in local Scottish traditions, as giants or warriors.

[499] Sìthichean (Fairy or Fae). Celts believed they were divided into those who were favourable towards humans (Seelie Court) and those with darker intent (Unseelie Court). Derived from sæl (blessed) and gesælig (unholy).

[500] Daoine Sìth or "People of the mounds", thought to be ancestors or supernatural beings.

In his dream, Stewart's mother felt her son's soaking clothing, remarking, as she led him past the open stone doorway, down the seven steps that led into the family crypt,

"You're soaked right through, come, dry yourself."

Once inside, Bella, Stewart's dog, proceeded to shake herself while Stewart took off his jacket and shirt, wringing the soaked clothing out and causing a substantial pool of water to accumulate on the dry flagstones of the crypt floor in front of him. The air inside the enclosed space was filled with the musty smell of damp earth and, now, wet dog.

Getting over his shock and delight at seeing his mother, Stewart asked, while he put the still damp shirt and jacket back on,

"Was that you just now by the main front door, Mam?"

His mother shook her head,

"No, Tavish. That was none other than the Daoine Sìth's queen herself, come to see the man who would return the Seann Rìghrean Gaisgeach[501] to their former glory."

While waiting for his body heat to return, Stewart sat down on one of the unused burial vaults, opposite the figure of his mother. Looking down to see the intended occupant of the empty vault, he noticed, with a slight start, it was none other than Tavish Stewart[502].

His mother noticed Stewart's reaction,

---

[501] Seann Rìghrean Gaisgeach are the "ancient warrior kings" who serve the queen of the Daoine Sìth.

[502] For some reason Stewart's knighthood and VC have been omitted from this inscription but he always did regard the titles as a rather ostentatious vanity.

"Aye, Tavish, you will take your place here alongside me in due course. But no one knows exactly when or where, except perhaps," She paused, "the Cailleach Bheartha[503]."

Stewart's mother gestured back towards the graveyard outside the crypt entrance. The rain was still pouring, and the gale-force winds were blowing, gathering the fallen leaves and branches into a single, large clump of foliage. As Stewart watched, the mass of accumulated leaves and branches appeared to pull themselves closer together and rise until they reached the height and shape of a small child.

To Stewart's shocked disbelief, the leaves shook themselves and transformed into the figure of a young girl wearing a dark red, hooded, full-length robe. She was around four feet high, with long, black hair and what could only be described as elfin features, slanted eyes and long, pointed ears. But the hands were the most disturbing and inhuman aspect of her appearance, as the fingers were twice the length of the palms and her nails were as long again as the elongated fingers.

The strange girl smiled directly at Stewart as she approached the crypt doorway. She moved with almost serpentine grace across the grass. Her legs and feet were completely hidden beneath the full-length red gown, and although she had a childlike appearance, she was clearly not human. There was, in fact, a distinct, otherworldly beauty about her. She continued to approach, and just as she reached the crypt entrance, another bright lightning flash

---

[503] "Cailleach Bheartha" or "The Veiled Hag" is an ancient, powerful and feared female spirit known in the more remote parts of Scotland. Some folklorists assert "The Veiled Hag" is the same preternatural entity known through the different Celtic tribes variously as Maev, Maeve, Medb, Meadhbh or Mab. Although Shakespeare portrayed "Queen Mab" as the comedic "queen of the fairies", to the ancient Celts she was anything but funny.

fully illuminated the figure and allowed Stewart a clearer look at his visitor.

In the bright light, it was revealed that the long, elfin ears were, in fact, oak leaves. The eyes were formed from twisted pine twigs, with shining blueberries within the formed sockets. The long, elegant fingers were revealed as elongated branches, held within bunches of beech leaves, and the long nails were, in fact, the tendrils from tree vines that had sprouted from the ends of the finger twigs. But, as the semi-darkness of the night returned, so did the illusion that this was a striking, elfin looking young girl of around six years of age. Taking a deep breath to make sure he had not passed out, Stewart noted that the air within the confined space of the crypt now smelt of fresh heather and tree blossom, like the early days of summer within a forest glade.

Still in his dream, Stewart looked to his mother to confirm what he was seeing, only to find that he was now alone in the crypt. All that was left was the oak coffin in the stone vault opposite where Stewart was sitting. With a pang of sadness at not being able to say goodbye to his mother, Stewart returned his gaze to the strange girl, only to find that in the brief moment that he had looked away, the figure had transformed from a girl into an adult woman. She now appeared to be around six feet high, with long, black hair that flowed down to her waist. She wore a medieval kirtle, combining a tight-fitting green and gold silk bodice laced up the entire length of its front, highlighting her classic, voluptuous figure. From the woman's shapely waist extended a full-length green silk skirt, pleated into a waist seam of red and gold. Around the woman's neck hung the Triquetra[504] symbol of three interjoined arcs

---

[504] The Triquetra is one of the oldest mystical symbols and in pagan belief is often associated with the triune nature of lunar

woven from dried grass; the same symbol that Stewart recalled was carved into some of the standing stones at the Neolithic circle.

At first, Stewart wondered if this new figure could be the mother or elder sister of the little girl he had seen earlier. However, the facial features were so strikingly similar that one had to assume the two figures were the same entity, who had, mysteriously and instantaneously, aged by some twenty years but that ageing had not diminished her. If anything, her transformation to adulthood had enhanced her otherworldly beauty. The Scotsman noticed that the scent of fresh spring blossoms had been replaced by dog roses and tree honeysuckle in the full bloom of summer.

Based on the woman's facial expression, she was amused by Stewart's shocked reaction to her transformation. She raised her right hand and gestured, with her eerily elongated fingers, to the crypt wall that lay immediately behind where Stewart was seated. Although the Scotsman knew that there should be nothing behind him except the crypt's cold, dry, stone wall, he felt compelled to look. He found himself gazing at a partially opened stone doorway leading to a long, narrow passageway with walls and ceilings of smooth, dry earth, held back by the roots of various trees that must have once grown on the site of the Stewart family cemetery. A faint, flickering light emanated from much deeper within the tunnel, along with the faint aroma of church incense and the sound of a group of male voices chanting in Latin.

Intrigued by what was within this concealed entrance, Stewart turned back to his mysterious visitor, only to find that she had performed yet another transformation. This time she became considerably shorter and bent forwards in

---

goddesses, (waxing, full and waning) or, in more recent times, the triune nature of the Christian God.

what looked like extreme old age. Stewart also noticed that the smell of summer flowers had gone. Now the crypt was filled with the distinct aroma of autumn, fallen leaves, and fungal decay's musky scent.

The strange figure still wore the same long, red cape but what was different was that now, sitting on the hunched shoulders of this older woman were two indistinct shapes, one of which, on the right shoulder, had the profile of a large, jet black raven. A small, short-coated animal was on the left shoulder, perhaps a stoat or a weasel. Whereas the young girl and the woman were unarmed, this older woman held the shaft of a long, wooden spear in her right hand, clearly using the weapon to support her in standing. The end of the spear was a foot taller than the hunched woman. The head of the spear was of gleaming bronze. The tip glowed and shimmered as if on fire.

Just as Stewart was about to address this strange woman, he noticed that the atmosphere inside the crypt was changing, fading away into the blackness of dreamless sleep, and the attractive autumnal scents had vanished, replaced by a mild smell of damp or decomposing organic matter. Stewart also became acutely aware of a foreboding sense of evil combined with a deep, penetrating cold, which leaked into every organ of his body. This sensation was so extreme that the Scotsman's body began to shiver uncontrollably. This physiological reaction to the growing chill in the atmosphere finally broke his strange dream and brought him back to consciousness with a sudden start. He found himself lying flat on his back on the foldout double bed beside Sinclair in the kitchen above his London showroom.

As Stewart's senses gradually returned, he realised that he had recovered consciousness too quickly, as he was fully aware but in what he assumed was a state of sleep paralysis[505]. Having experienced this unusual and sometimes unpleasant state before, when he had extreme fatigue, he relaxed by focusing on his environment as he waited for his motor control to return.

A cursory glance at the kitchen area confirmed that the sensation of cold that had awoken him was objectively real and not an element of the strange dream he had been experiencing. There was a noticeable amount of vapour rising from the standing water left in the washing up bowl, and the glass in the partition doors, which separated the kitchen area from the main corridor, had begun to form condensation on the outer side of the glass. For a moment, Stewart wondered if the fridge freezer doors had been left open, but from where he was lying, he could see they were firmly closed.

Stewart's shallow breathing was starting to produce thin trails of steam from his two nostrils with each exhalation of breath, just like on a cold winter's day. That could only mean that the temperature inside the small kitchen was close to freezing. The Georgian building's old wooden frame and floorboards began to creak and crack as the temperature continued its rapid fall. Stewart was able to move his eyes and, looking down the room towards the two sash windows that faced New Bond Street, he saw they had also become saturated with thick condensation on the outside of the window.

Stewart was racking his brain, trying to think what could cause such severe cold indoors during a warm, drizzle filled, early September night, when he noticed a distinct smell of decay, like an old blocked drain, that grew stronger as the

---

[505] A state where a sleeper regains consciousness before their parasympathetic nervous system has disabled the deep sleep movement inhibition that, for most people, inhibits sleepers from large scale body movement.

temperature continued to fall. Then he noticed that tiny specs of dust had started to rise into the air. He wondered if this was a known phenomenon related to low temperature when the dust specs began to flicker with light intermittently. The flickering speed increased until the dust particles glowed like fireflies and began moving in what looked like coordinated patterns around the room[506].

These patterns converged and formed a single mass around the size of a soccer ball. Sensing that something more sinister was about to begin, Stewart struggled to move and regain control over his body. However, his attempts only resulted in confirming that he was immobile. Continuing to watch with a horrified fascination, Stewart began to recognise that a face was forming on the ball of red and brown coloured, semi-incandescing material that floated four feet from the kitchen floor and around six feet from his own recumbent body. Even though Stewart had only briefly met her, he recognised the distinctive, spite filled face of the sari wearing female magician from the Wigmore Hall reception earlier that evening[507].

The Scotsman steeled himself as he realised he was facing some kind of magical attack, no doubt a misguided retribution for escaping the New Republic's plans for his demise.

---

[506] Classically called Orbs in the esoteric literature, they are asserted to be a preliminary stage of the physical manifestation of many forms of paranormal phenomena.

[507] Such projections are performed by an advanced adaptation of a Vedic technique related to tvikShepa-shakti (विक्षेपशक्ति) (the power of projection). The thought form is called the Mayavi-Rupa. This is a Sanskrit compound term, derived from māyāvin (मायाविन्,"illusory") and rūpa (रूप, "form"). It is an advanced form of so-called astral projection common in both Eastern and Western occult teachings.

The dark, earthy coloured, luminescing sphere, that held the image of the Priestess cast a slight shadow over the wooden floor as it moved closer and closer to where Stewart lay. The woman's projected image was now so near that Stewart could smell her rancid breath, combined with an overpowering scent of rotten fruit and onions from her body odour.

The clear, sharp image of a long-curved dagger was suddenly revealed in the floating luminous mass above him, causing Stewart to mentally prepare himself for the imminent searing pain of a deep cut on his body. However, curiously, the cruel-looking blade slashed the plasterwork on the wall above the head of the double bed. From where Stewart lay, the slashes and cuts in the wall formed an unrecognisable pattern. The strange figure then moved away from the wall and where Stewart lay. The red and brown light ball gradually dissolved back into a series of glowing dust specs. These, in turn, rapidly disappeared, leaving only the strange slashed patterns on the wall above where the Scotsman was lying.

Stewart told himself that Sinclair's "Sazerac" cocktail contained something significantly more exotic than alcohol when a distinct scratching noise started coming from the wall above the bed, where the Priestess's projected manifestation had viciously slashed the plasterwork.

It sounded like rats were in the wall cavity, except that Stewart knew that the specific wall was load-bearing and not hollow enough to house any vermin. As the scratching noise intensified, it combined with sinister scrabbling noises, as if something with long claws ran up the walls. The sounds began to spread more widely until they issued from numerous different places around the entire kitchen.

Suddenly, the sounds stopped, and there was complete silence that, inexplicably, felt more foreboding than the scratching and scrabbling noise ever had. The room grew colder again, and as Stewart struggled to move, two dark shadows slowly emerged from beneath the kitchen door.

Even though Stewart could not see any new light source to cast them, the shadows grew in length until they extended well into the kitchen area. They began to rise, like a column of smoke from a campfire on a perfectly still day, slowly upwards from the floor until they stood some three feet tall and three inches wide. Within minutes, these two columns of darkness had assumed the size and proportions of two fully grown men, standing side by side some four feet away from the end of the bed. Unlike the glowing sphere that had carried the astral projection of the Priestess, these two manifestations were not formed by orbs of light but instead by patches of intense darkness that blocked out everything immediately behind them. These two shadow forms moved and approached closer to the bottom of the folded-out sofa bed, then continued along either side of the bed until they were directly next to the prone figures of Stewart and Sinclair.

Back at the Wigmore Hall, less than a mile away from where Stewart and Sinclair were lying helplessly beside these two new shadow manifestations, Cortez had watched the Priestess, sitting cross-legged, in deep meditation for the past ten minutes. She had resumed her position at the Southern tip of the sacred cardinal point, focusing on the malevolent tantric ritual that would ensure Sinclair and Stewart would die violently and that their immortal souls would suffer the torments of hell.

Abruptly she opened her eyes and announced, with triumph,

"It has begun!"

The three adepts shared a conspiratorial smile, clearly delighted that such an advanced LHP ceremony could be successfully completed with such short notice.

Back in the kitchen area above Stewart's New Bond Street showroom, the dark shadow that had moved close beside the Scotsman's prone body was so intense that, although Stewart's eyes continued to function, he could no longer see anything beyond the visible contours of his nose. The rest of his field of vision was an impenetrable blackness. Stewart could, however, sense a human presence. Years of combat experience had developed an innate ability to tell when he was watched. This sixth sense that had saved his and others' lives on numerous occasions was prickled. He became increasingly confident that the two forms standing on either side of the bed were none other than "Kermit" and "Gonzo", the two blonde, Neo-Nazi assassins he had dispatched earlier that evening at the Wigmore Hall.

The air suddenly became filled with the pungent smell of menthol and herbs, such as are found in exotic oriental liniments[508]. Then the attack began. Stewart felt heavy pressure applied to his chest, limiting his breathing and asphyxiating him. Through the corner of his eyes, Stewart could see the same fate was befalling Sinclair beside him. He realised that if he was to retain enough strength to break free, he must act immediately for himself and Sinclair. Stewart rolled from the extended sofa in an enormous effort of will, crashing to the hardwood floor beside the bed. He gasped for air, then pushed himself off the floor and, standing on the bed, pulled Sinclair up to a sitting position, shaking her to wake her.

---

[508] Used in Tantric necro-reanimation, such as in the forbidden Yamarāja ritual.

Sinclair remained unconscious, but her breathing was now much more regular. Before Stewart could take any further action to help her, he noticed that the two dark shadows had now moved over to the kitchen sink.

One by one, the items stacked on a drying rack rose into the air and were thrown violently toward the Scotsman. Crystal glasses smashed into fragments, cutting Stewart's bare arms and hands, while shattered ceramic shards from broken plates rose from the floor and flew like throwing knives toward the Scotsman. Stewart had to drop the unconscious Sinclair back to the bed and duck to avoid being impaled. He then performed a spectacular flying Mae Ukemi (forward roll) that instantly took his body from a standing position on the bed to a place on the floor, some eight feet away by the kitchen sink. The Scotsman then rolled back up to assume another standing 'ready' position. Watching such a flawlessly executed advanced Jujitsu technique would have made even the most hardened professional fighter wonder if he had picked the wrong opponent to fight.

Numerous shards of glass, broken plates and the odd knife and fork were deeply embedded in the wall immediately behind where Stewart had just been standing. The impact of these projectiles caused the framed stone rubbings that had been on display to drop and smash into pieces. No sooner had the broken glass fragments from the frames hit the floor; they were back in the air, flying at speed, directly towards the Scotsman.

Pulling a small Turkish rug[509] from the floorboards, Stewart used it like a matador used his cape to swipe and divert the flying glass shards from embedding themselves all over his body. Thinking that light might help him see and react to whatever attack came next, Stewart reached for the light switch on the wall, bringing the kitchen spotlights on full

---

[509] A gift from Mohammed Sek in Istanbul.

and revealing the destruction that had taken place within the last few moments. The floor was covered with smashed debris and the walls above the bed, where Sinclair still remained unconscious, had knives, forks and large shards of glass deeply embedded into the plasterwork. The depth to which these items were buried into the wall indicated to Stewart that whatever was throwing the objects was able to exert considerable force.

This supposition was confirmed moments later when, in the full light from the kitchen spots, two of the heavy framed, birchwood, Ercol Shalstone kitchen chairs flew directly in front of where Stewart was standing, smashing full into him and knocking him violently to the floor. The remaining chairs landed violently onto Stewart's prone body before the Scotsman could gather himself back to his feet. These massive blows stunned him to such an extent that he could not respond when he suddenly felt himself being forcibly dragged across the room, picked up some four feet into the air and violently smashed into the wall beside the bed. By now, Stewart was severely dazed. He had been unable to take any evasive action to minimize the full brunt of these latest repeated beatings. All he could do was look up from the floor where he was lying beside the bed, covered in his own blood, and take some small comfort that Sinclair remained oblivious to all the mayhem unfolding around her.

Stewart's brief respite was sadly short-lived as, almost immediately, he heard the ominous noise of the large, wooden Ercol Corso kitchen bench, making a loud scraping sound as it was forcibly dragged at speed across the floor towards him. The heavy bench rose into the air, clearly being readied to repeatedly strike the last vestiges of life from the Scotsman's body.

Gathering himself for one final effort, Stewart looked down at his badly cut arms and hands, where numerous glass and ceramic shards were now deeply embedded in his flesh. His blood-soaked palm rested on one of the stone rubbings that had been smashed from the wall. With what would probably be one of his final thoughts, he noted the grim synchronicity, that the blood-soaked image on the stone rubbing was none other than the Triquetra symbol that had featured so vividly in his recent dream. Bracing himself for the pending deadly impact, Stewart uttered an oath that, should he survive, he would hunt down that bastard Cortez and put an end to his ambitions for his New Republic!

The story continues in:

THE NEW REPUBLIC: THE QLIPHOTHIC GATES

If you enjoyed reading this book, please leave a review on social media so others can also discover the adventures of Tavish Stewart.

ALSO BY K.R.M. Morgan

Bridge of Souls: Ancient Prophecy. Ultimate Evil.

An ancient esoteric object, once used by Elizabethan Magician John Dee in his infamous occult rituals, attracts a deadly interest from the clandestine world of outsourced military operations and leads Antiquarian and former Scottish Military hero, Tavish Stewart, to uncover a global conspiracy to control world leaders and enslave the whole of humanity.

Stewart's discovery leads him, and his friends, into a race across the globe to locate ancient maps, mysterious lost cities, magical relics and a forgotten civilisation so ancient and advanced that it would rewrite human history. Stewart must use all his Military and Martial Arts expertise to overcome the elite warriors, weapons and technologies that are set against him before a final apocalyptic confrontation in the desolate wastes of Asia, to preserve the greatest secret of all time!

ISBN: 978-1-5272-2595-4

What readers had to say:

"What an absolute cracker of a novel. Jam packed with action from start to finish. Well crafted with a cleverly woven plot, full of twists and turns.. K.R.M. Morgan is one heck of a storyteller. I loved it so much on Kindle, I bought the paperback to keep. Can't wait for the movie!" – 5 Star Review Amazon.co.uk

"Think James Bond versus The Omen. Fast cars, prophecy, gunplay, religion, martial arts, the occult, and an unlikely trio on a mission to avert the Apocalypse. If you liked Charlie Stross's "The Jennifer Morgue" you'll love this." – 5 Star Review Amazon.co.uk

"From the thoroughly gripping beginning this story takes you on a roller coaster of twists and turns, dark alleys and darker characters. Intelligently written its a must for anyone who likes a conspiracy. If you like James Bond, Indiana Jones, The Mummy, ancient history, or Dan Browne you'll LOVE this more! Why on earth isn't it a film yet?" – 5 Star Review Amazon.co.uk

About K.R.M. Morgan

After leaving school, Konrad worked to fund himself through several years of further and higher education. When he was not studying, he spent his free time practising various martial arts in his back garden, much to his neighbours' amusement. After finishing his studies, Konrad pursued an academic career that permitted him to work in several regions around the world.

During his travels, Konrad encountered some extraordinary individuals, including politicians, bureaucrats, mad professors, spies, ritual magicians, bankers and media moguls. Some were good, some were bad, and some were just bizarre. His experiences form the basis for his books' complex plots and characters.

Connect with K.R.M. Morgan:
Twitter: @KRM_Morgan

Printed in Great Britain
by Amazon

82382645R10224